Also by Diana Pharaoh Francis from Pocket Books

Bitter Night

CRIMSON WIND

A HORNGATE WITCHES BOOK

Diana Pharaoh Francis

Pocket Books

New York   London   Toronto   Sydney

Pocket Books
A Division of Simon & Schuster, Inc.
1230 Avenue of the Americas
New York, NY 10020

First Pocket Books paperback edition January 2011

POCKET and colophon are registered trademarks of Simon & Schuster, Inc.

For information about special discounts for bulk purchases, please contact Simon & Schuster Special Sales at 1-866-506-1949 or business@simonandschuster.com.

The Simon & Schuster Speakers Bureau can bring authors to your live event. For more information or to book an event, contact the Simon & Schuster Speakers Bureau at 1-866-248-3049 or visit our website at www.simonspeakers.com.

Designed by Jacquelynne Hudson
Cover illustration by Shane Rebenschied

Manufactured in the United States of America

10 9 8 7 6 5 4 3 2 1

ISBN 978-1-4165-9815-2
ISBN 978-1-4165-9820-6 (ebook)

To Tony, Quentin, and Sydney.
You give me strength.

Acknowledgments

THIS BOOK WAS A BEAR TO WRITE AND REVISE. THE STORY just wouldn't come out the way I wanted it to. So I want to thank everyone who talked me down off the ledge when I started looking wild-eyed and chattering about monkeys, dog biscuits, and flying dodos. Seriously, though, I really did get a lot of encouragement from a lot of people, as well as terrific feedback.

Thanks go specifically to: Jennifer Heddle, my wonderful and tough editor; Lucienne Diver, my erudite and thoughtful agent; Megan Schaffer, Christy Keyes, Missy Sawmiller, Barb Cass, all of whom read the book draft after draft; my family, who put up with my fits and my moods and my disappearances into the cave of my office; my parents, who took pictures of Weed for me; and finally, Ann Aguirre, who took time to read the book and give me pointed feedback that helped me finally figure out where the fractures were and fix them.

Thank you also to my readers. You mean so much to me and I thank you for giving my books your precious time. You are awesome.

As usual, I'm sure I forgot to thank someone and I must apologize for my lapse. Even if your name isn't here, I am grateful.

I

THE DREAM WAS NOT A DREAM. IT WAS A KIDNAP-
ping.

Max struggled. She hung pendant and weight-
less in the abyss between worlds. Tatters of magic
swirled like bright jewels in the black. They shimmered
and billowed like silk rags, and they sliced like razors
wherever they touched.

She twisted to avoid a swooping cluster that bunched
and spiraled like a deadly flock of birds. A gauzy wisp
of purple slid along Max's hip, and she wrenched away
from the liquid curl of acid that reached intimately
down inside her, causing a fierce ache in a place beyond
flesh and bone.

Max did not scream. She had done it just once, the
first time Scooter had dragged her here. She wasn't
going to give him the satisfaction ever again.

A force shoved her insistently toward the right.
Scooter. The fucker. She yanked away from the pressure, tumbling in the darkness and into a cloud of gray
magic. It clung to her with tenacious eagerness. It
melted into her. Her heart pounded frantically as her

healing spells kicked into high gear, drawing on her shallow reserve of calories from the food she'd eaten before bed. It wouldn't be long until they began feeding on her flesh. If she couldn't wake herself up, she was going to die.

She hesitated, tempted to let herself stop fighting. He wanted her bad, and she was worthless to him dead. She'd love to see his face if he killed her.

But he wasn't the only one who needed her. The thought spurred her. She resumed her struggle.

Again the demanding push. She snarled and hauled back against it. She couldn't keep Scooter out—she couldn't keep him from attacking her every time she fell asleep—but she didn't have to let him push her around while he had her trapped here. She didn't care if he probably *was* a half-breed god.

Something like fear quivered deep inside her. She ignored it. She could panic later. And there would be a later. She'd make sure of it.

She felt his frustration like an explosion of quills drilling through her insides. They curved like hooks and ripped through her. Pain burned like nothing she had ever felt. She opened herself to it out of habit, letting herself relax into the boiling cauldron of agony. It filled her, drawing her down into its depths. Far away, her body twitched and went as still as death as Max embraced the pain. Her breathing slowed, her heart beat evenly. She felt her spectral self smiling with vicious triumph as she drew perverse strength from the hurt. It was a skill she'd mastered the hard way. She refused to ever let anyone use her body against her, not if she could help it. And today she could.

Scooter hovered out of sight, waiting for her to capitulate. He prodded her again. It felt like she'd been Tasered. Max snarled, wishing she could pummel him to bits. But there was no fighting him here. She didn't know how. But that didn't make her helpless.

With slow deliberation, she reached out to her body. She told herself to kick and thrash. On her bed far away, her physical self responded, sluggishly at first, then began to jerk and convulse. She redoubled her efforts, evading Scooter as he sought to shatter the connection. It was a race. If she could wake herself first, she'd win.

Pain streaked from her hand to her arm, and Max woke. She lunged to her feet. Her ribs bellowed as she panted. Blood ran from a ragged three-inch gash that seamed across her palm. She closed her fist around it with a grim smile of triumph. For the last two weeks, every time she went to sleep, Scooter came for her, and every time, it was harder and harder to wake up and escape. This time, she had planned for it.

Max glanced down at the tack strips on the floor surrounding her mattress. Four-inch twenty-penny nails spiked from the wood in a six-inch-wide moat. She'd known that sooner or later as she struggled to wake, she'd impale herself and the pain would give her the means to wake up. Above on the wall was a dream catcher. Or it had been. The center of it was shriveled and twisted, and the smell of burned leather and feathers filled the room. She grimaced. It had been a long shot. The shaman who made it was powerful but nothing like Scooter.

She opened her hand. The wound had mostly closed, thanks to her healing spells. Her stomach cramped

sharply, and she wobbled dizzily. The spells were sucking more out of her than she had to give. For days, she'd
been eating enough to feed the entire Pittsburgh Steel-
ers defensive line, and it still wasn't enough.

She stepped over the tack strip and grabbed a power
bar from the stack on her nightstand, left there for just
this purpose. Her hand shook, and she steadied it with
an effort. She gulped the bar in two bites and then ate
another dozen in quick succession. She grabbed the
lukewarm bottle of flat Mountain Dew and chugged the
entire thing, making a face at the foul taste. The bars
and drink would give the spells some fuel to work with
until she could calorie-load in the dining commons.
Which, if she had any sense, she would do right now.

She ran her hands through her short blond hair, annoyed at the way they still shook. She clenched them
as anger seared through her. She was getting really
fucking tired of this. What she ought to do was go deal
with Scooter once and for all. The only trouble was that
seeing him might be the last thing she ever did in this
world.

Max drew a sharp breath and blew it out as her compulsion spells jerked tight. Tears burned in her eyes,
and she staggered, sagging onto the box spring of her
bed. Her legs felt like syrup. She drew deep, ragged
breaths, bracing her elbows on her knees and pressing
her hands against her face. Her compulsion spells didn't
like the idea of her dying in a Scooter confrontation.
She doubted Giselle had even thought what would happen when the witch-bitch promised to give Max to the
bastard. If just thinking about going to him set off her
compulsion spells—she was supposed to protect Horn-

gate and Giselle, not abandon them—actually going to him might kill her. But then, so would he if she kept putting him off.

Max snarled. Trust Giselle to make her the center of a game of magical tug-of-war and never think what it might do to Max.

Giselle held the *anneau* of Horngate—the knot of magic at the heart of a covenstead's territorial power. She was a powerful and smart witch, as she must be to hold an *anneau*, as well as ruthless and cruel. Max's mouth twisted. She knew better than anyone just how ruthless and cruel Giselle could be. The witch had taught Max everything she knew about pain. Max had spent uncountable hours being tortured on her altar as she was bound to Giselle's service, then thousands more as those bonds were strengthened and increased.

The memories were as fresh as when they were brand-new, and familiar fury swirled up inside Max as hot as on the first day she'd woken up to find herself no longer human. Giselle had turned her into a Shadowblade, one of two castes of warriors that every territory witch created as her own personal army. Shadowblades were creatures of the night—the magic that made them was fueled by the elemental force of darkness. They could not go into the sunlight without burning or melting—it was a swift and nasty death. They were preternaturally fast and strong, and many had other talents, depending on what spells the witch layered into them. Max was Giselle's Prime, the strongest of the Shadowblades and thus their leader. They answered to her, and she answered to Giselle.

She ground her teeth together and swallowed, forcing down the foul taste that rose on her tongue as the memories of those first years of enslavement played vividly through her mind. Quickly she thrust them away. No. That was history now. Four weeks ago, she and Giselle had called a truce, and as bitter as it was, Max was going to stick to it. She had agreed to put aside her hate and thirst for revenge and work with Giselle to protect Horngate. It was a sacrifice she was willing to make, as was giving herself to Scooter. Horngate meant more to her than almost anything else. Almost. She still had something important to do, and come hell or high water, she was going to get it done before she tied a red bow around herself and hopped under Scooter's Christmas tree.

Now she just had to tell him so.

She thrust to her feet. No time like the present. It was only about noon, so her Blades would still be asleep, and the Sunspears would be on patrol. No one would be around to try to talk her out of it.

As she crossed to her dresser, her compulsion spells coiled around her like razor wire. She panted shallowly. Usually she could think around them, twist her logic so that they loosened up and let her do whatever stupid thing she wanted to do. Not today. Compulsion spells didn't care if Giselle had traded Max away to Scooter. All they cared about was making sure Max protected the witch-bitch and Horngate. Committing suicide by visiting Scooter didn't cut the mustard.

She laughed softly and let the pain feed her resolve. One good thing about it was that it helped keep the predator Prime inside her from rising. If it did, all her Blades would come running, and she really didn't need to explain herself. They should just obey her orders and quit harassing her to be more careful. She rolled her eyes. Like there was any safety to be had anymore. Like there ever had been.

She stripped off her clothes and tossed them in the direction of her hamper, then dressed in heavy black cargo pants and a long-sleeved black T-shirt.

Next, she went to the spacious closet. Two walls were devoted entirely to weapons. The third was stacked with ammunition, grenades, flash bombs, whetstones, reloading supplies, cleaning paraphernalia, and boxes of power bars, jars of peanut butter, cases of Gatorade, and several jugs of Mountain Dew. Several one-pound bags of M&M's rounded out the cache. A scattering of boots and running shoes was strewn across the floor, and in the corner near the door hung a collection of jackets and two Kevlar vests.

Max examined the racks of weapons with narrowed eyes. What would she take with her? She wasn't going to see Scooter unarmed, though nothing she had would hurt him much.

Scooter was a poweful creature of Divine magic, which meant that, like witches, he could perform magic and create spells. Uncanny creatures like Max were made of magic but had no abilities to manipulate magic.

Although she knew he was Divine, Max had no idea what Scooter actually was. She didn't even know his real name. All she knew was that he was the child of Onniont, the horned serpent, and Nihansan, the spinner of webs—both legendary creatures of immense magic—and Scooter seemed to have inherited a hefty dose of it. Giselle had convinced him to guard a secret entrance to Horngate, one that only Max could open with her magical talent for opening locks. Giselle had foreseen the need for such an entrance in a vision. Scooter had agreed—for a price. That price was Max. He called her his gift, and even Giselle didn't know what that meant, but she'd still promised to give Max to him. Anything to get what she wanted.

The knowledge stirred up the forge of old fury in Max's chest. The witch-bitch hadn't even asked any questions.

She caught herself before the flames of her anger turned white-hot. The promise was made, and Max had agreed to it. It had to be done.

Just not yet.

Setting her jaw, she reached for her favorite weapons. First went on two flat-bladed knives. The sheaths strapped to the insides of her forearms with Velcro. She pulled her sleeves down over them. Next, she donned her shoulder holster. On the left side was her .45, and on the right was a pouch containing eight extra clips, half with hollow-point bullets, half with shot shells. Hollow points worked well on humans and even fairy creatures, if you hit them dead in the brain. The latter always healed, however. Shot shells debilitated them longer. The steel shot was mostly iron and stayed in the bodies, poisoning them.

She strapped a combat knife to her thigh and her new Glock .9mm to her ankle before lacing up her boots.

She ate another power bar as she went through her living room to her apartment door. She glanced around. There wasn't much to it. She had a long wall of books and scrolls—information about magic that she'd collected over the last thirty years. There was a brilliantly colored woven rug, several lamps, and a U-shaped black leather couch. On the far wall was a painting of a brilliant sunset over jagged mountains. It was the only sunset she'd ever see again.

She scanned the room. *I might not be coming back.* She quenched the thought as soon as it flittered through her mind, but not fast enough. Her compulsion spells flailed her and she braced herself against the back of the couch. Her legs shook as her body spasmed and her muscles knotted into stone.

She stayed there a moment, getting used to the pain, then turned stiffly and clomped to the door with ungainly steps that grew steadier with each forced movement. She opened the wards and slipped out as quietly as she could.

The corridor was smooth, unpolished stone. There were no lights—Blades saw in the cave darkness with no trouble, and Giselle didn't have the strength to waste on restoring the witchlights that had been destroyed during the attacks four weeks ago. There were more important things to do, like rebuilding the shattered shield wards and the rest of the covenstead.

Max's room was at the end of the passage. She went quietly to the stairway that rose from the center of the corridor, her teeth clamping together as she passed empty rooms. She'd lost six Blades in the attacks four weeks before.

A ball of molten grief bubbled in her chest. It was a pain she didn't know how to cope with. She had thought she'd figured out how not to care, how to keep everyone at arm's length. But it turned out she sucked at emotional armor and had let them get too close to her. Her hands clenched, and her fingernails cut half-moons into her palms as she drew a harsh breath deep into her constricted lungs. It didn't matter that they'd known the danger or that they were heroes. All that mattered was that Max hadn't been good enough to protect them. She was their Prime and she should have kept them safe.

Logic told her that they were Shadowblades and their entire existence was to fight and protect Horngate. Of course they would die. No one got to live forever.

But logic was cold comfort when she remembered their charred and mangled bodies. She bit her cheek, tasting blood. Enough. They were dead. It was her fault. The end. She didn't get to feel sorry because she fucked up. She had to do better next time—train harder.

She turned up the steps, bounding up them five at a time, her stomach still churning. She skimmed through the mountain fortress corridors like a shadow. Gravel still littered the floor, and dust hazed the air, despite the cleaning effort of the last four weeks.

She heard footsteps ahead and ducked into a side passage. Her nose told her it was Magpie before the witch appeared. Her long blue-black hair was streaked white on each side of her face, giving her her nickname. She was a witch of minor power and a great cook, unless you pissed her off, and then you'd be eating inedible food for as long as she had her panties in a wad.

She passed Max without turning her head, her body stiff. Her eyes were fixed and staring, and they had gone entirely white. Max eased back out into the corridor, a chill running down her back all the way to her heels. She'd seen Magpie look like that only once, just before she'd made a true prophecy meant only for Max. Now she was headed back in the direction of the Shadowblade apartments. Who was she looking for? Not Max. Magpie would have found her if so. So who?

Max twitched as if to follow, then caught herself. She drew a breath. No. Following might keep Magpie from speaking the prophecy, and that could be disastrous.

She swung around. She'd worry about it later. For now, she had an appointment with a homicidal godlet.

She kept to the more unused corridors, many of which remained partially blocked from the attack four weeks ago. She turned down one and was caught by the shine of white light coming from ahead. It grew brighter as she drew closer, but didn't bother her eyes. Witchlight, then. Sunlight and even some artificial light blinded her, but not witchlight.

She turned a corner and stopped at the bottom of a heap of stone. The light flared like a lighthouse beacon through an opening at the top. Max leaped up and through, quick and silent as a panther. She dropped to a crouch on the other side, gravel crunching beneath her feet.

In front of her was an angel, his back to her, his legs braced wide. He wore black leather jeans and a leather vest cut to allow his silver wings to emerge. They swept upward over his head, each metallic feather shining with razor edges. Black hair cascaded down to his shoulders in sharp contrast to his marble-white skin. He was beautiful, every muscle looking like it was chiseled from stone. The point of a massive sword rose four feet above his head. Its unearthly metal was sheathed in incandescent witchlight.

Suddenly the light winked out, and Tutresiel's wings snapped shut with a musical chiming sound. He turned.

The sword was gone, vanished into thin air. His red eyes gleamed, and his mouth twisted in irritation.

"Shouldn't you be asleep this time of day?"

Max rose to her feet. The angel was one of the most beautiful and deadly creatures she'd ever seen. He stood nearly six and a half feet tall, with an aura that screamed danger. If he wanted, he could shred her with one swipe of his wings. Not that she'd make it that easy for him.

"Yep," she said.

"Then what are you doing here?"

"Passing through," she said unhelpfully.

His gaze ran over her from head to toe. His lip curled. "You look like shit."

She couldn't help her grin. She liked Tutresiel. He was an ass and a jerk, but he was honest, and you always knew where you stood with him. Everybody else didn't trust him at all, but he was as true to his nature as the scorpion in the fable, and if he stung you, then you deserved it for being stupid.

"Aren't you a bright ray of sunshine. Did some bully on the playground push you into the mud and steal your candy?"

The corner of his mouth twitched unwillingly. "Sounds like you got up on the wrong side of the bed. Or maybe you just need to get laid."

Her brows rose. "You offering?"

He looked her over again. "I don't fuck corpses."

"I'm not dead yet," Max said, her grin widening. "But check back in an hour. Things change."

His eyes narrowed as his mood shifted into hunt mode. "What does that mean?"

Max sighed and shook her head. Talk about loose lips.

She needed to pull her head out of her ass and get her shit together before someone—namely herself—got killed. "Nothing for you to worry about, kitten. Go back to doing your yoga."

"Kitten?" He snorted, then folded his arms as she started around him, his wings still blocking most of the passage.

She stopped, tipping her head thoughtfully as an idea struck her. "You don't like me much, do you?"

He smiled, and it was as cold as arctic ice. "Don't take it personally. I don't like anyone, though you're better than most around here."

"Good. Then I need to tell you something."

He looked surprised. "Secrets? Are we going to braid each other's hair and have a slumber party, too?" His gaze ran over her again. "No offense, but even if I was a necrophiliac, I'd break you in half."

His smile turned wolfish, and Max shivered with something close to desire. *Holy mother of fuck*. She did need to get laid if *he* was turning her on.

Max rolled her eyes at him. "Get over yourself, chicken boy. I'm going to go down into the vault to see Scooter. He's the creature that's been trying to kill me for the last couple of weeks, and there's a decent chance he's going to finish the job. If I don't come back, mention it to Giselle, would you?"

She didn't give him a chance to answer, but swung into a quick walk. Her compulsion spells stitched fire through every cell of her body. She shook with the effort of walking, but forced herself to keep going. She turned her head in surprise as Tutresiel fell into step beside her. He was scowling.

"You aren't telling Giselle what you're up to?"

She shook her head. "No one but you, kitten."

"Why tell me?"

"Because you don't care enough about me to try to stop me, and I should tell someone, if only so they don't waste time and magic looking for me."

"Very noble."

She snorted. "It's the job. Nothing noble about it."

He said no more, but continued to pace along beside her. His razor-sharp feathers clanked lightly together.

Max frowned at him. "Going somewhere?"

"With you."

"What for?"

He glanced down at her. "I was wrong."

"What about?"

"Turns out I like you more than I thought."

"Sort of the way a crocodile likes a wildebeest. Feeling hungry?"

He stopped and grabbed her arm, pulling her around to face him. His brow was furrowed with genuine confusion. "Why don't you send me or Xaphan in to face this creature?"

Xaphan was a fire angel and as powerful and deadly as Tutresiel. She shrugged. "Not your problem. Besides, Scooter would probably swat you both like flies."

"I'm a hundred times more powerful than you. If this creature will swat me, then what will he do to you?"

"Like I said, that's my problem, not yours. Scooter wants me. If I send you in there, he'll kill you, and I'll still be on the hook. It's stupid and a waste."

"It could be Xaphan and I could weaken him so that you stand a better chance." His crimson gaze was fixed on her, pinning her in place.

Max felt the predator inside her rising in response to the challenge she read there. *Dammit. Not now.* She wrestled with it, trying to keep it chained, but it broke free, flattening her humanity and filling her senses. Her body tensed and volcanic power filled the air. She stopped struggling, reveling in the primal strength of her Blade. She felt her body becoming more fluid, her senses sharpening, her instincts turning hard and deadly. The pain of her compulsion spells faded into the background of her mind. They weren't important. Hunting was important, and fighting.

She glared at Tutresiel. "What's your point?"

"My point is that you protect your people and risk yourself, even when it's stupid."

"It's not stupid, kitten. It's common sense. Horngate can get along without me. If I don't happen to come back, you'll still be here to defend the covenstead. Like you said, you're a hundred times more powerful than I am. You and Xaphan are too valuable to waste when Scooter only wants me. Besides, I've seen the kind of fighting you do. Horngate wouldn't survive another one of your brawls."

"It's common sense for someone who isn't selfish, who will sacrifice herself for the good of her coven. In my experience, that makes you rather unique in the magical world."

"Why doesn't that sound like a compliment?"

"Because it's stupid. You ought to concentrate on saving your own skin."

"There's only one flaw in your thinking," she said.

"Oh? What's that, princess?"

"I made a promise, which means that any way you slice it, he's got me on his leash." Her mouth twisted.

"He's been yanking my chain for weeks, and I'm damned tired of it. It's time for me to get in his face."

She swung around and began to jog away, hoping she'd corked his mouth. Her Shadowblade Prime was fully roused now, power rolling away from her in uncontrollable waves. Her Blades wouldn't be able to ignore it. She had to get to the vault before they came running to stop her like a horde of hysterical nannies.

Tutresiel fell in beside her again, his wings soundless as he held them stiff behind him. "Promises are stupid," he said. "You put yourself fully into his power. I thought you were smarter than that."

"If you keep calling me stupid, I'm going to find a big pointy stick and jam it up your ass," she said.

He chuckled. "Any time you want to try, princess, I'll be ready." He sobered. "Do not misunderstand. I have no intention of going in your place or trying to stop you. But I will bear witness. You should have that." He grinned. "Besides, this could be fun. This place is as boring as a crypt."

She blew out an annoyed breath, wanting nothing more than to rip off his wings and tell him to go rent himself a hooker or stick his head in a vat of acid if he wanted entertainment. "Can I stop you?"

"You could try." He flicked a wing out, the edge of a feather slicing lightly across the back of her exposed neck. "But you wouldn't win."

Cocky bastard. Max wiped away the trickle of blood, even as the wound healed over. "Fine. Then do whatever blows your dress up, kitten. Just stay the hell out of my way."

2

ALEXANDER PULLED HIMSELF UP TO THE CHIN bar installed in the closet doorway. Sweat slicked his skin. He'd lost count of how many times he'd pulled himself up. He had done hundreds of push-ups, paced every foot of his small suite of rooms dozens of times, and gone through fifty fights with invisible enemies, but sleep still eluded him.

He dropped to the floor and instantly began to pace again. He deserved better than this half-life. He might as well be a prisoner, the way they watched him. He ground his teeth together, his lips curling in a silent snarl. For the love of darkness, he had helped this covenstead fight off both the angel attack and his own former witch! While he did not expect instant trust, he had earned a few points.

As the former Prime of another coven, he had the trust of no one at Horngate, except possibly Max, and lately that was looking more and more doubtful. She barely said a word to him, and what did come out of her mouth was usually scathing. The others only saw him as a threat to her. Once a Prime, always a Prime, and they could not comprehend that he was willing to never challenge for the role of Shadowblade Prime as long as Max held it. Giselle had made it more than clear that she would kill him before she let that happen, but that was not what kept him in check. Max commanded absolute loyalty from her people and most of the coven-stead, including him. She earned such loyalty with her strength and skills, as well as her willingness to sacrifice herself for them. Which is why she needed Alexander—even if she did not want him.

He slammed a fist into the top of his dresser, feeling a primal satisfaction in the way the wood splintered apart. He picked up the offending furniture and smashed it against the wall, then systematically began to shred it into sawdust.

Max was always likely to try fixing a problem by her-self before she called for backup. She hated risking her people, and after she had lost so many of her Blades defending Horngate four weeks ago, that tendency was only going to get worse. She was constantly put-ting her own life in danger—in the first week he had known her, she had nearly died three times. Horngate could not afford to lose her. *He* did not want to lose her. He slammed his fist into the wall. Bones shattered and spiked through his skin. The pain did nothing to steady his churning emotions. He shook his hand to straighten the bones, feeling his healing spells take hold.

She needed someone as strong as she was to break her out of her single-minded focus, someone who would not back down. Alexander was that someone. As a Prime, even if he no longer served as such, he could get in her face and stay there until she saw reason. None of her

Blades could do the same, and Max defied Giselle on principle.

She needed him. Horngate needed him. But how the hell was he going to make them see it?

He was tired of acting the part of the castrated lion to soothe their worries. He had kept his predator tightly leashed for weeks, pretending to be meek and safe. He was not fooling anyone. So why bother anymore? He started for the door. He was going to go for a run in the fortress halls, even if it made him look like a spy. He had not gone three steps when the locking wards on his door flared blue and faded and the door swung open.

He stopped dead. He only knew one person who could walk through locks like they did not exist.

Max.

Hope surged in his chest.

Finally.

Hope turned to bitter ash as Magpie stepped inside. She turned to face him, her body jerky. He froze. Her eyes were cloud white. She did not blink. His body corded, and he felt the Prime in him rising. He struggled with it, pulling it back under control. As much as he wanted to be let out of the limbo he was trapped in, letting his Prime loose would only give Giselle the reason she needed to kick him out. Or, more likely, kill him. He knew too much about Horngate and its devastated defenses just to let go.

Magpie shut the door behind her. Alexander's skin prickled, but he held himself still as she stopped just inches away. She looked up at him with those unworldly eyes, and a chill swept him. He scowled. Dense power surrounded her—she was far stronger than any circle-level witch was supposed to be.

"The amulet is coming to you," she said in a slow, guttural voice that sounded nothing like her usual clipped tones. "It will give you your heart's desire. You will be Prime."

All Alexander could do was stare as her words hammered him like bullets. "What do you mean?" he demanded. The amulet? How could she even know about it? And his heart's desire? What was that? Prime? Here? If he was Prime, then that meant he and Max would have had to fight, probably to the death. Or else someone else would kill her—Horngate had a lot of enemies.

He snatched Magpie's shoulders. "What the fuck do you mean? How can I be Prime?"

How could he prevent it? He shook her, and her head bobbled back and forth. Then she went limp as a rag. He held her up and felt her coming back to herself. When she looked at him again, her eyes were their usual near black.

"What did you mean?" He grated again. Max dead. He *would not* kill her. Nor would he let anyone else do it.

"Let me go," Magpie ordered.

When he did not immediately obey, she put her fingertips on his bare chest and sent a piercing burst of magic through his flesh. He dropped his hands as shards of lightning exploded inside him. Still, he did not back away.

"Tell me what you meant," he said, his mouth tight.

She glared at him, and then her expression softened slightly. "I don't know what I said. No." She held up a hand. "Don't tell me. If I was meant to know, I would remember. All I can tell you is this—whatever I said, you shouldn't ignore it. What I say is always true."

With that, she turned to the door. She pulled on the handle and looked at him. "Let me out."

He scowled. "You opened the door just fine a minute ago."

"And now I want you to open it. Or you can find somewhere else to eat for a while."

He grimaced and went to the door, swiping the wards. She swept out without looking at him. He shut the door and leaned back against it, scraping his fingers through his hair.

The amulet is coming to you. It will give you your heart's desire. You will be Prime.

She could only have meant the Amengohr amulet.

The breath went out of him and he closed his eyes. For years, he had thought it only a myth of his mother's people. She came from Caramaras gypsies whose history and magic were rooted in ancient Egypt. Alexander's mother had told him bedtime stories of the Amengohr, an amulet that granted the wearer invisibility at night and the power to walk in the day without harm. As a boy, he had never understood the point of the second half, but then he had been made a Shadowblade, and he knew what it really was: the Amengohr amulet allowed a Shadowblade to walk safely in the light of day and to become invisible in the dark.

The moment he realized what the amulet was, it captivated him. He did not regret being a Shadowblade, but to walk again in the sun . . . The want of that caused an unimaginable ache deep down in his soul.

He caught his breath. If he had it, Max would not be able to beat him in a fight. *It would be cheating.* No. He *would not* challenge her. He had decided that four weeks ago. She was the best Prime for Horngate—she was the heart of her Blades, and even the Sunspears followed her without question. They trusted her to look out for them and lay her life on the line for them, and in return, they did the same. He had never seen a Prime who enjoyed so much loyalty. He could never hope to replace her.

So if Magpie's prophecy really was true, then something else must happen to her. There had to be a way to stop it. Even if he had to reveal the prophecy to Niko, Max's second in command. He grimaced. That would go over well. Niko was insanely loyal to Max. He would kill Alexander before he could get a chance to become Prime. Or the little bastard would try.

Alexander's mouth twisted with brutal humor. He was not so easy to kill. Max, on the other hand, found trouble the way bears found honey. She needed a keeper, and not even a coven full of witches, Shadowblades, and Sunspears seemed able to do the job. But they would damned well have to do a better job now, or they would lose her.

He shoved himself away from the door and stripped off his pants before stepping into the shower. He turned on the cold water.

The amulet is coming to you. It will give you your heart's desire. You will be Prime.

His heart's desire? What was that? He longed to be a part of Horngate—no other coven would have him, and he never wanted to go back to Selange, his former witch. Not that she would have him. But it was not just that he had nowhere else to go; there was something special about Horngate. Part of it was Max and the loyalty she inspired. Part of it was Giselle—as ruthless and brutal as she was, she cared about the people of her covenstead more than she cared about power and prestige. He had never met another witch like her.

It took balls of steel to refuse to serve the Guardians, and she had. When all of the other territory witches were called upon to serve as generals in the war to destroy most of humanity and return magic back to the stagnating earth, she had refused, and the Guardians had sent two angels—Xaphan and Tutresiel—to destroy her and Horngate. But she had survived, and now the angels served her. It was a testimony to her power as a witch and her leadership. She also recognized that she needed help—without Max, without everyone laying themselves completely on the line, the place would have been destroyed.

You will be Prime.

He twisted the water off and got out of the shower, toweling himself off roughly before dressing in black jeans and a white T-shirt. Out of long habit, he slid his phone into his pocket and a knife into his waistband. He started for the door, not entirely sure what he planned to do.

At that moment, he felt the power of Max roll through him. Her Prime was fully roused. He nearly ripped the door off its hinges as he plunged into the corridor, unleashing his own Prime as he did, no longer caring what anyone might think. Protecting Max from whatever was out to kill her meant he needed to quit cowering in a corner and start acting like what he was. In a split second, the predator inside him rose to a killing edge. Smells and sounds sharpened. His muscles tightened, and he rolled onto the balls of his feet, his knees flexing. Power cascaded off him in palpable waves.

In moments he was joined by the other Blades, all in various stages of undress, most carrying weapons.

The power of Max's Prime filled the corridor. Alexander could almost smell it.

Niko eyed Alexander warily, his body taut. Alexander could see him brace against the thrust of Alexander's Prime. Like Max, he was about five foot seven, except he was built like a tree stump, with broad shoulders, powerfully muscled legs, and a square, blunt-featured face. His skin was naturally tanned, though not as dark as Alexander's, and his black hair was tousled.

Beside him stood Tyler. He was slender and graceful, with blond hair and a rakish three musketeers type of beard and mustache. He spun a knife in his fingers, and Alexander knew he could drill it through an enemy's throat in the space of a heartbeat. His hazel eyes were diamond hard, and, like everyone else in the corridor, his Blade had risen to the killing edge.

He and Niko were close to becoming Primes themselves, as was Thor. He stood near the stairs. He was an inch or so taller than Alexander, with shaggy blond hair that hung to his shoulders. His face was lean, with a square jaw, and his eyes were stormy blue. He wore an unbuttoned flannel shirt and a pair of threadbare Levi's. He met Alexander's gaze with a slight nod. It did not pay to be too friendly with his former Prime.

"Anybody know where she is?" Niko demanded. There was naked accusation in his eyes as he looked at Alexander.

There was a chorus of noes, and Alexander jerked his

head in the negative. A thought whispered in his mind: *Is this it? Is this how she dies?* He crushed it. *No.*

"Scatter," Niko ordered. "Search the mountain. Call when you find her. Then I'm going to fucking kill her," he muttered as he started away.

All seven did as they were told. Alexander lunged up the stairs, hard on Niko's heels, with Tyler and Thor just behind. They split at the cross corridor and then again. Alexander followed a path he could barely sense—a feeling of increasing strength as he drew closer.

His helpless fury grew as he hunted. What the hell was she doing? How could he keep her safe if she did not tell anyone when she was doing something dangerous and stupid? And what could be so dangerous inside the covenstead?

Realization struck him like a sledgehammer. "Mother fucking night," he grated aloud, reaching for his phone. He speed-dialed Niko.

"What?" came the other man's terse response.

"The vault. She went down into the damned vault. She is giving herself up to the bastard."

Alexander snapped his phone shut before Niko could respond, then flung it against the wall in fury. He began to run in earnest.

He raced through the main hall to the top of the entrance leading down into Scooter's vault. He remembered the creature—it had appeared as a man, but it was far more than that. It had held a territorial witch and fourteen Shadowblades in thrall without any effort at all. It wanted Max, and she had just walked in and given herself up without a word to anyone. Alexander was going to break her neck. He did not let himself think about what Scooter might do to her.

The vault was at the bottom of a deep shaft. Alexander leaped down to the first landing, swung through the turn, and leaped again. He had gone halfway when he stumbled to a halt. A chill ran through him.

The invisible trail of Max's Prime vanished like it had never existed. Alexander snarled and launched himself downward again. He caught the scent of her—the metallic, corrosive smell of the Uncanny mixed with a rich bittersweet flavor, like the darkest chocolate twined with a tang of winter snowmelt and the faintest hint of honey. It was a scent that was purely Max. Alexander tasted her on his tongue and jumped the last forty feet down into the open shaft at the center of the stairs.

He landed in a crouch, one hand on the floor. He scanned the room. The vault was a round room cut into the heart of the mountain. Veins of crystal, gems, and metals streaked across the polished floor and walls. A shimmering barrier of magic hung across the middle, cutting the room in half and separating the stairway from a dilapidated door on the other side of the stone room. It appeared to be made of scraps of wood, as if a mild breeze would blow it to pieces. Alexander knew better. That door was made of magic and opened only when its maker—the extraordinarily powerful creature Max had mockingly dubbed Scooter—chose to allow it.

He stood and turned to the wall beside the stairs, where a yellow starburst of quartz gleamed brightly on the wall. He slapped his hand against it and the ward within deactivated. The curtain vanished. The smell of Divine magic permeated the air—at once acrid and warmly mellow. He started across the room, jerking to a halt when Niko grabbed his arm and spun him around. He had been so intent on his purpose that he had not heard the other man arrive.

Niko flinched from the animal rage in Alexander's eyes but did not let go.

"Wait for the others," he said, then carefully lifted his hand. "I'm not your enemy. Not at the moment, anyway."

Alexander's lip curled. "If you keep me from helping Max, then you sure as hell are."

"She didn't invite any of us to her party."

Alexander stared. This was not like Niko. "Does she ever invite you to the bad ones?" His attention moved inexorably back to the door. "She does what she has to to keep you safe, even if it means walking into a death trap. She is in trouble."

"She's in trouble a lot. She can handle it." But Niko did not sound convinced.

"You are stalling."

The other man winced. "I'm being smart. We can't do this alone. I'm hoping a little help will show up."

Alexander's mouth flattened. As powerful a creature as Scooter was, he did not know if a hundred Blades could help Max. His jaw tightened. *You are the gift and the answer. I will wait for your return, and we will walk the web roads together.* Those had been Scooter's last words to Max four weeks ago. Alexander remembered them vividly. Her expression when she heard the words had been fatalistic and annoyed, as if she did not entirely know what they meant, but she was willing to pay any price, since it meant protecting Horngate. At the time, she had no doubt been certain of dying in battle, and she had probably figured the point hardly worth considering. But she *had* survived, and now—what gift and answer was Scooter expecting Max to be?

You will be Prime.

His stomach churned, and he ground his teeth together, feeling them crack, the momentary flicker of pain flashing through his jaws. *I have to get her back.* The need was raw, like a bloody wound, and astonishing in its intensity.

A soft metallic sound made them both jerk around. Behind them, Tutresiel seemed to emerge from nowhere. The angel flexed his silver wings, the knife-edged feathers gleaming.

"Where did you come from?" Niko demanded.

"I've been here since before you arrived."

"I didn't see you."

Tutresiel smiled thinly. "I didn't choose for you to do so."

Niko's mouth twisted and he looked as if he dearly wanted to put his fist through the angel's face. Alexander agreed wholeheartedly. Unlike Xaphan, Tutresiel made a point of being rude and abrasive.

"What are you doing here?" he asked.

Tutresiel shifted his red gaze to Alexander. "Waiting. Witnessing."

"Max told you to come?" Niko's lip curled and his face flushed hot. If there was one creature he liked less than Alexander, it was Tutresiel.

Not that Alexander could disagree, at least with the sentiment. Why call the angel? Tutresiel did not give a damn about her. Why not call one of her Blades? Or him?

The memory of the two kisses they had shared flooded his mind, and his body stirred in instant response. He shoved it away. This was no time for distraction.

The angel shook his head. "She told me she was coming here in case she did not return, so that someone would know. I chose to wait."

Alexander's jaw knotted. "You let her go in alone, knowing she thought she would not come back?"

"It was her choice. She could have sent me." The angel made an uncharacteristic shrug. "I told her she should."

"You could have volunteered," Niko pointed out through clenched teeth.

Again the shrug. "She didn't want my help. Said it was her problem, and he'd kill me anyhow, so she'd have to go in herself eventually. She said it would be a waste."

Fury snatched Alexander in a bone-crushing grip. He did not think. His hands locked together and he smashed Tutresiel's chest with a hammer blow. The angel crashed against the wall. Alexander ducked beneath a whistling whir of silver death, rolling under Tutresiel's slashing wing. Rock shards and sparks flew as the metal feathers chiseled through the wall. Alexander slammed into Tutresiel's knees and the angel tumbled over him. Silver feathers sliced into Alexander's back, scraping bone. Blood streamed down his back. He hardly felt the pain. He leaped to his feet, jumping high out of the way as Tutresiel's wings flayed the air where he had been.

He landed, and the angel caught him around the neck, speed blurring his hand. Tutresiel hoisted Alexander into the air. His feet dangled a foot above the ground. The angel was smiling like a cobra, his red eyes glistening. His wings fanned forward, each feather rapier sharp. His head tilted slightly to the side. "Are we going to play a game together, then?"

His fingers squeezed, and his wings curved around to brush Alexander's sides. His T-shirt shredded under the light pressure, and blood ran in ribbons down his skin. Alexander could not breathe. In the throes of rage, he did not care. His stomach muscles clenched. He swung his legs up, bracing against the angel's hold as he ran his feet up Tutresiel's chest and kicked him in the chin. Tutresiel's head jerked back with a cracking sound. At the same time, Alexander used his telekinesis to force the angel's fingers apart. He dropped to the ground, rolling backward to his feet and sucking in deep breaths.

Tutresiel was already coming at him, his smile wider now, his red eyes gleaming with delight. Alexander crouched to spring up into the air, but before he could, Niko and Tyler grabbed his arms and shoved him back against the wall, their bodies a pitiful wall against Tutresiel's menace.

"What the hell do you think you're doing?" Niko demanded as he strained against Alexander's struggles. "He's a fucking angel. And he's a member of Horngate."

You're not. The unspoken words hung in the air like lit dynamite.

"He needs a lesson in loyalty." Alexander's fury boiled hotter as the truth burrowed through his chest. He had no place here. His face contorted. He would be damned if they made him leave. He would *make* them give him a place here.

His hands clenched. He kicked out, and his foot rammed flesh. Tyler made a guttural sound and buried his fist in Alexander's gut. Fire spread along his ribs as bones fractured.

"One of these days soon, you and I are going to have a serious talk," Tyler said, shifting position and locking his arm around Alexander's neck in an iron chokehold.

"Anytime. The sooner, the better," Alexander rasped, never looking away from the angel. He did not have the strength or concentration to use his telekinesis on his two captors. It was a recent talent, and he was still learning to use it. Nor did he want a fight with them *and* Tutresiel. He would not win that battle.

"I think it is you who's in need of a lesson," Tutresiel crooned softly, his eyes crimson slits, his wings fluttering with a chiming sound. "Do you really think you can take me on and win?"

"I was holding my own," Alexander growled, jerking against the arms holding him. His healing spells had already repaired his ribs and back. He dragged Niko and Tyler a couple of feet before they hauled him to a stop. His Prime was savage and wanted blood.

"Only because I chose not to skewer you." Tutresiel rolled his head on his neck as if to loosen tense muscles, and his wings folded forward again, the razor feathers clashing together like two huge sword fans. Anything caught between would be shredded apart. "But do keep trying. I have been so bored these last few weeks. Killing you would be fun." His lips widened in a death's-head smile.

A hand fell on Alexander's shoulder, and Thor moved in front of him, blocking his view of the angel. "Easy, old son," Thor drawled with his Texas twang. "You can't kill him. Don't waste yourself on that son of a bitch."

Alexander stared into Thor's intent blue eyes. For a moment, he hated his friend with every fiber of his being. Hated him for being accepted to Horngate and hated him for being right. As much as he wanted to kill someone right now, it was pointless to fight Tutresiel. Slowly, he reeled himself in.

Niko and Tyler felt his withdrawal and let go, stepping back warily. His lips peeled from his teeth in an animal snarl. Good. He was not so weak or tame as they thought. *You will be Prime.* That was exactly their fear, and now they had seen for themselves that he was capable of battling Max, perhaps winning. His exhibition with Tutresiel would not endear him to anyone. His chin thrust out. Fuck them.

"I am going to get her. Come or not, as you please."

He shoved past all of them and went to the dilapidated door. He gripped the handle and yanked. It broke off and dissolved into a handful of blue sparks. They burned through his hand and the smell of burning flesh filled the chamber. He began ripping at the boards. They pulled away and dissolved. Blue sparks spun through the air, falling on his skin and burrowing through him like tiny stars, dying where they fell on the stone floor. More hands joined his. First Niko, then Tyler and Thor.

The stink of scorched hair and flesh thickened, and still they worked. For every board they removed, another sprouted in its place.

Suddenly an iron hand grasped Alexander by the collar and flung him backward. "Out of my way, cockroach."

The incandescent white light of Tutresiel's sword flared as Alexander flew across the vault. The air burst from his lungs as he slammed against the wall. He slid to the floor, his head reeling. He touched the back of his skull. His fingers came away bloody. Gritting his teeth, he climbed clumsily to his feet, swaying dizzily as he tried to catch his balance, feeling his healing spells going to work to knit his fractured skull.

"Stand back," Tutresiel advised the others.

His wings fanned wide as he slashed at the door. A resounding *boom* shook the mountain, and a wave of power smashed into Alexander. He dropped to his knees, his fingers curving against the floor to hold him in place as magic raked his skin. Then a fine mist of blue descended, and his body was on fire.

He ignored the pain and burns, his vision curling black as magic seared his eyes. He got to his feet, stalking past Tutresiel and running his hands over the scarred stone of the vault wall. The door was gone. Tutresiel's sword had left a shallow groove in the rock where it had been. *Holy fucking night*. The sword should have had more effect.

Helplessness warred with molten fury in Alexander's chest. Damn her for going alone. His hands flexed and tightened into fists. If she were here, he would strangle her.

He turned to Niko. "Get Xaphan. His battle fire will melt the wall."

"And bring down the mountain. Giselle won't like that."

"She does not want to lose Max," Alexander countered. "Besides, what she does not know will not hurt her, will it?"

Niko hesitated, clearly tempted.

"The wall isn't made of stone, it's made of magic. Will

his fire work if Tutresiel's sword hardly scratched it?" Tyler asked.

Alexander whirled on him. "Get Xaphan now, or spirits help you, because if Max does not return, I will take Prime, and I will make you suffer the rest of your despicable and very short lives."

"Careful," Niko warned. "You're only immortal if someone doesn't kill you first. The only reason you're still alive is Max doesn't want you dead. But if she's gone—" His face contorted and settled into a cold mask. "A bullet to the back of your head will take care of you."

Alexander smiled, his eyes narrowing to slits. He spoke softly, his voice flat. "Do you think I have survived a hundred years without knowing how to take care of myself? Do not think me an easy target. But since you and I both agree that Max needs help, fetch Xaphan. Unless you have a better idea."

Niko did not move at first, clearly not liking the idea of taking orders from Alexander. Finally he gave in. "All right. But don't think this is over. You and I will have a discussion soon. Tyler, go get him."

Tyler reacted with pleasing speed and launched himself at the stairs. In that same moment, Alexander's back prickled as a wash of magic filled the vault. He spun about. The dilapidated door on the wall had returned. Only now it stood ajar, a brilliant wedge of pale blue light pouring through the narrow opening.

Instantly Alexander moved forward. But before he could touch the handle, the door swung slowly open.

3

MAX STEPPED DOWN INTO THE BOTTOM OF THE vault with Tutresiel hard on her heels. She was surprisingly glad of his company. She winced. It felt like a symptom that she was going soft somehow, and that worried her. She needed her hard edges to survive the world of magic, especially as the Guardians went to war. She couldn't afford to let herself be distracted by anything. She was Horngate's Prime, and it was her job to protect its people, not get them killed because she was thinking of friends or—

Alexander's sharp-featured face rose in her mind, and she banished it instantly, but not before liquid longing pooled in her stomach. She groaned inwardly. He made her want to do bad, bad things to him and with him. Regularly and often.

Down, girl, she told herself, even as his image crept back into her mind with his piercing eyes, the smooth touchable planes of his muscular chest, and his lips— oh, holy mother of fuck, that man could kiss. *Shit*. She drew a breath and let it out slowly, trying to focus on the trouble at hand. Scooter.

She stopped and eyed the magical curtain cutting the space in half. What was it for? She didn't think it could keep Scooter out if he wanted in. He'd blow through it like it was wet tissue. Maybe it was there in case he decided to abandon Horngate. This way, their enemies wouldn't be able to just walk through the back door unannounced.

"Well?" Tutresiel asked. "Change your mind?"

She eyed him. He was leaning against the wall like he was settling in to watch a movie and wasn't sure it was going to be any good.

"So if you thought there was a decent chance you might disappear forever, would you feel bad not letting your friends say good-bye?" The question surprised her as it left her lips. Soft. She was going so damned soft. But if Scooter kept her, this would be the second time she'd left the people who mattered most to her without any word of good-bye. The first had been when Giselle turned her, and now—

Her throat went dry. Now, thirty years later, she was going to go drag them to Horngate for safety. What would they say when they saw her? Dread made her go cold. She'd made sure they thought she was dead. Would they be angry? Would they be glad to see her? Would they be afraid of her? Max looked just the same as she did when she vanished out of their lives, but she was nothing like that girl—Anne. Her name had been Anne. No one but Giselle knew that. She'd never intended to go back to them, although she had someone keeping an eye on them, just to be sure they were always safe and didn't need for anything. But with the Guardians waging war on humanity, she had to bring them to Horngate. They'd never survive otherwise. So now

she was going to have to face them. If she could make
Scooter let her go long enough to bring them back.

If.

She nearly laughed at herself. Here she was worried
about what her family would say when she went to get
them and what Niko and the others would say if she
disappeared without saying good-bye. Only one could
happen, but she was obsessing about both. *Idiot.*

Tutresiel's brows had risen as he considered her question. "You're supposing I have friends."

"You've been alive a long time. You'd be truly pathetic
if you hadn't managed at least one or two. Unless they
all died with the dinosaurs."

He smiled. "There are some who might miss me."

"So? Would you feel bad?"

"Guilty conscience?"

She looked away. "I didn't want them to stop me, and
they'd have tried. Probably would have succeeded, too,
in the shape I'm in. Then they would have gone inside
instead of me. I couldn't let that happen. All the same,
they're going to be pissed that I walked out on them
without a word."

"I take it you didn't leave a note?"

She shook her head. "I was in a hurry."

He shook his head, *tsk*ing. "Very thoughtless." He patted his über-tight pants. "And me without a pen and
paper." His brows rose. "What would you have said?"

She frowned. That was just it. Niko and Tyler were
her best friends, and they probably didn't even know
it. She'd kept them at arm's length. Lise and Oz, too—
Oz was the Sunspear Prime, and Lise was one of his
Spears. And Giselle. She was—

Max didn't know what the witch-bitch was anymore. What would Max have said to her? *Bite me? See you in hell?* Or maybe . . . *thanks.* She bit her tongue. Who'd have thought she'd ever *thank* Giselle for kidnapping and torturing her? But the witch had made her a Shadowblade and brought her to Horngate and given her a purpose in life. Not to mention giving her good friends. Just at the moment, all the pain she'd suffered seemed worth it. But telling the witch-bitch that—Max wasn't sure she'd ever want to.

And then there was Alexander.

What kind of note could she have left him? *Wish I could have licked you like a Popsicle?*

Only it went deeper than lust, as much as she hated to admit it. He knew what it was like to be Prime—the weight of responsibility, holding her people's lives in her hands. It was a burden that no one else at Horngate could understand the way he did, except Oz and maybe Giselle, and she couldn't talk to either of them. She'd never expose herself to Giselle that way. As for Oz, he was one of her best friends, but they'd been doing a flirting dance for so long that she didn't dare do anything to tip the balance into something more. She didn't want him that way—not the way she wanted Alexander. And man, she wanted him worse than a starving man wanted food. She rolled her eyes at herself. She really needed to get laid.

She sobered as she eyed the door again. She should have left him some word. She more than wanted him. She'd opened herself up to him in ways she'd not done with anyone since before Giselle turned her. And she trusted him with Horngate. He'd guard it with his heart and soul. She knew it, even if no one else did. But they'd come around, especially if Scooter took Max. Giselle had already lost too many Spears and Blades, and she didn't have the strength to make more at the moment. You didn't just make a Prime quick from scratch. It took many years. Niko and Tyler were close but were still a year or so away. And even if they jumped to Prime tomorrow, Max was certain that neither of them could take Alexander in a challenge. He'd slap them down like puppies. And if Max did survive Scooter, then Horngate would still need all the strong warriors it could get. They hadn't seen the last of war.

So what would she have really said in a letter? *Sorry I've been a bitch the last few weeks. Nothing personal, I was just trying to stay alive. Oh, and by the way, nice knowing you.* She snorted softly. That would have gone over well. Why did it always come down to words, anyhow? Her tongue always got her in trouble.

"I have no idea what I would have said," she said finally, answering Tutresiel's question. "It was a stupid idea and pointless, anyhow. I'd better get going." She eyed the dilapidated door on the other side of the magic barrier, then looked at Tutresiel. "I'll see you when I see you, kitten." She hesitated. "This really is a good place. You could've done a lot worse than fall into Giselle's lap."

"Strange words, considering how much you hate her."

"Yeah, but as witches go, she could be a lot worse. I'm just saying . . ." What was she saying? "I've been you. Hell, I *am* you. Chained up and pissed about it. But this place grows on you, if you give it a chance."

He folded his arms across his chest. "But you're the

only one I like, princess. And you're blowing out of here."

"Aw. You like me. Ain't that sweet."

"You like me, too, princess," he said with a taunting grin. "Don't try to deny it. So do me a favor and come back before I'm forced to skewer some of your annoying little minions."

"Well, good news, then. I have no intention of letting Scooter keep me today. I've got some things to take care of, and he's either going to have to kill me or wait till I'm good and ready."

"What makes you think he won't kill you?"

"Because he wants something from me. If I die, he's shit out of luck, so he's not going to kill me. Not today, anyhow. Of course, there's always tomorrow." She tossed a little wave at him, wishing she was as confident as she sounded, and then strode to the barrier.

Magic washed over her in a tingling shower, and then she was through. One of her talents was to go through any lock without needing a key. She went to the door and pulled it open.

Beyond should have been a wide cave that narrowed to a long tunnel leading out of Horngate. At least, that's what it had been when she went through it the first time. But Scooter had changed things up. Instead, a wall of magic filled the entry with pale blue fire. She stared at it a moment. Well, she'd known he wasn't going to make it easy on her. He'd made that clear enough in her dreams. She grimaced. If he wanted a little revenge, she couldn't stop him. She sucked in a breath and strode forward into fire.

It felt like she'd gone through a wood chipper. The

pain reached deeper into her soul than she'd ever felt before. It was like someone was carving at the core of herself with dull surgical instruments. It was intimate and horrifying, and she screamed. Except she had no mouth, no throat, no lungs.

She didn't know how long she drifted there. She felt Scooter all around her. He was angry and resentful and gloating over her pain.

Deep inside, smugness filled Max. The fucker had no idea what he was dealing with. There was only so much pain a person could feel before it became monotonous. Or maybe Max had too much practice with torture. Thanks to Giselle's endless ministrations, she'd learned long ago to embrace pain and turn it into something like pleasure, knowing that surviving without breaking was the same as winning in this kind of game.

She didn't fight. She simply waited as the waves of agony washed through her. On some level, she felt her healing spells trying to interfere, but they were impotent against Scooter's power. Still, she knew that she could very well die before he was done punishing her. Her spells could drain her to the point where she no longer had anything left. Part of her was willing. If he killed her, she won the battle. Or rather, if she died, he lost the prize, which amounted to a win for her. But no. She had things to do.

"I'm dying." She didn't know if her mouth moved or if she'd simply spoken the words in her mind.

For a seemingly endless time there was no answer. Then, suddenly, she was whole again and falling. She sprawled on the floor of the cave. She rolled over as copper-colored sand filled her eyes, nose, and mouth.

She coughed, inhaling the fine grains. She doubled over, nearly puking as she hacked violently.

Finally, the fit subsided, and she lay breathless. The sand was hot, like it had been in an oven, though not unpleasantly so. She sat up and looked around. The walls of the cave were made of faceted crystals of every color. They glittered in the soft blue light of Scooter's magic. The door was gone, and Scooter himself was nowhere to be found.

Max sat up. She was exhausted, and her body felt like taffy. She looked at her hands, loosely thatched together between her knees. They were little more than skin wrapped around bone sticks. Her wrists and arms were no better. She hadn't lied when she told Scooter she was dying. He was draining the life right out of her. Maybe she should have dubbed him Dracula instead of Scooter.

She looked around. "Well? I haven't got all day," she called.

For a moment, nothing happened. Then the sand began to shift. It rippled as if blown by the wind. A couple of feet in front of her, it rose in a tall, round shape, the sands whirling in a tight spiral. Then the bottom and the top split and a bulb grew on top, turning into the semblance of a man. A moment later, the sand contracted and firmed into a solid shape. It smoothed, and Max found herself staring at a naked Scooter.

He looked exactly as he had before. He had long blue-black hair that shone iridescent in the crystal light. His skin was the same color as the sand, and his features were hawklike. His body was muscular, and he looked like he might have been thirty years old, except that his onyx eyes were ancient. Flecks of blue magic swam in their depths, reminding Max that he was not human. As if she needed a reminder. She wasn't even sure if he was a *he*. Except that he had the right parts between his legs, and they weren't too shabby.

He stared down at her, his expression oddly impassive, while she could feel his anger pounding against her like a club.

"Can you tone that down a little?" she said, brushing away invisible cobwebs and propping her head on her hands. "I'm having a hard time staying upright as it is." The pounding sensation eased, though it didn't go away.

"You promised to come to me."

"Yes, I did."

"But you did not."

"I've had some other things on my plate. More important."

He made a low rumbling sound almost out of hearing, and the walls quivered. The crystals made a thin chiming sound that made Max ache in the marrow of her bones.

She was too tired for tact. "Look, Scooter, here's how it is. I'm a Shadowblade, and I'm bound to serve and protect Giselle and Horngate. Right now, my compulsion spells don't want me anywhere near you. So just walking in here costs me the equivalent of a stomach full of razor wire. On top of that, the Guardians are trying to kill off most of humanity, and I really want to go fetch my family and bring them to Horngate before they become casualties. So you come in third on my priority list."

"You are *my* gift," he hissed, and it sounded disturbingly snakelike. But then, his father was Onniont, the Horned Serpent, who dug the rifts between mountains.

"So you said. But I'm not ready to be unwrapped yet. I'll make you a deal. You stop invading my dreams and don't try to stop me from going to get my family, and I'll come back and let you do whatever you want with me."

"You are mine. You will stay."

Max gave a slow smile and stood. "Now, that's a problem for you, Scooter, because you want me alive, and I'll make sure you've got nothing but a corpse to play dollies with. Trust me, I'd rather die than lose this particular game."

He said nothing, just staring. Max didn't look away. His eyes seemed to pour out of his sockets like moon-dappled oil. The tide washed over her and she found herself shrouded in something that felt like an electric web. It laced her skin, and everywhere it touched, jolts of electricity sizzled. She leaned into it, feeling her strength ebbing. If he kept this up much longer, she'd be worm food. Still, she didn't argue or fight. It was a game of chicken, and she didn't mean to blink first.

Speckles of white and green flashed across her vision, and she recognized them as signs that she was losing consciousness. She sagged, slumping over onto her side. She felt oddly warm and comfortable, and though her compulsion spells flogged her like whips, telling her to fight, she didn't move.

Suddenly the black shroud vanished. Scooter was behind her. He lifted her, cradling her against his chest. His skin was as warm and soft as any man's, and he smelled of grass and dirt. Max's head fell back to nestle in the crook of his neck. He stroked his hands over her arms and breasts, then lower, to her belly and legs. She had no sense of what he was doing until he repeated his gestures twice more. Then she realized she was being cocooned in magic. She didn't struggle. He didn't want her dead.

Soon she felt the sludge in her head starting to thin, and the gray cleared from her vision. Healing energy seeped into her body, and she began to feel like she might be strong enough to hold up her own weight again. Still, she didn't try to escape Scooter's hands. She found the sensation both soothing and strangely erotic.

She drew a breath and turned to snuggle closer against him. He was still naked. And apparently the plumbing worked, because he was sporting a growing hard-on. Not for the first time did she wonder just what he planned to do with her.

"I have to go," she said, still resting in his arms.

His hands stilled. "Time is running away."

"Time for what?"

"For what must be done. What you and I must do."

"I need a week. Maybe a little longer. Then I'm all yours."

He nodded slowly, as if he had a choice. "I will wait."

"I'll come back to you." Max pushed herself to her feet. She felt back to normal strength. But then, he wouldn't want to send her out damaged. Better odds of her getting back safe if she wasn't roadkill when she left. She glanced pointedly at the wall where the door should be. "I'd better go."

"First," he said, standing up with unnatural fluid grace, "I will give you a gift."

She frowned and took a step back. In her experience,

gifts weren't something you wanted to receive, especially from creatures like Scooter. He smiled. It was the first time she'd ever seen such an expression on his face, and it was unnerving. She felt very much like the fly invited into the spider's parlor. She'd been congratulating herself because she thought she had him trapped over a barrel, but he wasn't taking it lying down.

She watched him closely, tensing herself to jump away. But he never moved. Instead, the sparkling crystals on the ceiling and walls suddenly flashed brighter, sending sequins of jeweled light dancing through the air and across the floor. They swirled and coalesced into a flashing disco ball. Before Max could do more than twitch, it dove and engulfed her left arm.

The disco ball contracted into a tight, hard sleeve that felt like a lead weight. It flared bright blue and faded from sight, but the tight heaviness remained. She rubbed her arm, feeling nothing. "Any chance you're going to tell me what this is?" she asked. "Or do I get to find out on my own?" At the worst possible moment, of course.

"You already have the power to travel the web. It is what makes you special to me. If you are in danger for your life, you will now be able to step through the web to somewhere else. Not far. Perhaps only a few feet."

Max considered a moment. "Thanks. I think." She had a feeling that invoking the spell would be less than pleasant. Scooter's slight smile told her she was right. When he only continued to look at her as if waiting, she shifted. "I should go. The faster I get my family, the faster I return to you."

"There is something else you might wish to see."

She scowled, her stomach twisting with foreboding. His expression had gone entirely bland, except for his eyes. They gleamed with angry fire. The hairs on the back of her neck rose. Whatever he wanted to show her, it felt like a trap.

"If you want to show me something, then get on with it. I don't have time to mess around."

"Less than you think." He smiled again, and it wasn't remotely pleasant.

Then he gestured, and the room fell dark except for the crystals on the opposite wall. Across them panned an image of a farm town. They were looking down on it from high above. On the eastern side was a wide black strip of freeway, and to the west rose steep hills. A long lake nestled behind a dam, surrounded by a thin fringe of trees and bare ridges. In between was the town, surrounded by checkerboard orchards and farmland. Max's mouth went dry. The town was Winters. Her gaze riveted on the finger-shaped patch of green that was her brother's orchard.

"Why are you showing me this?" she rasped, her throat tight.

"Watch."

He moved behind her, his hands sliding gently over her shoulders to her arms, his chest hot against her back. Max couldn't tell if he meant to be comforting or if he thought she'd turn away and was going to make sure she couldn't. Fat chance. She was locked in place.

"They come," he murmured against her ear.

At first, she didn't see anything. Then mounds of loose dirt rose in the surrounding fields like giant gopher holes. Out of them crawled animals and people. They were sleek and inhuman in their grace, their eyes jewel-like. They scanned the area like hungry wolves. There were hundreds of them. They were followed by ribbons of white smoke that hung low, curling across the ground to surround the town and outlying fields in a thick wall. It thickened, spreading inward. Before long, it would swallow everything inside.

"What are they?" Max fixed her gaze on her brother's farmhouse. The smoke was closing on it quickly.

"No questions. Watch."

She could see people running toward the house. Someone on a four-wheeler was overtaken halfway through the orchard. Others were swallowed as they dropped baskets and leaped from ladders beneath the trees. The smoke swept along faster. Suddenly the view telescoped. Max had a moment of vertigo like she was plummeting out of the sky. The picture yanked to a halt, and Max was there in the yard around the white-gabled farmhouse, with its wraparound porch and silo turret. Graceful trees surrounded it, and beyond were two long white barns.

She saw her father and mother. Her throat seized and she could hardly breathe. They were so close, staring straight at her. Then her father shoved her mother, and she raced up onto the porch, pushing ahead of her Tris—Max's sister—and a teenage girl, Tris's youngest daughter. What were they doing there? Any of them? They must have come to visit Kyle, the brother she had never really known. He owned the orchard.

Her father started running toward Max. His eyes were wide, and his tanned face was taut and gray. For a moment she thought he was going to snatch her into his arms, he was so close. But then smoke swirled from behind her, and the picture winked out.

"No!"

She spun around, shoving at Scooter. It was like pushing on a mountain. He didn't move.

"What was that?" she demanded.

"It is what is."

"It's happening now?" Max wanted to throw up. She scraped her fingers through her hair, pulling sharply. What was happening there? "What will the smoke and those creatures do to them?"

He shrugged. "I do not have the gift of foreseeing."

"Then show me. Show me what's happening to them."

His brows rose and his eyes gleamed. "What will you pay?" he asked softly. "Will you come with me now if I show you?"

"You motherfucker," Max spat, crossing her arms tight across her stomach to keep from stabbing him through the eye. "You know I can't. I have to help them."

"Will they be alive when you get there?"

She stared at him. The bastard was taunting her. She was making him wait, so he was getting a little revenge. Anger made her shake. She drew it in, pushing it down. She sank inside herself, feeling her emotions peeling away as she withdrew. She needed to be cool-headed and focused.

"If you want me to be faster, then why don't you send me there through the web? Surely you can do that," she said, lifting the arm he'd ensorcelled and tapping it meaningfully.

"You are not yet ready for such a journey. Nor am I willing to risk it."

"Risk what?"

Abruptly he pointed at the wall, and the door reappeared. "Go. I *will* hold you to your word."

The emphasis on *will* told her that what she suspected was true: the spell on her arm wasn't just a gift, it was also a leash. Apparently he'd been watching too many cop shows about GPS tracking.

"I'll be back," Max said, and started for the door, sidestepping so she could keep an eye on Scooter.

The crystal walls glowed with milky blue light and, within seconds, began to melt like wax. The magic pooled on the floor and ran toward her as if she were a magnet. Max turned and fled. She knew without asking that if it overtook her, she wasn't leaving. The bastard definitely had passive-aggressive tendencies.

She shouldered through the door, her spell-wrapped arm turning searingly cold. She staggered, bending double, the air rushing out of her lungs as the cold swept up her arm and into her chest. Her heart spasmed, and her lungs cramped. She looked up, finding the barrier down and Niko, Alexander, Thor, and Tutresiel staring at her. Panic flared inside her.

"The barrier!" She gasped. "Get it up now!"

4

NIKO SPUN AND LEAPED TO DO AS ORDERED. Alexander grabbed Max, swinging her up in his arms and jerking back to the stairs just as Niko slapped the starburst on the wall. Once again, the shimmering curtain of magic cut across the center of the vault. The blue light washed up against it and flared dirty yellow. Beyond, in the doorway, Scooter stood naked, blue magic swirling around him. Light flashed, and Alexander jerked away. He turned back a moment later, his vision dancing with spots. Scooter, the door, and the magic were gone.

He looked down at Max. She rubbed her left forearm up and down, her attention fixed on the curtain. Her body trembled—with fear, exhaustion, or anger, he could not tell. She met his gaze, and for once there was no bite there. There was nothing there at all. Her gaze was distant, like she was looking at him from far away. She had sunk into the depths of herself—it was her version of emotional Kevlar. Whatever had happened in there with Scooter, it was bad. Worse than bad.

"Put me down. I can walk."

He set her on her feet.

"What the hell were you doing in there? Alone?" Niko demanded.

Tyler had come back down the stairs, and they stood shoulder to shoulder. Tutresiel loomed behind, and Thor stood off to the side.

Max looked at him, then at the others, her gaze settling on Alexander. She frowned at the bloody shreds of his shirt. "What happened to you?"

He looked down at himself and back at her. "Hunting accident."

Her mouth curved reluctantly, and she shook her head before turning back to Niko. She rubbed her fingers over her arm again, holding it stiffly against her side. Alexander scowled at it.

"Scooter's been sending me love messages. I thought I'd better go see him before I stopped breathing."

"That's why you've been looking like death warmed over," Niko said. It was not a question.

Max shrugged.

"You shouldn't have gone alone," Niko said. "What the hell are we for if you don't bother to use us?"

"Don't you trust us to have your back?" Tyler demanded.

"Of course I do. Don't be dumber than you have to be," Max said impatiently. "This is my problem. Not yours. He'd have killed you."

"Looks like he almost killed you," Alexander pointed out as he shrugged out of the shredded remains of his shirt and dropped it onto the ground.

"A couple of times," she admitted. "But he didn't, because he needs me alive."

"For what?"

"That is the billion-dollar question. If you figure it out, let me know. Anyhow, it's over, at least for now." She pushed her hair behind her ears.

"What do you mean, for now?" Niko demanded.

"Scooter is going to be patient until I get back."

"Back from where?" Alexander, Tyler, and Niko asked in unison.

"California. My family is in trouble."

"Your family?" This time it was Thor. He looked astonished. "You have living family? How old are you?"

Before she could answer, her phone rang with a high-pitched sound few but Shadowblades could hear. She reached into her pocket and flipped it open. Alexander could hear Giselle's voice on the other end.

"Where have you been? I've been calling you for the last fifteen minutes. I need to see you. Now. There's news."

"I heard," Max said. "I'll be there in a minute."

She snapped the phone shut and looked at the gathered men and Tutresiel. She flashed a grin at the angel. "Scooter would have kicked your ass up to your throat," she said, then headed for the stairs.

Alexander fell in at her heels, followed by the others. Tutresiel brought up the rear, the shaft too small for him to fly up.

No one said anything. Alexander was too glad to see her alive and too worried about what might happen to her when she left. Was she going to try to go to California alone? His jaw set. He would not let her. She could order the others around, and they had to obey, but he was not part of Horngate, and he was not going to sit on his ass while she ran off by herself to get killed. *You will be Prime*. Not if he could help it.

They followed Max as she wound through the corridors toward Giselle's suite of rooms. She stopped and turned around.

"Don't you all have somewhere else to be?"

None of them answered, standing firm without so much as a twitch to suggest that they might be thinking of leaving.

She sighed exasperation. "Giselle wants to see *me*."

"Fine," Niko said.

"After that, you'll see us," Tyler said. "We'll wait."

She glared, then shook her head. "Bunch of fucking mother hens," she muttered, and started away again.

Alexander grinned with bitter humor. For once, he was one of them, a brother-in-arms. Tutresiel even seemed welcome in the effort to gang up on Max and make her cooperate. It was a twisted version of "the enemy of my enemy is my friend."

Giselle's suite lay at the bulbous end of a broad passage on the south side of the mountain fortress. Max approached the pair of polished oak doors, pausing outside to check her phone. Her expression was shuttered as she shoved it back into her pocket. Whom was she expecting to hear from?

She turned to look at her companions. "This could take a while."

"We'll wait." Niko crossed his arms, his square jaw jutting.

Max eyed him balefully. "Remind me later to kick your ass and show you who's in charge."

"Whatever lights your fire," he said, not moving.

She turned away and knocked on the heavy doors, then thrust them open. Beyond was a spacious sitting room decorated in shades of cream and purple. The walls were mostly bare, and everything smelled new. Like most everything in the keep, Giselle's quarters had been destroyed in the battle four weeks before and had only recently been repaired and refurbished.

Max took a step inside and paused, her body suddenly pulling taut, her head cocking. Alexander stiffened and followed her. Niko and Tyler were already moving. As soon as he crossed the threshold, Alexander could feel what had sent her hackles rising. Every hair on his body prickled with the swell of magic. It was a turbulent current, spinning through the room like the outer edge of a whirlpool.

Max plunged into it, heading for the door on the left. It was made of an enormous slab of stone. There was no handle. She put her hands flat against it and shoved. Complex wards flared, and vines of black magic wriggled over her hands and up her arms.

"C'mon, bitch," Max growled. "You made me to open doors. Don't think for a second you're going to keep me out." She shoved again. A second later, the magic retracted, and the slab of stone swung inward, rotating around a central pivot.

The five Blades and the angel slid inside. It was a circular room with another door on the opposite wall. Protective wards glimmered on every surface. Set in the flat stone floor was the *anneau* floor—a triangle, inside a star, inside a circle. It was lit. At the center of the triangle was Giselle. She hovered a foot off the ground. Her hands were held low and out from her body, and her head was tipped back. She stared upward into the darkness, and her lips moved in an unintelligible whisper. Black magic surrounded her in a crackling cloud.

"What the hell?" Max muttered. "She knew I was coming. Why start a spell?"

"Look," Alexander said, pointing at a melted blob on the outer edge of the circle. He smelled the burned plastic.

Niko picked it up. "Her phone," he said with a frown. He dropped it, shaking his hand. "It's hot."

Suddenly Giselle's arms rose over her head in graceful arcs. She pressed her palms together. Magic thickened around her hands. She lowered her arms, her fingers meshed tightly. Magic drained into the ball around her hands, growing dense. She bowed her head, still whispering. Then she thrust her hands down hard, flattening her palms so they were parallel to the floor.

The walls shuddered as magic exploded. It burst through the triangle. The star held it a moment and then winked out. Magic roiled within the circle, as Giselle, her thin face twisting with concentration, again lifted her hands above her head.

"What's going on?" Tyler asked.

"She's losing it," Max said, pacing along the edge of the circle, her hands clenching and unclenching, her gaze locked on Giselle. "She needs to shut this down."

"She is trying," Alexander said, his attention shifting between Giselle and Max. Although her expression showed nothing, her compulsion spells had to be ripping her apart, demanding that she rescue the witch. Between those and her own sense of duty, she might do something extremely stupid. Like try to break the circle and pull Giselle out of the maelstrom. The result could bring down the mountain. The circle and the witch were all that was keeping the wild magic from exploding like a nuclear bomb.

"Come on, come on," Max muttered. "Get your shit together. Stop fucking around."

Giselle sagged, and magic whirled like a tornado inside the circle. Max lunged. Alexander leaped to stop her, but his fingers only brushed her boot.

He hit the floor and leaped back to his feet. Max had passed *through* the circle. It was not possible. But then, she could open any lock, and a ward circle was a lock. A moment later, she and Giselle sprawled onto the floor on the other side.

The witch lay limp. She was pale and far too thin. Magic still snapped across her skin in sizzling threads. Beneath her, Max lay on her back, blinking blearily, her body twitching as magic zapped her. She was scorched. Her arms were a patchwork of black and red, and her hands looked like she'd stuck them into the heart of a fire. Her clothes were charred, her hair burned. The smell was awful.

Alexander glanced at the circle. It still held, but the magic it contained was growing visibly more chaotic. It would not be long before it broke through. What kind of idiot was Giselle, risking a powerful working like this without a coven to support her? When she was barely out of her sickbed?

"Get them out," he ordered the others as they hovered helplessly over the two women. "The circle will not hold. Hurry."

No one argued. Niko and Tyler lifted Giselle gently

away and carried her out into the sitting room. Thor grabbed Max, who groaned, her head lolling over his arm. Alexander and Tutresiel followed. They spun the heavy stone door back into place. The wards flared as it shut. They should be powerful enough to contain the explosion. But if not—

"Keep going. We have to get out of here," Alexander told the others.

Before anyone could move, a blast reverberated through the mountain. The wall between the sitting room and the workroom bulged, and a spiderweb of cracks wove across it and the ceiling. Two lamps shattered to the floor. Dust sifted down from above.

Giselle convulsed, her body flailing. Niko and Tyler held her firmly as magic whipped them, leaving behind red welts and blisters. Max struggled to stand, and Thor steadied her as she swayed. She closed on Giselle, grasping the witch's face between her raw hands, bending to get close in her face.

"Stop it. Giselle! Get your shit together before you kill us all!"

Her voice was thick and rasping. Magic writhed over her arms and up her shoulders. She did not seem to notice. Her attention was fixed on the witch. Giselle's eyes flickered.

"That's right. Wake up and shut this down," Max urged. "Come on, now. Remember, I get to be the one to kill you. Are you trying to commit suicide before I can do so?"

"Fat chance," Giselle whispered, and her eyes opened wide. She sat up. Her mouth pulled into a thin line, her face skeletal beneath the pale wrapping of skin. She had nearly drained herself to death fending off the attacks four weeks ago, and her recovery had been slow, despite the healing help of Xaphan.

She struggled to climb to her feet. Niko helped her. Stepping away, she clenched her hands, pulling them tight together between her breasts. Taking a long, unsteady breath, she pushed them out before her. As before, the magic chasing around her body slid down to ball around her fists. There was less of it now than there had been inside the *anneau* floor. Alexander held his breath.

Giselle brought her fists down sharply at her sides, flattening her hands and pointing her fingers toward the ground. She shouted a word that hammered Alexander's skull and sent him reeling. He fell against Tutresiel. The angel shoved him away. Alexander caught himself against the wall and spun about. Tutresiel watched him, his red eyes shining brilliantly, daring Alexander to attack.

"Later," Alexander mouthed, and then turned back to Max and Giselle. The smothering press of magic was gone.

Giselle stood inside a patch of burning carpet. Black smoke billowed as the thick pad beneath caught.

"Get her out of here," Max said, coughing.

Tyler swung the witch into his arms and carried her out into the foyer area. Niko and Alexander grabbed Max, picking her up between them.

"Can you put that fire out?" she asked Tutresiel as Alexander and Niko set her back on her feet, continuing to steady her as she swayed.

"It is magic fire. Xaphan must do it. Or a witch."

Max looked at Thor. "Go find him."

Thor took off at a dead run. Dense black smoke squeezed from the cracks surrounding the now-closed doors. It stank of chemicals and made Alexander's throat and nose burn.

"Tutresiel, wait here. When Xaphan's done, bring him. Giselle will need healing. We'd better keep moving before the smoke kills us," Max said to the others, shaking off Niko and Alexander.

The two men exchanged annoyed glances and followed. Tyler led the way with Giselle.

"Where to?" he asked Max.

Alexander answered. "Dining commons. You need to eat and heal," he said unapologetically when Max scowled at him. "Giselle could use something to eat and drink as well."

"Fine," she said.

She brushed away offers of aid, though clearly she was hurting more than a little. Typical. She never took help unless she had no other choice. He suppressed the urge to help her anyway. She might take it as a Prime challenge, and just at the moment, she might not be able to beat him.

The memory of Magpie's prophecy swept over him, and his skin went cold. He pulled away, falling back to walk behind.

The dining commons was empty except for Magpie. Alexander could hear her in the kitchen. The scent of baking bread and garlic filled the air. A cold buffet table ran down one side of the serving area, and two hot tables were on the other side. A beverage bar sat in one corner, and chairs and tables were scattered through the large space. Pillars and screens lent an air of privacy here and there.

Tyler set Giselle gently on a chair. She slumped, her eyes half closed. Her chestnut hair was pulled back from her face. Her face was pale and bruised-looking, and her clothes looked like they belonged on a much larger woman. Still, she emanated authority and power. Max slid into a chair beside her.

Niko went to let Magpie know they were there, and Alexander filled two glasses with apple juice and set them on the table before the two women.

"Drink."

He did not wait for a reply, but started gathering food from the buffet for Max. He stacked it on a tray and set it in front of her. Her glass was empty, and Giselle had at least sipped from hers.

Wordlessly, he refilled the glass and then fetched a milkshake from the machine. He gave it to Giselle.

"That looks good," Max said, eyeing it longingly.

"Your wish is my command," he said, and went to get her one.

"Why don't I believe that?" she said, rolling the cold glass he handed her between her palms and sucking from the straw. "Oh, holy night, that feels good," she said. "Cold."

Her skin was healing, and she no longer looked quite so raw. He sat down and Niko followed suit. Tyler remained standing behind Giselle to catch her if she started to fall.

"What the hell was that?" Max said, opening up a sub sandwich. Her voice was deceptively calm. "Are you trying to kill yourself? Because no need to go to all that trouble. Say the word, and I'll do it for you. With pleasure."

Giselle grimaced. "I thought you got over the whole hate-my-guts thing."

"Over you enslaving me and turning me into your own personal pit bull? Not so much, no. I just decided there were more important things to deal with. For now, anyway. Who knows what joys the future will bring? Like maybe pulling your lungs out through your nose. So were you just redecorating the place? Seems a little extreme. We just finished rebuilding in there. You could have waited a while before destroying it again."

Alexander saw Max rub her left arm surreptitiously— the same arm she had been favoring since she had come out of Scooter's den. What had the creature done to her? His jaw tightened with frustration. The chances of her telling him were zero, if not less.

"Sorry, I'm fickle," Giselle said.

The corners of Max's mouth lifted in a reluctant smile. "So what happened? If you wanted to burn me to a crisp, you could have sent me out into the sun."

"Sorry."

Max's brows rose. "You've done worse to me. No sense feeling sorry about it now."

"But now—I was trying to scry," Giselle said. "I wanted to know exactly what was going on in Winters."

"Should have asked me. I can save you the trouble. The place is under siege by shape-shifting creatures."

Her tone was devoid of any emotion, but Alexander could see her sinking inside herself. The ability to do that—to separate her feelings from her mind and body—made her terribly strong, but it also terrified him, because it always meant she was about to take on serious trouble, maybe more than she could handle. He corrected himself: *probably* more than she could handle.

"Your contacts told you that? So fast?" Giselle stared in surprise.

Max shook her head. "Scooter showed me."

"Right. Scooter," Giselle said, and her mouth pulled down. "What did you see?"

"Smoke. Shape-shifters. My whole family is at the orchard. They're trapped. Maybe dead by now." Her phone chirped. She pulled it out of her pocket. "It's a text. From Jim. He watches the place for me." She flipped open her phone and read it. Her expression did not change. "Nothing new. He's going to try to circle around to the lakeside and go down to the house."

"Will he make it?" Giselle asked.

Max shrugged. "He's a hex witch—circle level."

Giselle eyed her, clearly wondering where Max had met Jim and how many other powerful friends she was keeping secret. "You'll have to go. Tonight."

Max stared down at her phone for a long moment. She went rigid, and her mouth was rimmed white. The tendons in her neck corded. Her breathing quickened, and her body shook, her burned hands clenching on the table. Finally, she shook her head. "Can't." She slumped against the table, panting raggedly. "Fucking compulsion spells aren't going to let me leave you. 'Specially not when you're in this shape." She waved her fingers at Giselle.

"Yes, you can. I promised you that you could get them, and that's what you're going to do."

"Yeah? Going to take these damned spells off me?"

"You know better. But I've got the angels and Oz and your Blades and the Spears. They'll be enough."

"Not enough to talk down these damned compulsion spells. I won't survive ten miles."

"But all the same, you will go, and you will survive."

"Oh, yeah? Who's going to knock your ass out of the fire when your magic gets the best of you? Not that we don't all want the chance to smack you around, but I'm the only one who can cross a circle and live."

"You almost sound like you care what happens to me."

"I do. If something happens to you, then Horngate implodes, which means people I care about will die."

"I'm touched."

"And apparently the potency of the compulsion spells increase exponentially once you decide your witch-bitch master shouldn't die screaming after all. At least, not yet."

"Aw. That's so sweet. Almost like a Hallmark card. But let me make it real simple for you. If you don't go, then I will. I'll sneak off without anyone to guard me. So you can decide. You go tonight, or I do."

Niko's chair scraped back suddenly, and he lunged to his feet. Tyler stood on the other side of Giselle, his jaw jutting as he spun his knife in his fingers. At Giselle's threat, their Blades had risen back to a killing edge. Their compulsion spells would not like the threat of their witch leaving the safety of the covenstead, especially in her weakened condition.

Neither Giselle nor Max paid any attention to them. The witch's gaze was fixed on Max, who leaned over the table, her hands braced flat as she glared down at Giselle.

"Why? It makes no sense. With all the Guardian attacks, it isn't exactly safe out there, and you have told me time and again how much you need me." She slowly sat back down, her fingers drumming on the table. "Of course, if I stay here, then I go to Scooter. You have me on borrowed time either way."

"I promised you that you could bring your family back here to safety," Giselle said.

"You don't give a shit about promises. You're all about the bottom line, and going after my family doesn't add anything to Horngate."

"Doesn't it?" Giselle smiled mysteriously. "I'll be the judge of that."

Max sat forward. "What aren't you telling me?"

"So many things. And none of them is any of your business."

At that moment, Thor came in with Xaphan close behind. The fire angel was as tall as Tutresiel and shared the crimson eyes and perfect physique, but that's where their likeness ended. Xaphan's hair was short and white, and his expression was slightly gentler than his steel-winged cousin. He wore jeans, and his chest was as bare as his feet. His wings were iridescent black—like oil—and blue and orange flames licked the edges.

He eyed the group around the table, smiling at Max, who returned the greeting with a tight smile of her own that faded as quickly as it appeared.

"This isn't really about my family at all," she said slowly. "This is about Horngate. You've had a vision. That's why you want me to go."

Giselle smiled, but it didn't reach her eyes. "If it makes you feel better to think so, then sure."

Max scraped her burned fingers through her charred

hair. "Can't you give me a straight answer for once?"

"What would be the fun in that? It's so much more entertaining to jerk the string and watch you pounce on the catnip."

"One of these days, I *will* kill you," Max said, her eyes glittering.

"You'll try. One more thing. Take Alexander with you."

At the mention of his name, Alexander started and stared.

"What? Why? What's he got to do with this?"

"Call it precaution. If he goes with you, then he can't take Prime while you're gone."

Neither woman looked at him. He might as well have been on the moon. Fury twisted into a hot tornado inside him. He held himself still, waiting to hear the rest. He was not impulsive like Max. He liked to know what he was getting into before he jumped into the fire.

"You haven't bound him to Horngate," Max said to Giselle. "He can't be Prime."

Giselle snorted. "Don't underestimate him. He's strong and he's motivated. Being Prime is in his nature. He won't be able to help himself, and if he takes it far enough, I'll have to bind him."

"Far enough?"

"Taking over while you're gone. Killing you when you return."

"You think he'd beat me? Your confidence in me is underwhelming. I'm so flattered. Anyhow, if he is better than I am, you *should* want him to be your Prime. Only the best for you, right?"

Giselle's mouth tightened, and she spoke quietly, her words as hard as iron. "I've told you before—I only want you. Horngate needs you. And I'd be very surprised if you didn't beat him in a challenge. But it is a risk I don't intend to take. I searched for you too long and worked too hard to make you. He's not worth nearly what you are to me."

"And so he shoots me in the back of the head when I've got my back turned. My family is fucked and I'm dead. I'm better off going alone."

Alexander thrust to his feet, ready to protest Max's accusation, but the look both women directed at him sealed his lips before he could speak. This was part of their ongoing war. He sat back down, crossing his ankles out before him and folding his hands with a look of casual ease. Inside, anger burned white-hot. Soon he was going to have his say. He was not a toy for their tug-of-war.

"You need someone to help you, and if I know you, you'll refuse anyone else, even if it kills you. So as not to rob Horngate of defenders if the Guardians attack again. Am I wrong?"

Max made a face and gave a grudging shake of her head. Score for Giselle. But Max wasn't done. "So I take him with me, and what? Let's suppose he doesn't stab me in the back. What then? Do you want me to take him out? Hell of a way to pay him back for all he's done for Horngate. Anyhow, I told you before, you claimed him, which makes him one of my Blades. I don't abandon my own."

Giselle looked up at the ceiling, fury knotting her hands. She gusted a sigh, and Max grinned ferally. Alexander's lips curved along a knife edge. She wasn't easy, that was for certain. But she made him want to toss her over his shoulder and drag her back to his quarters like a caveman.

"Here's the deal. Since he's been here, you've been jumpy as hell. There's clearly something between you, whether you want to admit it or not, and you need to settle it. You need your focus. Look at you—you look like hell. It's eating you alive and has been since he got here. Right now, he could probably snap you in half with his pinkies."

"Of course, you trying to burn me alive couldn't possibly have anything to do with how I look," Max muttered. She pointedly did not mention Scooter.

"You've been looking like crap for weeks, and you know it. I need you to get your shit together."

"And he has to be the reason, because nothing else is going on around here, like, say, for instance, the near total destruction of the covenstead and the end of the world? Besides, what do you think I'm going to do? Go all Ophelia over him?"

Giselle shook her head and laughed, then pressed her hand against her side and coughed. Max glanced at Xaphan, motioning with her head. He stepped behind Giselle and settled his hands on her shoulders. She tried to shake him off, but his fingers tightened and she sat still, her expression sour as he began to pour healing energy into her. Alexander bit back his chortle at her annoyance, then gave a wry shake of his head. Max's attitude about the witch was catching.

Suddenly Giselle pushed herself to her feet, despite Xaphan. "You take him with you. He's too much of a threat here. Make sure he knows his place, and if he can't learn it, take him out. I don't need him coming back to cause trouble. If you do bring him back, get whatever's between the two of you sorted out. Consider it an order."

The witch's glance swept Alexander. He looked back through sleepy eyes. Her mouth tightened. He smiled.

"Did you hit your head or something?" Max said. "Four weeks ago, you let Selange walk out of here unharmed. A territory witch. Compared to her, Alexander is a cuddly puppy. Selange hates us, and she has a full coven to back her. I'd be worrying about her. As for him and me, there's nothing between us."

"I have my reasons for releasing Selange," Giselle said. "Not that it's any of your business. As for the two of you, I'm not stupid. You nearly explode whenever you're within twenty feet of each other. I almost have to smoke a cigarette when you leave the room. I'm sure everyone here would say the same."

Not a single person—man or angel—so much as twitched when Max's razor gaze scraped over them. When she looked at Alexander, he felt the heat flash between them like a lightning strike. His skin fairly sizzled. She turned away, her cheeks flushing.

She shrugged. "What can I say? He's pretty to look at, and yeah, I wouldn't mind having a ride on his merry-go-round, but I'm not pining away. I don't mess around with the men in the covenstead. You know that. "

"So what's turning you into a ghost?" Giselle demanded.

Max's lips curved maliciously. "I can't imagine what you're talking about."

The witch's eyes narrowed. "I need you healthy. Something's wrong. Fix it."

Max touched her forehead in a mock salute. "Whatever you say, boss."

Giselle's mouth twisted, and then she turned and stalked out. Xaphan winked at Max, then followed.

Alexander slid his chair back and stood.

"Going somewhere in particular, Slick?" Max asked, using her favorite nickname for him.

"Yes," he said, and strode after Giselle.

"Hey, Slick."

Alexander turned in the doorway, his expression carefully neutral. He wanted to tear someone in half, and right now, Max was the one he wanted to hit most. *He's pretty to look at.* Like he was a boy toy. She had dismissed him without a thought, and it churned in his gut. But he would be damned if he let her see the effect she had on him. At least, not until he had her alone on the road. Then they would settle things.

"When you're done chatting with Giselle, I want to see you."

"Do you?" he asked, and walked away. He was not bound to Horngate, and she had no right to command him. He would see her when he got around to it.

Giselle had not gone far. She walked by herself, although she was wobbly. Xaphan paced behind and to the side. He turned as Alexander approached, his wings flaring protectively in front of Giselle. He said nothing.

"I want to talk to her," Alexander said.

"Let him through," Giselle said.

Xaphan hesitated, then lowered his wings and stepped aside. "Your funeral," he told her.

"Alexander isn't going to hurt me, are you?" she asked. She motioned him to accompany her inside a small sitting room. A dusty assembly of chairs, couches, tables, and shelves was stacked against one wall. Wide cracks zigzagged across the walls and ceiling. The room was still waiting for repair.

He glanced over his shoulder. "I would rather we were not heard," he said.

Her brows rose, but she scraped a wide circle in dust on the floor with her foot and stepped inside. He followed suit. She bent and drew a sigil, and power flickered around them.

"No one will hear," she said, crossing her arms as she watched him. "What do you want?"

He rubbed a hand over his mouth. This was absolutely a bad idea. Still, he did not have a better one. "Magpie came to see me."

Giselle stiffened, her eyes hardening. "What did she say?"

"She said I would get my heart's desire. And that I would be Prime."

The witch did not say anything for a long moment. Instead, she paced slowly inside the circle, her brow furrowed. She looked at Alexander. "I don't want you to be Prime. Not here."

"Neither do I."

Her brows rose. "I wish I could believe that. You could be useful here." She frowned again. "But you knew I wouldn't. You knew telling me would make me want you dead, just to be sure. What's your game?"

"I want a place here. That is my heart's desire. So I am going to go with Max to California, and I will keep her alive and bring her back. When I do, it should prove I can be trusted. So I will want you to bind me."

"Or what?"

He shrugged. "I will think of something."

Like threaten Max. He could see her racing to the conclusion. He did not bother to contradict her; she would not believe him.

"So this is blackmail? I'll have Xaphan burn you to a crisp the moment you walk into the hall."

"It will not work. Magpie's prophecies always come true," Alexander countered. "She told me so. Therefore, I must become Prime." The words were like hot lead on his tongue. He must become Prime. But he could put it off for a hundred years—a thousand. Shadowblades did not die naturally—they had to be killed. All he had to do was keep Max alive.

"She runs after trouble like starving sharks after blood," Giselle pointed out.

"Yes. No doubt that will make the trip more interesting for me. But I will keep her alive."

She cocked her head at him. "I'm curious about one thing. Why haven't you voluntarily bound yourself to Horngate as Thor and the angels did?"

"What would be the point? Unless you want me, any oath I make is meaningless, not to mention stupid. I would be chained here, unable to leave."

"It could be taken as a sign that you want to be here."

He bared his teeth in a snarl. "I nearly killed myself defending this covenstead from Selange and from the angels. Surely that tells you that I want to be here." The words were hot and hard.

"Or it tells me you are very clever. Selange could be trying to plant you inside my covenstead to spy."

He snorted. "You really believe that? She cut my bindings and kicked me out. She does not want me any more than I want her."

"Your loyalty to her is underwhelming."

"Is that it? You want me to be more loyal to her? Despite all she has done to me?" He crossed his arms, looking down at her, his gaze hard and unrelenting. "This is not about me at all, is it? It is about Max. You have tortured her for thirty years, and you fear she will turn on you. After all, if I turned on Selange, who treated me reasonably well by comparison, then what might Max do?" He shook his head. "You are stupid if you think she would betray Horngate. She is not capable, no matter what you deserve."

Giselle's lips pulled tight. The corner of Alexander's mouth quirked up with malicious humor. He had hit close to the heart of the matter.

"You want to protect her from me, but who protects her from *you*?" he asked softly.

"Careful. Remember who you are talking to," Giselle said, her cheeks spotting red.

He grinned, feeling his Prime pushing for escape. "Or what? You will kill me? You could have done so any time in the last four weeks. You want me here. You want me serving Horngate. With the Guardians attacking all over the world, you need all the warriors you can find. I am an asset."

"You are," Giselle agreed. "But only if you don't challenge Max. You are a Prime. How could you be content serving when you could lead?"

"Before long, Niko, Tyler, and Thor will step up to Prime level. What will you do then?"

"None of them could win a challenge against Max," Giselle said with a dismissive wave of her fingers.

"But I could."

"Very possibly."

"I do not want to. I am content to follow her."

"I'd like to believe that."

"How do I prove it to you?"

She shook her head. "I don't know. Figure something out. Bringing her back from California alive is a start."

Something in the way she said it made his skin go cold. "You are hiding something. What?"

She stared at him a long moment and then gave a little nod. "My visions refuse to show me how things will turn out. They have never been so disjointed. What I do get are fragments. I don't know when anything will happen or what the pieces mean, except that you and Max are together and you are fighting someone or something." She licked her lips. "One vision in particular bothers me. It involves a living void."

"A living void?" Alexander repeated, frowning. "What do you mean?"

She folded her arms, rubbing her skin as if cold. "It is the opposite of life. A feeling of sterility—of complete annihilation. I think—" She broke off, looking at him warily. She came to a decision. "I think the Guardians have let loose something they didn't intend to. They wanted to bring back the balance of magic to the world, but I think they brought back something else, too. Or it's coming. I can't tell. Whatever it is, it's dangerous. Worse than that. You're going to run into it."

"And?" There was more. He could tell. "You did not tell Max this."

Giselle gave a jerking shake of her head. "I think she gets killed. You have to prevent it."

Alexander felt like she had punched him in the gut. His Prime exploded, driving out anything but the need to hunt and kill. It was a wild, primitive feeling. Max *could not* die. The thought of it was so full of pain it nearly dropped him to his knees. *What the hell?*

He had no time to consider the burst of feeling. He carefully stepped back from Giselle as Xaphan filled the doorway. The angel could kill him easily, and he would if he thought Alexander was threatening Giselle.

"Are your visions always true? Like Magpie's?" he demanded hoarsely.

The witch shook her head. "Sometimes. I can usually tell if an event is fixed or if it can be changed. Not this time." She stared at him, her eyes cold. "Stop it. Or don't come back."

She hesitated. "One more thing. I don't like blackmail." Then, with a movement that was as sharp and fast as a cobra strike, she flicked her fingers at him.

A hard ball of black magic struck him in the chest and sent him staggering backward. The magic permeated Alexander's chest and exploded inside his ribs. He gasped and convulsed, his arms and legs jerking wildly. His back arched as the shards of magic whirled like a hurricane of glass inside him. He dropped to the ground. His heart and lungs shredded, and blood filled his throat and ran from his nose. He choked and fought for breath, pain racing through him like a forest fire.

Then, just as suddenly as it had begun, the hurricane inside him turned to something different. He felt the magic soften and heat. His flesh mended, the blood draining into its proper channels, his heart and lungs coalescing back into themselves and starting to beat and pump as they should.

He panted, every muscle quivering with the aftermath. Still, he refused to show weakness. He levered himself to his feet, bracing his legs wide and facing Giselle defiantly. He smelled Niko, Tyler, Max, and Thor as they came into the room, the ward of silence keeping him from hearing their footsteps.

Giselle was watching him with cold implacability. Magic curled in her eyes like ribbons of smoke. His stomach clenched. Even this depleted, she still had deep reserves of power.

"Never forget what I can do to you," she warned.

"That?" He shook himself. "Cleared my sinuses is all. Surely you can do better." He wiped the blood from his nose with the back of his hand.

She smiled. "Don't tempt me." She glanced past him, then back. "One last thing. Did Magpie's prophecy say anything else?"

"Yes." He walked out of the ward circle. He scanned the others, his gaze lingering a moment on Max.

She eyed him with that thousand-yard stare he hated. She was so far from him at the moment that she might as well be on another planet.

"What was that about?" she asked.

"Meeting of the minds," he said, and headed past her toward the door.

"Remember I want to see you, Slick." Her voice was edged.

"Yeah? Take a picture."

He turned and left.

5

DAMN. THAT LOOKED LIKE IT HURT," NIKO SAID, following Alexander. "Glad it wasn't me."

"Me, either. What do you think he said to deserve it?" Tyler asked as he joined them.

"Maybe he told her she was fat."

"Or that she looks old."

"Never good to say to any woman," Niko said. "Even if it's true."

Alexander ignored them. He needed to think, to calm his Prime, and to figure out just what the hell he was going to do next. His fingers clenched. He felt like ripping something apart. He glanced over his shoulder. Niko and Tyler were exchanging knowing looks. Alexander turned forward before they saw him. So it was going to be an attack, was it? What did they want from him?

He headed for his quarters. The two Blades continued to trail behind him. After a while, they fell silent. Alexander turned a corner. Now, he thought. Now they spring the trap.

Niko snatched his shoulders and slammed him against the wall. Before Alexander could react, Tyler dug the point of a knife into Alexander's ribs above his heart. Blood trickled down his side.

Alexander did not move, reining himself in. These were his brothers now, and Horngate could not afford to lose either of them. Still, they needed a lesson in manners, and he meant to give them one. Just as soon as he learned what they wanted.

"Here's the deal, Slick," Niko said, using Max's nickname for Alexander. From her, it was annoying. From anyone else—intolerable. He hissed and his muscles flexed. Tyler's knife jabbed deeper.

"I will make you very sorry," Alexander rasped past Niko's grip on his throat.

"Easy, now. Don't get ideas," Tyler said. "You won't heal so well if I hack your heart into stew meat."

"We just want you to be very clear about the rules of your trip to California. If Max doesn't come back alive, then you'd better be sure you don't, either. And just so you don't get any bright ideas, we want your promise on that. Understand?"

Alexander did. It was an oath he could give easily, but he was in no mood to indulge these two. It was time to take them to school. He gave a minuscule nod.

"Good," Niko said, and released his grip a fraction, enough to let Alexander speak freely. "Get to it."

Their first mistake was thinking that they could force him. Their second was forgetting that he was tele-kinetic.

With a thought, he twisted the knife out of Tyler's grasp, sliding it back to slice the tendons of the other man's hand. In the same moment, he kicked Niko's left knee, shattering it with a wet, crunching sound. He grasped the hand clutching his throat and twisted, snapping Niko's wrist.

Tyler lunged, coming in low. Alexander whirled as he struck, gripping his elbow and flipping him over his hip and slamming him to the floor. Tyler rolled smoothly to his feet, and now Alexander was between his two attackers. Clever. Both darted in. Niko's injured leg dragged, but it hardly slowed him. Such were the Blades that Max trained.

Alexander whipped a roundhouse at Niko, kicking him in the jaw before the other man realized he had moved. He clobbered Tyler in the head with a downward jab. Then he was dodging and weaving as the two kept coming. He was never where they expected. More than once, he lured them into punching the stone wall. Bones crunched and blood spattered.

It was a beautiful, violent dance, and Alexander found himself smiling fiercely as he twisted and lunged with velvet fluidity. This was what he was made for.

Niko and Tyler were worthy adversaries, and soon he saw that they were smiling, too. They attacked again and again. Although Alexander took some punches and kicks, he gave better than he got. At last, both of his opponents were lying on the ground. Tyler's eyes were black and nearly swollen shut. His nose was broken, and his mouth was pulpy. He was panting. Niko did not look much better. He sat up slowly and eyed Alexander with careful respect.

"Nice moves." His voice was slurred. He rubbed the side of his jaw. There was an imprint of Alexander's boot rising on his skin and another around his neck from a Brabo choke. "Wouldn't mind learning a few of those."

Tyler rolled onto his side with a groan. "When did you get so damned fast?"

"I always have been."

"You've been holding out," Niko said.

Alexander could hear the suspicion in his voice. He sighed. "You saw me with Tutresiel this morning. I held nothing back with him. Before that, I wished to be welcomed here, and you already distrusted me. It seemed smarter not to add more fuel to your fire. But you know that I was Shadowblade Prime. It should come as no surprise that I have skills."

"We saw you with Tutresiel, sure, but you see things better when you're the one getting hit. You're faster than Max," Tyler said as he clambered to his feet. He staggered to the wall and leaned against it.

"I might be." Alexander watched them carefully in case they decided to renew the fight. "Is that a problem?"

"Depends," Niko said as he stood.

"On whether you think I am loyal to Horngate?"

"On whether you are. And whether you plan to challenge for Prime."

"Max would say that whoever was strongest should take it."

"Maybe, but strength—and speed—aren't everything. Brains, instinct, heart, loyalty—they matter, too. And Max is neither weak nor slow," Tyler said.

"Then she will win. So there should be no problem, should there?"

Neither man said anything. There were no guarantees, and Alexander was a threat. That was why they had come after him in the first place, and their fight had only demonstrated how much of a threat he was.

The corner of Alexander's mouth twitched upward. Max, as much as Giselle, was the heart of Horngate. If Alexander took Prime—presuming that he could, and he had his doubts about that—none of her Blades would follow him. He knew it without a doubt. Just as he knew that Giselle would not suffer him to live.

But he had no intention of challenging her. Neither did he intend to grovel to make these two or anyone else believe him. They would just have to figure it out on their own.

He glanced down at his swollen, bloody hands and flexed his fingers. "So do you want to start again, or are we done?"

"We're done," Niko said, rubbing his jaw again. "For now."

"Anytime you want another go at me, I am ready. Now, if that is all, I am going to go clean up." He started to turn but stopped when Niko spoke again.

"You know, someone might think you've got your panties in a twist over Max," he said, spitting to the side. "You're not exactly acting like someone who's after the Prime job."

Alexander snorted. "No kidding. Have I not been telling you so?"

"Could be an act," Tyler said. He was leaning over with his hands on his knees, his breath sounding liquid. He was bleeding inside.

"Could be. But I do not need to prove myself to you."

Niko smiled slowly. "No. But it's awfully fun to dance together." He rubbed his chest. "Hurts a bit, though."

Alexander stared, then chuckled, feeling the Shadowblade inside him retreating. "You are a fucking bastard." He glanced at Tyler, who had found his knife and was wiping it on his pants leg. "Both of you."

Niko grinned. "So they say. Don't see it myself. Women love me."

Tyler snorted.

Niko turned and started limping up the corridor. Alexander fell in beside him. Tyler came along more slowly.

"How much do you have to pay them before they love you?" Alexander asked.

Niko put a hand over his heart. "You hurt me. I am simply adorable, and they can't resist me."

"Adorable as a black widow spider, maybe."

"Compared to Max, I'm a kitten. I almost feel sorry for you."

Alexander grimaced. "Me too. But I would not bet against me. I mean to win."

"She beat you once already," Tyler pointed out. "That's how you got here in the first place."

Alexander glared over his shoulder. "I remember. But this time, I am more motivated. She is the prize, after all."

"She is at that," Niko said. He stopped and held out a battered hand. "I'll wish you luck. You'll need it."

Alexander stared a moment, then grasped the proffered hand. "Imagine that. Miracles do happen," he murmured.

"So I've heard. Like angels serving a witch. Or a Prime deciding he doesn't want to be that anymore."

"Do not make that mistake. I am a Prime, and I always will be. It was stupid to pretend otherwise. But Max is Horngate's Prime, and I do not plan to try to change that. Just as when you and Tyler rise to Prime, you will not try for it. Or am I wrong?"

Niko drew back with a frown and then nodded. "Nope. Not a snowball's chance in hell."

"She's our Prime. End of story," Tyler said flatly.

"Then we understand each other at last."

"Yeah. I guess we do," said Niko.

"I would take it as a personal favor if you would enlighten the others while I am gone. I would rather come back to friends than enemies." *If* he came back.

"We'll make it happen. Just take care of our girl."

"All that I can get away with before she kills me," Alexander agreed.

Niko grinned. "I don't envy you. She's been in a foul mood."

"And I make it worse. I can hardly wait."

He turned up the corridor to his apartment. He ached from where their punches and kicks had landed. They'd broken his ribs in at least three places, and he was pretty certain that his right shin was cracked as well. He went into his bathroom, rinsing the dried blood from his face. Niko had broken his nose, and there were swiftly closing cuts on his forehead and along his cheeks. Bruises splotched his lower back, chest, and arms. He'd be mostly right in a few hours, but their wounds were more severe and would take longer to heal. Satisfaction made him grin.

It faded abruptly as he recalled Max's family. He squatted down and opened the undersink cupboard. Reaching back under the bowl, he felt for the hole where the pipe ran back out of the cabinet. He reached behind and hooked a string that was attached to the pipe and carefully fished out the phone tied to the end in a crude net. He unfastened the phone and dropped the string in the wastebasket. If anyone searched his apartment while he was in California, they wouldn't find anything damning.

He turned the phone on and saw that there were two dozen text messages and one voice message. He wiped his mouth with the back of his hand. Most of the messages were from his network of contacts in the magic world. They were the reason he had bought this phone and kept it hidden. They were too valuable to lose, but he knew that Max and Giselle would think it too risky for him to keep a phone number he had had when he was with Selange. Or they would think he was still working for her. Either way, if they found the phone on him, he was dead.

He punched in a number. It rang three times, then went to voice mail. "It is Alexander," he said. "I am looking for information on magic activity in Winters, California. I need all you can tell me as soon as you can. Send a text."

He pressed the End button and glanced again at the messages. They could wait. He dialed his voice mailbox and punched in his password. There was only one message. Valery. He stiffened, his breath catching in his chest. Magpie was right. The only reason for Valery to call was that she had found the Amengohr amulet.

The rich tones of her voice filled his ears and rolled through his body like a caress. "Alexander, my sweet. I have found it at last. Do not take too long to call me back. It will not remain where it is for long."

He replayed the message. She really had found it. Alexander reeled. He had never believed she really could. Not even after Magpie's prediction. And now—

He stared unseeing at the wall. What did he do now?

The amulet could give him the power he needed to keep Max safe. But he did not have time to go get it. And even if he did, Giselle had seen her die.

Once again, violent emotion crashed over him. He shuddered as it swept him up. He was drowning. He was burning up. He was falling off a cliff. He dragged his fingers through his hair, sucking in a painful breath as he fought for calm. Ever since Magpie's visit, he'd been thinking of how he could keep Max safe, although the chance of her dying had hardly registered. He could not really wrap his mind around it. She was too vibrant, too smart, and too strong.

Giselle had seen her die.

You will be Prime.

The two ideas collided in his head like two semi trucks. Giselle was not sure that her vision was true. It could not be true. But then how else did he become Prime?

Alexander stood mechanically, setting the phone down carefully on the counter. It was all he could do not to let his Blade go on a rampage. But he needed to stay in control. He needed to think. He drew a long, slow breath.

Giselle's vision might not be fixed. So he could change

the outcome. He brought his battered fist down hard on the countertop. Cracks webbed across it. He would change it. He was not going to lose her, not now, when he had just realized how badly he wanted her. Needed her.

Abruptly, he stripped away his bloody pants and underwear. Every muscle in his body was clenched tight. He was not ready to feel this way. It was stupid. It was insane. And yet he wanted Max like he had never wanted another woman in his life. He grimaced at himself in the mirror. Of all the women to choose—she was thorny, foul-mouthed, reckless, and as hard as tempered steel.

And just thinking of her made him ache with want. *Damn.*

He stepped into the shower and washed the blood from his skin, then stepped out, dried himself, and dressed in a pair of black jeans and a black turtleneck he pulled from the wreckage of his dresser. He found his duffel in the closet and stuffed spare clothing into it, followed by his emergency kit, which included a light-sealing tent, a box of power bars, a healing salve, two spare combat knives, a .45, a .9mm, a dozen full magazines of both shot shells and regular bullets for each gun, two window- and door-sealing kits, two quarts of orange Gatorade, and a set of bandages.

He looked around the room. He owned next to nothing. He had left everything at Aulne Rouge, his former covenstead. All he had now were the clothes he had bought and the phone that he had tossed on the bed. He stared at it.

I have found it at last. . . . It will not remain where it is for long.

He picked up the phone, turning it in his fingers as he considered.

Valery was a Caramaras smoke witch and a thief. She had broken into a Beltane witch gathering near Big Bear, California. Valery had managed to get inside safely enough but had tripped the wards on the way out. She had been wounded, and Alexander had been the one to find her hiding in a bathroom.

There had been instant recognition. That they were both of Caramaras blood was written on both their faces. They had the same dark hair and skin, the same sculpted jaws and cheekbones. Valery could have been his sister. That, more than anything else, made Alexander take her to his room and later sneak her out to freedom.

They had become friends. She was determined to repay her debt to him, and the Caramaras people were not so many that she was willing to lose touch. By her accounting, they were blood kin. He did not remember telling her about the Amengohr amulet, but it had become her mission to find it for him.

He would have the ability to walk in the daylight. A thought struck him. With the amulet, he could pass for an ordinary human. He would not need a covenstead. He would have freedom. Freedom to court Max—after all, he would no longer be of her covenstead. She could not refuse him on that basis.

The thought brought little comfort. He did not want to leave, and even if he did, he could not watch her back if he was not here. He wanted her and Horngate both. He would be damned if anyone kept him from getting what he wanted.

He retreated to the bathroom, turned the faucet on to

mask his voice, and punched the speed dial for Valery. She answered on the third ring.

"I've been waiting for you, sweetness. Where have you been? I called days ago." Her voice was husky and quiet, as if she had been asleep.

"Long story. I am no longer with Selange."

His terse announcement was met with silence. Then, "Sounds like an interesting story. I'd like to hear it."

"Not now. Can you still get the amulet?"

"I am leaving with it right now, sweetness, so we'd better keep this short."

Alexander choked back a laugh. Only Valery would answer her phone in the middle of a job. "Where are you?"

"Near Seattle. But I'll be moving along fast. Holt's not far behind." A grim tone sharpened the edge of her voice.

"He has not given up?"

"He never will. Not until he gets what he wants. Too bad it isn't me." Bitterness filled the words. "But I don't want to catch you up in this. He'll kill you."

Alexander's lip curled. Holt was a mage, which made him very powerful, but he was not invulnerable. Valery had been running from the bastard for more than three years now, and the chase was wearing on her. She needed a chance to rest. "Head for Portland. I should be there tomorrow. I will call and tell you where."

"I'll be there." She hesitated. "Is everything all right with you? You sound tense."

"Things are . . . complicated. But I am working on it. See you in Portland."

He hung up, not wanting to distract her any further from making her escape. She was a free spirit—wild and reckless, with a joy about her that reminded him of eagles playing on the wind. She took risks that curdled his blood, for no better reason than to experience the thrills that came with them. She played her cards all in, never holding anything back. But she was a witch, and her powers were substantial. He did not worry about her as he did Max.

Max never held back, either, but she only had Shadowblade magic to protect her. She was also more inclined to go running into battle with powerful creatures than Valery was.

He turned off the faucet just as a knock sounded at the outer door. It was Thor.

He leaned in the doorway, wearing the same flannel shirt and threadbare Levi's as earlier, but he'd put on a pair of scuffed cowboy boots, and his .454 Super Redhawk hung on his hip, tied down like he'd stepped off the streets of the Old West. On the other hip was a combat knife.

"What the hell happened to you?" Thor demanded, straightening as he took in Alexander's injuries. His eyes went flat and cold, and the air around him seemed to drop twenty degrees.

Alexander smiled thinly. "I had words with Niko and Tyler."

"Who won?"

"You have to ask?"

Thor's shoulder rose in a half-shrug, his temper mellowing. "Not really. But they are not easy opponents. So what did they want to talk about?"

"They wanted me to swear an oath that I would protect Max."

"You didn't, did you?"

"No." Alexander grimaced, feeling hollow inside. "I would do it, do you know that? If I was bound to Horngate, I would swear it and never think twice. But if I have to walk away from this place, I cannot carry that burden with me."

"You'd walk away?" Thor's brows rose. "Old man, I thought you were in this for the long haul."

"I am not sure I have a choice. If Giselle will not bind me, what can I do? Sooner or later, they will chase me off or kill me."

He thrust to his feet and paced, violence filling him. Thor eyed him warily from beneath his brows, his head lowered in a stance of submission.

"Max wants to see you," Thor said.

"Good for her," Alexander said, although his blood pounded. "She knows where to find me."

"You want me to tell her that?"

Alexander hesitated only an instant. "Yeah. Tell her exactly that."

"You know that's just going to piss her off?"

"I am counting on it." Because she would want to tear him a new one in person, and at least he would get the chance to talk to her face-to-face.

"Going to make for a fun trip to California."

"Just like wresting porcupines."

Thor grinned and shook his head, then started to turn away and stopped. He looked at Alexander. "Her family is still living. How long has she been a Blade?"

"Thirty years."

Thor's mouth fell open. "I'm older than she is. How can she be so . . . *Prime* . . . after just thirty years? That's—" He shook his head. "I figured her to be as old as you, at least." He whistled. "I'm surprised Giselle is letting her go. Family ties? Selange wouldn't have tolerated anything or anybody that might have divided our loyalties."

Alexander knew that very well. It was why he had obtained and hidden a secret phone. "Giselle is not exactly an ordinary witch, any more than Max is an ordinary Prime. Besides, I am not certain Max would stomach that sort of coercion."

"Most of us don't have a choice."

"Most of us would not die to make a point. Giselle wants her alive more than she wants to win this particular argument." *Giselle had seen Max die.* No. He would prevent it.

"And yet you're blowing off Max when she's asking to see you. Seems like maybe she isn't the only one willing to be suicidal to make a point."

Alexander shrugged. "It is a point worth making."

"Your funeral. I'll go tell her. Do me favor, though, save me a front-row seat for when she breaks your legs and yanks your lungs out your ass."

"I have no intention of being her punching bag. I am done with that."

Thor frowned, giving Alexander a long look. "You aren't planning anything stupid, are you?"

"Depends on how you define *stupid*."

The other man shook his head. "I can't have your back. I gave myself to Horngate."

"I can take care of myself."

Thor shook his head. "Not if Max turns us loose on you. We'll kill you for sure."

"Then it was good knowing you."

"You don't think she'll do it?"

Alexander's mouth quirked. "I think . . . I think I will find out very soon."

6

MAX WAS STUFFED. SHE'D EATEN EVERYTHING Magpie had put in front of her. Tutresiel perched on the back of a chair opposite her. She had no idea where Niko and Tyler had made off to, and Giselle had refused to say anything about what she and Alexander had been discussing.

"I made a circle of silence for a reason. I don't actually want you to know what we talked about," the witch-bitch had explained slowly, as if Max were a three-year-old child. Then she had gone off with Xaphan.

Max scowled down at her plate.

"Eventful morning," Tutresiel observed, watching her.

She made a face. "Too damned many secrets around here."

"Too much truth can be unsettling."

Her brows arched. "Is that so? Personally, I'd rather have more than less."

"You didn't tell anyone but me that you were going to see Scooter. Or that he has been attacking you in the night. Why not begin with sharing your own truths?"

"What are you, a lawyer? Jiminy Cricket? Or maybe

one of those good angels who sit on your shoulder and talk you into behaving properly?"

He smiled. *Damn.* It made him go from austerely beautiful to downright touchably gorgeous. Were those dimples? Max swallowed.

"I would never talk anyone into proper behavior. And I'm just pointing out the obvious: you like secrets just fine—as long as you are in on them."

She couldn't disagree there. "All right. So there are too many secrets being kept from *me*. Satisfied?"

"Truth stings, doesn't it?"

"Bite me."

His gaze ran over her. "You don't look quite so much like a corpse anymore. I might be talked into it."

A shiver ran through Max, and she stretched like a cat. "Kitten, don't tempt me. I haven't been laid in months."

"Months?" He shook his head. "Pitiful. Maybe I should fuck you for first aid."

Heat swept through Max. The offer was tempting. If she screwed him, would that make her forget Alexander? Somehow, she doubted it. She sighed. "Sorry, kitten. I've got business to take care of. Maybe next time."

"Your loss."

"Cocky bastard, aren't you?"

"You wanted truth. I'm telling it straight."

She snorted.

He sobered. "One more thing. I will not let anything happen here while you are away. I promise." As he said the last two words, a coruscating ring of silver light pulsed outward, rolling through her. The walls glowed for a second, and then the magic swept away through the mountain.

Max stared. For any magical creature to make a promise was a momentous thing. It carried the weight of magic, and it made the person vulnerable. Promises were the strongest chains, because they were self-imposed. Tutresiel hated being enslaved to Giselle or anyone else. For him to bind himself willingly was a gift beyond measure and wholly unexpected.

"Are you sure?" Stupid question. The deed was done and he knew very well what it meant. "Why?"

He lifted his shoulder in a shrug, his face shuttering. "I told you. I like you more than I thought. You should have a place to bring your family back to."

"They might be dead." She forced the words out. He was right. The truth sucked sometimes.

He stepped down from his perch. "They might be alive. Do come back. I would not like to be stuck with that promise forever."

"Sounds like buyer's remorse. Maybe you should have thought it through harder."

"Call it self-interest. I do not want to go back to Mithra. If Giselle dies, I'll have to. So I'll protect the place."

"You didn't have to promise."

"It's motivational. So I don't forget myself and let everyone die out of spite. Plus, despite current appearances—" His gaze ran over her disparagingly. "You've been a decent bet so far."

"Let's hope your luck doesn't run out, then."

He smiled thinly. "Nor yours."

*   *   *

Tutresiel was gone, and Max had just finished bus-ing the last of her dishes when Niko and Tyler returned. They limped in, both looking like they'd had a fight with a tank. Max examined them, her arms crossed.

"Did you win?" she asked, certain that they had gone after Alexander. They had disappeared when he left Giselle. It was too much of a coincidence not to draw the obvious conclusion.

Niko grimaced. He had black eyes, and his nose was swollen and crooked. His mouth was pulpy, and his exposed skin was black and blue with hints of healing yellow and green. Tyler looked much the same. They had washed away the blood, and both had damp hair. Tyler held Niko up, the other man's leg dragging.

"Nope," Niko said with surprising good humor. "Got our asses kicked."

"A hell of a lot more than our asses." Tyler groaned as he started them both toward the food tables. "I don't think I've ever been hurt this bad."

"Then apparently I have to work you harder," she said sardonically. "What about Alexander?"

"Got some hits in on him. Shit, but he's quick," Niko said, stuffing a bread roll into his mouth. "And he has a lot of moves I've never seen. He's been holding out on us."

"He's also not stupid," Max said, torn between laugh-ter and annoyance. "What brought this on?"

"We wanted to make sure he was going to have your six going to California," Tyler explained, piling a plate up with one hand while trying to steady Niko. "Wanted to make him promise."

Max boggled, fury spinning hot in her gut. "You were going to *force* him into a promise? For me?"

"For us. We want you back," Niko said unrepentantly. "Seemed like a good idea. Next time, I'll take more Blades to the party."

"You're lucky he didn't kill you," Max gritted. "I might still do it. When I get back from California, we're going to have a serious talk about rules."

"If you make it back." His voice had turned to stone. He shook off Tyler's help and limped to the table. "Were you going to tell us about it or just sneak off without a word? And are you going to tell us about that wave of magic a minute ago? You promised something. What? To whom?" He glared at her furiously, the humor of a few moments ago gone. His Blade had risen, and his lip curled in a snarl.

Tyler set his plate down with a sharp click and glared at her, his thumbs hooked in his waistband. "So are you going to tell us? Or are we mushrooms—kept in the dark and piled with shit?"

Max hesitated. Too many damned secrets. She blew out an annoyed breath. "All right. I didn't promise anybody anything."

Niko frowned. "Then who?"

"If you must know, Tutresiel promised to guard this place until I get back."

Both their jaws dropped. Neither thought much of the angel.

"He did?" Tyler asked.

"He did."

"Why?"

"Ask him."

She glanced at the door. Thor stood outside, looking like he'd eaten a rotten egg. He caught her look and came in reluctantly. She looked past him.

"Where's Alexander?"

He winced. "He's in his apartment. Says you know where to find him if you want to see him."

Max's eyes narrowed dangerously, her Prime rising. Her fingers curled into claws. "He said what?"

"That you know where to find him if you want him."

"I see."

She glanced at Niko and Tyler. "Have Magpie put a cooler together for the trip, and prep a vehicle for me. Make sure it's got a full weapons kit and emergency supplies."

With that, she stalked away, her fury growing with every step. Before she'd gone ten feet, her Prime had gone into a complete rage.

Max slammed open Alexander's door without bothering to knock. His wards flared and gave beneath her lock spells.

He was waiting inside, dressed in black and leaning back against the opposite wall, his arms and legs crossed. His eyes gleamed. His Prime was as roused as hers.

"Took you long enough," he said, straightening.

She shut the door hard. "What the fuck makes you think you don't have to answer to me?" she demanded.

"What makes you think I do?"

"Because Giselle claimed you, and that makes you one of my Blades. Unless you want to challenge me for Prime? Is that what you want, Slick?" Her voice dropped to a low singsong. She was ready to explode, though whether she wanted to hit or kiss him more, she didn't know.

"I am not bound here. I am nothing here." He spat the words with equal fury. "Neither one of you will give me the time of day. So I might as well act the part you have given me. So no, I do not think I have to answer to you. I am tired of this limbo."

That caught her up. She'd told him once to leave, that he could have his freedom—he was unbound. There was nothing keeping him here. But he'd been determined to stay, and she'd begun to get used to that. Now, the thought of him going made her heart ache. And that pissed her off.

"So you have decided to leave?" she said, her throat tight.

"No, dammit." He lunged forward and grabbed her arms in a bone-crushing grip. "I want to belong here. What is it going to take? Do I need to promise never to take Prime? I will, if that will put things to rest. But I am done with this half-life. Choose whether you want me here or not."

He stared at her, waiting. Her tongue clung to the roof of her mouth, and her heart pounded painfully against her ribs.

"Not my choice. It's Giselle's. Take it up with her."

"The hell with that." He shook her hard, then slid his hands down to hold her hips. He pulled her against him, his lips inches from hers. "I want to know what *you* choose. That is all that matters."

Crap crap crap. Being this close to him made her stupid. Heat pooled in her stomach, and want tingled through every single one of her cells. Tutresiel was pretty, but Alexander made her want to rub herself all over him.

"I told you. I don't fool around with the men in my covenstead," she said hoarsely.

"I am not of your covenstead," he said, his mouth inching closer. "You have made that all too clear. So that must mean there is nothing to hold us back. Unless you do not want me. For the record, I want you, and I want to do a lot more with you than just fool around."

With that, he closed the distance between them. His lips pressed hard against hers. His tongue slipped into her mouth and tasted her with strong, determined sweeps. She gripped his shoulders, her fingers digging hard into him, and kissed him back. She tipped her head and pressed herself closer. He groaned, and his hands came up to grip her head as he deepened the kiss.

Heat and pleasure rocketed through Max. Her body ached for his touch, and she ground her hips against his with hungry eagerness.

Suddenly she pulled back, pressing the back of her hand against her throbbing lips. She was breathing hard, and so was he. His fingers were tense against the back of her neck. He looked down at her, a hard, cold look.

"Are you saying no? Should I be leaving here?"

Her eyes narrowed. "If I say I don't want to screw you, then you'll walk out? Is that the deal, Slick?"

She shoved against his chest, and he fell back a step, his arms dropping to his sides. Her stomach knotted, and the euphoria she'd been feeling turned sickening. She'd stopped the kiss to catch her balance. His touch drove her out of control, like she was being tossed around in a tornado. She wasn't sure how she liked it. But now, anger warred with contempt and disappointment.

"Good luck with that. Giselle will send you out of here with a toe tag. She doesn't want you spilling our secrets."

He gave a harsh laugh. "I am not worried. I will leave when I want, and she will not send anybody to hunt me. She cannot spare anyone from guarding Horngate."

He stepped closer until he was barely an inch away. Max bristled, standing firm.

His breath brushed her face, his eyes hot with a churn of emotion. "I want you. More than I can say. But I am done waiting for you and Giselle to figure out what to do with me. I will go with you and help you get your family. I will watch your back. But if you have not chosen me before we return, then I will disappear, and you will not see me again."

"I don't like ultimatums, Slick."

He spun around and picked up his duffel, sliding the strap over his shoulder. "And I do not like swinging in the wind. It is almost dark. Are you ready to go?"

It was a dismissal. Max clenched her teeth. He was right. He did deserve better from Giselle. He'd proven himself loyal to Horngate. But this—

It was more than she was ready for.

"See you topside," she said, and walked out without looking back.

Inside the door to her own apartment, she sagged back against the closed door, her eyes shutting. Her body still felt the rush of Alexander's touch, and it was good. So damned good.

She pushed herself upright and went to her bedroom. She stripped off her clothes and headed to her bathroom. It was half the size of her bedroom. In the center was a ten-foot-wide tub cut into the stone floor. Hot spring water bubbled up from the bottom and spilled over a set of inch-wide notches around the top. Beside it was a teak basket of shampoo and soap. Beyond was a glassed-in shower with dual heads. Opposite was a towel cupboard and a granite sink with a broad mirror above it.

Steam rose to the ceiling and vanished into the spell set there to collect it. Max stepped down into the tub, grabbed the soap and scrubby, and began washing away the stink of the fire and her sweat from dealing with Scooter. She rubbed her arm where the magical sleeve felt cold against her skin. LoJacked. She'd been Lo-Jacked like a fucking car. He'd know where to find her no matter where she went. She clenched her fist. Her grip was strong enough. A prickle like an electric pulse ran from her elbow to her wrist. She grimaced. It was a small price to pay for the freedom to retrieve her family. She snorted. She wasn't free. Scooter had put her on a leash. If she didn't come home soon, he'd be dragging her back.

Her mind ran back over the images in the vision Scooter had showed her. Was her family still alive? Or had they become food for those creatures?

Fear screwed through her. It went deep, piercing through all of her armor to prod at her where she had no defenses. She curled her knees up to her chest, pressing her head against them, her mouth open in a silent cry. While her family was safe, she'd always felt like she could survive. But now she felt helpless, and the fear of what might be happening to them—what might have happened already—was more than she could bear. What if she lost them? She was supposed to be strong enough to protect them.

She thought of her sister, Tris, with her two girls and her brother, Kyle, with his stepsons and her parents—

They would have been like wheat under the thresher when the creatures overran the house.

Hard shudders ran through her. They were dead. They had to be. But then she remembered Jim. Had the witch made it to the house? If anyone could have, it would be him. He'd fought the blue goblins—these creatures couldn't be any worse.

If he *had* made it, there was hope. Which meant she had to stop wallowing and get her shit together before they were all slaughtered.

Spurred by the thought, she climbed out and rinsed off in the shower, then dressed and combed her hair before tossing clothes and an emergency kit into her duffel. She added a bag of M&M's and a couple of Gatorades.

She straightened and grabbed a pair of sunglasses from her top drawer. She shoved her cell phone into her pocket and hooked the glasses in the neck of her shirt before glancing in the mirror. Thanks to Scooter's healing, she no longer looked like a refugee from a Nazi death camp. Which was something. After all, she'd been awake for all of a few hours and was already over the day's quota on near-death experiences. She could hardly wait to see what happened next.

She did not have long to wait. When she got to the

lobby inside the main entrance to Horngate, she found Oz waiting for her. He was about a mile past pissed off.

"You were leaving without saying a word to me?" he demanded, folding his arms across his broad chest in front of the door.

He was tall, with wide, muscular shoulders and sun-streaked dark blond hair. With his square jaw and dimpled cheeks, he looked like an all-American frat boy. He was, in a word, gorgeous, though not Max's type. She liked her men wiry and dark like Alexander—

She yanked her mind away from that thought and scowled at Oz.

"I'm in a hurry," she told him. "My family is in trouble. I don't have time to waste. Or is there something specific you needed to talk about?"

His mouth rimmed white as his lips pinched together. He looked up as if praying for patience and took a deep breath. He looked down at her again and spoke with a slow deliberation that told Max just how furious he was. "We're friends. You haven't seen your family in thirty years. They're not only going to be a little surprised that you're alive and haven't been in contact for three decades, but the notion that you're also a supernatural creature might startle them just a little bit. Add in the fact that they are under magical attack, and I thought I might wish you good luck. You might need it. And friendship aside, as Sunspear Prime, I thought I might check in with your plans for the Blades while you're gone. I don't think I'm being unreasonable, expecting you might take a minute to give me the time of day."

She winced. "Sorry," she said, rubbing a hand over the

back of her neck. "The last few hours have been a little tougher than I expected, and I'm not thinking all that clearly. Thank you. I appreciate having all the luck I can get. As for my Blades, Niko's in charge. Hopefully there won't be any trouble before I get back, but you've got the angels. They're worth a small army by themselves."

He relaxed fractionally at her apology. "What about Alexander? He's going with you? I don't like it."

"I'm not exactly jumping up and down either, but those are Giselle's orders. She doesn't want him here if I'm not here."

"She's got the angels to keep him in check."

Max lifted one shoulder in a shrug. "Yeah, well, she thinks he and I have some issues to work out. If we can't, I'm supposed to make sure he doesn't come back."

He scowled. "Issues?"

Max suppressed a sigh. She and Oz had been flirting with each other for years, but it had never been more than a little fun for her. She doubted he had deep feelings for her, but men didn't like other men peeing in their territory. She grimaced. In that metaphor, she was their handy fire hydrant.

"That's right," she said.

He stood there waiting for more. She wasn't in the mood to give it.

"I've got to go. I'll see you soon. Call me if you need me."

She stepped adroitly around him. He spun and caught her arm. She stopped and looked up at him, her expression icy. He didn't back down.

"I deserve better than that," he said through gritted teeth. "You know I do."

She sighed. "Look. I've had a bad time of it already today, and mostly I want to hit someone. You're the one in front of me, so you're getting it."

Oz's expression thawed slightly. "All right. Be careful. Call me if things go sideways."

"Sure," she said, but if—*when*—the shit hit the fan, she doubted there would be time for help to arrive. He knew it as well as she did. "I'd better go."

He nodded and stepped back. Max hesitated. She sucked at good-byes. She'd rather just make her escape without having to see anybody. "Take care of yourself," she said lamely, and brushed her fingers across his shoulder before heading out into the night. He didn't follow. Not that he would. Darkness poisoned Sunspears. They only ventured into the night for very good reasons, like the covenstead being under attack.

Outside, the mountain looked like a wasteland. The ground was rippled and charred black where Xaphan's battle fire had struck. The stone had run and pooled, and what was left of the trees were ominous black skeletons. The moon was shining, and blisters instantly rose on Max's exposed skin. Sunshine was deadly to Shadowblades. The less powerful ones would melt into goo; the more powerful would simply burst into flame. Even the reflected light of the moon was painful, the full moon particularly so. She slid on her sunglasses and felt a wave of itchiness spread across her eyes as they healed.

She jogged down the ridge to the valley. The grass here was parched and it crunched beneath her boots, but the ground had not burned. A dozen cars and trucks were parked in a flat dirt lot near the river. Across it were the greenhouses. They remained intact after the battle, but all the plants within had shriveled and died. Horngate had a reputation for growing some of the finest organic fruits and vegetables in the Pacific Northwest. It was the covenstead's cover—no one thought of witches when they saw the place. Everyone saw hippie organic farmers, which fit perfectly with their location outside the granola city of Missoula.

She stopped when she saw the truck that was waiting for her. It was a red crew-cab Chevy. There were scratches in the hood from where blackberry brambles had scraped it. Hidden beneath the shell on the back was a light- and dark-sealed steel box. It was about four feet tall and five feet deep and as wide as the bed of the truck. It was a safety retreat for Shadowblades and Sunspears caught out at the wrong time of the day or night. Alexander was leaning against the driver's side, flipping the keys around his forefinger. Niko and Tyler waited beside him. They were all watching her like they expected her to fall apart or blow up.

Max swallowed the rock that had risen in her throat. Of course. They didn't have many vehicles to spare, and her Tahoe had been blown up. It made sense to use Akemi's truck. Akemi wasn't going to need it. She'd been killed in the battle with the angels. Still, it hurt. Max had hardly had a chance to grieve for the men and women who'd died. She hadn't wanted to think about it and had instead focused all her attention on rebuilding the covenstead and fighting off Scooter's dream attacks. Now she was going to be wrapped in Akemi's scent.

She strode forward, keeping the emotion from her face.

She eyed Alexander. He didn't look nearly as bad as Niko and Tyler. The bruises on his face were healing quickly, and his cuts were fading to pink. Soon they'd vanish. She met his eyes. He was staring back at her with a hooded gaze. Her mouth tightened. This was going to be a fun trip.

"Time to get on the road." She held out her hand for the keys.

He shook his head. "I am driving. You can sleep, since word is you have not been doing a lot of that lately."

There was accusation in his voice that made her want to punch him. It wasn't his business. She didn't need a nanny.

She scraped her teeth over her lower lip, wondering if it was worth the time or energy to take him down a peg. She glanced at Tyler and Niko, who both looked ready to back him up against any protests she might make. Apparently, they were not so much against Alexander that they wouldn't join forces against her.

Not being stupid, Max chose not to argue. "Sounds good," she said, and went around to the passenger door and climbed in.

Niko and Tyler followed her.

"Do you think she's sick or something?" Tyler asked Niko. "Or maybe someone has taken possession of her body? I've never seen our Max agree to anything that quick, except maybe food."

Niko frowned and examined Max's face closely. He leaned through the window and lightly tapped a knuckle against her forehead. "Can you prove you're Max?"

"Step away from the truck, or I'll cut your balls off and roast 'em on a stick."

Niko glanced at Tyler. "Sounds like her."

"I don't know. Usually she's more creative. Roasting them on a stick? Very cliché."

They both looked expectantly at Max. She rolled her eyes. "Fine. I'll cut them off and make earrings out of them. I might even let you wear them sometimes. Once we drill holes in your pretty little ears."

"Still pretty weak," Tyler said doubtfully.

"Very."

Max looked at Alexander. "Can we go now?"

"Yes, ma'am," he said with a mock salute. He turned the engine over and put the truck in reverse.

Max looked at Niko and Tyler. "Try to keep everyone alive while I'm gone."

"Aw, Mom, do we have to?" Tyler asked. "I was planning a trip to Vegas by way of the Bahamas."

"Remind me to kick your ass when I get back."

"Make sure you make it back," he said, the humor fading from his expression, "and I will."

"With you two waiting for me, why would I ever want to stay away?"

"Hey, I have good idea. Just for something new, why don't you mix it up a little and try not to be too stupid on this trip?" Niko said.

"Stupid? I thought I was audacious and brave, spunky even."

"Spunky?" Tyler repeated. "Audacious and brave I can buy. But spunky? That's like calling Godzilla a little bit accident-prone."

Max shrugged. "Poor Godzilla—she gets such a bad rap. Tell you what, I'll only be as *brave* and *audacious* as I have to be," she said, and she waved as Alexander drove away.

She sat back in her seat, listening to the sounds of the night through the open window. The smell of Akemi rose up around her, undispelled by the night air blowing through the window. It was a musky, sweet scent, like oolong tea and beeswax. There was a hint of pepper to it, too, and a tang of old sweat.

Max swallowed the sudden knot in her throat and stared out the window, trying to ignore the memories of her dead friend and her fears for her family.

They wound through mountains on the nameless dirt road that led away from covenstead. A short distance from Lolo Creek Road, they drove under the arch of antlers that marked the entrance of Horngate. Max's attention snagged on a gleam of metal up high on the rimrock. Tutresiel perched barefoot on top of a thin finger of basalt. The top couldn't have been more than a few inches square. He crouched there with preternatural stillness, his wings furled around him, his elbows resting on his knees.

Suddenly he leaped up into the air and dove down at the truck. He swooped past her window, his wings flared and silent. The sweet and caustic scent of Divine magic washed through the cab as he winged upward and disappeared over the ridge.

"What the hell?" Alexander said, slamming on the brakes and glaring after the angel.

"I don't know," Max said, but in the palm of her hand was a tiny curled feather, an inch long and a half-inch wide. It was made of silver, and she had no doubt it had been plucked from his wings. Her fingers closed around it. The edges were sharp, and she loosened her grip as it cut into her skin. A flash of cold seared her palm, and she snapped her fingers open.

The feather was gone, and where it had cut, a scar remained. She rubbed the thin white slice in astonishment. She was a Shadowblade—she didn't scar. She didn't take tattoos, and her ears wouldn't hold a piercing. And yet . . . Beneath the scar, she felt a rigidness. She flexed her hand. There was no restriction in her movement and no pain. Still, she was certain the feather had sunk inside.

Her hand curled into a fist. It was the second time in the last few hours that someone had given her a gift. She knew Scooter's came with strings. What the hell had Tutresiel given her? And just when was the surprise going to jump out of the closet and clobber her over the head?

She sighed, tilting her head back against the seat.

"You okay?"

She looked at Alexander. "Don't I look it?" Her voice was sharper than she meant it to be, but she was on edge. He put her on edge.

He faced back to the road, his expression granite. "You have been looking a bit like the walking dead lately. Though you appear to have made a remarkable recovery today."

"Thanks to Scooter."

"Scooter," he repeated, his lip curling with distaste.

"Yeah," she said.

"Do you want to talk about it?"

Her instant response was no. But it melted to ash on the tip of her tongue. They were going to be stuck together for the next few days. Might as well try to get along. Telling him about Scooter might ease the tension between them. Or piss him off more. But what the hell?

The truth was, as much as she'd kept Alexander at arm's length the last four weeks, he was the one she *wanted* to talk to. In fact, she wanted to do a lot with him, and most of it was a really bad idea. But talking—that much was safe enough.

"He's been pretty irritated that I haven't come to see him. So a few weeks ago, he started trying to drag me off whenever I went to sleep. It was killing me, so this morning I decided I'd better put a stop to it, and I went to see him."

He turned his head to look at her, his brows raised. "You remember who I am, right? You have not wanted to share the same air for weeks, much less talk to me."

"A girl can change her mind. Besides, who else is there?"

"You like your secrets. Why talk to anyone at all?"

She growled low in her throat, a sound of aggravation. "Whatever blows your dress up, Slick. You asked, I said yes. No one's twisting your arm." She reached out and turned on the radio.

He flicked it off. "Tell me."

Irritation scraped at her. She yawned exaggeratedly. "Maybe I should sleep like you said."

He reached over and grabbed her hand, squeezing gently. "Tell me."

She looked at his hand on hers. His touch sent a jolt through every one of her nerves. She ought to pull away, but she didn't want to. *Stupid.*

She remembered his threat—or had it been a promise? If she didn't choose him, he'd leave. She didn't want him to go. Neither could she imagine starting up a relationship with him or anyone else. A shiver pimpled her skin with goose bumps as her body clenched at the thought. *Never*. She didn't want to care that much for anyone. It was too . . . dangerous.

But Alexander would leave.

Her mouth dropped open in a silent gasp as hurt drove through her like a spear. The wound felt gaping and raw. She closed her lips and stared blindly out the window. Was it too late? *No*. Even if she had developed real feelings for him, they hadn't had time to take root. She could dig them out. With a chain saw, if she had to. So that if he did leave, she wouldn't care.

But she did. Her Prime rose, borne on the raw emotions of her dread for her family's fate and the thought of losing Alexander.

His hand tightened. "Max?"

His voice was almost guttural. It sent a tremor through her. His Prime had risen with hers, wild and primitive. She looked at him. He bent toward her. His expression was taut and his eyes were molten. Her eyes widened. He wasn't afraid. But then, why would he be? He was as scary as she was. Instead, he was turned on. So was she. She dug her fingers hard into her thigh, touching the tip of her tongue to her lips. His gaze jerked and narrowed on the movement.

Then abruptly he pulled his hand away and drew a sharp breath. He clamped his hands on the steering wheel. "Not that way," he rasped.

"Sure, Slick," Max said, hiding her disappointment. She felt like he'd tossed a bucket of ice water on her head. The predator inside her snarled in frustrated fury, but it was no longer in danger of overwhelming her human reason. "I can always find a bed buddy for a night."

He jerked the wheel, skidding to a halt on the side of the road. His hand whipped out. He snatched her arm and yanked her halfway over the console, his face twisting. "Do not dare," he said between gritted teeth. "When you decide to come to me, you will do it because you want me as much as I want you, not because your Blade took possession of you."

He thrust her back as suddenly as he'd grabbed her.

Max grinned. "Wow, you can't make up your mind, can you? Must take you hours to pick out something to wear every night."

He goggled at her and then gave a short laugh as he once again grasped the steering wheel, like he didn't quite trust what he might do with his hands if they didn't have something else to do. "You are a . . ." He searched for words. "Remarkable woman."

"I'm pretty sure you mean raging bitch."

"That too."

"Not to mention pain in the ass."

"Of course. That goes without saying."

"At least I'm not boring."

"Oh, no. Never that," he agreed, rubbing a tense hand over his mouth.

She couldn't resist poking at him. It was fun seeing him off-balance for once. "I'm beginning to wonder about you, Slick. You ever think about seeing a shrink?"

He slanted a look at her. "Maybe I know something special when I find it."

Max snorted. "Special? Like the bearded lady at the freak show?"

"I was thinking something more along the lines of a

pirate treasure. Of course, it is buried under a mound of fire ants at the bottom of an active volcano and guarded by dragons, but a treasure nonetheless."

"Tell the truth—you're on drugs." But despite herself, Max was hanging on every word like a pimple-faced fifteen-year-old girl drooling over the captain of the football team.

"I would like to know something, if you will tell me," he said, turning to face her, his mood shifting suddenly.

"What's that?" she said cautiously. He wasn't off-balance anymore.

"You are attracted to me. You do not deny that." He waited.

She nodded reluctantly. It was pretty pointless to lie.

He made a frustrated gesture. "Then why?"

Max went still. Why not tell him? There wasn't much point in secrecy. Maybe he would back off if he knew. "Giselle."

His brow furrowed. "Giselle? She does not want us to be together?"

Be together. What exactly did he think could happen? Marriage and a baby carriage? "No. She couldn't care less. Right up until the point where she decided that she could use you to force me to do something I don't want to. You'd be a hostage."

"I thought the two of you came to terms. You are working together."

"For now. Until we butt heads, and then we'll be back at it. If she didn't think she'd need to push me around now and again, she'd have freed me."

"So instead of living your life, you live like a militant nun."

"Something like that," she said, resenting the accusation in his voice. "Except I do find some time to have a romp in the hay."

He gave a silent snarl, but didn't respond to that, staying focused on the subject at hand. "And if she chooses Niko? Or Tyler? She has plenty of hostages against your good behavior. She has for years. What makes me different?"

He was too smart for her own good. She knew it wasn't logical. But she was terrified of what would happen if she let Giselle get ahold of someone she really cared about. And she could care about Alexander. She already did.

"What about your family?" he pressed when she remained silent. "You are bringing them here. Will she not use them?"

"I'd kill her," Max said. "No matter what it took." Pain flared around her in a spinning tornado of razor wire as her compulsion spells reacted to her threat. She thrashed and clenched herself, letting the pain take her. She would never give in on this one.

Alexander grabbed her shoulders and shook her hard. Her head snapped back. "Max! Giselle is not here; she is not threatening your family. Let it go before you kill yourself."

His words permeated the haze of pain slowly. She forced herself to relax. He was right. More importantly, she still had to rescue her family, and killing herself wasn't going to help a whole lot.

The magic receded, feeling like it was peeling away her flesh as it went. She sucked in a breath and let it out slowly, feeling her heart slowing back to normal. Alexander's hands fell away.

"The truth is, she has plenty of hostages to hold against you already, and you are about to give her more," he said. "You cannot hide behind that excuse."

Max stared out the bug-speckled windshield. He was right. She had no good excuses. "The last time I dated anyone was in 1980."

When she didn't say anything more, he prodded, "And?"

She lifted a shoulder. "He was cheating on me. Right after we broke up, my best friend in the world turned me into a Shadowblade. I may have some trust issues."

He was silent for a long minute. "I can work with that," he said finally, putting the truck in drive and pulling back out onto the road.

She looked at Alexander. "You're awfully sure of yourself."

"I am. You admit you want me and that you do not have any good reasons not to be with me. It is only a matter of time." His eyes laughed at her, daring her to deny him.

Max's stomach curled in anticipation. She ruthlessly crushed it. "You forgot something."

"Oh? What is that?"

"I am already spoken for. Giselle gave me to Scooter."

He was silent a long moment, negotiating the sinuous mountain curves, the truck's wheels squealing as he swerved around them.

"Tell me about Scooter," he said finally, the words pushed through gritted teeth. "What did you mean when you said he tried to drag you off while you were sleeping?"

Max eyed him sideways, feeling reluctant to begin again. Instead, she changed the subject.

"So you know you don't use contractions, right? Like *isn't* or *wasn't* or *can't*. You know it makes you sound pretentious and arrogant, like you've got a stick stuck up your ass?"

He stared, then shook his head. "I was not aware that my speech was so . . . stiff."

"There you go again. 'Was not aware.' Couldn't you say, 'I wasn't aware'? 'I didn't know'?"

"I expect I could."

"Then why don't you, already? Welcome to the twenty-first century."

"In my younger years, my mother impressed upon me the need for proper speech."

"And that's proper?"

"According to my mother."

Max's lips pinched together. Saying any more would be an insult to his mother, and she had a feeling that would be crossing a line. Not that she minded crossing lines, but families were off-limits.

"So are you going to tell me about Scooter? What did he do to your arm?" he asked, not letting her off the hook.

She tightened her hand into a fist, feeling the cool heaviness of the spell along her arm. "How did you know?"

"I am not blind. You have been favoring it since you came out of the vault. What happened?"

She considered putting him off again, but he was likely to drive off a cliff. Or try to throttle her. Besides, he needed to know. Then he would give up on her. Why did that make her want to vomit?

She swallowed. "Scooter's been a little irritated with

me. I kept putting off going to see him, so he started coming to me while I was sleeping. At first, he just kept me from resting. I kept waking up. After a while, when I still didn't go down to see him, he decided he wasn't going to wait anymore." She rubbed her forehead between her eyes, remembering the first of his visits. "He'd come into my dreams and push at me to go somewhere with him—on an astral level, not physical. It wasn't so bad at the beginning. He was gentle, if demanding. But when I still didn't come to him, he started attacking—trying to drag me off. It got to be that I would put off sleeping as long as I could, but it didn't matter. He was always waiting. Fighting him got harder and harder."

"That is—" Alexander caught himself. "That's why you started looking like death warmed over."

"Did I? I thought I was fashionably corpselike. I could have been on the cover of *Vogue*."

He didn't laugh. His face had gone cold, and the air in the truck thickened with the weight of his mounting fury. "So then what?"

"It's been getting harder to wake up. He's been—" *How to explain?* "He takes me to this place." She closed her eyes, seeing the gray world again, with the spinning shards of cutting magic, the billows of silk that burned like acid, the clouds of flittering beauty that cut through her like flying razor blades. "It's like a minefield, and if I don't follow the path he's laid out or if I try to escape, I get hurt."

That was an understatement.

"My healing spells have had a hard time keeping up, especially with the lack of sleep." She paused. "This last time . . . I almost didn't get away."

"Why didn't you say something?" he said, enunciating each word through clenched teeth. "Ask for help?"

"What could anybody do? It's his right. I told you, Giselle sold me to him. He just wants to collect on their bargain."

"Fuck that," he said with a snarl.

"Oddly, when I told them the same thing, neither Giselle nor Scooter found it to be a very compelling argument," she said. "They seem to think that they can do whatever they want with me."

Bitterness filled her mouth and made her want to spit. Old hate for Giselle welled up inside her, and she swallowed it down, forcing herself to remember that things had changed, and she wasn't fighting the witch-bitch anymore. But she hadn't forgiven, and she sure as hell hadn't forgotten.

"So what happened when you went to see him?" Alexander's fingers had tightened on the steering wheel, and she wondered if he was going to snap it into pieces. He'd sped up, and she felt the left wheels of the truck leave the ground and then settle back down. They skidded on the loose dirt and gravel that lined every Montana road, fishtailing across the rumble strip before he straightened it out.

"If you don't want to flip the truck, then you might want to ease up, Slick."

He growled but slowed down. She said nothing for a while, watching the steep sides of the wooded ridge beside them.

"I knew I was going to have to confront him," she began again. "I'd been trying to wait until Giselle was stronger and Horngate had recovered some so I could go get my family, but I couldn't put it off any longer, or my healing spells were going to eat me alive. So I went to see him. I made a deal. He's going to leave off the dream attacks until I can go help my family."

"A deal?"

"I told him if he lets me go get my family, I'll go to him as soon as I get back, and he can have his wicked way with me. Otherwise, he was going to have to kill me to get me to cooperate. Apparently, he wants me breathing."

"And your arm?"

"Says it's a gift. If my life is seriously in danger, it will help me jump through the abyss or the web between worlds or whatever, and I'll land a few feet away. But really, it's a leash, to keep me from wandering off or taking too long. If I'm not careful, he'll drag me back, and that will be that."

Alexander sat silently for a long moment. He was seething. She could feel his body shaking, and his face was pulled into a harsh mask of fury. What exactly had crawled up his ass and died, she didn't know.

"So you will go to him when this is done," he said.

"That's the deal."

"Forever?"

There was a wealth of bullheaded tenacity in that word. Like he meant to fight the sentence with all his might. Scooter would wad him up like toilet paper and flush him, but Max appreciated the sentiment. Giselle hadn't offered even that much.

She grimaced, exhaustion pulling at her. "Maybe. Probably. You'd have to ask Scooter or Giselle. Good luck with it. Neither has given me any straight answers. But then, it's just my life. Why should I care?"

"I would like to strangle Giselle," he grated.

"Get in line." Max yawned. "Now, if you don't mind, I want to sleep a little."

She leaned her seat back and closed her eyes. She'd fallen into a doze when she felt Alexander's fingers wrap hers. He pulled her hand to his mouth and whispered a kiss across her knuckles. As he lowered her hand back to her lap, he didn't let go, holding firmly. Max didn't try to pull away.

7

ALEXANDER STOPPED IN KENNEWICK FOR FUEL before heading across the Columbia River Gorge. He rolled his window down, smelling the wet of the river on the right and the dry of the sunbaked grass and dirt on the left. The wind was unexpectedly calm. He pressed the gas, going faster than he ought to. The speed limit here was a paltry sixty-five, and he was going nearly ninety. There were only a few hours left before daylight, and he meant to be in Portland by then, or at least to Troutdale.

His chest churned with a wash of violent emotions. He was not going to let Scooter have Max. Yet how could he stop him? Giselle had made the bargain and so had Max. And Scooter was a powerful creature. He chewed his lower lip. He was not bound to Horngate or to Giselle. He did not have to obey their rules. Everybody had an Achilles' heel. All he had to do was find Scooter's.

His mind skipped ahead. He should tell her about Valery. About the Amengohr amulet. She had told him everything about Scooter and had not seemed to hold anything back. *Hadn't* seemed. He smiled in the darkness of the truck's cab, remembering Max's admonishments about his too formal language.

He wondered then if, in fact, she had told him everything. He scowled. He thought she would not tell him anything at all about Scooter, and then she had surprised him. But did that mean she had told him all there was to tell? He gritted his teeth, wanting to shake her awake and demand full disclosure. Not that she would give it. No one made Max do anything. Not without spilling a lot of blood.

He smoothed his thumb over the back of her hand. She shifted in her seat and sat up, pulling away from him to stretch.

"Where are we?"

"Coming up on Hood River."

She eyed the clock and nodded approvingly. "You've made good time." She paused. "I'm hungry."

She leaned over the seat and dug in the cooler Magpie had made up for them. She returned with two thick roast beef sandwiches, handing him one. She reached back again for two bottles of Coke and a sack of barbecue chips. They ate in silence as the river rushed by on the right and the summer-dried hills flashed by on the left.

Alexander finished his sandwich, and Max handed him another.

He should tell her about Valery. Max was going to learn about her soon, anyway—it would be better if he came clean up front. He wanted her to trust him. Keeping secrets would not win him any points, especially when that was all Giselle did to her. He thought of Giselle's vision that Max would die. Did he tell her that, too? His stomach clenched. What did he say? A living void would kill her? What the hell did that mean?

He heaved a silent sigh, feeling trapped between a rock and a hard place. Deep within, the predator inside him stirred, sensing a battle. Alexander quelled it. Now was definitely not the time.

He checked the clock. It was almost five. They had a little under an hour before sunrise. Before then, they needed to find a hotel and make it light tight, and he had to get in touch with Valery. Max followed his gaze.

"Cutting it close."

"When don't you?" he said, forcing himself to use the contraction.

She grinned. "That looked like it actually hurt, Slick. To answer your question, I try not to, but it seems events conspire against me."

"Of course, you have nothing to do with such events."

"Me? Never. It's all just bad luck."

They had just passed the Benson State Recreation Area when his secret phone vibrated. He'd broken the one Giselle had given him. His foot pressed down, and the truck leaped forward. Max glanced at him with a frown. He eased up and made his decision. He pulled out the phone, glancing at the caller ID. It was Valery.

"Hello," he said, putting it to his ear and knowing full well that nothing the Caramaras witch said would be lost on Max. Her Shadowblade hearing was too good, and she was paying attention.

"Where are you?" Her usually rich voice was thin with tension.

"About ten miles from Troutdale."

"Good. I'll meet you at the Holiday Inn Express. You can get under cover for the day."

"You all right?"

"Holt's hard on my heels. You might want to hurry." She took a drink of something, her voice tight with something like fear, or maybe it was anticipation. She and Holt had a peculiar relationship. "Maybe I'd better leave the amulet at the hotel where you can find it. You don't need his kind of trouble."

"He does not scare me," Alexander said. "Wait for me."

"He's a mage, Alexander. He scares everybody." She paused. "I'll see you at the hotel if I can."

The phone went dead. He put it back in his pocket and pushed the gas pedal until they were flying through the steep-sided gorge. He glanced at Max. She had turned to face him, leaning back against her door. She was tapping her fingers on her thigh, her face as expressionless as a stone wall.

"Friend of yours?"

"A little more than that," he said.

"Do tell," she said, her voice as dry as dust.

Was she jealous? He could not tell. More likely, she was raging angry. But she was not jumping to conclusions; she was giving him a chance to explain.

"Do you know what the Caramaras are?" he asked.

"No."

"They are gypsies. Their bloodlines trace back to Egypt. Today, many live as Travelers."

"The thieves? Con artists?"

"Yes."

Her brows rose. "And this woman is one of them?"

"Valery. She is a Caramaras witch. I met her when I helped her escape after she broke into a witches' retreat."

"You have hidden depths, Slick. Why would you help a strange witch?"

"I am also Caramaras. And blood is family."

"Selange must have loved that."

He smiled tightly. "Selange did not need to know about Valery."

"You shock me. You kept secrets from your witch? Here I thought you were a Boy Scout," Max said. "So what is this amulet she has for you? And who is Holt?"

Alexander hesitated a bare second and then decided that honesty was the smartest course. Lying to Max would win him nothing. "My mother told me stories of an ancient Egyptian amulet called the Amengohr amulet. It was said to grant the wearer invisibility in the night and the power to walk in the daylight without harm."

She stiffened. "In the daylight?"

"So it is said." He swerved around a bend. Not far now. He had better tell her the rest quickly. "Valery is a thief, and a good one. Most often, she comes and goes without anyone noticing. That night I helped her, she was off her game. She decided to repay me by searching for the amulet. I thought if it had ever existed, then surely it had been destroyed or locked away in some museum collection somewhere. A few days ago, she left a message for me. She had found it."

"And the mage—Holt?"

They were coming up on Troutdale. He could see the green and white sign of the Holiday Inn Express just off the freeway. "Logan Holt. She was married to him. A few years ago, she divorced him. She also took something from him—I do not know what. But he wants it back. He has been hunting her ever since."

Max leaned her head back against the window, staring up at the truck's headliner. Alexander veered onto the off-ramp, hitting the brake hard and squealing the tires. He stopped for the light, then gunned the gas again as it turned green. There was no traffic.

"Take it easy, Slick. We don't need someone calling the cops."

"I have to help her," he said abruptly. "She is the closest thing to family I have. Holt is very powerful."

"Never heard of a mage who wasn't," Max said, straightening in her seat. She slid out her .45 and made sure there was a bullet in the chamber and the safety was off. She holstered it again and checked the gun in her ankle holster. Her fingers touched lightly over her knives. She glanced at the eastern sky. "Not much time before we're ash in a pan. We need to get inside quick."

"And Valery?"

"She'd better not snore."

Alexander felt a surge of wonder. Max was not angry, nor was she cutting him loose. Just that much was astonishing, but clearly she meant to help him. He pulled into a parking space near the entrance and jumped out. Max was still inside, rifling through the weapons locker beneath the backseat. After a moment, she got out.

"I smell Divine magic," Max said. She frowned, her nose wrinkling. "It's peppery," she said just as Valery stepped out from behind a thick clump of bushes.

Max tensed, jerking around to face the witch. Valery

stopped, looking like she might leap away. She was tall, with sun-gilded skin and black hair cut in a dramatic jagged fringe around her face and cheeks. She wore torn blue jeans and a faded blue T-shirt with purple tennis shoes. Her eyes were shadowed, and her expression was tense. Energy snapped around her like fireworks. She was always that way after a successful job.

"It is all right," Alexander said. "This is Max. She is a friend."

Her dark gaze scanned Max from head to foot, and then she relaxed slightly. "I am Valery."

"So I hear," Max said. "You've got some trouble on your ass, too. Is that right?"

"You don't need to be involved. I only came to give Alexander this." She strode over to him and held out her hand, dropping a heavy metal object onto his palm. "I'd better go before Holt gets here."

"It's a little late for that," came a liquid masculine voice.

Neither Max nor Alexander hesitated. Alexander dragged Valery behind him, and Max stepped to his shoulder so that the witch was shielded from the parking lot where the voice had come from.

"What are you idiots doing? Holt is my problem," Valery said, shoving at her protectors' backs. Neither moved.

"Tonight he's ours," was Max's reply. "Besides, we need exercise after that drive."

Alexander grinned, hearing the playful tone of her voice and feeling the surge of her predator rising. His own leaped to the surface, and he felt a crackling wave of violence pressing at him to be unleashed.

"We'd better make this quick," Max murmured. "We only have ten minutes or so before dawn."

"Get out of the way. I am perfectly capable of managing my own problems," Valery said as she started to step around Alexander.

He shoved her back with a snarl. "Stay. Put."

"You're nuts. Holt won't hurt me, but he'll turn you into hamburger. He's a *mage*. That's a witch squared or quadrupled or something. I don't have so much family that I want to waste one because I was a coward."

"I know what you can do. So be ready, and let us have a little fun," Alexander said.

"Fun?" she sputtered, but then Holt stepped from the shadows.

Except that there were no shadows that a Blade could not see through. It was as if the mage materialized from thin air.

Holt was not an imposing figure. He stood a little over six feet tall, with a slim waist and brown shoulder-length hair. His jaw prickled with stubble as if he had not shaved in days. He had thick, straight eyebrows, and beneath them, his eyes were the color of new spring leaves. He wore canvas pants, an untucked faded jeans shirt and scuffed brown boots. He stood hipshot, his hands in his pockets, his head tilted slightly to the side.

"Alexander. I should have known she'd come running to you," he said, looking like he'd just swallowed anti-freeze. "I really wish you'd go sniffing after someone else's wife. Valery belongs to me."

There was a sound of spitting fury from behind Alexander. Valery tried to thrust herself between him and Max, and both held firm. "I am not your wife. I haven't been for a long time," she called loudly from behind her Shadowblade wall. "You really need to get that through your cement head."

"Caramaras witches can't divorce. You will be mine forever." His expression had turned molten.

"If we are married still, then where are your marriage marks?" she retorted. "I don't know why you are getting your boxers in a twist. You never really wanted me. You made that clear enough. So why don't you just shove off already and leave me the hell alone?"

"I want you. I always wanted you," he grated, as if the words were dragged out of him against his will. "You're the one who quit us. You're the one who stole the marks. I want them back. And the rest of what belongs to me, too."

"Never," she said. "You might as well give up, because I'd rather die before I give you anything."

A ripple of emotion flashed over Holt's expression, and then his face turned almost serene. Both Alexander and Max stiffened. The mage was clearly done talking.

"Let's make this very quick," Max said in a voice too low for any but Alexander to hear. "Distract him." She turned her head, still watching Holt. "You can handle yourself, Val?" she asked.

"Of course I can," the witch snapped.

Alexander felt her gather power. An invisible wind brushed past him full of magic. She was a Caramaras smoke witch, and her power was unlike Giselle's or Holt's. Alexander had never seen her use it for more than minor spells. She did not believe in relying on it. He hoped she was strong enough to fend off Holt until Max took him down.

Despite Holt's appearance, Alexander knew very well that the other man was dangerous. He was a mage, which meant he had all the power of several witches combined, and he was more than willing to use it. Holt was vicious, brutal, and a cold-blooded bastard, and why Valery had married him, Alexander did not know. Holt had been looking for Valery since she had walked away from him, and it was clear that he had no intention of letting Max and Alexander keep him from snatching her back, no matter how much blood he had to spill.

"Who is your friend?" Holt asked, studying Max like a snake examining breakfast.

Alexander snarled, sudden possessive fury making him want to smash the mage's smug face to a pulp. He clamped his teeth together before he could say something stupid. Max was perfectly capable of taking care of her own business.

"I don't really care if I kill you," Holt told her. "But if you want to get out of here with your skin, go now. You've got two seconds."

A thin smile curved her lips. "And miss the party? I don't think so. Besides, I don't like bullies."

"So it's going to be that way, is it?" The mage pulled a hand out of his pocket. It was covered in a complex pattern of blue hex marks. "Valery, you really need to find a better class of friends." He held his arm out straight before him, palm up, his fingertips bunched tightly together. Then, without a word, he snapped his hand flat. A ball of silver witchlight streaked through the air, bullet fast.

Alexander and Max were already in motion. They split apart, leaving Valery standing alone. Alexander knew she could handle a few blasts from Holt, especially since she was right—Holt didn't want to kill her.

Alexander launched himself to the side. The heat of Holt's magic flared across his skin as he landed on his shoulder and rolled to his feet. He never stopped moving as he lunged at the mage, who was humanly slow.

Holt jerked around to level a blast of magic at Alexander. The Shadowblade ducked under the bolt, flattening to the ground as it crackled through the air above him. His hair and shirt burst into flames. He rolled to his back, but the magical fire did not die. He hardly felt the pain as he flipped onto his feet. He charged the mage, whose hands were outstretched, brilliant white magic swirling around them.

Before Holt could release his attack, Max dropped from above and smashed him to the ground. The mage went sprawling, the white ball of magic exploding wildly like whirling shards of jagged glass. It slashed Max like the blades of a blender, shredding her clothes and skin. Then the leading edge passed her and ripped into Alexander.

The hail of magic sliced deep into his left eye, blinding him. More embedded themselves in his chest, stomach, and legs. He doubled over as each fragment struck. Flames still seared his back, and he smelled the stink of burned hair, cloth, and flesh.

He forced himself upright and staggered toward Max. She glanced at him, her eyes blazing. Was her rage for him?

She hooked her fingers on something around her waist and pulled it loose. Silver witch chain coiled through the air like a cracked whip. Max knelt down on Holt's back and slid the chain around his neck, tying it tightly. She kept the end in her hand as she turned to Alexander and wrapped it around him, unmindful of the white flames that licked her arms as she reached behind him.

As the chain slid around his waist, the flames died. The witch chain smothered witch magic, making witches and their spells impotent. The shards of the exploded spell had already faded to nothing. Alexander sucked a breath through clenched teeth, feeling his flesh cool and his healing spells kick in, even as blood ran out of him like he was a sieve.

"Thanks." He looked at her through his one good eye as Max drew back. "You look like hell."

The wild magic had cut through her nose, lips, and cheeks. One ear was cut in half. Her entire shirt was drenched in blood.

"We're a matched pair," Max said. "The jokers in the deck. C'mon. We don't have much time." She looked past Alexander to Valery. "Get us a room. Fast as you can. Bottom floor near an outside exit, if possible."

Valery loped away without a word.

"Help me with this bastard," Max told Alexander.

They hooked him under the arms, dragged him to the rear of the truck, and laid him on the ground. He was unconscious. A purple lump had risen on his forehead, and his nose and lips were bleeding. As Max grappled with the latches on the shell and the tailgate, Alexander scanned the parking lot. No lights had popped on in any of the nearby rooms, and he saw no signs of observers. He looked up, trying to piece together the battle. He frowned. Max had leaped down on top of Holt, but from where? There were no trees or light posts nearby.

She pulled out her duffel and got the cooler out of the backseat. She set them on the ground and went to dig out the first-aid kit.

She hit the locking button on the key fob and shut up the rear of the truck before propping herself on the bumper. Now all they had to do was wait for Valery.

"Nice move, hitting Holt like that. He never saw it coming," Alexander said, searching the parking lot again to see how she'd done it.

She looked down at her right hand. She spread her fingers wide and stared at her palm, then rubbed a finger gently across it as if tracing a pattern. "Damned son of a bitch," she murmured.

"Who?"

She looked up at Alexander with a wry expression, then held up her hand. A white hashmark that looked impossibly like a scar crossed her palm. Glowing faintly gold beneath her skin was a feather wisp, like the down from the breast of a swan.

"What's that?"

"A gift. Or a joke. Maybe both. From Tutresiel."

"What does it do? Make you fly?"

She made a face. "More like hang glide. And maybe I can even jump tall buildings in a single bound."

"So you are Superwoman. Why am I not surprised?" He reached out and rubbed at a trickle of blood from her cheek with his thumb. It only smeared.

"I'll have to look into getting blue long johns and a cape."

He looked at her hand again. "You did not have to tell me."

She shrugged. "I seem to have a habit of telling you

things I don't mean to. Just don't say anything to anybody back home. I don't want them knowing. Not yet."

"I will not. I broke the Horngate phone. All I have is my spare," he said, warmth spreading through him.

He almost did not feel the pain of his wounds. She had given him her trust. More even than she gave it to Niko or Tyler. It meant she cared for him, whether she knew it or not.

"What about him?" He nudged the unconcious Holt with his foot.

"We'll take him inside. After that? Snap his neck, maybe, and leave him under the bed for the maid to find in a few weeks."

She surveyed the parking lot, picking out the security cameras. "A few weeks ago, I'd have been a lot more worried about being seen. But the Guardians are moving. Did you hear about the series of earthquakes in South America and Indonesia? Or the lightning fires in Colorado and Arizona? Or the tornadoes across the South? It's only a matter of time before they kick their war into high gear, and what people think of us isn't going to matter." She looked at Alexander, her brown eyes troubled. "Winters is a small town, but if it's been attacked magically, then the escalation has already begun. The whole world might be under attack."

She did not mention her family, but he could see her worry. He wanted to reassure her, but there was nothing he could say.

They both heard footsteps at the same time and whirled to see Valery coming around the corner. She jogged to them, glancing over her shoulder at the brightening sky.

"Room 128 on the end," she said, flashing the key card. "I fogged the security tapes, too." Her gaze ran over Max and then Alexander. Her mouth tightened. "You should have let me fight my own damned war," she said before reaching for the cooler.

"You're welcome," Max said. She looked at Alexander. "She's unusual, your witch sister. Most of them send us off to do their dirty work for them and never think twice."

"I told you she was unique."

"Excuse me. I am standing right here," Valery said, annoyed. "Dawn is coming. Want to speed up a little?"

Alexander bent and flipped Holt over his shoulder. An itch under his skin told him to hurry. Valery was right. The sun was very close. Max handed him the end of the witch chain before snatching up their duffels and the cooler and followed Valery as she led the way to the side entrance. The Caramaras witch keyed open the outer door and then their room.

Valery had rented a small suite. It contained a kitchenette, a large bathroom, a king-size bed, and a sitting room with an easy chair and a fold-out couch. There were two windows.

Alexander dumped Holt onto the floor beside the bed and went to help Max with the windows. They shook out the thin silver blankets from Max's duffel and taped them over the glass with duct tape to seal out the sunlight. Next, Alexander taped over the cracks of the door.

Max was tugging off her boots and socks. She stood and looked down at herself. Like him, she had stopped bleeding, and her wounds were closing, but more slowly than they should have. His mouth twisted, his teeth grinding together. Scooter had healed her, but her body was still too depleted to suffer such wounds. Guilt knotted in his stomach. He should not have involved her in this.

"Well, I don't know about you two, but three near-death experiences in one day is a little over the top, even for me. If this keeps up, I'm going to run out of clothes."

"You should have stayed out of it," Valery said. "Both of you. I could have handled Holt."

Max eyed her, rubbing at her ear. It had nearly grown back together. "There's only one little flaw in your logic."

"What's that?" Valery was tapping her fingers against her thighs, and she kept looking at Holt. It was obvious that she was still in love with him. Whatever had happened to make her divorce him and run for the hills, it was not that she had stopped caring for him.

"As I see it, Alexander was going to jump in no matter what. Right?" Max asked him.

He nodded, and Valery made a frustrated noise and shook her head. "Stupid men."

Max laughed. "I can't argue that. But either way, he's my—"

She broke off, and Alexander just barely resisted the urge to shake the rest of the sentence out of her.

"Anyhow, I don't let one of my Blades walk into trouble by himself," Max told Valery.

The witch gave a little nod of understanding. "What do you plan to do with Holt?"

Max gave her a long look. "I take it you don't want him dead."

Valery flushed. "No."

"Then I guess we let him live. You might want to hit

the road. He'll be crawling up your ass the minute he's freed, and you'll want a head start." She unzipped her duffel and started pulling out a change of clothing. Her hands stilled, and she stared a moment, lost in thought. Then she looked at Valery consideringly but said nothing.

"She needs sleep. At least through today," Alexander argued when Valery nodded agreement.

"I'll be fine," she snapped.

"Better if you sleep today and run tomorrow. We can keep him occupied for a day or so to give you a head start." He glanced at Max for confirmation.

"Sure," she said, and Alexander could not read what she might be thinking. "We can do that."

The witch licked her lips, and Alexander could see her hands shake with the aftermath of the theft, running from Holt, and the battle. He put his arm around her, and she nestled against him like a kitten.

"Now that that's settled and the two of you are getting cozy, I'm going to get cleaned up," Max said, and gathered her clothing before disappearing inside the bathroom.

Valery slowly turned to face Alexander. "I think you've got a story to tell me. What happened to Selange? Who is Max?"

"I am not with Selange anymore. And Max is . . ." He trailed off, rubbing a hand over his mouth and shaking his head ruefully.

Her eyes widened. "Holy shit. You haven't gone and fallen for her, have you? You have! I never thought I'd see the day a miser like you would let loose the heartstrings for anybody. Does she know?"

"She does not want to know. But I am working on it."

Valery smiled, and her glance slipped down to Holt. "At least *she* isn't trying to kill *you*."

"Not at the moment. But tomorrow is a whole new day."

She smiled. "Big brother, why do we choose such hard-asses to love?"

"We like a challenge?"

She yawned. "I think I'm challenged out." Her glance fell to Holt again, and her expression turned grim. She stepped back. "Do me a favor and put him on the couch for me. I need to check his head wound."

"You cannot take the chain off him. He is too dangerous," Alexander warned.

She shrugged. "No problem. This chain can't touch Caramaras magic. It's meant for elemental witches. Mages are just elementals on steroids."

She went to unfold the couch, and Alexander laid the unconscious man down on it. As he did, Holt opened his eyes. Alexander wondered how long he had been awake listening. The mage lifted a hand and touched the witch chain around his neck.

"Why am I still alive?"

"If it was up to me, you would be dead."

Holt turned his head, searching the room before riveting on Valery. He scowled. "What are you still doing here? I'd have thought you'd be halfway to Timbuktu by now."

"There's no need to hurry. You're looking a little toothless right now."

His jaw knotted. "You can't keep me tied up forever."

"Sure we can," Alexander said cheerfully. "We can bury you in the chain and let you rot for all eternity."

Holt glared up at him, missing the way Valery flinched at the words.

"One of these days, I'm going to make you regret interfering in my business."

"But Valery *is* my business. She is family."

"Maybe a thousand years ago, you had a common ancestor," Holt scoffed. "That doesn't make you family."

"I disagree. No matter how far back, we are blood, and you—" Alexander ran a hard finger over Holt's collarbone, where the marks of his marriage to Valery had once been. "You are an arrogant bastard. You never deserved her."

The expression in Holt's eyes was murderous. He flung himself upward and punched Alexander in the jaw. Alexander shoved him back down.

"Did I touch a nerve?"

"I swear I will kill you," Holt seethed through clenched teeth.

"You can try. But I am not the one with a chain around my neck."

With that, Alexander taped up the mage's hands and feet. Valery watched without a word.

Alexander glanced at her. "You are sure this is what you want?"

"I don't want to be responsible for killing him."

"He doesn't seem to mind if he kills you."

"Valery knows me better than that," Holt growled. "Don't you?"

She shook her head. "I know you'll do anything to get your property back. It doesn't matter what happens to me." She stood and folded her arms over her chest, pacing away as far as the small room would allow.

"You're wrong," Holt said.

"Am I?" she asked without turning around. "Then stop chasing me, and leave me alone."

"You know I can't."

"Because you want the Nur-dagan tablets back."

"It's not that simple. You know that."

"I know better than to ever trust you again."

"Enough," Max said, coming out of the bathroom and tossing her ruined clothes in a pile behind the door. "The divorce is final. You can stop arguing any time now."

She yawned, reached into the cooler, and pulled out another sandwich and a bottle of Mountain Dew before sitting cross-legged on the bed. The slashes on her face were pink and fading, and her blond hair was slicked tight to her head.

Alexander fished a change of clothes out of his bag and went into the bathroom to shower. It was still full of steam. He set his weapons next to the sink and stripped off the remains of his shirt and pants. He pulled out his cell phone and was about to toss the ruined jeans on the floor when he remembered the amulet.

He drew it out. The back of it was a disk made of smooth gold almost the size of his palm. At the center was a round black diamond larger than a quarter. Set in a circle around it were a series of orange opals. Arrows pointing outward toward the edge were interspersed between like the rays of a sun. Around the rim was inscribed a series of archaic words in a language Alexander did not recognize. They were not traditional Egyptian hieroglyphics. The words spiraled around the back to the center to end at a small eye.

He ran his fingers over it. The metal was warm from

his pocket. He sniffed it. It smelled of Divine magic. He turned it over in his fingers and then set it down beside his belongings on the counter. It could allow him to walk in the daytime again. Of course, the only way to test it was to try it, which could mean death if it did not work. Just at the moment, he did not care to die, not with Max thawing out as she seemed to be. Or maybe she was just too tired to know what she was doing.

He groaned his frustration and finished undressing before stepping into the shower. He had wanted time alone with her, and now they were stuck with Valery for the night and Holt for at least another day, if not longer. He reached for the soap.

He was nearly done when he felt Max's Shadowblade rising. It rolled through the walls like a tide of boiling tar. He shoved the spigot off and pulled his pants on without bothering to dry off.

He pushed open the bathroom door and lunged out into the room. He stopped short. Max was standing at the foot of the bed, staring at the TV. Her mouth was rimmed white, and her body shook.

"What's going on?" he demanded, searching the room. Holt remained bound, and Valery stood near the wall, smoky magic wreathing her arms. His attention returned to Max. "What is it?"

She began to shake and sway. Alexander caught her around the waist as her eyes rolled up into her head and she slumped.

"Max!"

He laid her down on the bed. Her skin was gray and cold, and the presence of her Shadowblade snuffed out like a candle. Everything inside him seized tight. He reached out to grab her shoulders and stopped himself, instead smoothing his fingers over her forehead. "Valery? What is wrong with her?"

Valery knelt next to Max and held her hands above the prone woman. She closed her eyes as the smoke wreathing her fingers turned silver-green and drifted down over Max. Soon magic cocooned her in a gauzy shell.

A minute passed. Then five. Alexander held himself taut. His hands curled into white-knuckled fists on his knees. Max's breathing was shallow and quick, and her body was too still.

"What's happening?" Holt demanded from the couch. He managed to get to his feet and hop awkwardly over to the bed, the witch chain dangling down his back. His gaze narrowed, and his face hardened. "Stop her," he told Alexander. "Valery's too tired for this. It's drawing too much out of her." His bound hands hovered behind her back like he was going to grab her hair and yank her away.

Alexander studied the woman he considered a sister. She was trembling like a plucked guitar string, and her neck tented with strain as sweat trickled down her flushed cheeks. He hesitated, but then gripped her shoulder. "Stop, Valery. You have done enough." He hoped.

She gasped and pulled her arms around her stomach. She put her head down on her knees and rocked back and forth, drawing rasping breaths. The smoke cocoon wavered and slowly faded. Beneath it, Max was still gray and waxy. Her eyes were open and dilated to black. She stared unseeing at the ceiling.

"Max? Max!" Alexander gripped her face between his palms and angled her to look at him. She did not respond. She was as rigid and indifferent as a plastic doll.

His fingers knotted in her hair. Unthinking, he picked her up and pulled her tight against him as he sat against the headboard. He held her, stroking her back as he whispered against her ear over and over.

"Hear me, Max. This is the way back. Follow my voice. I am waiting for you."

8

SHE FELT HIM COMING FOR HER BEFORE HE EVER got close. It was like standing on an empty beach watching a towering tsunami rise higher on the horizon.

Every sense went on alert, her body tensing. Her left arm went frigid inside Scooter's spell. She leaped to her feet. There was a rushing sensation, as if something was flying at her on an invisible gale. She braced herself. Whatever Scooter was up to, she wasn't going down without a fight.

A funnel cloud swept her mind. It whirled around her, full of glittering magical shrapnel. It flayed her spirit, wrenching her arm. She felt herself tearing loose from her body. She scrabbled to stay, but the shredding wind spun her away.

She was back in the black abyss of her nightmares. The wind died, but she felt a pull, like a rip current. She dug in against it as feral magic descended on her. Yellow blobs swarmed her. Festering poison flooded her, and far away she felt her body shake and collapse. The current twined around her arm and dragged harder at her. The poison of the yellow jellies turned her perception watery. Colors wavered, and the abyss tumbled and spun. Light flared bright and strobed as pain chewed her.

She clawed for a moment of stillness, but the world toppled and whirled. More magic erupted out of the abyss. It looked like a collection of streaking green ribbons. They coiled and knotted, then sprang at her like rattlesnakes. They fastened, and if she could have, she would have screamed as their icy fangs stabbed through to the center of her being.

She flung herself away from the pain and the sense of deep violation, following the drag on her arm along the rip current. As if in reward, the agony ceased, leaving behind an aching throb.

Somewhere at the end of the river carrying her across the abyss between worlds waited Scooter. She had no doubts. What was the bastard doing? He had agreed to wait for her. So what was this? Had he lied?

Fury swept her, and she gathered herself to fling herself in the opposite direction. She stopped as logic grabbed her.

Scooter wouldn't lie to her. It wasn't his style. He had a thing for truth. So why was he attacking her?

There was only one good answer. He wasn't attacking at all. Which meant— Could it be?

The moment the thought struck her, Max knew she was right. Scooter was making a telephone call of sorts. If she could have, she would have rolled her eyes. First thing on her to-do list when she got back to Horngate was to get him a cell phone and put her number on speed dial. She did not need to do this ever again.

Max considered only for a split second before decid-

ing what she had to do. He wanted her alive. To attack
her this way must mean he needed to talk to her pretty
badly. He obviously couldn't cross the abyss—weeks of
nightmares had proven that. Whatever he wanted had
to be important enough to ambush her while awake and
threaten her life. He wasn't going to stop until she answered his call, so she'd better get on it.

She gathered herself and, without another thought,
flung herself in the direction of the current. Searing
cold slid up her shoulder and spread through her body
as she raced through the darkness on a black river. Tatters of magic in a rainbow of colors blurred and ran
together as her speed increased.

Ahead, she saw a thin stripe of fluorescent purple
running side to side like a horizon line. It thickened
and quickly became a wall. It rose abruptly as far as she
could see. The current didn't slow as she rushed toward
the barrier. She braced herself and slammed against it.

She expected pain, but instead she was enveloped in
a soft warmth. It cradled her, although it did nothing to
break the cold grip of Scooter's spell. She found herself
drifting slowly. She no longer felt the pull of the current
to guide her.

"Scooter?" she said. Or thought. Who the hell knew
in this place? When he didn't answer, she tried again.
"Dammit! I don't have time for your shit. You called. I
came. Now, tell me what the hell you want."

A tiny blue light bloomed in the purple near Max. It
grew larger, and then suddenly Scooter faded into sight.
He wore his human guise, except that he was covered in
a pattern of red-brown scales. Running through it was
a webbing made of thin strands of gold. Each strand of

his long hair was limned in gold and floated around him, moving like it had a mind of its own. Only his eyes were the same—that onyx black flecked with bits of shining blue. His shape wavered and steadied. Again, Max wondered what his natural shape was.

"Why is it that every time I even think about sleeping, you have to mess with me? What's going on?"

"The Guardians are summoning magic through the world webs."

Max waited. He said no more. Finally, she asked, "Care to expand on that? What are the world webs?"

"The world webs are the ties that bind all of the worlds together in the abyss. This—" He gestured at the purple around them. "This is one strand of the web. That is unimportant. Summoned magic must be used quickly, or it will dissolve back into the web and take with it the strength of the summoners. The Guardians must strike quickly or suffer great harm. For many years, the magic of your world has drained away into the web. The Guardians are drawing it all back and will release it into your world. You are in danger." He spoke quickly, his expression wooden.

If she'd had a face, Max would have scowled. Like she needed more bad news. "There must be a couple million square miles of world out there, and they plan to conquer it all. What makes you think they'll come anywhere near me?"

"They will not come to you; you will go to them."

That caught her up short. "Explain."

"A major vortex lies in the land you call California. You must hurry." His voice was taut now.

"How many vortexes are there?"

"Thirty that I have sensed."

"Thirty? What will they look like? What will the returning magic do?"

He shrugged. "It is wild magic. It will change the face of all. I must go."

"I'm surprised you're not trying to drag me back to Horngate before I get into trouble."

He tipped his head to the side. "I said I will wait for you. You said you will return. Has that changed?"

Talk about the letter of the law. It didn't leave any room for pesky little complications like death or imprisonment. But if he was willing to ignore such minor details, so was she. "No. I'll be back."

"Then farewell."

With that, he stepped backward and simply vanished. Max stared after him. "How the hell do I get out of here?" she asked the purple emptiness. There was no answer.

She twisted around, searching for a way out. But she could not tell up from down or backward from forward. There was only dense purple. *Fuck*. "Scooter!" He did not answer. The bastard. He warns her about the Guardians and tells her to hurry but then leaves her twisting in the wind. Just like a damned fairy.

Well, she couldn't stay here forever. She had to pick a direction and go and hope to hell it took her where she wanted to go. Then an idea struck her. She quieted herself, reaching out with all her senses, searching for the thread that still tied her to her body.

Nothing.

But wait—yes. Not the link to her body but something else . . .

She listened. *This is the way back. Follow my voice. I am waiting for you.*

Alexander. How did he know? But then, he wasn't remotely stupid, and she'd told him about Scooter.

She pushed in the direction of his words, following his voice like a breadcrumb trail. She slid out of the purple into the abyss between worlds. She thrust her spectral arm out before her, picking up speed as she leaned harder into the direction she wanted to go. His voice became a strand of web that she could almost see. Magic flashed, and she plowed through a flittering orange cloud. Bits of it clung to her like rose petals. She smelled them—sweet like nutmeg and caramel. She drew a breath and felt them flowing inside her.

Her body tingled, and exhilaration flooded her mind. Her body? She could feel it now. It was close. Alexander's voice was louder, and she could hear its ragged edge. More, she could feel the pressure of his arms around her, his lips whispering against her ear—

Between one moment and the next, she snapped back into herself. She opened her eyes and pushed back from Alexander. He loosened his arms only slightly. His dark eyes were nearly black with fear, and his face was rigid. The power of his Shadowblade filled the room with smothering waves.

"Max?"

"The one and only," she said, trying to shift herself away. He was too damned close. How was she supposed to stay out of his pants if he insisted on mauling her?

He tightened his grip. "Are you all right?"

She frowned. She felt no pain. She was tired, but not exhausted, not the way she expected to be after her little journey across the abyss between worlds. "I'm fine."

"What happened to you?"

She shifted, trying to straighten up. He let her, but refused to let her off his lap. His gaze challenged her to fight him. She shrugged inwardly. There was nowhere else she wanted to be at the moment, and she wasn't in the mood to argue with herself over the subject.

"Scooter called me. His version of a cell phone."

"Called?" Alexander asked.

"Scooter?" Holt echoed.

Max twisted. Holt had come to his feet off the sofa bed, and Valery sat in a chair with her feet propped on the edge of the nightstand. Her face was pale, and she was having a hard time keeping her eyes open.

Max turned back to Alexander. "He wanted to warn me. He says the Guardians are opening vortexes all over the world to release magic back into the world. He suggested we might want to light a fire under our asses."

"Vortexes?" Holt echoed. "What do you mean? Who is Scooter?"

She shrugged. "Scooter is— Hell if I know what he is. I don't even know his name. He's powerful, anyhow. He said something about how the Guardians were summoning magic through the world webs, power that drained into them over time from our world."

Holt made a sound of disbelief, and Max turned to look at him. "That means something to you?"

"They are pulling power from other worlds, other dimensions—it's like a bottomless well. How much magic they can draw up is limited only by the strength of their summoning. They could draw far more than what this world has lost. It will shake the entire earth—a storm of magic beyond anything you can imagine. You need to let me loose. Valery, this is no place for you. We have to get out of here."

The witch yawned and shook her head as she stood up. "I wouldn't cross the street with you, and I'm too damned tired to go on the run today. Somebody wake me when the sun goes down."

With that, she stood and stumbled around to the other side of the fold-out couch, slipped off her shoes, and crawled under the covers, pulling them up over her head. Holt glared at her. His jaw looked like it might splinter apart, he was clenching his teeth so hard. His lips pulled back like he was going to swear. Then he caught himself and hopped back to the sofa bed. He lay on his back beside her and put his bound hands behind his head. He stared up at the ceiling as if praying for patience.

Max couldn't help her grin at his annoyance. The man rubbed her up and down the wrong way, not to mention that he'd tried to kill her and Alexander. Normally she didn't take that sort of thing personally, but his know-it-all superiority reminded her just a little too much of Giselle.

She turned back to Alexander, who was still watching her like the proverbial hawk. She let out a quiet sigh.

"We'd better sleep, too. Make sure Holt is secure, would you? We don't need him getting loose and killing us in our sleep."

She waited as he considered. Finally, he gave a short nod and slid out from beneath her. He went to Holt and bound his hands to his waist, then tied the loose end of the chain to the lamp. It would come crashing down and wake everyone if Holt moved much.

He flipped off the lights and turned back to Max on the bed. He stalked toward her, and a chill swept down her arms and curled deliciously up into the pit of her stomach. He wasn't wearing a shirt, and his pants hung low on his hips. His stomach and shoulders rippled with muscle beneath skin that looked like pure silk. She wanted to trace each line of him with her fingers, with her tongue. She swallowed, her mouth dry with anticipation and sudden hunger.

He sat down beside her and stretched his legs out in front of him. Wordlessly, he reached for her, pulling her onto his lap. She straddled his legs as he tangled one hand in her hair, his arm coming around her back like an iron bar. He pulled her tight against him. His lips met hers with raw need. There was no gentleness as his mouth slanted over hers and his tongue licked inside. She met him with equal passion, grinding her crotch against his swelling groin as she wrapped her arms around his neck.

He made a sound in his throat, and his hands ran down her back and fastened on her hips. He yanked her closer. Spiraling pleasure ran up into her stomach at the friction. She wanted to feel his skin on hers; she wanted his weight pressing her down as he made love to her.

Unexpectedly, he drew back. His breath rasped loudly in his throat. His eyes devoured her. "Much as I want to keep going, we have guests."

Max leaned close, resting her forehead against his. "This cannot end well. Scooter owns me."

"But you agree that there is something between us— that *this* is *something*?"

She nodded, not letting herself find an excuse. She

wanted him so damned bad, and she was tired of pretending she didn't. "Yeah. This is something."

He closed his eyes and took a deep breath, letting it out slowly. "Thank you." He kissed her again. It wasn't as desperate this time. He took his time, nibbling and teasing as his hands slid caressingly over her back. Max gave as good as she got, letting herself taste him. She traced the contours of his shoulders. His skin was hot and satiny soft. Her body ached with need, and she wanted nothing more than to rip off his pants and explore the rest of him. But Valery and Holt were ten feet away, and she wasn't interested in putting on a show for them.

She drew slowly away. "This is going to have to wait," she whispered. Her stomach clenched. Wait for when? There would be little enough chance for privacy before they reached Winters, and then they'd be surrounded by her family. Next stop would be Horngate, where Scooter waited impatiently. Why had she been pushing Alexander away instead of grabbing what she could while she could?

She bit down hard on her lower lip, sliding off Alexander and turning so that she sat beside him. She was breathing fast, and her body throbbed. He snugged her tight against him.

"Soon," he whispered, pressing a trail of light kisses down her neck.

Chills ran down to Max's toes, followed by a wave of liquid heat. She took a breath, then slid determinedly down, turning onto her side away from him and stuffing a pillow under her head. "I'm going to sleep," she said unnecessarily.

Alexander was still a moment, then he eased down and spooned up against her. He slid one arm under her neck, and the other arm draped her waist. His quiet breaths brushed over her hair and cheek. She stiffened. She'd not actually slept with any man in the fifty years she'd been alive.

"Relax," Alexander murmured. "I will not bite. Not tonight, anyway."

There was a smile in his voice and the delicious promise of things to come. That was supposed to relax her? She jabbed him in the ribs with her elbow. He laughed silently, the rumble in his chest quaking through her and sending her pulse racing again. She suppressed a groan. The bastard was killing her. She closed her eyes and forced herself to breathe slowly, counting each breath like sheep.

The heat of his body wrapped around her, and Max soon slid into the sleep her exhausted body craved.

She woke just before nightfall. She'd not moved in the day, and Alexander still wrapped her from behind. Max lay still for a long minute, savoring the feel of him against her. Then she reluctantly sat up and scrubbed her hands across her face. She felt groggy, but sleep had done a lot to restore her. Her stomach growled.

Valery and Holt were still asleep. She turned to look at Alexander. He was leaning on his elbow, a frown between his eyes.

"What's wrong, Slick?"

"Just wondering if you are going to revert to form and pretend last night did not happen."

"And if I did?"

He reached out and traced her mouth with his fingers. "Then I would not let you out of this bed until you got over your amnesia."

She pretended to consider. "That only tempts me to say nothing happened." Then she remembered where they were going and Scooter's warning. Her expression tightened. "But we've got places to go and people to kill. We'd better get moving."

She started to get up, and he caught her arm and pulled her down. His kiss was slow and deep and hungry. He let her go at last, looking like he wanted to say something else, but he only levered himself up off the bed and went into the bathroom.

IT WAS A QUARTER AFTER NINE BEFORE THEY WERE READY to go. Holt's hands were still taped in front of him, but the bindings around his legs and waist had been cut loose. Alexander held the end of the witch chain. Valery was rumpled, but her eyes snapped with energy. Max's stomach was appeased for now. They'd polished off the food that Magpie had sent.

She took down the window covers and packed them up. "Ready? We'll take Holt with us. We'll leave him somewhere in a day or so."

"You won't kill him?" Valery asked.

"No."

She nodded, then said slowly, as if the words stuck in her throat like fish hooks, "I want a minute with him alone."

Max looked at Alexander and shrugged. He looked like he'd swallowed a hammer sideways, but he handed Valery the end of the chain and followed Max out to the parking lot. The moon was up, but clouds hid its brilliance, saving

Max a case of itchy blisters. They put their gear back into the truck. Max reached into her pocket and dialed Jim's number. Once again, she got his voice mail. "Dammit," she said as she snapped her phone shut.

"Maybe the magic has cut off the signal," Alexander suggested.

She nodded. It was possible. Though more probable was that he was dead or captured. She glanced back at the hotel doors. "We haven't got all fucking night," she muttered. How long to get to Winters? Going down Highway 5, it was close to six hundred miles. They had about eight hours of darkness to get there. It could be done, barely, although they'd have to lie low until the following night. And that was only if they didn't hit a lot of traffic or get pulled over.

Max paced back and forth as the minutes ticked past. Finally, Valery and Holt pushed through the exit doors. Holt looked murderous, and Valery looked resolute. She handed Alexander the end of the chain and then hugged him tightly.

"Watch yourself. Try not to get killed." Her glance flicked to Max and then back to Alexander. "Good luck with your project."

He smiled. "It is coming along. Thanks for the amulet. Keep your head down, would you? Things are going to get ugly in the world soon. Do not get yourself hurt. Maybe I should gut Holt. I would be doing you a favor."

She shook her head, her mouth flat. "No. He deserves a lot of things but not that. Just give me a day's head start. He won't find me."

"Don't do this, Valery," Holt ground out. He started toward her, and Alexander caught him by the collar. "You don't know what you've gotten into," Holt said to her, ignoring Alexander. "I need those tablets back. You're in danger as long as you've got them, and I can't keep you safe much longer. Especially with what the Guardians are doing to the world."

She snorted derisively. "Safe? Is that what you call it? You need a new dictionary, baby, and a new line. Figure it out. You and I are done. I don't need you, and I'll never give those damned tablets back. Consider them my divorce settlement. So you might as well get over yourself and move on."

She turned her back on him and held out her hand to Max, who shook it.

"I hope you find your family and get them out," Valery said. "Thanks for your help with Holt. If you ever need anything, I owe you a favor. Alexander knows how to find me."

Max nodded. "Good luck."

Valery got into her car, waving one more time at Alexander as she pulled away. Max opened the door to stuff Holt into the backseat. He yanked away, pushing against her with his bound hands, his neck craned as he watched the retreating car.

"Dammit, let me go! She's in danger. I have to get those tablets back before someone else finds her first."

Max shoved him into the backseat, her hands splaying on his chest as he fought against her hold. "Cool it, Zippy. You're stuck with us for a while."

"Please," he pleaded, although it looked like he was swallowing poison. He wasn't the sort of man who asked for anything. He was the sort who made demands and was not often refused. "She doesn't understand what she's gotten into."

The soul-deep desperation was real and demanded curiosity, at least, if not sympathy. "Did you tell her?"

He grimaced. "I can't. It's . . . complicated."

"Always is, Zippy." Max glanced at Alexander, whose lip curled in skeptical disgust. "But we're all stuck with the beds we make. She doesn't strike me as all that helpless. Maybe you should have trusted her enough to tell her."

"She's going to get herself killed. Or worse." Holt pulled uselessly against the tape around his wrists. "Let me go. It's not too late. I can still catch her."

"Not going to happen. Might as well sit back and relax and wait for the ride to be over."

Fury suffused his face, and if looks could kill, Max would be flayed and gutted. Then his expression shifted as he reined himself in. "What would it take for you to let me go? I am a mage. I can give you the world. Just let me go now."

"Sorry, Zippy. I'm a lot of things, but I am not for sale."

With that, Max shut the door and circled the truck to climb into the driver's seat. She started the engine and put the truck in reverse. As she did, her cell phone rang. She checked the caller ID. It was Jim.

Her mouth went dry as she flipped open the phone. "Are you okay? What's going on?"

It was hard to hear him. Static crackled on the line, and his voice sounded hoarse and far away. "Don't have much time. My cell is running out of juice. I worked around toward the dam. I got high enough to look out over the orchard. I can't see much, but it looks like there might be a thinning up near the house—like something's keeping the smoke creatures away. I'm going to try to get through and see what's going on."

She wanted to tell him to go ahead. But she couldn't ask him to risk himself. Her stomach churning, she said, "No. That's not your job. If things go right, I should be down there before sunrise. Wait for me."

"Sorry, babe. Gotta do it. You'd do it for me. Besides, if they are somehow managing to keep the critters at bay, they could use my help." He stopped and coughed raggedly. "I wouldn't mind if you hurried up. See you soon."

With that, the line went dead. Max closed her phone slowly. "That was Jim," she told Alexander as if he hadn't heard everything. Her voice was sandpaper dry, and her stomach twisted. She wanted to throw up. She hadn't let herself think that she would get there too late. "We should hurry."

9

As she put the truck in gear and headed out onto the highway, Max sank deep into that cold place where Alexander could not follow. He wanted to shake her, to keep her with him. But he held himself in check. This was her armor. It was how she kept going when pain was too overwhelming to deal with. In the cold place, she could withdraw from the bite of her emotions and the suffering of her body, and focus on what she had to get done. It made her more lethally strong than any Shadowblade he had ever met.

But it meant she was also retreating from him and the fragile bridge they had forged the night before. It made Alexander want to put his fist through the dash.

Once she passed Salem, she opened it up, no longer caring about the speed limit. In Eugene, she pulled off for food and fuel.

"Take him to the bathroom," she told Alexander, jerking her head toward Holt, who'd said nothing more since they'd left Troutdale. She turned a cold look on the mage. "Try anything, and Alexander will drop you like a sack of onions, understand?"

She didn't wait for his answer, but instead strode inside the McDonald's to order.

Alexander opened the rear door of the truck and slid out his knife. He slit the tape on Holt's wrists and wrapped the witch chain around his neck beneath the collar of his shirt. "Do please try something. I would not mind having a reason to kill you," Alexander said.

Holt's mouth twisted, but he said nothing and came along docilely enough. They returned to the truck, and Alexander retaped Holt's wrists. He watched Max through the broad wall of windows on the front of the building. She filled three drink cups and then leaned casually against a table while she waited. There were a dozen other customers in the place and four employees that Alexander could see. They all watched Max nervously. Her Shadowblade was tightly leashed, but in this mood, nothing hid what she was. Every survival instinct those people had was telling them she was dangerous and they should run. A minute or two later, every single customer evacuated, leaving their food half-eaten on the table.

The instant they emerged, they veered away from the truck, feeling Alexander's presence.

"I always thought you had a thing for Valery," Holt said, surprise coloring his voice.

Alexander glanced at him, his brows arching. "She is my sister."

"Not by blood."

"We are Caramaras. We do not measure family the same way you do."

Holt was silent for a long moment, staring at his retaped hands. Quietly he said, "She really is in trouble.

Those tablets she stole are too powerful for her to hold. I am not the only one looking for them. If someone else finds her first—"

"Someone?"

"Just as you serve someone more powerful than you, so do I. I have kept him off Valery's trail, but the Guardians' war is changing everything. He's no longer willing to wait for me to find the tablets. If he gets to her before I do, he won't just kill her. He wants her, too. A Caramaras smoke witch is a rare commodity. Now that she's removed my marriage marks, any loyalty he might have felt to me is gone. He'll take her."

His voice was bitter, though whether it was directed at Valery or his mysterious master, Alexander didn't know.

"She is not a commodity. And she is not going to let that happen," Alexander said.

"She won't have a choice. She'll go to him, and he'll make her like it. She'll never think it wasn't her idea." His lips twisted. "I have to find her before he does. You have to let me go. She thinks she knows what he's capable of, but she doesn't. This thing the Guardians are doing—pulling magic through the webs. They'll unleash it into this world, and when they do, my master will be more powerful than before. Valery won't stand a chance against him."

"Nice of you to warn her," Alexander said, disgust coloring his voice. As soon as he could, he would call her and let her know.

"I—" Holt turned away, his narrow jaw tightening. "She wouldn't believe me if I did."

"Which makes me wonder why I should. She knows you better than anyone. Why should I trust you when Valery does not?"

"You stupid son of a bitch. I'm telling you the truth. If you care about her as much as you say you do, then you'll help me."

Alexander shook his head. "You will have to do better than that."

"All right. Then what about this? What if I am telling the truth? What if she is being hunted right now by my master? When he finds her, he'll brainwash her. When he's through wrapping her up in his spells, she'll be his puppet. I've seen him do it before with more powerful witches than Valery.

"I might be able to stop him if I can return the tablets and get her to restore our marriage. Then she won't be nearly as tempting." When Alexander still looked unconvinced, Holt made a guttural sound of frustration, clenching his bound hands. "At least think about it."

Just then, Max thrust through the doors of the McDonald's. She handed a tray of drinks and the sacks of burgers through the window and climbed in. She went to turn the key and stopped, tilting her head. "Do you feel that?"

Alexander spread out his senses into the quiet of the August night. Cars raced past on the highway, and all around was the pulse of people living ordinary lives. The smell of magic was thin here. He pushed farther. There. A sound that wasn't a sound—more a rumble beyond hearing. He felt its tremor deep in the marrow of his bones. "I feel it."

"I do, too," Holt said. "It's the magic the Guardians are pulling through the web. It's building. It won't be long before they unleash it."

Alexander glanced back at the mage. His mouth was

bracketed in white, and his green eyes were half closed. He leaned back in his seat as if bracing against an avalanche. Max twisted the key and squealed the wheels as she pulled out of the parking lot. When she got back on the freeway, she sped up to a hundred miles an hour. Wordlessly, Alexander opened a box and handed her a hamburger. He passed another to Holt and then set to eating his own.

An hour and a half later, they crossed the border into California. Fifty miles or so ahead, they could see Mount Shasta rising up alone from the floor of the valley like a shining fang. Snow blanketed the peak despite the August heat. To the east and west, the Sierra and coastal mountain ridges ran south.

The tremor of magic reverberated in the air and ached in Alexander's lungs and teeth.

"It's close," Holt said, and he was breathing hard. His expression was a mix of pain and euphoria.

They passed through Weed, a dusty little town just north of Mount Shasta. The mountain loomed ominously, its shining white peak of snow scraping the starry sky.

They had gone another four miles when Holt groaned loudly. He lurched sideways and convulsed. The truck shimmied, and it felt like all four tires went flat at the same time.

"What the hell?" Max said, and veered off onto the shoulder.

They skidded to a stop, and she jammed the truck into park before yanking open her door and leaping out. Alexander did the same. The ache had spread through his body, and his head spun. The ground twitched and jumped beneath his feet. He staggered drunkenly to the front of the truck, where Max stood watching the mountain.

"Holy mother of fuck," she murmured as she swayed.

Suddenly the top of the mountain exploded. Ash and smoke doughnutted outward and then surged up in a tall plume. A wave of something else followed, smashing into Alexander like an invisible wall. He fell flat on his back, his head bouncing off the ground. His head spinning, he clambered to his feet. He looked for Max. He did not see her. He lurched around the front of the truck. She was slowly sitting up. Blood ran from a gouge on her cheek.

"Get in," Alexander said, grabbing her arm and hoisting her up. "We have to get out of here. There is going to be a hell of a mud flow coming at us in nothing flat."

She shook her head to clear it, then flung herself into the driver's seat. He jumped in on his side, glancing at Holt. He was toppled onto his side, facedown on the seat. Max put the truck in gear and then stopped, her mouth falling open as she stared up at the mountain. Alexander followed her gaze.

The smoke and ash were already thinning. The top of the main peak was flat and black, and runnels of water, mud, trees, and boulders were streaming down its sides. But what caught their attention was the thin streamer of gauzy red that rose from the black cone like a towering flame. As they watched, it curled and flattened on top, coiling through the air in a widening spiral.

The column in the middle thickened until it was as broad as the mountaintop, and the spinning cloud widened. Max spun the wheel to turn around. Before she could gun the motor, something smashed into them from behind. The truck jolted forward with a screech of tires, and there was a sound of crumpling metal and the smell of hot oil, burned rubber, and antifreeze. They were pushed fifteen feet before shuddering to a stop.

They'd been rear-ended by a Jeep pulling a fishing boat. Its front end was smashed, and the trailer had flipped onto its side, jackknifing and spilling duffel bags, coolers, tackle boxes, and sleeping bags all over the road. They blocked both lanes. Inside the Jeep, a man bobbled behind the wheel, dazed. The airbag had deployed and was already deflating. In the back were two teenage boys. Steam spurted from the Jeep's radiator, and oil and red transmission fluid puddled on the ground.

Alexander ran to the back of the Jeep and pulled the two boys out. He carried them off to the side, well out of the way should more cars come along and smash into the pileup. Max helped the driver out and settled him next to the boys. None looked any the worse for wear— all had been wearing seat belts.

"What is that?" The man asked, pointing at the sky.

Max looked up. The red cloud had turned turbulent, shredding apart into streamers and clumps as if stirred by a sharp wind, though the night was still and humid. Its color had thickened, and a mass of it pushed southward. As they watched, bits of it began to fall like bloody dandelion fluff. She looked over at Alexander.

"We've got to get out of here. I'll check the truck."

The truck's rear bumper was made of cement-filled steel pipe, and the Jeep had done little damage. Max and Alexander loaded their passengers into the back beneath the shell, ignoring their protestations, both eyeing the drifting fluff of the clouds. Wordlessly, they turned in unison to push the boat and trailer out of the road. Seconds later, they climbed back into the truck. Max got them turned around, jouncing through the median and pinning the gas pedal to the floor.

"Can you wake Zippy up?" she asked.

Alexander leaned over the seat, pulling the mage upright. Holt's head flopped. His eyes were open and unseeing. He breathed hard, with deep, clutching breaths. Alexander slapped his cheeks gently. "Wake up, Holt."

When that didn't work, he grabbed a half-drunk water bottle from his seat and splashed some on the mage's face. "Holt! Wake up!"

The mage shuddered and blinked, bracing his hands on either side of himself. "What's happened?"

"See for youself." Alexander pointed behind them.

Max rolled the window down so Holt could stick his head out and see behind. A moment later, he pulled back in.

"If you can go faster, you should," he told Max.

"What is that stuff?"

"Magic. Wild magic," he amended.

"That's what Scooter called it," Max said. "What's it mean?"

"You can't control it. It's like—" Holt broke off and rubbed his mouth with his bound hands. "Witches— most of us, anyhow—deal in elemental magic: earth, water, flesh, hex, air, fire. Caramaras witches deal in other kinds of magic," he said with a nod at Alexander. "But the elemental magic that we draw on is tempered—

it's already chosen what it will be. Wild magic hasn't. It plants itself and grows. It is extraordinarily fertile, even primordial. Who knows why or what it will become? Think of the enchanted forests of the fairy tales. Think of crystal mountains, rivers of milk and blood, giant bean stalks—it can be anything and turn anyone into anything. The only things safe from its effects are those things that have already been claimed or tamed by magic. So you and Alexander and I are safe enough."

"Why did you pass out?" Alexander asked.

"The shock wave. So much magic erupting back into the world . . ." He closed his eyes and swallowed. "It is overwhelming. Even the witch chain couldn't completely protect me from it. My guess is that any witches within a couple hundred miles passed out cold and won't be waking for a while."

Max veered around a car stopped on the side of the road, blaring her horn at the couple standing behind it, staring openmouthed at the sky. "Idiots," she muttered. "They are going to get themselves killed. Or worse."

Suddenly she slammed on the brakes and thrust the truck into reverse. She floored it, and they swerved back and forth before she straightened up and came flying back. She squealed to a halt beside the gray sedan.

Alexander leaned out his window. "Are you all right? Do you need help? You cannot stay here."

The man had his arm around the woman, who looked wilted and dazed. They could not have been much older than twenty-two or twenty-three. They were dressed in button-up shirts tucked into their khaki pants, with carefully styled hair and almost-new hiking boots. They looked at Alexander as if he was a ghost.

"What's happening?" the man asked. Husband, Alexander realized, seeing the gold band on his left hand.

"Does your car work?"

The man looked vaguely behind him at the sedan and back at Alexander. "Yeah, I think— I don't—" He looked at Alexander as if he couldn't remember the question. Then his wife moaned and swayed. He pulled her tight against his chest. "Amanda? Are you all right? What's wrong?"

"She's a latent witch," Holt murmured inside the truck, eyeing the couple with narrowed eyes. "Probably just starting to come into her powers. She's lucky. It protected her from the full weight of the blast."

Just then, there was a sudden squall from the back of the car. Max started at the sound. "Is that a baby?" she asked.

Alexander caught sight of the baby carrier in the backseat. He nodded. "It is."

"Shit."

He knew what she was thinking. That her family was under attack and there was no time to waste.

"Whatever you're going to do, get on it," Holt said. He was leaning out the window, peering back the way they'd come.

Alexander followed suit, pulling himself up onto the sill to get a broader view. His stomach clenched. A fine mist of red was slowly falling behind them. It drifted and swirled like ash as it descended, hanging a crimson curtain across the valley. He could no longer see Mount Shasta. As he watched, bits from the leading edge settled on the road no more than two hundred yards behind them. Instantly, the ground buckled and twisted.

Orange tentacles that could have been plants or something else entirely shot twenty feet into the air. A second
later, the mist thickened so he could see no more.

He dropped back inside. "We have to go. Now."

"We aren't leaving them. Load them in the back."

Alexander did not argue. It would only waste time,
and the stubborn thrust of Max's jaw told him she was
not going to change her mind.

He snatched up Amanda first. She was feverish, her
cheeks flushed splotchy red. Her head rolled back to
dangle over his arm, and her body went limp as he
swung her up. Alexander carried her around to the back
of the truck. The father of the two boys was already
pushing open the tailgate. Alexander set his burden
down and went to drag her husband to the rear. The
man struggled.

"My daughter! I can't leave her!"

Alexander picked the kicking man up and tossed
him over his shoulder, dumping him in the back with
the others. Without a word, he went to get the baby.
He leaned in through the window and yanked out the
seat. Plastic snapped, and the seat belt uprooted as he
pulled the baby free. He handed the crying baby to her
distraught father and shut the tailgate and shell before
jumping back in the truck.

Max gunned the motor before he shut his door, and
they squealed away up the freeway, back toward Weed.

Alexander looked behind them. A clump of crimson
fell to the left, only a hundred yards away now.

"How far can this magic go?" he asked Holt.

The mage shrugged. "It took a lot of effort to pull
it into this world. I doubt the Guardians have much

strength left to push it very far. Using a volcano was smart—made it easier to disperse. That's probably how they're doing it everywhere. From here, they can shove it down the valley and cover most of the state. I wouldn't bother to go north where hardly anyone lives. Not that it will matter. Eventually it will fall into rivers and drain to the ocean and spread everywhere. Water is the one thing that doesn't transform."

"Will the mountains contain it?" Max asked. She had gone cold again and seemed almost relaxed as she raced ahead of the falling wild magic.

"For now. If the Guardians have any strength to push it, they'll use what wind they can find and the summer heat to keep it aloft as long as possible. It takes less effort. Forcing it over the mountains is a lot of work for little purpose. You have the ocean on one side and desert on the other. They get more bang for their buck by staying in the valley and letting the rivers take care of spread."

"All right. Then once it stops coming at us, we can turn west to the coast and see if we can beat it to Winters," Max said.

Neither man answered. It was a long shot, and Alexander knew it. As fast as the mist was overtaking them, they could not go fast enough south to get around it.

Max swerved to miss a downed motorcycle, jamming on the brakes and sliding sideways as she did. Alexander leaped out before the truck skidded to a halt and ran to pick up the man struggling to walk down the shoulder of the road.

"Leg's broke," he told Alexander. "Hey! I'm too heavy for you!"

But Alexander swung him up easily and trotted him back to the truck, shoving him in beside Holt. The back was stuffed full already.

The big man groaned and swore. "Goddamn that hurts!" A couple of minutes later, he recovered enough to examine his companions. "What's going on here?" he asked, staring at the tape binding Holt.

"He is dangerous," Alexander answered.

"And you're not? I weigh two fifty, and you picked me up like I was a rag doll."

Alexander smiled. "Maybe I am dangerous, too. But I just saved you, so that should offer you some comfort."

"What the hell is that stuff coming out of Shasta? That's no regular volcanic eruption."

"You don't want to know," Max said. "What's your name?"

"Call me Baker," he said. He grimaced and wiped the sweat off his forehead. He was dressed in a black leather jacket and pants, and he wore a green bandanna tied around his head. The leather was scarred from where he'd slid across the blacktop. The stubble on his jaw was a mix of gray and brown, and his face was weathered and tan. "You going to tell me what's going on?"

"The end of the world," Max said. "Hold on."

She veered off into the median, hardly slowing down. The truck jolted and bumped, spewing dust behind it in a long plume. A pileup of six cars blocked the road, and a dozen others had stopped to help. They jounced over a rise, and a loud crack sounded beneath them. The truck slewed from side to side and finally rolled to a stop. The smell of burning oil filled the cab.

"End of the line," Max said. She looked at Alexander. "Get the others out. I'll help Baker and Holt."

He went around to the rear. The curtain of wild magic was only fifty or sixty feet away. They were not going to outrun it. He opened the shell and the tailgate, waving everyone out. "Come on. Let's go!" His passengers were pale and breathless with fear. Each sported new bumps and bruises from the rough ride. "You have to hurry. It is coming on quick."

The father who'd been pulling the boat and his two sons scrambled out and pulled the still unconscious Amanda out with them. Her husband crawled forward, clutching his daughter's car seat to his stomach. Alexander took it from him and lifted him out before passing the baby back. Ignoring their questions and rising panic, he swung around to the side of the truck where Max was helping Baker and Holt.

He stopped dead. She had ripped the tape from Holt's wrists and was unwinding the chain from his neck. She pulled it free. Her eyes met Alexander's, reading his shock and anger. She held the chain up.

"This is the best chance these people have to come out of this. We can't waste it on Holt."

She was right. With luck, the witch chain would counter the wild magic and keep their passengers safe. He nodded shortly. She flipped up the backseat and pulled out a second chain. She looked at the mage. "Can you do anything about Baker's leg? He'll only slow us down."

Holt eyed her, scrutinizing her from head to foot like she was an alien from another planet. Alexander sympathized. Max never did the expected.

"You want me to help you?" Holt asked incredulously.

"I want you to help him," she said, jerking her chin at Baker, who was biting his lips, tears squeezing from the corners of his eyes. "After that, if you've got a few minutes before you start stalking the woman who's been trying to ditch you for the last few years, I want you to help us take these people to safety."

Holt crossed his arms. "And if I don't?"

"Then you don't. But if these people get fucked because you didn't bother to help, then I'd probably take it personally. I'd probably make a point of getting revenge. We're out of time. What are you going to do?"

He smiled. "You know, your threats don't scare me."

"That's because you don't know me very well yet, Zippy."

Holt smiled wider. "What's in it for me?" He turned a speculative glance at a seething Alexander. "I might be willing if you tell me where Valery went."

Alexander looked at Max. If she demanded it of him, would he do it? He couldn't. But if Max asked—

His stomach turned to cold lead as he silently begged her not to make him choose.

"The only thing in it for you is the warm, fuzzy feeling you get when you do a good deed," she told Holt. "And since you've probably never experienced it in your entire sorry life, you might get a real high out of it. So what's it going to be?"

"You're a real bitch on wheels, aren't you? All right. We're headed in the same direction anyhow. Might as well give you a hand."

"What a prince," she said. "Help Baker."

She handed one of the witch chains to Alexander. "Put a loop around everybody's wrist. Hopefully the magic isn't stronger than the chains. Oh, and one more thing—Holt's right. I *am* a bitch. But did you really think I'd tell you to sell out your sister, Slick?"

There was a wealth of fury and hurt in her voice. Before he could answer, she walked away.

Holt followed his glance. "That's one hell of a woman," he murmured appreciatively.

"Keep your damned hands to yourself," Alexander snapped, and was rewarded with a gloating laugh. He started to put the chain around the baby's wrist, but Holt stopped him.

"Better take the baby out of that seat. It might turn into something that will eat her," Holt said.

"What?" Baker exclaimed. "You can't be serious."

Alexander blew out a harsh breath and started to unbuckle the seat, pushing aside the father's resistant hands. "Unfortunately, things do not get more serious."

10

MAX APPROACHED THE FATHER OF THE TWO teenage boys, anger sizzling inside her. She didn't throw innocent people under the bus for any reason. Alexander ought to know that about her, if nothing else.

"Give me your arms."

The man glowered at her, unmoving. He was probably around forty years old, slim and fit, with brown hair clipped close over the ears. His sons were lanky, with torn jeans and faded T-shirts. One had hair dyed solid black and combed over his eyes, and the older one wore the short bleached tips of his brown hair pushed up in a ridge down the middle of his head. They stood just behind their father, hands jammed into their pockets, looking terrified. Amanda was lying on the ground, unconscious.

"Tell me what the hell is going on," the father demanded. "Who are you, and what is that?"

He pointed at the nearing curtain of wild magic. It was like the leading edge of a rainstorm, except this rain fell in swirling, twisting clumps and droplets. It was so thick it was difficult to see more than twenty feet or so inside.

How did she tell this ordinary man that it was magic? That fairy tales were true and that he was about to walk into the worst one ever? No happily ever afters, just wild magic that could do just about anything, if Holt was telling the truth. Max didn't think he was lying. The ground continued to shudder and buckle with the force of what was happening inside the growing magical storm, and what she could see inside the leading edge had lumped and writhed before vanishing behind the fall of crimson.

Still, she had to say something, or they would stand here like idiot deer and get butchered. She scraped her fingers through her hair.

"All right. All of you, listen to me. I'm only going to say this once, and you don't get to ask questions. We don't have time. Here's the nutshell version, and as much as you aren't going to want to believe it, there's your proof."

She pointed at the closing curtain of red. Except it really wasn't a curtain. The leading edge dropped the red seeds of magic like embers from fireworks. The mist closed in behind it, or rose up from it—Max had no idea.

"What you're looking at is pure magic straight out of Grimms' Fairy Tales. This chain should protect you from it. Let go, and you might turn into goblins or trolls or rocks. We're going to try to lead you to safety. There's a good chance it won't extend too far north."

"Who *are* you?" Baker asked, staring down at Holt, who was chanting, his hands clasped around the other man's thigh.

The mage's hex marks writhed, and coppery light twined around the injured man's leg.

"I'm Max, that's Alexander," she said, pointing to him, "and the man healing your leg is Holt."

"*What* are you?" asked the baby's father, his voice low and breathless.

"We're what is going to keep you safe, if you let us. Now, let us fasten this chain on you before it's too late."

The father of the two teenage boys held his arm out reluctantly.

"What are your names?" Max asked as she tied the chain firmly to his wrist. Witch chain tied like twine and yet ran through her hands with the liquid heaviness of finely worked metal.

"I'm Geoff Brewer. These are my sons, Josh and David."

She finished tying them together. "No matter what you see, don't pull loose of this chain for any reason. It might be the last thing you do."

Alexander was finishing with Matthew, the father of the baby. "What about Amanda?" he asked, his voice rising in panic as Alexander skipped her and chained up Baker.

"She doesn't need the chain to protect her," Holt said, straightening from his crouch.

Baker took a tentative step, shock making his mouth drop open. "How did you do that? I couldn't walk—the pain—it's all gone!"

"I'm a mage," Holt said smugly.

"What do you mean, she doesn't need it?" Matthew was struggling against his bonds. Alexander had tied a length of chain around the man's waist and looped it around both of the baby's legs before tying in Baker.

"Witches don't need protection," Max said bluntly.

Matthew's mouth gaped.

"Witch?" one of the boys repeated, as if he wasn't sure he'd heard her correctly.

Holt bent over the prone woman, brushing his fingers over her forehead. He straightened and nodded. "No doubt about it."

"I will carry her," Alexander said, picking her up and slinging her over his shoulders. One arm wrapped her thighs, and the other held one of her arms. He looked at Max. "I'll take the lead."

She nodded. "Holt and I will watch our flanks. If trouble comes, don't stop. Get them out of here."

He nodded and turned away without arguing about her taking risks or admonishing her to be careful. She'd braced herself for both, expecting to have to remind him of her capabilities and that she was a Shadowblade Prime. She let out a small sigh, her anger toward him cooling. Maybe she didn't know him as well as she thought she did, either.

He took the lead, holding on to the end of the chain tying Matthew and his daughter to Baker. Max tied off the end of her chain to Baker's as well, and she and Holt walked on either side of the small column as guards.

She glanced back. The creeping mist was maybe twenty feet away. Inside it, she could see shadows, some as tall as skyscrapers. Shapes twisted and moved, sprawling over the ground and rising like waves hitting a rocky headland. It was like the world inside was re-arranging itself.

The ground rumbled and growled and jolted. She

felt drunk as she staggered over the moving earth. She slipped a knife into her hand. What if it wasn't just a magical forest or a glass mountain sprouting up in there? Fairy tales came loaded with a horde of vicious beasties. Keeping the wild magic from changing her little band of survivors into eggplant Parmesan was one thing; staying alive was another kettle of piranha altogether.

Alexander broke into a slow jog. Amanda's head bounced against his shoulder, and behind him, Matthew struggled to run with his daughter pressed to his chest. Max fell back behind. Holt soon joined her.

"So if we're attacked, are you going to cover your own ass or help me?" she asked. "I'd rather know now if I can count on you."

"I said I would help."

"How far are you willing to take it? Valery didn't seem to think you're the till-death-do-us-part kind of guy. If you bailed on her, what kind of loyalty are you going to have for someone like me who tied you up and held you prisoner?"

His face hardened; his eyes turned scorching. "Valery left me," he said tautly. "I never *bailed* on her."

"You must have done something to piss her off. She didn't strike me as all that flighty and impulsive."

"I—" He broke off, his face twisting with the violence of hard-held emotions.

"Did I hit a nerve?" Max asked.

"As I told you before, it is complicated," he said, enunciating each word carefully.

"When isn't it complicated? But hey, not my problem. That's between you and your ex. All I want to know is if you're going to throw me to the wolves when they're gnawing at our feet. After all, saving these people doesn't require covering my ass, now does it?"

"And if I say yes, you'll believe me?"

"I might. If you say it with feeling."

He laughed suddenly. "You're a bitch coming and going, aren't you?"

"So they tell me." Max grinned. Despite herself, she liked Holt. She could see what had drawn Valery to him in the first place. He had a kind of razor charm and an unexpected humor that made him likable, despite being a mage and an arrogant ass.

"I guess you'll have to wait and see what I do," he said. "Don't you love a good surprise?"

"Only if I'm the one springing it."

"I couldn't agree more." He chuckled, then sobered. "Why are you helping these people? What's in it for you?"

She shook her head. And the rat bastard came scurrying back. "Does there have to be something in it for me?"

"What's the point of risking yourself if not?"

"Is it always about the bottom line with you? Do you ever do anything without expecting something in return?"

"Not really."

"No wonder Valery divorced you."

"She didn't divorce me," he said through gritted teeth. "Caramaras don't get divorced. When I catch up with her, we'll get that settled once and for all."

"If you catch up with her."

"She'd better hope I find her first," he said, and a flicker of fear danced through his eyes so fast that Max wasn't sure she'd actually seen it.

"So why help us? If you only do things for payment, what are you expecting?"

"Alexander will owe me. You saw him. He'd have told me how to find Valery if you'd ordered him to. If I happen to save your life, then he might just feel obligated to share the information."

"I wouldn't count on it. She's his family."

"And he's in love with you."

Max ground to a halt, staring slack-jawed at the mage. "Where the hell do you get that from?"

"Aw, is that one of those surprises you don't like?" He grabbed her arm and jerked her forward. "Stopping is probably a bad idea right now."

She started her stumbling jog again. "He is not in love with me."

But electricity was racing through her, and her blood pounded with the possibility. What if he was? No, she didn't want that. Did she? *Fuck no.* Even if Scooter wasn't waiting for her, there were a dozen other things that made it an insane idea. Like the fact that Giselle wouldn't hesitate to use him against her; like the fact that no one at Horngate trusted him; like the fact that screwing around with one of her own Shadowblades would make everyone question her decisions. Not to mention the fact that letting people get that close made you stupid.

She sought out his form ahead of the others. He'd made it clear that he wanted her, whatever that meant, but love? That was too much. Holt was wrong. And if he wasn't, it was a can of worms she didn't want to open.

"Ready now," Holt said, looking upward.

A rain of scarlet fell softly toward them. It clumped in

thick tufts, some the size of melons. Some of it was no bigger than an eyelash. It whirled and drifted on a wind Max couldn't see or feel.

She and Holt closed the distance on their companions.

"Things are about to get weird," she told them. "Don't let go of that chain."

They all were looking up now, fear making them bunch together and stop.

"Keep moving," she ordered.

Alexander tugged on the end of the chain, and they started forward again.

More of the wild magic filled the air, swirling around them like a red blizzard. A heady, sweet smell filled her nose and flooded her mouth. It tasted of honey and oranges and burned down into her lungs with every breath. The heat was searing, and yet it filled her with strength and energy like she'd never felt before. The ground lifted and rolled like a wave in the ocean. Max staggered and fell to one knee. Holt lurched against her, and she held him steady.

Then the world around them exploded.

The weight of Holt vanished. Dust and clods of dirt filled the air, and Max was blinded. She coughed, her mouth filling with dirt. Something hit her cheek, slicing her to the bone. Flying rocks and debris hammered her from every side.

The ground dropped away. Max swung her arms wildly. They tangled in a vine. She clutched it with one hand, swinging like a pendulum in the dirt-choked air. The surface of the vine was warm and nobby. It stretched in her hand, growing and widening, splaying her fingers apart until she could no longer hold it. She dropped her knife and reached up to grip it with her other hand, clawing her fingers into it. The outer layer gave, and sticky coldness seeped down over her skin. The massive vine jerked and swung her from side to side.

She kicked, trying to swing her legs up to grab the vine for a better hold. Before she could, something grabbed her left ankle, and sharp pains drilled into her calf. A second later, her right foot was captured. Both legs went numb, and something smooth and wet slid up to her waist.

It was like she was caught in cement. She could swivel her hips but little else. Max gripped harder on her handhold above and tried to draw herself up. She didn't budge. She could hardly feel her legs now, and sharp prickles circled her waist.

"Alexander! Holt!" She coughed again as dust filled her mouth and nose. No one answered. She called again and thought she heard a faint noise off to her right. She strained to listen. Not far away, she heard a guttural panting and a high-pitched whining-buzzing sound like flies and ants arguing over a picnic. A thrum vibrated through the air, the sound so deep it could only be felt, not heard. Other sounds rose now, too—chirps of birds, barks of squirrels, squeals, purrs, squeaks, and so much more. In the distance, she heard splashing.

The dust began to settle. Max caught her breath in amazement. The panorama that spread out before her was primordial. Gone was the flat plane of the valley. All that remained was Mount Shasta, still spewing wild magic from its cone. The snow looked glassy and sparkled like cut crystal. The lower slopes vanished into a lush forest that spread over a broken landscape of hills and gorges, bald tors and sharp ridges. The foliage was dark green, almost black. Wild magic still spun in the air, but Max could see that Holt had been right. The bulk of it was blowing southward on a crimson wind. She swallowed. She had to get to Winters before the wild magic did. *If anyone is still alive.*

She refused to consider it. Instead, she examined her predicament. She was on the edge of a cliff. Far below, a gold river cut through the steep-sided gorge. She was naked—her clothes and weapons no doubt changed by the wild magic. Her legs were encased in a sickly green, nacreous material that was solid from the knees down, breaking apart into a delicate lace patterning over her thighs and waist. Blood welled from beneath the filigree and was absorbed into the shiny green casing with a faint wet sound.

Bile flooded her tongue. It was eating her.

She looked up. She was gripping a long orange and black limb as big around as she was. Its smooth surface was studded with flat calluses. Where her fingers dug through its skin, she could see pale yellow flesh. Yellow liquid ran down over her hands and arms, smelling faintly like carrion.

Suddenly the limb trembled and lifted. Max let it go as her body stretched, her tendons pulling taut. The limb—no, a tentacle, she realized— curled, and the end of it whipped back toward her. The last four feet or so flattened out into a kind of webbed fan. The underside was covered with puffy ovals with a slit down the middle of each one. It came at Max like a big flyswatter. She flung herself sideways, and it passed over her, wind whistling around it. The sharp edge of her prison cut into her, and blood streamed down her side as she readied herself for the next pass.

The swatter came at her again. Max ducked and slammed it with a two-fisted hammer blow. There was a scream like tearing metal, and the tentacle flailed wildly. More sprang up around it, and Max realized that they grew in a cluster. Whether the one tentacle was attached like an arm to the others or whether it was a little patch of individuals, she didn't know. What she knew was that they were going to batter her to death and likely eat her.

Just then, the stuff around her legs made a sound like a burp and rippled upward over her no longer bleeding belly wound. Inside, her skin prickled and itched. Max grimaced. The tentacles might be late to the buffet.

She glanced at the quivering tentacles. They would certainly kill her if they came at her at once. Which meant she had to free her legs fast.

She bent as far as the lips of the mouth holding her would allow and swung her fists at the outer shell with all her might. The creature shuddered and clamped tighter on her. She swore and pounded it again, all the while keeping one eye on her tentacle friends. They quivered, the fan ends rubbing gently together. It wouldn't be long before they attacked.

Suddenly the creature's grip on her waist loosened. Encouraged, Max kept up her battering attack. Abruptly, the mouth opened and shrank back down into the ground with a wet groan. Max flung herself headlong as the tentacles crashed down where she'd been in one united blow.

The creature below was still feeling hungry; it snapped up and circled a group of six or seven tentacles, hardening almost instantly. The tentacles tugged furiously, and those that hadn't been caught thrashed madly at the ground. Max dragged herself out of the way, her legs clumsy and weak. Her thighs were mottled blue and black, and her lower legs were pale gray. She crawled around a wet gash in the ground that looked too much like another mouth and eyed the trees around her carefully.

The trees were scattered widely, allowing for a carpet of lush grass pocked with bright flowers that bobbed in the heat. Many were familiar—tansy, goldenrod, lupine, golden poppies, and horseradish. Others she didn't recognize at all, not that she was much of a gardener. They could be common, and she'd never know it.

Something caught her eye. It was a small grove of trees with smooth gray-orange skin and dark oval leaves gathered in small fronds. Rowan. Max lurched to her feet and limped toward it. Small creatures scuttled away, twitching a telltale path through grass.

Max went into the grove and found a low-hanging branch about two inches in diameter. She pressed her palm against the trunk. It felt warm and silky.

"Sorry about this," she said. "But I need a weapon if I'm going to get out of here alive."

With that, she snapped off the limb. The tree made a moaning sound, and the grove rustled, though no wind blew. Max hesitated. Rowan wood was powerful against most Uncanny and Divine creatures. But taking it without some kind of payment when the tree was protesting seemed incredibly stupid. The trouble was, she was stark naked and, aside from blood, had little to offer. But maybe that was enough. Blood was life, after all, and sacrifice was honored.

She didn't have a knife or anything to cut with, which meant this was going to be messy. She dug her right thumbnail deep into her wrist at the base of her left thumb, looking for the radial artery. She nicked it, sending a small fountain into the air. She aimed at the splintered stump of the branch she'd stolen. It took only a few seconds for the wound to heal. She stared in surprise. Even in perfect health, it should have taken a minute to close. But the wound was already a pink scar, and as she watched, even that faded.

She looked down at her legs. The bruises had disappeared, and the gray was now looking more pink. It had to be the wild magic. It was feeding her healing spells. Thank goodness. She looked back at the tree. Her blood had disappeared, the end of the branch was smooth, and a new twig rose from the center.

"Thank you," she said, and then headed out to find her companions.

She went north, away from Mount Shasta, hoping that any of the enchantments traditionally associated with magical forests wouldn't work on her. Otherwise, she'd wander in circles forever or until she got captured or eaten or worse.

Max carried the rowan branch like a club, making her way carefully so that she didn't step into any traps. She didn't let herself think about what was becoming of all the people caught up in the spreading eruption of magic. She hoped to hell Alexander had gotten clear with his charges.

She'd gone maybe a mile, following a zigzagging track

as she avoided clear pools of inviting water, sand pits, suspicious glades, and strange plants, when she heard him yelling for her.

"Here!" She started in his direction, going into a small copse of what looked like dwarf oak trees. Beside her, something unfurled from a stout branch. It was four feet long and covered with a thin layer of white hair. A black stripe ran down its red center. It dangled like a thin flag. Or a tongue. Max eased around it. More of the things uncurled until she was standing in the middle of a swaying maze. She dropped to the ground and wiggled forward on her stomach. The tongues sensed her passing and stretched toward her. She pushed them away with the twiggy end of the rowan branch and pulled herself along faster. She reached the other side and rolled clear before jumping to her feet.

Alexander called for her again, and she didn't answer, following his voice and hoping for his sake that no one else was doing the same thing.

She topped a low ridge and stopped short. The downslope was covered in short silvery white grass. She hesitated. It didn't look threatening, but then nothing ever did in fairy tales. That was the point. She prodded the nearby edge with the end of the rowan branch. Nothing happened. That was a good sign.

She looked to either side. Trees crowded up the ridge, their shadows black and dense. Who knew what hid within? A rustling caught her attention, and Alexander emerged from a tangle of bushes at the foot of the hill. He was fully clothed, one of the witch chains wrapped around his waist. Just her luck. The chance to see him naked, and she was the only one streaking.

"Max!" he said, relief coloring his voice as he caught sight of her. His gaze traveled down and back up. "Nice. A little dirty, though. Care to turn around so I can see the rest of you?" He turned his finger in the air.

Men. "Did you get the others out? Where's Holt?"

"The magic stopped just short of Weed. I got the others out, mostly none the worse for wear. I have not seen Holt."

Damn. They couldn't just leave him, either. "I'm coming down," she said, and reached out a tentative foot. The silver grass was as stiff as its color. The tips slid into her flesh like needles. Max jerked back, swearing. She was going to have to go around through the trees after all. Then she remembered Tutresiel's feather in her hand. Could she just jump over it?

"Wait. I am coming to get you," Alexander said.

He pushed his booted foot out, bending the blades of silver down with a crunching sound. He scuffed up the hill, making a long double-ribboned track behind him. At the top, he reached for Max and pulled her into a swift kiss before swinging her up into his arms. "My kingdom for a bed and a few minutes of privacy," he growled as he leered down at her.

"I wouldn't be bragging too loudly about how fast it takes you to get your business done," Max admonished. "You don't want a reputation for getting off the freeway an exit too early."

He snorted and kissed her again. "If that was a dare, I will take you up on it."

"You're getting awfully grabby, aren't you?" Not that she minded his kisses or being wrapped up in his arms. In fact, she liked it too damned much. Suddenly she remembered what Holt had said about Alexander being in love with her. She started to pull away, then stopped herself. What if he was? Did it matter? She was promised to Scooter. It couldn't last. He knew that as well as she did. So if he was willing to play for a few days, why shouldn't she?

"Are you complaining?"

"I'm . . . crap," she said, and then pulled him to her. This kiss was as fast as the other two, but it left them both breathless. She could hear his heart thudding in his chest. Hers wasn't any slower.

Close by, a whispery howl cut through the night, followed by two more. Alexander tensed. Without another word, he followed his path back down, the leaves of silver grass already springing back upright. He set Max on her feet at the bottom.

"What now, boss?"

"We can't leave Holt. We have to look for him," she said.

He grimaced and nodded. "I know."

He stripped off his shirt and handed it to her with the second witch chain. She pulled the material over her head. It fell to midthigh and smelled deliciously like Alexander. She wrapped the chain around her waist like a belt. He passed her a knife, and she used it to sharpen the end of the rowan wood branch.

"Where do we start?" he asked when she was done.

"I have no idea. I haven't seen or smelled him since the wild magic hit us." She glanced up at the sky. The crimson mist hung thick overhead. They probably had two or three hours to sunrise. Not a lot of time to find a safe place to hole up in, much less track down the mage. If he wasn't hurt, he'd probably make out all right on his own, but if he was— She'd pushed him into this mess, and she owed it to him to get him out if she could.

"Any signal we make will just bring trouble down on us," Alexander said.

"That didn't seem to bother you when you were bellowing for me," Max pointed out.

"I like you more than I like him. I would leave him to rot, but Valery would gut me."

"For a divorced woman being stalked by her ex, you'd think she'd be pleased if he fell off the side of the planet."

"You would think," he agreed, but said no more.

"Let's angle back that way and see if we can pick up some sign of him," Max said, pointing. "If we don't find him in two hours, he's on his own. We'll have to look for cover."

She started walking, and her thoughts turned to Jim. She wondered if he'd made it through to her brother's house. She wondered if her family was still alive and if Jim had told them she was coming, that she'd be there before sunrise. Her stomach churned, and she felt nauseous. She wondered if they were waiting—praying for help that was going to be very late in coming.

II

MAX STALKED AHEAD, HER HEAD SWIVELING back and forth warily. Alexander drifted to her left, leaving a good twenty feet between them. He watched the ground and trees, periodically lifting his gaze to scan the skies. Wild magic still fell. He could hear unfamiliar sounds, and they set him on edge. He could not tell how normal they might be to a forest or what dangers they might hint at. He had spent most of the past hundred years or so in cities. Even at Horngate, he rarely made the perimeter patrols.

Smells tickled his attention. Bitter musk, sour mold, mealy ash. He stepped over a mound of crumbled dirt and then another and another. There were a couple of dozen altogether. He eased through on the balls of his feet, wondering what hid inside them.

A rumble shook the ground just as he reached the last of the mounds. Suddenly black and blue beetles spilled from the tops of each. They were as big as sparrows and covered in glossy feathers. They had rounded doglike snouts full of sharp teeth. They instantly honed in on Alexander, pooling together and flooding toward him.

Alexander sprang away, grasping an overhead limb and swinging up into a tree. They followed, swarming up the trunk. He crouched on the branch and sprang fifteen feet to another tree, catching himself with his hands. He pulled himself up and made two more leaps before dropping lightly down, trying not to jar the earth and call attention to himself.

He turned to find Max right behind him. He breathed in her scent and bit the inside of his cheek with the sudden flush of desire that spilled through him. Every time he saw her, every time he was close to her, he re-acted like a thirteen-year-old boy. But there was nothing juvenile in his hunger for her. He wanted to rip his shirt off her and see her bare body again; he wanted to push her up against the tree and drive himself into her until neither of them had the strength to stand.

He ground his teeth together. Now was not the time. But soon, if he had anything to say on the matter.

Max started away and Alexander followed her, then grabbed her wrist as a faint scent hooked him. Blood, and it had a coppery taste. Human, or close to it. He glanced at her. She'd caught it, too. She nodded. "It might not be him, but it's the only trail we've got," she murmured.

He led the way this time. He climbed a hill, and the sound of rushing water came to him, and the smell of blood grew stronger. He went down the opposite slope. The trees grew thicker, the gnarled limbs twisting and knotting together in a thick tangle, making it nearly impossible to pass through.

White streamers of what looked like torn cobwebs hung like rags in the thicket. Three-inch thorns glistened wetly through the gray foliage. Alexander stopped. There was a presence here, as if something was waiting. The back of his neck prickled. In front of him, the weaving branches untied themselves, leaving a narrow tunnel. It was about thirty feet long. On the other end was a clearing.

He looked at Max. "Go through or go around?"

She looked over her shoulder. "Not sure we have a choice."

He followed her gaze. The path was gone; the trees had woven themselves together so tightly that there was not a hole big enough for a squirrel to get through. As he watched, thorns grew out like porcupine quills, covering every handhold and leaving only the enticing emptiness of the exit.

He snarled in fury. "It is a trap. I blundered right in."

"Both of us did," she said, her eyes narrowing on the tunnel. "One of us might get through before it snaps shut, but not both." She stroked her fingers over the rowan wood spear she'd made. "I'm not sure how much help this will be." She looked up, and a smile curved her lips. "That's interesting."

Above was open to the sky, as if the trees were taunting them. Max looked down at her hand, where Tutresiel's feather was embedded.

"I can distract it with the rowan spear while you run through, and then I'll jump out," she said. "It can't be more than twenty feet up. If the feather works, I should clear it easy."

Alexander shook his head. "First jump out and make sure you can. Then try attacking from the outside."

She raised her brows at him. "You'd better be fast."

He smiled smugly. "You are worried about me."

"You know you're about to be lunch food for a big, bloodthirsty bush, right? You might want to focus and get your priorities straight."

"Then get going. Feel free to be naked again when I get to the other side." He ran his knuckles over her bare thigh just below the hem of his shirt. "That is a lure no sane man could resist."

"No one ever said you were sane," Max said, pushing him away. "Here." She thrust the rowan spear into his hand. "If you come out of here dead, don't think I won't make you regret it. I'll find a Voudon witch and bring you back to life just so I can kill you again."

"I am not so easy to kill," he said, delighting in the fact that she seemed truly concerned. "Just tell me you will be waiting, and nothing will stop me."

She rolled her eyes. "Cool it, Slick. This isn't the movies."

With that, she bent her knees and sprang. As a Shadowblade, she could easily jump twenty or thirty feet into the air. But the feather made her soar. She rocketed up and in a moment vanished from sight.

Alexander let out a relieved breath. She was safely out of this mess.

Gripping the rowan staff, he turned to the tunnel trap. He crouched and sprang forward. There was not enough room for him to remain upright, and that made him slower. He was halfway through when the tunnel began to collapse, the limbs writhing and clutching at him. He used the spear, rapping it back and forth against the shrinking walls, roof, and root floor. The woven wood maw flinched, but otherwise the rowan had little effect.

He was ten feet from the end, and the mouth of the tunnel was puckering closed. Poisoned thorns grew in from every angle. He could not get through without scraping himself many times. If the toxin was quick-acting, he would be dead or possibly paralyzed before he escaped.

He did not stop moving. He smashed at the thorns with the rowan spear, clearing room for himself. Outside, he heard Max and saw the flash of her knife as she hacked at the entrance. In another moment or two, it would be too small for him to get out. He dove, flinging himself through the tunnel mouth. Wood and thorns scraped his bare chest and caught at his pants as he plunged through.

He landed on his shoulder and rolled onto his feet. Instantly, his vision fuzzed, and he staggered. Max caught him around the waist.

"Easy now, Slick. I've got you."

"But will you keep me?" The words were slurred. His tongue felt like a stone.

"Depends. How are you with cleaning bathrooms and making the bed? Or are you one of those men who leave their wet towels and dirty underwear on the floor?" She hitched him closer. "Come on. Get in the water. Let's try to rinse away some of the poison."

She pushed him back. He staggered. His legs were stiff, and every muscle in his body was seizing up. The toxin was paralytic. He hardly felt the chill of the water as he fell headlong into it. Max put her arm under his neck and rubbed gently at the scrapes along his torso.

"Come on, Slick. You're wasting the night. Hurry up and heal," she said, sounding tense.

He tried to speak, but his mouth wouldn't move. His heart stuttered, and his lungs felt like bricks. He could feel his healing spells fighting, spreading fingers of heat and light through his body. His head spun as he fought to breathe.

"This is a trick to get me to kiss you again, isn't it? You think I'll give you mouth-to-mouth. It's pathetic, Slick."

He felt the sensation of movement as she lifted him out of the water and laid him on the grass beside the pool. There was pressure against his numb nose and lips and a remote push into his chest. He heard her take another breath as she repeated the action four more times. Then he heard a cracking sound and felt a weight against his chest as she did compressions.

She repeated the sequence five more times, and each time more sensation returned to him as his healing spells did their job. By the sixth time, he could feel the warmth of her lips on his. Sluggishly, he lifted his arm and caught the back of her head with his hand. He pushed his tongue inside her mouth, kissing her. She froze an instant, then kissed him back, her hands sliding up to cup his cheeks. Her taste made his head spin. He lifted his head, pulling her closer, slanting his mouth and kissing her deeply. She made a sound in her throat, her fingers curling into fists against his face.

He pulled away, panting, though whether from want of her or lack of capacity in his still healing lungs, he did not know.

"So I guess you're feeling better," she said.

"I could use another kiss to really make me well."

She grinned and shook her head. "C'mon. We had better get looking for Holt."

She stood and helped him to his feet. He grimaced. His jeans were sopping wet, and his boots squelched. He stretched clumsily. His muscles were still stiff, but every moment made them less so. He looked around.

They stood in a small grass-filled cup. A spring bubbled merrily in a pool at the center and rushed away in a brook. The thorn tree thicket spread across the upslope and down the left and right, cut apart by the brook that ran uphill, against all nature. The downslope ended in a drop-off. Alexander went to the edge and peered over. A gorge opened up below. A golden river wound through it, and a herd of something that looked like buffalo grazed along the far bank.

He lifted his head, searching for the smell of coppery blood. It was close. "That way," he said to Max, pointing to the left. The thorn trees grew to the edge of the cliff, blocking their way.

"I hope he didn't get eaten already," Max said.

"They probably spit the bastard out."

"He does leave a bad taste in the mouth, doesn't he? So how do you want to get out of here? Do you want to try the creek?" She went to the edge of the cliff and leaned over. "We could probably climb across, if there aren't any rock traps."

Alexander grabbed her hand and pulled her back. "Better to take the creek path. Magic will not transform things in running water. It does not care for it much."

"Let's be quick, then. Holt might be bleeding to death."

"One can hope," Alexander said dryly, and followed her.

She picked up the rowan spear and splashed into the

pool, rinsing any poison off the spear before following the creek. Alexander followed. On either side, the gnarled thorn trees twitched and writhed, limbs winding through the air like snakes as they honed in on the two invading Blades. But Alexander was right. They could not break the boundary of the running water. He and Max trotted through the thicket, emerging into a meadow on the other side.

Along the edge of the cliff were what appeared to be three black and orange plants. Each was made up of six or seven tall, arching stems that pushed up out of the ground in a massive clump. The stems varied in size from several feet in diameter down to a foot. The ends of each flattened into fan shapes, the undersides of which were covered in slitted blisters. The stems slapped the ground and one another with angry ferocity.

"Déjà vu all over again," Max murmured. "There's Holt."

The mage was lying on the ground among the three plant creatures. A dome of white energy covered him, holding off the pounding blows. But even as they watched, the dome shrank.

Alexander and Max moved at the same time. She stabbed at the attacking tentacles with her rowan spear and knife. A squealing shriek cut the night, and the tentacles jerked back, flailing about. They did not like the taste of cold iron or rowan. Alexander grabbed Holt and dragged him out of range. Max followed, backing up and driving off the striking tentacles with sharp swipes of the spear.

Holt was bleeding from several wounds. He had a deep gash in his left side below his ribs and another on the inside of his left thigh. Blood trickled from the corner of his mouth and matted the hair on the side of his head. He blinked dazedly at his rescuers.

"You look like shit, Zippy," Max said. "And I know what I'm talking about."

"You lost your pants," he pointed out, and coughed painfully.

"Well, his brain isn't quite fried," she told Alexander.

"Too bad," he said, and unbuckled Holt's belt, using it to tie a tourniquet around his leg.

In the meantime, Max sat the injured mage up and pulled off his shirt, making a makeshift bandage for the wound in his side. Holt gasped and gritted his teeth beneath their ministrations, but he did not cry out. Alexander had to admit to grudging respect for the other man's strength.

They helped him up and carried him between them. Alexander guided their steps back north. They were able to avoid any potential trouble until they were a bare hundred yards from the edge of the enchantment, when a chorus of howls erupted from the trees and rocks littering the ridge behind.

"Is it me, or do those beasties sound hungry?" Max said.

"We could leave them Holt to feast on. That should give us plenty of time to escape," Alexander suggested. At her exasperated look, he shrugged. "Worth a try. Take him. I will keep our howling friends occupied."

She passed him the rowan spear and hoisted Holt up into her arms. The mage's head lolled against her shoulder and dangled over her arm. He had fainted. She started away, picking her way carefully as she looked for traps.

Alexander followed close behind, watching over his shoulder. When the hunters came, they flowed silently over the ground like a rolling fog. They were grizzled gray, with narrow heads, long pointed jaws, and skeletal bodies. They stood about three feet tall at the shoulder, with a ruff of long fur that ran thick around their necks and down their bellies. Their bones protruded sharply through the hairless skin covering the rest of their bodies, and a long wedged tail like an alligator's slid through the air behind. Their feet were broad paws with wickedly hooked claws. They loped across the ground, splitting and braiding back and forth. There had to be forty of them. They were silent now, heads dropped low as they hunted.

They spread out as they approached, circling wide. Max hurried faster. Twenty yards more, and she and Holt would be clear. The trouble was, the beasts had to be following the scent of blood; nothing Alexander could do would distract them.

"Jump with him," he ordered. "Break the blood trail."

To his surprise, she did not argue. Instead, she collected herself and leaped. She flew up into the air like she'd been thrown. Ahead, he could see the southern edge of the town of Weed, the highway lined with cars, and dazed-looking people wandering about, staring toward the erupting mountain. Between that old reality and this was a shimmering curtain, like heat waves rising off desert sands.

Something grabbed his foot. He jerked it back and look down. A hairy green hand with pointed black nails slid back beneath a clump of purple-headed clover. The plant twitched and stilled as if the creature waited.

More clover spread away in an apron of rich green. How many of the little beasts hid there, waiting to swarm some blundering idiot? He glanced over his shoulder. The noose of gray hunger was closing on him. He could see the snarling lips and yellow teeth of the hunting beasts and hear their soft panting breaths.

His grip tightened on the spear. With the other hand, he drew his .45. He edged sideways until he reached a smooth boulder humping up out of the ground. He leaped on top of it. It was barely five feet across and no more than two feet high, but it gave him the advantage of high ground.

He knew he could not hold them off long. He scanned the terrain again. The clover field narrowed considerably about thirty yards away. If he could kill some of the gray beasts, he could toss them into the clover and perhaps distract the hidden hunters. He could then make his escape.

He hefted the spear and tensed as the circle of beasts closed around his perch. There did not seem to be a pack leader. The animals paced in a narrowing spiral, watching Alexander with white eyes. Their pupils were slitted like a cat's. He shifted his weight, and six of them instantly leaped at him. Almost as one, they dug into the ground and lunged up, teeth snapping.

Alexander swung the rowan spear, smashing the ribs of one and knocking it into two others. They fell in a snarling tangle, biting and tearing at one another. He shot a fourth one, ducking down as the fifth came at his chest. He twisted and thrust his shoulder under it, flinging the creature off. Hot streaks flared as its claws raked down his back. The last one fastened on his right forearm. He heard his bones snapping, and he dropped his gun. He thrust the spear deep into the animal's stomach. Black blood spouted over his hand and sprayed his legs. The beast yelped and dropped away.

The other gray beasts ignored their fallen comrades and watched Alexander. Drool dripped from their jaws. They continued to circle. His back prickled, and he turned, trying to keep an eye on those behind him. His right hand hung at his side, next to useless. Another rush, and there was a good chance he would go down. He had to move.

He backed up to the edge of the boulder and lunged for the clover. He landed on something that wriggled and screamed. Alexander did not miss a beat. He ran flat out for the edge of the enchantment.

Things grabbed his ankles, and something hitched up his right thigh, digging its claws in as he ran.

Alexander reached down, snatched the creature, and flung it away. Its body felt like bones inside a moist sack of jelly. More fastened to his legs and clambered up over one another, biting and clawing. They gibbered and shrieked. He was forced to slow down as he knocked them away.

Paws slammed against his back. He felt the snap of teeth in the air by his neck. He fell, thrusting himself instantly back to his feet before the green creatures could swarm him. A single gray beast faced him, gathering itself. Behind it, green hunters leaped and ran through the clover. Their faces were a paler shade of green than their bodies. Their eyes were obsidian beads, and their features looked squashed. Their mouths cut their faces in half and were filled with several rows of black serrated teeth. There had to be hundreds of them.

They overran the gray beast, pulling it down. It snapped and fought, but there were too many of the little green monsters. Alexander smashed at those on his legs with the rowan spear and flung another away as it clambered up his stomach. He started running again. It was not far now.

Then Max was in front of him. She was carrying a tire iron in each hand. She pounded at the hunters gnawing on his legs. They fell away, and she smashed at those that followed. Another minute later, they ran out of the enchantment, back onto the parched dirt of the valley.

Alexander ran a few steps, then turned around. Several green hunters followed but quickly scrabbled back under the cover of their clover when Max started at them, the tire irons swinging menacingly.

She turned to look at Alexander. Her arms were slimed to the elbows with lime-green blood, and her legs had been bitten and clawed. She grinned at him as she scrutinized him from head to toe.

"That was fun." She wrinkled her nose, dropping the tire irons and shaking her hands off. "Could use a shower, though. And some clothes. You too. Those pants are about to fall off."

Alexander looked down at himself. His jeans were slashed to ribbons, and the skin beneath was in no better shape. A memory struck him. He reached into his pockets. His right hand was weak but already healing. He found his cell phone in one pocket, and in the other was the Amengohr amulet. He gripped it, feeling the hard curve biting into his fingers. Thank the spirits, he hadn't lost it.

"Alexander?" Max asked sharply. Her expression had gone hard, and she was looking wildly about. "Where did you go?"

He pulled the amulet out of his pocket and stared in wonder. He had thought it did not work. He had not gone invisible when Valery had given it to him. The difference, he realized, was blood. He had inadvertently smeared a layer of his own blood over the amulet when he pulled it out of his pocket.

"Alexander!"

Max was sounding furious now. And she was using his name. Not Slick. That made him smile. He was tempted to stay silent to see what she would do, but he doubted he would survive when she realized he was playing possum.

"Right here," he said.

"Where?"

"I have not moved." He scuffed his foot in the dirt to show where he was.

"The amulet? It works?" Her eyes were wide.

It was the first time he had ever seen her surprised out of her normal rigid control. She looked almost like a child.

"So it seems."

"That means you can be out in the sun." Her expression went from shock to longing to a kind of shuttered blankness.

He scowled. What twisty little thoughts were breeding in that thick skull of hers? He wished he could break it open and find out.

"Handy piece of jewelry, that," she said without any inflection in her voice. "What are you going to do with it?"

His wonder at the idea of having the opportunity to walk out in the sunlight again for the first time in more than a hundred years melted away. What *did* he plan to do with it? More important, what did *she* think he planned? Because she had clearly drawn a conclusion, and it was not in his favor.

"I do not know," he said honestly. In fact, he had no idea. So much of what he wanted depended on Max and Giselle.

"Come on. Surely you've got something in mind." Her voice had grown colder.

His jaw jutted. "Obviously, you think I do. Tell me, so I can be in on the secret, too."

"I'm not going to stand here and talk to thin air," she said, and started to move away.

He shoved the amulet into his rear pocket. "I wish to hell you would stop walking away from me," he said, grasping her arm and yanking her around.

"Hands off, Slick."

"A minute ago, you called me Alexander."

"Did I? Can't remember."

She twisted her arm, and his fingers slipped on the green blood coating her skin. He clamped tighter. "If we are going to argue, stand still and argue," he seethed through gritted teeth. "But quit acting like you will leave me behind. It is not going to happen. Get used to it."

She jerked out of his grasp but stood her ground. "What's your problem, Slick?"

"You are pissed off at me."

"Am I?"

"Tell me why before I pry it out of you with a crowbar."

"All right. How's this for a little truth? It just occurred to me how convenient it is for you that the amulet shows up right now. I mean, you're not bound to any coven-stead. It's your shot at freedom—the freedom you claim you don't even want. I'm beginning to think maybe the gentleman doth protest too much. Why else would you want it? But then again, the other possibility is that you plan to use it to take Prime from me. You could drag me out into the sun, and that would be the end of it. So now I have to wonder, are you playing me? Have you been playing me all along? Is that what all this business between us has really been about?"

Alexander stared, unable to find words. Could she really think that? Of course, he had thought about walk-ing away—living among humans. But it was not what he wanted. Nor did he want Prime, no matter what Magpie and her prophecy said.

"Wow. Silence of the guilty? I guess we're done, then."

She started away again, but he caught both her arms. "That is not the way it is. You know it."

"Do I?"

"You damned well should. I have not lied to you." He forced the words out. His anger was white-hot. He shoved her away from him to keep himself from hitting her. "If this is the way you want it, then, fine."

"So we're done, then?"

She was giving him that thousand-yard stare again—cold and lifeless. It was on the tip of his tongue to agree when realization struck him. She went inside to that cold place when she could not handle what she was feeling. Which meant— She felt something for him, enough to pull away inside. Triumph surged inside him. He smiled.

"Oh, no. We are not done. Not by a long shot. We made a good team out there fighting, and we make a good team when we are not. But you want obstacles— you want to make it impossible for us to be together. If not Giselle, then your Blades or Scooter. Now this amulet. Just when I think you are going to give in to what you clearly want as much as I do, you turn into an ice bitch and start throwing down roadblocks."

"Wow. You're whining like a kid who just lost his puppy. You need to go get a pair of big-boy pants on."

He stepped closer. "And that—a mouth like a rusty saw when you want to dodge the subject. You will not get rid of me that way, either."

She opened her mouth, then closed it, scraping her teeth over her bottom lip. She took a breath and let it out slowly. "I don't want to get rid of you, Slick," she said grudgingly.

She looked like she was about to say more, but Holt's voice interrupted her. Alexander could have happily slit his throat.

"You two had better get moving. Sun will be up soon. You need to find clothes and shelter."

Max turned gratefully, and Alexander glowered at him. Holt was walking on his own with the help of a cane. He was pale and gaunt, his eyes sunken and bruised-looking. He looked like he had lost about twenty pounds. He had scrounged a white button-up shirt that was still creased from the package and a pair of dark blue Wranglers. He limped stiffly, holding his hand pressed against his ribs. It glowed white, the hex marks brilliant blue against his tanned skin.

Alexander stared in awe. The bastard was healing himself. Most witches could not even manage minor self-healing. But then, Holt was a mage, and ordinary witch rules did not apply to them.

"You're going to live," Max observed.

"Thanks to the two of you," he said with a grimace. "Last person on earth I want to owe is Alexander."

"Since you do, leave Valery alone. Let her go."

"That's not going to happen." Holt looked down, rubbing his chin with his knuckles. He looked back up. "I'll protect her with my life," he said, and it sounded like a vow. "That's going to have to be enough for you." He turned to Max without waiting for Alexander's reaction. "If you ever need anything, call me."

And then he did the impossible. Blue and white sparks whirled in the air, obscuring him from view. A moment later, they drifted to the ground. Holt was gone. All that was left was a folded piece of white paper. Alexander picked it up. On it was a phone number scrawled boldly in black ink. He handed it to Max.

"This is yours, I believe."

She took at it and shook her head. "He knows how to make an exit, anyway."

"So should we. You need clothes, and we have to find shelter from the sun."

"Wrong, Slick. We need clothes and a vehicle and a way to keep me out of the sun. You have the amulet. We aren't going to hang around waiting for dark before we skip town."

She started walking, and he caught up with her. They

circled around the people gathered along the freeway and climbed a broad, dusty, tree-covered hill. Below them, Weed curled in a comma shape around the hill.

Alexander looked back the way they had come. The enchantment's edge followed a ragged path, rising and falling over the foothills to the west. It zigzagged back and forth, cutting south around Mount Eddy. Shasta continued to spew forth wild magic, but it was streaming entirely south now, as if pushed by a sharp wind.

"What will it all turn into?" Max said. "All those people down in the central valley—what is going to happen to them?"

"The Guardians want to rid the earth of most of humanity. Undoubtedly, that is why the enchanted area is so full of hungry predators. Most people will not survive." He took a slow breath. "There will be more of this. All over the world. How many vortexes did Scooter sense? Thirty?"

"All those people standing around down there have no idea. They should be running for their lives."

"To where? Where can they go that is safe?"

She looked at him, her expression granite, and then she started down the hill into Weed. Once again, he overtook her, not letting her leave him behind. He wondered if this was how it would always be.

12

THERE WASN'T MUCH TO THE TOWN OF WEED. No big chain stores and no malls. Max wondered where Holt had found his fresh clothing. On Main Street, they found a little thrift store. Max pulled open the doors, her unlocking spells making it easy. Inside, she and Alexander split up as they searched for clothes.

She found a pair of faded Levi's and a plain brown T-shirt, socks, and a pair of black canvas tennis shoes. She went into the back, looking for a bathroom or a sink to wash off the dried green gore slathering her arms and hands. She found the bathroom and peed. She pulled the knife that Alexander had given her from where she'd sheathed it in her witch-chain belt, then unwound the chain from her waist and pulled off Alexander's shirt. It still smelled like him. She resisted the urge to rub her face in it and sniff, and instead dropped it onto the back of the toilet.

There was a bar of gritty white soap by the sink that felt like sandpaper. She scrubbed off all that she could and dried herself with a couple of handfuls of paper towels. She dressed, wrapping the witch chain around her waist again and tucking the knife into her rear waistband. She'd have to find underwear someplace else. Not to mention money and a car.

She came out, carrying Alexander's shirt and her shoes and socks. He was waiting outside. He pushed past her without a word. She grimaced. She didn't really believe he'd been playing her. At least, his reaction had been angry enough that if he was acting, he was doing a damned fine job. He was still furious.

She rolled her shoulders to loosen them and made herself focus back on what needed to be done. She'd told Jim she'd be in Winters by sunrise. Now, if Alexander drove through the day, they might make it by nightfall, but they'd have to go north and catch a road to the coast and go down Highway 101. It would be a lot slower than shooting down Highway 5 as originally planned. Not only that, but they didn't have a car or money to pay for gas or any way to keep her sheltered from the sun. They might not get there for another twenty-four hours or longer.

Her stomach churned. If her family had survived, they could even now be fighting for their lives. And the wild magic of Mount Shasta was heading right for them. She might get there only to find they'd become breakfast for some magical saber-toothed tiger or, worse, they'd been transformed into bloodthirsty, ankle-biting critters from hell.

She yanked on her socks and shoes, then hunted around until she found a small office and ransacked it for money, finding only a five-dollar bill and a handful of loose change in the top side drawer. She pocketed it and picked up the phone. She ought to call Giselle and let her know what was going on. There was no dial tone. It was probably too much to hope that there would be. She set the phone back down, her mouth twisting with aggravation. The witch-bitch probably had foreseen this whole mess.

Just then, Alexander appeared in the doorway. He'd found a pair of blue jeans and a black V-necked T-shirt. It fit snugly, emphasizing the muscles of his arms and chest. Of course she'd notice that. Right now, in the middle of a crisis, and she was admiring the scenery. *Brilliant.* Worse, he'd noticed her noticing, and a faint smile quirked the corner of his mouth. *Smug bastard.*

"What now?" he asked.

"Let's go swipe a car. Something with a trunk. We should be able to seal that up well enough for me to ride in."

"I tried to call Valery to let her know Holt was on the loose. It would not go through. Tried Horngate also. Nothing."

"Landlines aren't working, either," Max said, gesturing to the phone on the desk. "Maybe they'll work when we get farther away from the eruption."

Her stomach growled loudly. "I guess we should find some food, too."

"There has to be a grocery store. As long as we are stealing, that is our best bet."

He was right. Without money, breaking into a grocery store was always a good choice. They might even find what they needed to light-seal a car trunk. Max grabbed a yellow pages, found the list of stores, and jotted the address for Ray's Food Place. There was no handy map inside the phone book to tell where it was.

They went back outside. Alexander retrieved the rowan spear from where he'd leaned it inside the door. They turned in unison back toward the freeway. There were people out on the street, talking in low, worried voices and milling about and pointing at the erupting mountain. Most were in their robes or pajamas, and many were barefoot.

Max and Alexander dodged down a side road and found themselves in a quiet neighborhood. They pushed farther in, keeping to the shadows as much as possible. Too many windows were lit. Stealing a car here was going to be next to impossible.

"Freeway is a parking lot," Alexander whispered. "We will have better luck there."

He was right. Max nodded, and they kicked into a ground-eating run.

It was only a few blocks away. Just before they got there, Max dug to a halt, pointing at the street sign. "Grocery store is around here somewhere."

They turned right toward the north end of Weed Boulevard. Ray's Food Place was only a few hundred yards away. They broke in as easily as they had the thrift store. Max grabbed a shopping cart. They breezed through the store, piling the cart high with an assortment of food and drinks. They grabbed paper plates and plastic silverware and napkins, then parked themselves at the deli tables to eat.

They attacked their foragings, ignoring each other as they bolted down their food. Max opened a jar of sweet pickles, fishing out four before passing them to Alexander. He offered her green olives.

It took a half hour before they were sated. Then they

went back, grabbing boxes of power bars, jerky, yogurt, cheese sticks, and a variety of other high-calorie quick snacks. They loaded their bounty into canvas bags from the checkout aisles. Next, Max found six rolls of duct tape—all they had. She also grabbed a dozen silver reflective windshield screens.

Last, she went to the office and opened the safe, pulling out the stacked cash drawers. She took all of the paper cash—just over twelve hundred dollars. She found a bag of deposits and emptied it out, finding another two thousand.

"There's gas and food for a while," she said, pocketing the money. She shut everything back up, not bothering to wipe away her fingerprints. She didn't have the time, and with Shasta erupting and the Guardians escalating their war against humanity, she doubted it would make much difference in the long run. No more than stealing would.

She tried the phone again, but there was still no service. She came out of the office and found Alexander waiting. He was holding a bouquet of knives from the butcher room in the back of the store. She took two of them, tucking one into each sock. He followed suit, then added two more to his rear waistband.

Outside, they went around back, crossed a narrow treed lot, and found themselves back on Highway 5. Cars clogged it in a solid mass. There was no way to drive on the road in either direction. *Terrific.* They'd have to hoof it back north until they could find both a car and some room to drive. Max started to tell Alexander so and then hesitated. There was one last thing she had to do. It would take a little time, but— She didn't finish the thought. Stupid or not, crunched for time or not, she wasn't going to just abandon the people they'd saved—Matthew, Amanda, their baby, Baker the biker, Geoff Brewer, and his two sons. Besides, Horngate needed witches, and Amanda was certainly one of those.

"Where did you leave them?" she asked Alexander.

He surprised her when he didn't ask whom she was talking about. "Up the road a ways."

"Show me."

She started away, and he overtook her. They broke into a run, their canvas bags bouncing awkwardly. They must have made quite a sight, Max thought. Not that anyone was looking. Mount Shasta, its red eruption, and the shimmering curtain of the enchantment held every eye hypnotized.

They had not gone far—not even two miles—when they met up with the group they were looking for. Geoff was carrying Amanda, who remained unconscious. He was red and sweating. Matthew walked stoically beside them, the baby crying. Behind came the two boys and Baker. They all looked dour and determined.

They came to a stuttering halt when they saw Max and Alexander approaching. Matthew stepped protectively in front of Amanda, holding his daughter tightly. Baker stepped around on the other side, shielding the rest of her. The boys edged closer to their father. They all smelled of sweat and fear. Like she and Alexander hadn't saved their asses. Why would they come back and attack? Still, she appreciated the way they protected one another, strangers as they were. They were good people. Horngate needed good people.

"Where are you headed?" Max asked.

"He told us to get out, go north," Baker said, jerking his chin at Alexander. He'd lost his green bandanna. His hair was mostly brown and clung wetly to his scalp. It was as hot now as it had been earlier in the day. "So we're heading north."

"Our mom is in Redding. Is she going to be okay?" one of the boys asked, the one with black hair. His hands were jammed into his pockets, and he was doing everything he could not to look scared. Tough kid.

"I don't know," Max said. "Probably not," she amended more honestly. Telling them lies because she didn't want them to worry wasn't doing anybody any favors. "If she survived the initial fall of magic, then she'll be facing a lot of trouble." She shrugged. "The odds aren't good."

"Dad! We have to go get her," urged the other son with the bleached hair tips and the half-assed mohawk.

"Then you will all die," Alexander said. "Max and I almost did not get out of there, and we are a lot better prepared for that world than you are."

"So what do we do?" Baker asked. "We all live down there—Matt and Amanda are from Sacramento, and I'm from Yuba City. Where do we go now if we can't go home? Where is safe?" His voice was clipped and hard as flint. Max wondered if he'd been in the military. He had the look of resolute determination she associated with men who'd been ordered into battles they couldn't win.

"There's a place in Montana where you can be safe."

"Safe?" Geoff barked harshly. "Who the hell can be safe anymore with *that* going on?" He pointed toward the bloody magic pouring out of the top of Mount

Shasta. His face was deeply lined, and he swayed under Amanda's weight.

Alexander set down the bags he was carrying and plucked the unconscious woman out of the other man's arms.

"'Safe' is a relative term," Max admitted. "Horngate has had its share of troubles, and we'll be seeing more. But it's a place to go where you'll have shelter and food and some protection. But you'll have to agree to keep the place a secret and obey its rules."

"What kind of rules?" Baker demanded.

"The kind that keep everybody alive. Any more than that, you'll find out when you get there. If you want to go."

"And if we don't like these rules? If we don't want to stay at this Horngate place?" Geoff asked.

"Then you can try your luck somewhere else. But this isn't the only volcano going off, and it isn't the last magical attack."

"And Amanda? Is she going to be all right?" Matthew was staring at his wife, looking both worried and fearful.

"She'll wake up eventually. And then she'll need some help. She can get that at Horngate."

He gulped. "Help?"

"Training in her craft."

He made a face like he had eaten a raw onion. "Witchcraft."

No doubt his head was dancing with images straight out of *The Wizard of Oz*.

"That's right."

"I don't— Will she— What—" Matthew couldn't put his questions into words. He stroked his daughter's head, tears running down his cheeks. "Is she still going to be herself?"

Max nodded. "She'll just be able to use magic."

"We have to get moving," Alexander said before Matthew could ask anything more. He backed away, forcing the others to follow after him.

Max picked up the sacks that Alexander had dropped and fell in behind, chafing at their slow progress. She glanced at the eastern sky. Dawn was maybe an hour off. That left them precious little time.

Alexander must have come to the same conclusion, because he increased his pace so that the others were panting as they hurried along, sometimes breaking into a jog to keep up.

"What's the hurry?" Baker asked breathlessly.

"We have some other business to take care of," Alexander said. "It is urgent."

"What's more urgent than this?"

Neither Max nor Alexander answered.

People watched curiously as they threaded between the parked vehicles, which included motor homes and semi trucks. The stink of diesel fumes could not cover the overwhelming smell of magic.

At last, the stream of cars began to thin. There was no other traffic coming. Police must have diverted it, maybe up by Grenada or Yreka. Max wondered where the emergency vehicles were—she would have expected to see them and the National Guard, too. But maybe they'd been sent elsewhere, like to evacuate the valley cities. Or maybe Mount Rainier had popped its top, too, and there wasn't enough emergency help to go around.

Alexander stopped, turning in a slow circle. Max eyed the cars around them. Most were empty. Maybe their drivers had gotten out and walked. More than a few were trapped in place by other cars. A gray minivan caught her attention.

"There."

Alexander passed Amanda to Baker and followed Max. The van was locked, but Max opened it without a problem. Inside was meticulously clean. Satchels of prescription drug samples and a small suitcase filled the rear, and a bar of hanging clothes stretched across the rear seat.

They removed the drugs and the clothing, stacking them on the side of the road. Then they lifted the van and carried it out from between the cars that wedged it in from front and back.

"Ho-ly shit," Baker said with a low whistle as they turned the vehicle around. "What the hell are you two?"

"What we are is in a hurry," Max said shortly, waving at them to get in.

They put Amanda in the rear with her husband and baby. They were going to have to do without a car seat. The two teenage boys took the two middle seats, and Baker volunteered to drive while Geoff sat shotgun.

"We need a screwdriver," Max called to Alexander. "See if you can find a tool kit."

"A screwdriver won't work," Baker said. "You need a lot more . . ." He trailed off. "Never mind. If you can lift a car, you have all the torque you need to break the lock pins and start the car."

Max grinned at him. "Perks of magic."

There were no tools in the van, but Alexander found

a screwdriver in a rusty ranch pickup a few cars away. Max jammed it into the lock, then backed away.

"You'd better do it," she told him. "The lock will open for me, but then they'll never get it restarted if they need to shut it down. Break the pins, and it won't be a problem."

He leaned in and twisted. There was a crackling noise as bits of metal snapped, and then the engine roared to life. He stepped back, and Baker got in.

"So how do we get to this Horngate place?" he asked after a moment of awkward silence.

"Wait! I don't know if I want to go there," Matthew said from the rear. He held the baby against his shoulder, rubbing her back. Amanda was propped against the window.

"Where else is there?" Geoff asked quietly. "None of us can go home. Do you have family or friends somewhere else who could put you up?"

"There have been eruptions all over the world," Max said. "Anywhere you go, you'll probably find trouble."

"You think this isn't the only one?" Geoff asked, looking like she'd clubbed him in the side of the head.

"I know it's not."

"So what makes you think this Horngate place is safe?" Baker asked.

"That's a long story. But it *is* safer than most places for you right now."

"Are there more people like you there?"

Max nodded. "And some who are even more . . . interesting."

He scowled. "They'll welcome us?"

"They will." She hoped. Giselle had claimed that she

wanted to make Horngate a sanctuary for humanity in this war the Guardians were waging, but the witch-bitch had never said whom she was willing to take in. Maybe she was looking for Nobel Prize winners or people she considered more deserving than a biker, a father, two teenagers, and a young family. On the other hand, fuck what Giselle wanted. Horngate was Max's home, too, and these people needed a place to go.

"Give me that pad of paper and pen." She pointed at the console. She wrote down directions and drew a map to Horngate. "Call this number first," she said, writing down Niko's cell number. "Hopefully they'll still have phone service. Tell them I sent you. If you can't reach them, then drive to Horngate. Someone will stop you, and you should give them this note. She jotted a few lines and handed the pad back to Baker. "Tell them what happened here."

She stepped back, bumping into Alexander, who stood silently behind her. He put a hand on her shoulder to steady her. She twitched as she started to shake him off, then stood still.

"Things will be strange there," she warned Baker.

His brows rose. "Stranger than that?" he asked incredulously, pointing toward the enchantment.

She shrugged. "You might think so." She wondered what they'd think of the two angels. If any in the van had a religious bent, they might be a little thrown to find out that angels were creatures of magic, not holy messengers of God. "You'd better get going."

Baker hesitated. "Maybe we should wait for the two of you to come with us."

She shook her head. "We might not make it back."

He sucked his teeth. "Then we go by ourselves. Good luck to you." He put the van in gear, then looked out the window again. "Thanks for your help. We wouldn't have made it out of there if not for you." He pressed on the gas and waved, and the van sped away into the night.

Max watched the taillights grow smaller. "Our turn," she said. "We'd better hurry."

"Right this way," Alexander said, pointing at a blue Toyota Corolla.

Max opened it up and popped the trunk.

"Nice talent, that one. Valery would envy you. You could be partners in crime."

"You've got the amulet. You be her partner," Max said, regretting the words as soon as they slipped out. She didn't know why the question of the amulet was chewing on her so much. She had told Alexander to leave, to escape living under the control of a witch. Why should it bother her that the amulet might make going easier for him? She ought to be happy for him.

"I have a partner already," he said, his eyes glittering.

"Me?"

"No one else."

He was looking at her with that hungry look that curled her toes. It made her want to hit him. He was demanding so much more than she had to give. She had no *time*, dammit, and if she did— And if she did, what would she do with it? She thrust the question away. It was stupid to even think about it. Scooter was waiting for her.

"Primes don't have partners," she said curtly, and turned her back before he could reply.

She looked down into the trunk. It was full of clothes,

ratty shoes, bats and mitts, greasy rags, empty oil bottles, a deflated car inner tube, three stained ties, a collection of hats touting various businesses, a plastic tarp, a sleeping bag, and a half dozen empty cartons of cigarettes. She started grabbing junk and dumped it onto the road. She wrinkled her nose. It smelled like the bottom of an ashtray that had been dropped into a Porta Potty. Riding inside was not going to be pleasant.

"We should find another car," she said.

Alexander looked over his shoulder and grinned maliciously. "No time. Everything around here either has no trunk or is too small." He waved his hand at the surrounding cars. "And we are in a hurry, right, boss?"

He made *boss* sound like an insult. And he was right. *Bastard*. She bared her teeth in a silent snarl and started grabbing the debris again.

Alexander abandoned her to unfold the windshield screens and start taping them together in a large silver quilt. When she'd cleared the trunk, Max went to help him, overlapping the screens before taping them. This was going to be her light-tight shelter inside what protection the trunk would offer—if the stench didn't kill her first.

In a few minutes, they'd folded together a soft-sided rectangular box. The top remained open. Max would climb into it, and Alexander would finish taping it up and put her in the trunk.

"We'll have to find another screwdriver if you want to be able to shut down the car," she said.

"You forget, I am telekinetic. I can turn the lock with my mind."

She *had* forgotten. "Then let's load up and get going."

"Hey! What are you doing with my car?"

A man in a wrinkled brown suit was jogging toward them, threading his way between the vehicles. His hair was thinning, and his face was florid. He had a cigarette pinched in the fingers of his right hand.

Alexander leaned his hip against the car. "You want me to handle this, boss?"

Max glowered at him, resisting the urge to kick his ribs in. "Oh, look. It's Mr. Helpful. Where were you when I couldn't find any underwear?"

She flushed as his gaze dropped, his eyes sharpening as if he could see through the denim of her pants.

"I said get away from my car!"

The car's owner had stopped a few feet away. He was panting, and Max could smell his strong odor, like he hadn't showered in three days and had dumped a bottle of cologne over himself to mask the stink. It hadn't worked. He pointed with his cigarette hand.

"Back off! I mean it."

"I'm sure you do, Spanky. But it isn't going to happen," Max said. "We're taking your car. We need it more than you do at the moment."

"Like hell you are, bitch. I'll call the cops." His face turned a darker shade of red, and he was spitting.

"You do that. C'mon, Slick. Let's go."

Spanky leaped in front of her as she started for the car. He was shaking as he stabbed the air in front of her face with his finger. He might need it broken to teach him some manners. Course, she *was* in the middle of stealing his car. He might deserve some leeway for that.

"You bitch! I am going to teach you a lesson." He flicked his cigarette butt at her.

Max batted it aside. "You know," she said, "the point-ing was rude, but I was going to let that pass, because I can see how you'd be upset. I mean, sure, the world is going to hell in a handbasket, and you're probably going to die screaming any day now, but I get that seeing someone steal your car would make you mad enough to lose your manners. But the cigarette? That's just un-called for."

She snatched him by the collar and lifted him off the ground. He gagged, and his feet kicked helplessly. His face turned more red, and she could hear his heart gal-loping like a frantic goat.

"Seeing as how I'm in a hurry and you've got some right to be pissed, I'll let you off easy," she said. She carried him over to the rear tire of a battered old pickup truck. "Hand me that inner tube," she told Alexander.

He brought the discarded inner tube from the trunk to her, and she set her prisoner down on the ground beside the truck. She snapped the tube in half and then pulled away two long strips. Spanky watched her with openmouthed terror.

"Put your hands behind your back," she said.

He complied slowly. She tied them tightly together, then used the second strip to make a large loop off his shackles. She motioned for Alexander to lift the truck up and slid the loop under the tire. Alexander eased the truck back down, and Spanky wasn't going anywhere for a while. Not until someone came along to help him. A thought caught her. She bent and patted his pockets, then reached into his front right and fished out the keys.

"Let's go," she said, tossing them to Alexander.

Spanky said nothing as they loaded the trunk with the

silver cocoon, the grocery bags, and the rowan spear. They lifted his car out from between the bumpers of the vehicles trapping it in place. They climbed in, and Alexander fitted the key into the ignition. The car roared to life, and they sped off north.

Max rolled the windows down, trying to clear the stench of stale food, cigarettes, and spilled coffee from the car. She looked into the backseat. It was knee-deep in snack wrappers, drink cups, and fast-food bags and boxes. Her tennis shoes clung stickily to the floor mat.

"Maybe we did him a favor, stealing this cockroach hotel," she said.

She popped open the glove box. A bottle of Tums fell out. She riffled through the papers and found a map of California. She unfolded it, searching. "Looks like if we get off at Edgewood, that will take us to Gazelle. From there, we can get to the coast." She showed him on the map. "That might be cutting it a little close, though. We could also go up to Yreka and not have to go back quite so far south."

"Let us do that," Alexander said. "We will not lose much time by it, and it gives us better odds."

Max sat back and folded up the map before crushing it in her hand. She stared blindly out the window, wondering what was happening in Winters.

The last memory she had of her family was of the big picnic just before she went back to college. It was a long-standing tradition. They cooked barbecue ribs in a smoker and made enough food to feed half the town. Then they invited friends over and played softball. It never ended before dawn the next morning.

That last one, Kyle had only been a few months old.

He was a bubbly, happy baby, and everyone wanted to hold him. She remembered how her mother had laughed and passed him around.

Her mother. Max hadn't thought about her in years. Her eyes burned. Her mother was an artist—she made the most beautiful ceramics. Or had. She quit after Max disappeared. Guilt burned in her gut. And hate. Giselle had done this. Max cut the thought off. Old news.

At that picnic, she remembered her parents telling stories of how they met and of the embarrassing things Max and Tris had done over the years. Max and Tris had fought back with stories of their parents, and soon they were all laughing so hard that Max's stomach hurt. Then she and her mother had made ice cream. They'd talked about Max's boyfriend, about school, about what she wanted to do when she graduated. Her mother had confided that she had planned a big surprise party for Tris and that Max would need to be sure to come home for it.

Time had flown, and all too soon it was morning, and Giselle had showed up to drive Max back to college. But she still remembered the safe, warm feel of her mother's hug and her promise to visit soon. Max hadn't told her mother she loved her or that she would miss her. That always went without saying. After all, they would see each other soon enough. Now she wished she'd forced the words out.

Tris and her father had been asleep when she left. Max had left her sister a note, promising to let her come visit over Halloween. It had never happened.

Max swallowed the ache in her throat, her hand clenching. They couldn't be dead. And if they weren't?

How would they react to seeing her? She bit her lips, tasting blood. If they were okay, it didn't matter what they thought.

She felt the itch of the sun just as Alexander pulled over. They were only a few miles from Yreka. She got out and went around to the rear of the car, pulling the cash from her pocket and handing it to Alexander.

She hopped up onto the fender and slid her feet into the silvery cocoon and stopped.

"Better get that amulet on. Let's make sure it's working."

He pulled it out of his pocket. He'd found a piece of curly ribbon at the grocery store to hang it on. He took out his knife, cut across the pad of his thumb, and rubbed it over both sides of the disk. Instantly, he vanished. Max blinked.

"Well, it works. You might refresh that blood every so often, just in case. I'd hate to see you barbecue yourself."

"That is nice to hear," said the air. "It looks like you want to cut my throat."

"And lose my taxi driver? Not a chance."

He reappeared. He'd wiped the blood off and was dangling the amulet from his finger. "There is that chain saw mouth again. Maybe you need a nap so you are not so cranky."

She chewed the inside of her cheek. They didn't have a lot of time for—whatever this was. She was wasting too much by finding reasons to be pissed at him. Old habits died hard. Part of her wanted desperately to keep him at a distance, and the other part of her wanted to be in his pants. Not just that. She didn't just want to screw his brains out, though the idea of it about made her drool. No, she wanted him. He was gasoline to her fire.

"Thanks," she said finally.

His brows rose. "For what?"

"Staying. Helping me." She gestured at the amulet. "You could leave anytime. And I haven't been the best company."

"I told you. I have no intention of leaving until you tell me to go. As for your crap company, it is better than not having you around."

Max shook her head. "You are batshit nuts, you know that, Slick? Or else you're sadomasochistic, which amounts to pretty much the same thing in my book."

"Maybe. If so, I am in good company."

Almost reluctantly, he reached out and trailed his fingers down her cheek to her neck and ran them along the collar of her shirt.

Max's toes curled, and her mouth went dry. Her heart sped up. He couldn't help but hear it. His own was thudding urgently. She thought he might kiss her. He didn't. She scowled. What was he waiting for?

"Sun's about to come up," she said to hurry him along.

"It is. You should get in so we can tape you up." He kept running his fingers along the collar of her shirt, slipping slightly under the edge.

She ground her teeth together in frustration. "What are you doing?"

"I want you to tell me what you want. I want you to ask for what you want."

"At the moment, I want to break your jaw."

"I do not think so," he said, smiling arrogantly. "I think you want me to kiss you. But you have to tell me." His breathing had gone shallow and fast. He was not nearly in as much control as he made out.

"I—"

She stopped. She felt like a twelve-year-old. Except that most twelve-year-old girls knew a whole lot more about relationships than she did. Sure, she'd had sex with plenty of men, and she'd dated a few before she was turned into a Shadowblade; one had even been serious. But that had been a long time ago, and she had no clue how to handle Alexander or the way she felt about him.

The urge was there to tell him she wanted him to kiss her. It would be the truth, just not all of it. Sort of like the tip of the iceberg that sank the *Titanic*. The question was, did she want to chicken out that way? She had little time left. She could easily be killed helping her family, and if not, then Scooter was going to take her. She was pretty sure he didn't intend to give her back. So what was she waiting for? Did she want to regret not telling him how she felt the way she regretted not telling her mother?

Alexander's hand dropped. She reached out and caught him. His muscles hardened beneath her touch as he clenched his fist.

"I want you," she said baldly.

He said nothing. She could tell he was waiting for a qualifier—*I want to screw you, I want to kiss you, I want to hang out with you for a while*—something more and less than what she'd admitted. But it was time for the truth.

"I want you. That's all."

13

ALEXANDER CLAMPED HIS HANDS AROUND MAX'S head and yanked her to him. There was no finesse in his kiss, only his hunger. He opened his mouth on hers, thrusting his tongue inside. Her teeth ground against his, and he started to pull back, then realized she was holding him as hard as he was holding her. He slid his arms around her, clenching her shirt in his fists and lifting her up.

She wrapped her legs around him, her arms tight around his neck. Her tongue licked his and flicked teasingly along the inside of his lips. He felt his cock swelling and he slid a hand down to cup her ass and grind her against him. She moaned and arched her back, wiggling her hips as she pulled away from the kiss. He nibbled down the taut line of her neck.

"You really do pick the worst times to get me all hot and bothered," she said hoarsely. "But I need to get in the trunk. We don't have long."

She was right. Slowly he let her go, pressing his lips against hers one more time.

Max stepped up into the trunk and slid down into the

cocoon. She grabbed a bottle of water, a Gatorade, and a bag of chocolate candies from one of the grocery bags. Alexander passed her a roll of duct tape, then bent and kissed her one more time. She lifted herself up, meeting him with bold eagerness.

He could smell her desire—musk and salt. It was almost more than he could stand.

He pulled back with every ounce of willpower he could muster. All he wanted to do was climb in with her and spend the day between her legs. But her family was waiting, and whatever Giselle had foreseen was still ahead of him. His jaw hardened. He would not let anything happen to Max. Not now, when she had finally admitted she wanted him as badly as he wanted her.

He folded the top of the cocoon closed and tacked it in place with a couple of tape strips. He could hear Max inside peeling tape free and pushing it into place over the seams of the cocoon. He did the same, making sure every seam was sealed. When he was done, he closed the lid of the trunk and got back behind the wheel. He smeared the amulet with his blood again, then slid it over his head and settled it against his chest beneath his shirt.

The first rays of sun crept up over the horizon.

"Are you still alive out there?" Max called from her hiding place. She sounded worried. "Alexander?"

He loved the way she said his name. It was only the second time he could remember her doing so. "Still here," he said, looking down at himself, then out the window at the sunrise. "Beautiful," he breathed.

The colors unfurled across the sky—pinks, oranges, yellows, and reds. He squinted, expecting his eyes to burn, but no, the brightness did not bother him. His throat ached as color swept over the greens and browns of the countryside. Above, the sky turned sapphire blue. He drew a breath and let it out slowly. He had never expected to see this again in his life.

A chill rolled over him as something in his body reacted, clenching him tight. His heart felt like someone had wrapped it in barbed wire. He sucked in a ragged breath as he convulsed. His head bounced off the steering wheel, and his feet kicked wildly.

"Alexander?" Max called. "Alexander!"

He could not answer. His stomach lurched, and he flung himself to the side, spewing his earlier meal out the window. The taste of it filled his mouth, overwhelming the flavor of Max. He heard her rustling around in the trunk. Would she come out and try to help him? She would die.

That fear overcame everything else. He reached for control. He had not burned up. He was safe. His body was just fighting an instinctive fear of the sun. Being out in it was *unnatural*. He twitched and shivered, clenching his hands on the steering wheel as his body settled.

"I am okay," he called out to Max.

The sounds in the trunk quieted. "You're sure?" The relief in her voice was sweet to hear.

"I am sure."

"Then hit the road, Slick. We've still got a long way to go."

"Yes, boss," he said, putting the car into drive. "I aim to please."

The road through the mountains to the coast was winding and slow. It was only two lanes, and there was little room to pass and more traffic than he expected. At night, few people drove, he realized. He was too used to that. But even after the eruption, people were still going about the business of their lives, which included clogging the mountain roads and making his progress ridiculously slow. Or maybe they had the sense to flee.

It took almost five hours to drive the hundred and seventy miles to Eureka. He stopped there for gas and got back onto the road immediately. The road to Ukiah was not as winding, but there was far more traffic. In places, it was stop and go. People with loaded cars drove erratically, and there were frequent fender benders. He did not get there until almost seven o'clock. Max slept through much of it.

Just before Ukiah, he pulled off onto Highway 20 heading toward Clear Lake. It would take them around the north side, and from there they could catch Highway 16 toward Woodland and then make a quick jump to Winters down Interstate 505.

The only question was, how far had the wild magic progressed? He could not see it from this side of the coastal mountains, but they would cross the bottom spur of the mountains as they passed Clear Lake and dropped back into the central valley. They might be driving straight into the enchantment.

He drove through Nice and Lucerne before there was any hint of trouble. He crossed an invisible line, the kind that marks the edge of a witch's territory. As soon as he crossed, he knew there was something terribly wrong. He felt sick. It was an echo of the unnaturalness he had felt when the sun had come up. Only this was not caused by the amulet; this came from something else.

He slowed and pulled over. On the right was the lake, shining and flat beneath the orange rays of the falling sun. It would not be long before Max could escape the trunk.

"What is it?" she demanded. "What's wrong?"

"I do not know. It feels like the *anneau* here is off-kilter. Sick."

"Sick? What does that mean?" She sounded frustrated. Like she was getting ready to kick her way out of the trunk.

"I felt something like this once before," he said. "It was back in 1954. A witch died, and her succession had not been settled, and so the *anneau* went unclaimed for several days. Everything became unsettled and started to unravel. Left too long, the *anneau* will fall apart."

She was slow to reply. "I didn't even know that was possible."

"The *anneau* is the heart of the territory, but it is gathered and woven by the coven and the territory witch. It must be bound."

"Do you even know what you're talking about, Slick? You sound like you're making shit up."

He smiled. That was his Max. "Only witches really understand it, and they do not talk about it much."

He could almost hear her shrug of exasperation. "Fair enough. Giselle tells me nothing unless she absolutely has to. So you think the territory witch has died?"

"I know nothing else that would cause the *anneau* to become so unsettled."

Except . . . the living void. Cold fear burrowed into his gut. It was coming. Max was going to die unless he prevented it. If he could.

"What about the eruption and the wild magic?"

"It has not reached here," he said, his tongue stiff. He could not tell her what Giselle had seen. That in itself could get her killed. She might be so busy looking for enemies that she missed a deadly trap. "Wild magic would not undermine an *anneau*," he continued. "It causes life, not death. Perhaps the witch here failed to respond to the Guardians' call to arms, and they had her murdered. Perhaps the entire coven was destroyed, as they tried to do at Horngate."

"I don't think so. The Guardians sent Alton to take over the *anneau* when they came after Horngate. It doesn't help their war any to let the *anneau* fall apart. They'd want a witch they trusted to take it on."

Alexander agreed. "We should keep going. This is not any of our business. Give me a second." He walked away to a nearby tree to relieve himself. There was no one around. In fact, the lack of any cars was almost eerie, given the bumper-to-bumper traffic on Highway 101.

He frowned, and the hairs on his neck prickled. The silence was too complete. Even the birds and insects were mute. Something was terribly wrong here. *Living void*. Giselle's words whispered insistently. He felt his Shadowblade rising. It came sluggishly, fighting against the smothering magic of the amulet. The trade-off for being able to walk in the sunlight unharmed was a considerable weakening of his Blade.

He growled deep in his chest. Right now, with Max helpless in the trunk, he was the only thing that stood between her and certain death. He needed all his strength to keep her from harm.

He zipped his fly and returned to the car. His senses

were dull. He got back inside and started it. He could feel Max's Shadowblade pushing out as she rose to a killing edge. She was so strong. And she was *his*. His lips pulled back from his teeth in an animal snarl. The hell with Giselle's vision. She was wrong.

He jammed the car into drive and gunned the gas. The tires squealed, and dirt and gravel plumed behind them. His skin itched with the feeling of being watched—of being hunted.

A few minutes later, he rounded a blind spur. He saw the spike strip too late. It lay flat across the entire road, made out of a two-by-four studded with long nails. It was crude but effective. He slammed on his brakes, turning the wheel. The car slid sideways over the strip. *Pop*s sounded, like champagne corks. The sedan flipped over, slammed onto its roof and skidded across pavement, metal shrieking protest.

Alexander was not wearing his seat belt and crashed against the ceiling—now the floor. Windows broke, splattering him with chunks of safety glass. As the car rocked to a halt, he found himself wedged between the headrest of the passenger seat and the roof. The smell of burned rubber, gasoline, and exhaust filled the crushed space of the car's interior.

The wheels were spinning, and the engine squealed. Alexander shut it off.

"Max? Are you all right?" The seat was pressing hard into his chest. He shoved against it. It gave more slowly than it should have. As soon as the sun went down, he was taking off the damned amulet.

"Yeah, but I think I want to drive next time," she said with a little groan. "What about you?"

"Fine. There was a spike strip in the road."

"Shit. Any sign of who put it there?"

He shook his head, then remembered that she could not see him, "No. But all I can smell is fuel. I am getting out."

He pushed on the seat again and squirmed free of it, then pulled himself slowly out, looking around, sniffing the air. There was no sign of anyone. That did not mean they were not there. But what were they waiting for? Smart hunters would be closing in while the wreck still had their prey disoriented. So either their enemies were not very smart, or they had something else in mind. He edged around to the trunk, keeping to a crouch.

Getting Max out would require lifting the car up. After that, everything depended on who was after them and why. How many were there?

He glanced at the western sky. A few more minutes, and the sun would be gone far enough to let him free Max and take off the damned amulet. He was feeling heavy, like he was encased in cement. He rubbed his eyes and shook his head. His brain felt thick as syrup.

He scowled. Was the way he felt an attack? "Max? Are you feeling this?"

"What?" Her voice was sharp.

His tongue felt clumsy and foolish. "Tired. Flat. Like breathing is an effort."

"No." She was quiet a moment. "It's that damned amulet. It's got to be. It feeds on you to power its spells. You've been wearing it for too long. Fucking witch tricks."

It made sense. Now that he thought about it, the exhaustion had been growing all day. He had chalked it up to the long previous night and not getting any sleep, but those things would not do this to him.

The car rocked as Max moved around inside. She swore softly, a long chain of epithets. "What the hell are they waiting for?" she asked suddenly.

"I do not know. Unless—" An idea struck him, and he knew he was right with an almost preternatural certainty. "It is almost sundown. If Sunspears set the attack, they might be waiting until it is safe for the Shadowblades to come out and finish the job."

She was silent a moment. "Any idea what they want with us?"

He shook his head. "I am not interested in finding out. I want to get this amulet off and get you out of there. Then we can run before they corner us."

He scanned the surrounding area. They were already pretty well cut off. Except for the car, there was precious little cover. Across the road were two ridges that came down in a wide V. The hills were covered with boulders and scrub brush, giving plenty of cover to anybody hiding above. Behind them was the lake. They could try swimming to escape, but chances were their enemies were prepared for that. Only the road offered any escape, and a couple of good shots with rifles could easily pin them down and make it easy for others to come in and scoop them up.

He felt the moment when the sun disappeared far enough for Shadowblades to safely be outside. He ripped the amulet off his neck and shoved it into his back pocket, then lifted the car onto its side. It was almost heavier than he could manage. His stomach felt hollow. His legs and arms shook.

There was a loud thump, and the trunk lid opened, the edge of it scraping over the road. Max emerged. She looked at Alexander, then reached back inside and grabbed a bottle of Gatorade. She tossed it to him, and he guzzled it down. She handed him some power bars. He ripped into one and shoved it in his mouth, then tucked the others into his pockets. She grabbed the rowan spear and scanned the hills behind them.

"Eat," Max said absently, still searching for signs of movement.

Alexander obeyed, eating two more bars. He felt a small surge of strength, but he still felt heavy and ungainly.

Max took a sharp breath through her nose, tipping her head. Alexander caught a whiff. Uncanny magic. He had expected no different. He felt his Shadowblade Prime rising, pushing away his exhaustion. The animal in him clawed with savage fury. Max glanced at him. Her Prime was riding high. Her entire body radiated strength and animal power.

"Welcome to the party, Slick. It's about time you woke up."

"What do you want to do?"

"I want to stop wasting time." She looked back out at the hills. "All right. You've got us stopped. What the hell do you want?" she yelled.

For a moment, there was silence. Then came a woman's voice, shrill and thin, like she was walking the knife edge of sanity. "Drop your weapons."

"And if we don't?"

A rifle report echoed across the water, and a bullet struck the tire above Max's head. She glanced at the hole it tore in the rubber. "I guess they want us to know they mean business. How many do you think there are?"

"I can smell four."

"That's what I've got. They stink like fear and desperation. That's never good. But no point hanging out here.
They've got us for now. Let's go find out why."

She pulled her knives out and set them on top of the
car—the passenger door that was now facing up to the
sky. Alexander followed suit. She hefted the rowan spear
and regretfully leaned it against the wheel.

"What about the witch chains?" he murmured.

"Leave them on. They aren't exactly weapons. If they
notice them, they can take them."

He reached into his pocket for the amulet and turned
it in his fingers. It was too valuable to let it be taken.
But what to do with it? He could throw it into the lake,
but then it would likely be lost forever. And what if they
needed it to escape from these faceless enemies? Could
he hide it on himself? Or use it now? But going invisible
would allow only him to escape. Their captors had seen
him and would torture Max to bring him out of hiding.
It was what he would do. He could not stand by and
watch that. It was not an option.

"Quick, give it to me." She pulled her shoe halfway off
and stuffed the amulet beneath her instep. "That's going
to be annoying," she muttered, lacing back up. "That's
it," she called. "Come and get us."

"Where are your guns and flash bombs? Where are
your grenades?" This time it was a man. His voice was
hoarse and ragged.

"Sorry, man. If you're shopping, we don't have anything for sale. We stole the car a ways back," Max said
dismissively.

Silence.

After about half a minute, Max made an annoyed sound. "Look, if you want to talk, come on down. I'm done otherwise."

"That's awfully brave, considering we have you at gunpoint," the female speaker said.

Max made no reply. Another shot rang out. This time, it went through the crumpled roof of the car.

"Do you think that's what they were aiming for? If not, they can't shoot for shit, and we can start running now." She said it loudly enough for their enemies to hear.

"I think that whatever is wrong with the *anneau* is affecting their minds," Alexander said more quietly. "Possibly their aim also," he added, the corner of his mouth quirking.

She grinned at him, and then her head jerked up. "They're coming."

All four of them had been perched up on the hills, two on each ridge. They picked their way down, rifles trained on Max and Alexander the entire way. There were three men and one woman. She was clearly the leader, although she was no Prime. None of them was.

The three men came down first, making a ragged line as they descended. They were filthy, their clothes ripped and stained with blood. They wore bandoliers of flash bombs and grenades and were armed to the teeth with knives and handguns. They looked as if they hadn't slept in days, and all of them were too thin.

The men closed around Max and Alexander in a loose triangle. Stupid. It set up a crossfire that could just as easily kill them as their captives. Two of them looked like startled rabbits. They were twins, with blue eyes and blond hair. The only thing differentiating them was their clothing and the buzzed hair on one of them.

The third man was undoubtedly the one who had shot at them. He swaggered, his lip curled in a sneer that was probably permanent. He carried a .30-30 covered with smears of blood and mud. His eyes were dark except for bands of white around the edges. Alexander growled low in his throat. The man's Blade had him in thrall, and he was close to going feral. It happened occasionally, usually with young Blades. Their minds broke under the magic it took to make them. But this one was no young Blade. What had driven him to the edge?

The woman came down last, and the others deferred to her, easing aside to give her room. She carried her rifle over her forearm. Her eyes were sunken, and she was holding herself so tight her body seemed to hum. Her hair was cut raggedly above her ears, as if it had been done with a knife. She wore a leather vest and jeans. Both were filthy, and the jeans were riddled with burn holes. From her left hip to her ankle was a patch of crusty brown blood, long since dried.

"Are you Max and Alexander?" she demanded.

"How the hell do you know that?" Max said.

"You were foreseen."

Alexander scowled. He was getting very tired of fore-tellings. It was a rare talent, and here in the space of a few days, he had run into three different witches with it.

"Who are you?" he asked.

"Your new boss."

"Funny, I thought we already served a witch," Max said

"Then she should have kept you on a shorter leash.

You're mine now." She motioned at her companions.
"Bring them."

She walked away up the road. Max and Alexander followed, the three men trailing them in a half-circle.

A dusty black pickup truck waited around the bend.
The woman climbed into the driver's seat, revving the
engine.

"Up there," the nontwin ordered, pointing to the
truck bed.

Max and Alexander hopped up and sat down with
their backs to the cab. The men climbed in behind, sitting on the fenders. The rifle muzzles never wavered.

"Who are you?" Max asked.

"Shuddup," said the twin with all his hair.

"Really, Sneezy? That's the best you've got?"

"Quiet, or I'll close your lips for good," said the sneering Blade. He said it in a quiet singsong.

Alexander stiffened, eyeing him warily. His Blade Prime
slammed against the cage that kept him from running
wild. Alexander could tell that the other man recognized
his danger. Still, he did not flinch in the slightest.

"And you must be Grumpy," Max said. "Where are the
rest of the dwarves? And the Wicked Witch? She must
be around somewhere."

That got a reaction. Grumpy's face went blank, and
his finger jerked on the trigger. Alexander knocked Max
to the side. The bullet shattered the rear window and
drilled through the windshield, passing just over the
driver's shoulder. The woman slammed on the brakes,
jumping out before the truck was completely stopped.

"What the fuck?" she yelled up at Grumpy. "You
could've taken my fucking head off!"

"But I didn't," he said, levering the bolt on his rifle, aiming again at the prisoners.

"Are you going to kill them?"

"Maybe just one. We don't need a spare," he said.

"Don't we? Since when? Judith said to bring them both, and that's what we're going to do."

He sucked his teeth and spat on the bed of the truck but did not object further. She took that as agreement, returned to the wheel, and began driving again.

The truck pulled off on a dirt road after a couple of miles and turned up into the folds of the flattening mountains, going another five miles, until they came to a broad, flat hilltop.

The moment they drove onto it, Alexander felt waves of twisting, wrong magic. His stomach lurched as it had when he had put the amulet on and the sun had come up. He swallowed, forcing himself to keep his food down. Sweat sprang up all over him, and his skin went clammy. He looked at Max. Her face was taut and slightly gray. Her jaw was clenched and she, too, was sweating.

This was the living void. Somewhere close. No wonder Grumpy was near to going feral. Alexander could feel the chains slipping from his Prime. His hands knotted. He had to keep it together, or he was going to lose Max.

You will be Prime.

Not if he could damned well help it.

The truck rolled up onto a smooth drive made of a flat black rock mortared together and edged by two lines of bricks. It wound through what appeared to have once been a verdant park. The grass, trees, and bushes were now black as if they had been burned, but there was no ash. The water in the creek was stagnant brown, and the plants floating on its surface were corpse white. The air was thin and bitter, and it hurt his lungs to breathe it.

"What happened here?"

The nose of Grumpy's gun twitched in Alexander's direction, but otherwise, there was no answer.

They pulled up outside a sprawling mansion. Or at least that was what it had been once. Now it looked like an ancient ruined castle from the backwaters of Ireland or Scotland. The mortar was cracked and crumbling, and many of the walls were collapsed or leaned drunkenly. It looked like the place could fall in at any moment.

Their captors got them out, and the woman stopped to stare at the building. For a moment, her concrete look of desperate determination gave way to stricken horror. She bit her lips and strode stiffly away.

She led them around the side and through a courtyard garden. Like everywhere else, it was barren and broken. They came to a set of stairs leading downward beneath the mansion. At the bottom was an iron door. It swung open without a squeak. Beyond it was a narrow corridor that led into a broad room filled with couches, televisions, exercise equipment, and a wall of books and games. The ceiling sagged pregnantly.

They went in and the door shut with a clang. Alexander's nostrils flared. He smelled Sunspears and witches and illness.

The Spears came through a door on the right. There were three of them, and they looked haggard. Black lines traced beneath their skin like fractures in old fine

china. They had been dark-poisoned, no doubt in helping to set the trap for Alexander and Max.

The three carried handguns, and, like the four Blades,
they bristled with weapons. The first was a slight man
with copper hair and darting blue eyes. The second
man had dark hair and a round face. The last was a tiny
woman, only five feet tall. She had wheat-blond hair
and a pink mouth. She looked like a doll. But there was
no doubt she was more than capable of killing. The aura
of danger surrounded her. She was not a Prime—none
of them was—but she was as close as Niko, Tyler, and
Thor. A few years and a few more spells, and she would
come into it.

She flashed a look at the two prisoners and then at
the brown-haired woman escorting them.

"Come on. No time to waste. Oak and Steel, come
with us. The rest of you, take up watch."

Oak and Steel turned out to be Grumpy and the twin
with the longer hair. The blond woman led the way
through the rec room to a smaller room. Whatever it
had been once, it was a sickroom now. Smudge pots
squatted in every corner and in a half-circle around the
narrow bed in the corner. Pungent smoke rose from
them—sage and a strange combination of butterscotch,
licorice, and celery.

On the bed lay a still form—a witch. His breathing was quick and shallow and labored. Another witch
leaned over the first, muttering and wiping his face with
a damp towel. Alexander hoped she was not using water
from anywhere near. He was fairly certain anything
within a few hundred yards of the place at least was
completely dead. Not just dead in the normal way that

provided fertile ground for other things but sterilized with no hope for any future life. It was a blight, and he doubted that even the wild magic from Mount Shasta could find a foothold here. Whatever had created it was the living void.

"What happened?" Max asked the witch in a voice devoid of any emotion. "What do you want of us?" Her expression was cold. She'd withdrawn deeply into herself. She was ready to fight.

The witch looked up. She was skeletal, much the way Giselle had been after the battle to save Horngate. Her brown hair was lank and stringy, and her skin sagged from her body. Her fingernails were purple, as if they had been crushed with a hammer, and her eyes were blotched with broken blood vessels. She looked like she had been through a war. She barely glanced at Alexander and Max before turning back to her patient.

The short blond Blade stepped forward. "Judith, are these the ones your vision showed you?"

The witch looked up again. She stared first at Max and then at Alexander. "Yes," she said in a papery voice before going back to her muttering chant.

"Good," the Blade said, turning to examine Max and Alexander speculatively. She had not put down her gun. It was a .454 Casull, made to bring down elephants. "We have a job for you."

"A job?" Max repeated. Her entire attention riveted on the blond Sunspear. It could not have been comfortable. "What makes you think we want to work for you?"

"Oh, I don't think you want to. But you're going to. Or you'll die."

Max shrugged. "I won't die alone."

"No, you won't. He'll die, too," the blonde said, gesturing her gun at Alexander.

"And so will you. All of you," Max crooned. She rolled up onto the balls of her feet, her knees flexing.

Alexander tensed, shifting so that he could go after Oak and Steel. Their rifles continued to be trained unwaveringly on their two captives, although once again, their crossfire could easily take out the blond Spear and the brunette Blade. Stupid. Who had trained them?

The blond Spear stared. Her jaw was clenched so hard it was shaking. "You'll do what we tell you, or I'll put a hole in your chest the size of a grapefruit. You won't walk away."

"Everybody's gotta die sometime. Why not tonight?"

She was bluffing. She had to be. Max's family was waiting, possibly dying or dead. She had no interest in dying today. But even knowing that, Alexander believed her.

The Spear's face contorted. The nose of her gun wavered. Then she jerked it at Alexander, shoving it hard against his chest. "You're very willing to stop breathing, but what about him? Are you going to watch me kill him?"

Alexander did not wait for Max's reply. He did what he should have done already. He used his telekinesis to fuse the trigger on her Casull and did the same with the weapons of the other three.

"Try it," he said, knowing that Max would understand.

And then all hell broke loose.

14

MAX'S RAGE WAS COLD AND METHODICAL. THREAT-ening her life was one thing, but Alexander—he was *hers*.

She snatched the barrel of the heavy Casull and smashed the gun into the mouthy blond Spear's stomach. The woman looked horrified and startled at once, like she'd figured that the gun and superior numbers made her invincible. She doubled over with a grunt. Max kicked her in the face, sending her flying. Alexander was caught up in a fight with Oak and Steel. The brunette Blade's gun swung around, cracking Max in the thigh. Her leg went numb. She pivoted and dropped, tackling the other woman.

None of them seemed to be that well trained. They fought with the ferocity of desperation, but they were not prepared for two angry Primes who had plenty of fighting skills and the willingness to use them.

The four went down in less than half a minute. They weren't dead. Max didn't kill unless she had to, and neither did Alexander. That was one of the things she liked about him. She pulled her witch chain free and had it wrapped around Judith's neck before the woman could react to the fight. Max knotted the chain tight and straddled the sick witch, planning to do the same to him.

"No! Please! He'll die. Let me help him," Judith pleaded. Her voice cracked, and tears streamed down her face. "Please. We won't hurt you. We can't. Neither of us have much left to use."

Max hesitated. "Never trust a witch" was her own personal motto. But there was no doubting this one's fear and desperation. Something terrible had happened to this coven, and those who were left were barely hanging on. She bit her bottom lip. *Don't be stupid. Just finish this and get the hell out.*

Apparently, "stupid" was her motto on this trip. With a heavy breath, she hopped down off the bed and unfastened the chain from the witch's neck. "Don't get cute," she ordered.

The witch blinked. "Thank you," she said, and went back to her chant.

Max looked at Alexander. He stood by the door, holding a steel police baton and looking none the worse for wear. Oak and Steel were in the middle of the room, where he'd dragged them. They lay next to the two women. The others were bloody and weren't healing very quickly. Max wiped the back of her hand over her chin. Blood came away on it. It wasn't hers.

"Shit," she said.

"We should be able to make it back out to the truck without much trouble," Alexander said, but made no move to open the door.

It was like he was reading her mind. That should have

annoyed the hell out of her. "Let's find out what's going on around here first," Max said.

They pulled the three Blades up and sat them up against the wall, stripping away their weapons. "Wish we had some water to wake them up with," Max said as she paced in front of them. "We're running out of night fast."

It had been less than an hour since their capture. They could still make it to Winters in plenty of time before the sun rose. Still, something was terribly wrong here, and she couldn't bring herself to just walk away without knowing what. Everyone looked shell-shocked. It reminded her too much of Horngate after the angels had attacked four weeks ago. Where were the rest of the covenstead's witches? Where were the rest of the Spears and Blades?

It was a good five minutes before any of the four stirred.

The blond woke first. She groaned, blinking and looking first at Max and Alexander and then at her companions. She made a sobbing sound and fell back against the wall, her eyes closing. It was the picture of defeat.

"That's it? You're giving up?"

The blond snapped upright, her eyes blazing. When she spoke, her voice was slurred. Her lips were pulpy, and her jaw was swollen, no doubt broken by Max's kick. She was too depleted for her healing spells to work. Max knew all about that.

"What do you know?" she said. "You were our last hope."

"Then you probably ought to have talked nicer," Max

said, squatting down in front of her. "You know what they say about vinegar and flies."

"Fuck you," the woman said, and tears rolled down her cheeks.

"You aren't all that tough as Sunspears go, are you?" Max said. "Not very smart, either. That's a bad combo. If you're going to be dumb, you should at least be tough."

"You don't know anything about me."

Her anger was starting to spark back to life. *Good.* Max wanted her mad.

"So why don't you tell me, Tinker Bell?"

"My name is Maple."

Of course it was. Max rolled her eyes. Witches and the stupid names they pinned on their Spears and Blades. "All right, Maple. What's going on here? Where is the rest of the coven? Where are the Primes?"

The other woman bit her lips, then released a shaky breath. "We were attacked. Two days ago."

"By who?"

Rage hardened Maple's expression. "Her name is Lacey." She swallowed, her mouth twisting. "She was one of us."

"One of you? A Spear?"

Maple shook her head. "One of the triangle. Patricia, our *anneau* witch, got sick. No one knew what happened, but suddenly, she was dead. Then Lacey stepped forward and said she was going to take the *anneau* in order to keep everyone safe. If the *anneau* fell apart, we'd all be covenless."

A full coven was made up of twenty-two witches. There were thirteen in the outer circle, five for the points of the pentagram inside the circle, three for the points of the triangle inside the pentagram, and one for the center point. The witch who held the coven held the center and the territory *anneau*. Once Patricia had died, the *anneau* would unravel and leave everyone homeless, unless someone else could take it and hold it.

"But some of you didn't like Lacey and refused," Max guessed.

"Not at first," said the brunette Blade who'd helped capture them. The side of her face was a solid purple bruise. She rubbed a finger inside her mouth, feeling the back of her teeth. "You kick like a horse," she told Max.

"Remember it. So what happened next?"

"Lacey said she was the strongest of the triangle, and it only made sense for her to ascend to the center point. Gregory and Judith were the other two points of the triangle, and they disagreed. She was strong, but she wasn't a good leader. They said Gregory made more sense."

"And Lacey didn't like that."

"No. She got furious. She said she already had the support of the star and most of the circle. Gregory and Judith just needed to get with the program. Most of the Spears and Blades didn't know what to do. Patricia's death broke our bindings and we weren't all there for a while."

"Compulsion-spell backlash," Alexander said. "It can drive Sunspears and Shadowblades insane, if not kill them altogether."

"Some of us were pretty bad off," the brunette Blade agreed.

"So what happened? The condensed version. We're in a hurry."

"Gregory and Judith accused Lacey of killing Patricia. She just laughed and told them they ought to watch themselves, or they'd end up dead, too. It looked like there was going to be a witch battle when another three witches showed up. If that's what you want to call them. Looked like they were carved out of ice—white hair, white skin, and silver-blue robes. They were so beautiful they were hard to look at. Made us want to crawl on our stomachs to lick their boots. And they were cold—so very cold. It felt like we'd all been stuck in the deep freeze. I don't know where they came from. One minute there was no one there, the next they appeared."

Max looked at Alexander, her brows rising. She'd not heard of anything like the three.

"Fairies, maybe," he suggested.

That wasn't particularly helpful. There were about as many kinds of fairy as there were homeless cats in the world.

"What did they do?"

"They told Lacey she'd done a good job. That's when we knew for sure she'd killed Patricia." There was a catch in Maple's voice.

"What then?"

"Then they said they wanted to give her what she wanted—the center point of the *anneau*.

"They told Lacey to go stand on the center point and told the rest of the witches to take their positions. The idiots did it. Even Lacey, though she could tell something wasn't right. She was sweating and looking around like she wanted someone to save her ass. And all we did was watch. We were so stupid. But it was like we were dreaming; we didn't even think about resisting. All except Judith and Gregory." She gestured toward the two witches in the corner. "That's them. All the rest went like sheep, but those two tried to fight. Then Gregory went down. We never saw what they did to him, but we thought he was dead. It was so sudden, so silent—" She broke off, swallowing hard. "Judith was the only one smart enough to run.

"Before we even knew what was happening, the three ice queens turned the rest of the coven witches into ice statues. Literally."

Maple stopped her torrent of words, breathing hard. Oak and Steel were awake now. Oak was looking malevolent, blood running from the cuts on his forehead and cheek. Steel just looked wiped out, like he could barely sit up. He was mottled with swellings and bruises.

"So then what happened, Pippy?" Max prompted the brunette Blade. Maple looked as if she wouldn't be able to talk for another few minutes, and Max was all too aware of time slipping down the drain.

"Pippy?" She made a face. "I'm Ivy."

"All right, Ivy. What happened next?"

"After the ice queens froze the coven, they went to stand around Lacey. They held hands and made a triangle but stood on the lines instead of the points. They opened their mouths like they were going to sing, only they made this noise. It was like a wind howling across ice. It was deafening and so empty. It felt like it was pulling our souls out of us. Then it changed. It felt like there was no hope for anything anymore. I wanted to cut my own throat.

"That's when the Primes decided we'd done nothing long enough and organized us into an attack. I don't know how they were able to resist that sound, but they did, and they kicked our asses until we could, too. We started to jump the ice queens, and then something exploded. Only there was no force to it. It was like something dead pulsed through the air—through us. It kept going, destroying almost everything all the way to the shield wards." She shook her head, looking haunted.

It startled Max when Oak picked up the story. "We got knocked on our asses. Couldn't think straight. When it ended, we couldn't even move. We lay on the floor like sitting ducks. They came around. Said we shouldn't have challenged them. They didn't care about us, only the witches. But they couldn't let the attack go unpunished. So they said they would give us a chance. Fight each other, and when enough were dead, they would let the rest of us live."

"Fight each other?" Alexander repeated, revulsion clearly written on his face.

"Yeah. At first we refused. Then each of them pointed at one of us. Before we knew what to expect, the three unlucky bastards crumbled to dust. We had no choice."

Max stared, appalled. What would she have done? Would she have tried to kill her own people? "So you tried to kill each other?" She could not keep the disgust from her voice.

"No." Steel spoke at last. "How could we?"

She frowned, confused. "So what did you do?"

Oak snorted derisively. "We fought. Not to kill, but about half of the other Spears and Blades had other ideas. They wanted to save their skins. So they came after us and each other."

"When it was done, we were all that were left," Maple said, her hands clenching tight. She stared straight in front of her as if seeing it all again. "The ice queens turned to us and told us they hoped we had learned our lesson. To prove it, we are to bring them Judith and Gregory. They said they had to destroy the entire coven. They'd return in a couple of days for them. That's tonight."

"That's why you want us? To fight these things? Why didn't you just run?" Max asked.

"Where do we go? What do we do? No witch will take us in. Besides, this is our covenstead. We're supposed to protect it."

"There's nothing left to protect. This place is dead. Can't you feel it? Hell, you're all not even healing properly," Alexander said. "I bet it has everything to do with what they've done to this place. The smart thing to do is to take the two witches you have left and get out. Start a life somewhere."

"That's not what Judith's vision said," Ivy said stubbornly.

"You know they don't understand half the shit they see, right?" Max said.

"She saw the two of you. She said you'd know how to get rid of the ice queens. You're here. She was right about that, she must be right about the rest."

Max thrust frustrated fingers through her hair. "I

don't even know what the fuck these three bitches are. How do you think we're going to stop them if your entire coven and a full squad of Blades and Spears couldn't?"

Maple gave a little shrug, but it was clear she wasn't changing her mind. Max thrust to her feet and paced away. "This is futile. We should just get the hell out of here," she told Alexander.

"I agree. We should leave. But you are not going to, are you?" Shadows moved in his eyes, and his face was pulled into a harsh mask. His Prime felt rabid.

She frowned at him. What had set him off? She shrugged inwardly. She'd find out sooner or later, and right now wasn't the time. "Not my style, Slick. You know that."

She winced inwardly. What was she? The patron saint of lost causes? Why was she such a sucker that she rescued witches with angry mage ex-husbands and pathetic Blades and Spears without the sense the Spirits gave rocks?

It was a character flaw. Or maybe it was such an ingrained habit to do exactly what Giselle would have hated that Max did it without even considering what she was doing. Or maybe she was just as much an idiot as these people she was trying to help.

Max swung around and went to the witch by the bed. "What did you see in your vision?" she demanded.

Judith paused in her chanting and looked wearily up at Max. "I asked the question, who can stop these three beings? The answer was you and him. I saw your car, and I saw you here. It was very clear. But beyond—I do not know. Just that you are the answer."

"That's—" *A boatload of horseshit. And not at all help-ful.* Max didn't say it. Judith was half dead. No point beating her up now. "All right," she said, and turned back to the others.

The heart of everything was knowing what the ice queens really were and how to kill them. Over the years, she'd studied a lot of mythology, folklore, and fairy tales, so that she wouldn't run blind into situations like this one. Unfortunately, these ice queens didn't fit anything she'd read or heard about.

"What do you think?" she asked Alexander.

"We can try the usual tricks: iron, rowan, salt—" He glanced at the smudge pots. "I suspect they already put all of that to work."

Maple nodded, her brow crimping as she looked up at them. "We're burning sage and osha. Both are pro-tective. The bed is made of rowan and iron, and we've made a salt barrier around the room."

Max looked. She'd not noticed it before, but there was a white strip of the stuff running around the base of the walls.

"You are going to help us?" Maple asked in surprise.

"Maybe," Max said. She wasn't sure what she and Al-exander could really do. But Judith had foreseen them, and that meant that they could do *something*. If it was a true foretelling. Though that left a lot of room open for pain and death. Helping was a matter of perspective, and hauling these idiots out of here at high speed was the best help she could imagine. But they weren't going to budge. That much was obvious. Which left finding a way to get rid of the ice queens.

"Chopping off heads tends to be a good solution," Max mused.

"If we can get close enough. If they do not turn us into dust first," Alexander replied.

"Got any better ideas? I'm all ears." Her gaze dropped to her foot, where the amulet was hidden. She looked back up at him.

He'd followed her look and was already nodding. "You wear it. I will make a diversion."

"Sounds good, except you'll wear it. You're more tired than I am. I stand a better chance of not getting killed the first second they set eyes on me."

His lips tightened, but then he nodded.

"We'll help," Maple said.

"Damned right you will," Max said. "Let's get going. There's no telling when they'll be back."

They gathered in the rec room with Steel's twin, Flint, and the other two Spears, Eagle and Stone. They looked haggard and swayed on their feet.

"What's wrong with all of you?" Max asked. "You should have healed by now."

"Healing spells aren't working. And we can't keep food down. It tastes terrible, and we throw it back up," Steel said, slumping into a chair.

"What about food from the outside? Have you gone to a store?"

Maple shook her head. "We didn't want to leave Gregory and Judith. There's already too few of us."

"And about to be fewer if you drop dead." They were like children. Worse. Like blind kittens. "All right. I need weapons. Guns with shot shells if you've got them.

And swords. At least two. Got any steel shields? Better bring those, too."

Oak and the three Sunspears went off to fetch the weapons.

"How long do you think we have?" Max asked Alexander as she pulled off her shoe and handed him the amulet.

"Moonrise is soon. Maybe then. Or midnight. But who can tell why they waited so long to come back or what gives them power?"

"I wish we knew more about them. Or anything about them at all."

"They need each other to work their strongest magic," Alexander said. "They untied the *anneau* when they held each other in a triangle. Keeping them apart is crucial."

"So kill them fast."

"I will. Do not let them hurt you. I do not want to carry you around in a jar. Making love to you would make me sneeze. It would be entirely unpleasant."

Her brows rose. Despite the joke, he looked anything but amused. "I try never to get hurt."

"Try not to very hard," he said.

A thin band of yellow circled his irises. He was edging into feral territory. What was driving him? She had reached out to put a hand on his arm when Ivy interrupted.

"How is it that two Prime Shadowblades are . . . working together?"

Max pulled back, slowly shifting her gaze from Alexander. "Long story. And none of your business. Do you guys know that you stink and you're covered in blood?"

Ivy looked down at herself. She touched the dried blood on her jeans, and her throat jerked as she

fought against tossing her cookies. "We've been sleeping in short shifts and guarding Judith and Gregory. I
didn't even think—" She broke off, her mouth clamping shut.

Max wondered how old she was. How old all of them
were. None of them was trained that well. In the human
world, they'd be scary and tough, but in the world of
witches, they were pathetic.

The others returned carrying a pile of weapons.
Maple had retrieved the ones from the sickroom and
offered Max her .454.

"Keep it," Max said. "Start shooting when you see them.
Only, for all our sakes, try not to set up a crossfire where
you're sure to hit your team when you shoot. I'd appreciate it especially if you didn't hit me or Alexander."

They all looked vaguely startled and shamefaced.

"Sorry," Maple muttered, red-cheeked.

"Did no one train you?" Max asked.

The other woman lifted her shoulder in a half-shrug.
"Patricia thought we were good enough."

"You aren't. Not by a long shot. If you were mine—"
But they weren't. "Give me the swords."

She took them from Oak and turned to Alexander.
"Do it," she said. The others would see what the amulet
was, but there was no way to keep it a secret and still
get this done.

Alexander sliced his hand across the palm and
smeared the blood over the gold disk front and back.
He put it around his neck, sliding it beneath his shirt.
And vanished.

"What the hell?" yelped Oak.

"How did he do that?" Ivy asked.

"Where did he go?" Maple said nervously.

"Here." Max handed two swords to Alexander. As she hoped, they disappeared like his clothing when he took them. She turned to the others, not bothering to answer the obvious. "When these ice witches come, he'll cut their heads off. We have to distract them first. Shoot on sight. You'll stand in ranks. Two of you crouching down, two on your feet, and the last two up on the bed. Don't shoot each other in the back. Alexander will be behind the door. You'll face the opposite corner. He'll be going for their heads, so be aware of him, and don't shoot in that direction. Keep on target—please tell me you can at least hit what you aim at."

They nodded at this last, but none seemed all that confident. Max fought the urge to slap each of them. "I'll be down on the floor, hopefully keeping their attention on me. I shouldn't be in your line of fire, but if I am, try not to blow holes in me."

A wave of nausea rolled through Max. She felt sick and wobbly. She saw it hit the others. She drew a deep breath. Now or never. "Looks like they're here. Give me a shield and let's get in there."

She'd already taken two .45s and a sword. Now she led the way inside. These ice queens had the power to just show up wherever they wanted to be. There was nothing saying they would bother with the door.

Judith looked up, her lips pulling down. She said nothing, but crawled up next to Gregory, holding him in her arms. The Spears and Blades took up their positions. At least they could follow directions. They looked resolute despite their fear and sudden sickness. That was something in their favor. Max took up a station near the closed door.

"Scrape away the salt on the threshold," she told the air where Alexander was. Then she smashed the smudge pot nearest her and stamped it out. Oak and Ivy did the same with the rest of them. The salt and smoke might have held the ice queens back or not. But at this point, Max wanted them in the room in her trap. She didn't want to have to walk into theirs.

Nausea hit again and a feeling of exhaustion. More than that—it was a sense of futility, that the world was hollow and empty and nothing mattered anymore. It slid over Max like sticky water, pulling her down into despair. She made a face and shook herself, clearing her mind. Her companions froze in place, staring blankly at nothing. Max slapped the back of Oak's head. "Come on, fight it. You're stronger than that." She did the same with Flint and Eagle. They blinked and woke the others from their catatonia.

The temperature dropped. Max's breath plumed in the air. She saw where Alexander stood as his breath did the same. She pressed back against the wall, waiting for the door to open. Instead, it crumbled to dust. Parts of the walls on either side also crumbled. The smell of Divine magic washed into the room, and the three ice queens came with it in a triangular formation. They seemed to float rather than walk. They stood more than six feet tall and were exactly as Maple had described them—white hair and skin, with silver-blue robes that shimmered iridescently.

Max didn't wait to see more. She started shooting,

aiming for their heads. Gunshots exploded in the small room as the others did the same.

As soon as she pulled the trigger, the room became smothering, and Max wanted nothing more than to slide to the floor and rest. Breathing became almost impossible. Her heart slowed, and she tottered dizzily, the gun sagging in her hand as the witches cast a spell over the room.

A second later, a sound like nothing she'd ever heard before cut across her mind. It was like a chorus of wails from one of Dante's hell circles. It filled her head and scrambled her brain. She might have screamed with it. Beside her, she vaguely heard her companions fall to the floor. She smelled blood and something bitter, like burned onion and sulfur. Bile rose in her throat, and she could neither spit it out nor swallow it.

The sound continued to vibrate through her, shaking the foundations of her reason. A part of her remembered what Maple had said happened the first time the witches visited. First the sound, then the blast of death. Max wasn't going to allow it. She still had her family to rescue, and these bitches were done killing.

She pushed one of her feet forward a few inches. Then the other. Her hand spasmed and went slack, and the shield slipped to the floor with a loud clang. Her gun followed as her other hand did the same. *Dammit.* Max reached for her other gun. Her arms felt dead; she could barely feel them. She fumbled her fingers around the handle and gripped it loosely. Another step. Where was Alexander? She blearily looked around her. One of the ice queens lay on the floor. Or what was left of her. She'd turned to granular bits of white and silver sand.

The two remaining ice queens clutched hands, their mouths open wider than should have been possible as they screamed.

Max edged forward, forcing her legs to move when all she wanted to do was fall down. She wanted to be close enough that she couldn't miss, even if she couldn't keep hold of the gun.

Another four scraping steps put her in position. The ice queens either didn't notice or were ignoring her. No doubt they figured the racket they were making had incapacitated everyone. She raised the gun. It rattled in her hand. She tightened her grip, forcing her other hand up to help hold it. She thumbed the hammer and held herself firmly, locking her elbows as best she could, her muzzle aimed point-blank at the ear of one of the ice queens. She fired.

Her hands jerked upward, and the gun went flying. But the ice queen dropped to the floor in a pile of sand. The other one turned to look at Max, rage making her almost ugly. She never stopped screaming. Her hand came up, and she pointed.

Dust, Max thought. *She's going to turn me into dust.*

Suddenly magic flared along her left arm, burning through her body. She felt a yank, and she was in the web between worlds. It was made of rainbow magic, and it stretched through a black plain as far as she could see. A sleeve of Scooter's blue-white magic sheathed her forearm. Before she could even think, her body cramped and pain flared along every one of her synapses. She'd known that using Scooter's gift would hurt, but at the moment, she didn't mind. It had also saved her butt.

A second later, she found herself being dragged through the web. Or, rather, strands of it reached for her, passing her along toward . . . somewhere. When they touched her, it was like being twined with vines of acid. She swallowed the pain out of long habit and just waited. She had a sense of place, of where she'd been. She needed it to hurry up—she had to get back to help Alexander fight. If he was still on his feet. Her heart clenched, and that was a pain that was far more unbearable than the web or anything else.

Suddenly the strands of the web curled away, and she found herself falling.

15

THE AIR WHISTLED ALONG THE EDGE OF THE SWORD
as Alexander swung it around and chopped
through the neck of the first ice queen. Cold
forked like lightning through his body, stabbing his heart
and lungs. Her head went flying and her body collapsed
in a fall of white and blue sand. At the same moment,
the other two opened their mouths, and the noise that
issued forth was like the cries of tortured demons. He
fell back against the wall as the sound filled him, tearing at every sinew. His body went limp, and he wanted
nothing more than slide down to the floor.

He forced himself up, gripping the hilts of the two
swords. There was a stench of something dead and
spoiled. He looked for Max. She was inching herself
forward toward the two screaming ice queens, a harsh
mask of grim determination on her face. Her eyes were
splotched red with broken blood vessels, and blood
dripped from her nose. The other Spears and Blades
had collapsed to the floor.

Alexander told himself to move. If Max took out one
of the remaining ice queens, he could finish the last

one. His arms were heavy. He did not know if he could force himself to swing a sword with enough speed to kill. He let one fall, putting both hands around the hilt of the other and lifting it high, ready to chop.

Max reached the shoulder of one of the ice queens. Slowly, her gun came up. She squeezed the trigger. The sound of the blast pounded through his skull, and her hands jerked up with the recoil. The gun went flying as the ice queen dropped in a shower of blue and white sand. The last one turned. Her face hardened, and her mouth pulled into a gaping rictus. She could have swallowed a melon whole. She lifted her hand, pointing.

No! Alexander surged forward, bringing his sword down with all the strength he could muster. Just as he chopped into the ice queen's neck, Max disappeared.

The noise ceased as the last ice queen fell in a heap of sand. But Alexander hardly noticed. His entire body was wrapped in an agony of loss. Sobs lodged in his chest, the pain too deep, too vast, for release.

He dropped to his knees, reaching blindly for the dust that had been Max. He'd failed. He groped at the stone floor. Nothing. He yanked off the amulet, certain it was interfering with his vision. He scrabbled, looking. No dust. She was—

"I never thought I'd be saying thank you to Scooter, but the bastard saved my ass big-time," she said as she walked through the gaping entrance that used to be the door.

—*alive.*

He lunged to his feet and caught her up in his arms, clamping her tightly against him. She hugged him back with fierce strength. He could not speak. The feeling of desperation and loss still clung to him with such force that he hardly knew how to cope with it.

Max loosened her hold. "Hey, Slick. I missed you, too, but we've got a lot of work left to do tonight."

He took a deep breath, filling himself with the wild, sweet smell of her, then stepped back, forcing himself to let her go. He could not let her know the depth of his feelings. Not here, not now. He did not want to scare her off. She was already too skittish.

Max bent, helping Oak to sit up. He wiped the blood from his face, looking halfway to being a ghost. He was even thinner than before the ice queens had arrived, and his skin was ash gray.

"Everybody still alive?" Max asked.

There were positive replies all around, including from Judith.

"What about Gregory?" Maple asked as she lurched to her feet. Alexander steadied her.

"He's alive," the witch said tiredly. "But I don't know for how much longer. I am nearly depleted."

The others stood slowly, none making a sound. They looked lost. Until now, the need to protect Gregory and Judith and get revenge against the ice queens had driven them and kept their grief and loss at bay. Now they had to face their future, and it was very bleak. They were covenless, and one of the two witches they had left was probably dying. Certainly Judith might have the power to form her own coven eventually—she was triangle-strength, after all—but she was looking like she might blow away in the first good wind.

"Why did they come here? What did they want?" Steel

asked, sounding more like a lost child than a Shadowblade.

"A new home, maybe?" Max said. "A well of power?
Who knows for sure? But you can't stay here. I doubt
they'll stay dead for long. They died way too easily. A
bullet shouldn't have killed them, and probably not
beheading. You need to move on." She glanced down.
"Look."

The piles of sand were starting to shimmer and shift.
Max kicked through them, scattering the grains. She
scraped some salt into the mix. The shimmering movement died. Alexander did not think that would last long.

"Move on? To what? There's nothing left for us. Just
glass statues," Maple said. Weariness hung on her like
a lead coat.

"And two witches," Alexander pointed out. "You
fought to protect them tonight. They still need you."

Maple nodded slowly, then stood straighter. Her lips
trembled and then firmed as she took hold of herself.
She looked at Max and Alexander. "Thank you. You
helped us when you didn't need to. We owe you. *I* owe
you."

"Just don't make it a waste of our time. Get out of
here and survive."

"We will." Strength and purpose were returning to the
other woman. "The least we can do to repay you is give
you a vehicle. I'll take you to one. In the meantime, everybody get together what you need to go. We get on the
road tonight. Oak, gather weapons." She looked at the
twins. "Steel and Flint, pack up Judith and Gregory's
things. Eagle, search the mansion for money and jewelry—anything of value that we can carry. All of you,

collect whatever you can't live without. We won't be coming back."

The others continued to look shell-shocked for a moment longer, then, like her, they pulled themselves together. Alexander was impressed. They were inexperienced and only half-trained, their coven had just been destroyed, and they were exhausted and wounded, but they were not cowards, and they were not going to give up.

Maple led the way back outside and they got inside the pickup truck. Neither Max nor Alexander pointed out that she was hardly in any shape to be out in the night. Healthy Spears could handle the dark for a couple of hours, and Maple was nothing close to healthy. Nor was she a child, and she had a right to make her own choices. She drove them around to the rear of the house. A long, three-sided pole barn provided cover for a line of vehicles, from motorcycles to a couple of RVs.

"Take what you want. The keys are in them," Maple said. "I'd offer you food, but everything we have is tainted."

"The weapons you gave us will be enough, with the car," Max said. She and Alexander had collected several boxes of shells, two bandoliers of grenades and flash bombs, and the two swords.

They got out. Max started to walk away, then stopped, closing her eyes. "I am such a sucker," she murmured with a sigh, then turned. She glared at Alexander. "What are you grinning at?"

"You. Have you ever passed by a stray in need?"

"Horngate lost most of our witches and a lot of our Spears and Blades. We need to rebuild quickly, and these people need a home. It's perfectly reasonable."

"Of course it is," he said sardonically. He could not tear his eyes away from her. It still felt like she could disappear into nothing. He would be having nightmares about that for a while.

Max made a face at him and leaned back through the open window. "Where will you go?"

Maple's expression tightened. "I don't know. We'll figure it out. What about you? Where are you headed?"

"My family is in trouble in Winters," Max said baldly, surprising Alexander with the truth. "We're going to help them."

"Family? Seriously? But you're—how old are you?"

"Old enough to know better. But I want to make you an offer. My covenstead is called Horngate. It's up in Montana." She opened the door and grabbed a pencil and paper off the console. It was an ad for a big arts fair in Ukiah. She turned it over and wrote down Niko's number and directions to Horngate. "If you want a place there, call this number and tell them I sent you. If there's no answer, go to the covenstead. Just you, no one else. Tell them your story, and tell them I sent you."

"Why? Why would you help us again after we kidnapped you?"

"I've got my reasons. If you decide to go, take Highway 101 up north. Don't get mixed up in the magic in the valley."

Maple frowned. "Magic in the valley?"

"You didn't know? Shasta started erupting last night. It's spewing wild magic into the valley and it's very dangerous. Stay out of it."

"We haven't heard anything about it." She hesitated. "But Winters is in the valley."

"If only that was the worst of our problems. Someone attacked the town three days ago."

Maple's eyes widened. "Then you should go. You're losing night."

Max handed her the paper. "Horngate is a good place to go. Better get inside now. You're turning black."

With that, she and Alexander went to select their car. They picked a new Mustang with a light-sealed box built behind the front seats and into the trunk. Alexander got behind the wheel and Max did not argue. They reached the main road and turned east, following the shore of the lake. Neither spoke. Alexander could not help replaying that moment when Max vanished and he thought she had died. The pain of it still pulsed through his body.

He pressed the gas pedal down, squealing around the curve. He glanced at the dashboard clock. It was just past midnight. They still had time to get to Winters and find out what was going on before the sun came up. They still had time to die tonight. Giselle's prophecy had not come true, but there was still Magpie's: *You will be Prime*.

He smothered the thought. He and Max were always going to be looking in the mirror at death. That was what they were made for. He was going to have to learn to deal with it if he wanted to be with her, and there was nothing else in the world he wanted more. He remembered the first part of Magpie's prophecy: *You will have your heart's desire*. That was Max. He knew that now. It had become more than clear when he thought she had died. But how could he have her and still be Prime? If part of a prophecy was true, then it all had to be. He had the amulet. The rest would fall into place whether he liked it or not. It was just a matter of time.

His hands jerked on the wheel and the Mustang fishtailed. He straightened out, forcing himself to concentrate on the road before he wrecked them again.

"Want me to drive, Slick?"

"No," he said curtly.

"Then do you mind staying on the road?"

He did not answer.

"Something bothering you, Slick?"

"None of your business."

"I thought you wanted to be my business."

He grimaced. She had him there, and he sure as hell did not want to destroy the fragile roots of their budding relationship. Neither did he want to tell her about Magpie's prophecy. "I am just hungry," he said finally.

This time it was her turn not to answer. She gave him a long look and then rolled down her window and stared out at the black water of the lake.

They came through Clearlake and stopped at a Taco Bell for food. Just outside of town, Alexander was about to follow the split to Highway 20, when Max stopped him. She had a map open on her lap. "Take 53 south. It will hit Morgan Valley Road, and that will bring us in the back door of Winters."

He did as told and soon they found themselves winding through the foothills leading down to Lake Berryessa, just west of Winters. Max tapped her feet and twisted her fingers together nervously. It was not like her.

"How pathetic is it that I don't know if I'm more wor-

ried that they'll be dead or that they'll still be alive and
pissed at me for pretending I was dead all these years?"
she asked suddenly.

"What if you had told them?" he asked.

She grimaced. "They probably would have tried to
come and rescue me. Even knowing what I'd become.
Especially Tris."

"Giselle would have taken that well."

"The witch-bitch would have killed them, if she
couldn't stop them some other way. Then I would have
killed her, no matter what it took." A flicker of pain
crossed her face and smoothed away. No doubt her
compulsion spells telling her she should never even
think about killing Giselle.

"So in letting the lie that you were dead stand, you
protected your family."

"They won't see it that way. They'll just see that I lied
for years and that I hid from them."

"They will have to get over it. You could not have done
anything different."

She snorted, but did not argue. He started to reach out
and grip her hand, but pulled back. He felt as explosive
as dynamite. One spark—one touch from Max—would
ignite him into a conflagration. This was not the time
or the place.

"Any chance your cell phone is working?" she asked
suddenly.

He handed it to her. Hers had disappeared with
her clothes and weapons in the enchantment around
Shasta. She tried it, then tossed it onto the dash. "Nothing. If we don't make it back, I hope Giselle takes in
everyone I sent her."

"We will make it back," he said.

"You sound awfully certain. You got a crystal ball I don't know about?"

He shook his head. "I have no intention of dying before I get you into bed."

"Oh? Do I get a vote on that?"

"Not anymore," he said, unsmiling. She had told him all she needed to when she told him she wanted him.

"You sound like a caveman."

"If that is what it takes."

She said nothing after that. He drove the next sixty miles as quickly as he dared. The road was winding and narrow, and it was still more than an hour later when they passed the Lake Berryessa dam. As they started a descent toward the valley and Winters, Max sat forward in her seat, staring out the windshield.

The land was dry and rucked up like a blanket, with a sparse sprinkling of trees. They wound through the progressively lower hills, following a river that ran alongside the road.

They came around a bend and Alexander slowed to a stop. Ahead, the way was blocked by a wall of white smoke. It was too thick to see through, and it swirled as if stirred by wind, but maintained a static line across the blacktop. Outside of it, the night was calm. Crickets chirped, and birds called.

Max opened her door and got out. Alexander shut off the car and did the same.

"Where is your family's orchard?"

"Over that ridge and southeast a little ways." Max pointed to the left. "Maybe a couple of miles at most." She walked toward the white wall of smoke. "Smells like woodsmoke. Sweet, though. Like honey and hay, too. Ever seen anything like it?"

He frowned. Something tickled at his memory. He walked closer until he was only a few inches away. He closed his eyes, smelling and tasting the air. Yes— woodsmoke, honey, and hay. Those things for certain. But also— He tilted his head, concentrating. There, under it all. A sift of musky fur and a hint of dry death. He stepped back. "I think—yes, it must be *obake*."

"What is an *obake*?"

"*Obake* are shape-shifters from Japan. They begin as animals or even objects with souls and can transform into human form. Some are ghosts that can transform. This smoke is of the *bakemono*—the ghost variety."

"So what do they want here? Winters doesn't strike me as a top-of-the-list target for the Guardians."

"My guess is territory. Japan is a small place and the Guardians are ridding the world of the human infestation. These *obake* might have been given this place as a reward for their service to the Guardians."

"How do you fight them?"

"Same as most Uncanny creatures. Steel slows them down and cutting them apart kills them. *Obake* are not particularly strong, but they are clever, and they have numbers."

"And this smoke? How dangerous is it?"

"The moment we enter it, they will know where we are. It hides them, and it tells them about their enemies. Breathing it will probably not be healthy."

"How long can someone survive in it?"

He shook his head. "I have no idea."

"So the less we're in it, the better," Max said.

He knew she was wondering how humans could have survived it for three days. But her face was calm and focused, her emotions shoved down where they could not interfere.

She turned around. "Let's go that way." She started up the hill.

"Wait." Alexander went to the car and took out the two swords. He shoved one into the witch chain around his waist and handed the other to Max, who did the same. Next, he grabbed the bandoliers of grenades and extra ammo clips, doling them out between them.

At the top of the hill, they stopped to survey the expanse of smoke that hovered like a low fog for miles. Alexander looked north, putting a hand on her shoulder to draw her attention to the smudge of crimson on the horizon.

"It's close," she said, her jaw knotting as she squinted at it. "We'd better hurry. We've only got a few hours before dawn. We can't wait till tomorrow to escape, or we'll be caught up in the wild magic."

She ran down the slope to the bottom and turned to follow the long V between the ridges. Alexander kept pace with her. They came again to the smoke wall and stopped.

"How far from here?"

"Maybe another half-mile or so. Jim said he thought he saw a thinning near the farmhouse. Let's climb up there and see what there is to see."

She bounded up the hill and scanned the smoke above the orchard. "He's right. See it? Over there—you can see through it a little. Do you see a light?"

A spot of orange flickered and did not disappear. "It could be a fire or a signal."

"Maybe that's for us. Maybe Jim wanted us to know he got through," Max said.

"Either way, it is at the farmhouse, right?"

"Pretty close."

"How far can you jump with that feather?"

She narrowed her eyes thoughtfully.

"With a passenger," he added. "We are going together."

"Never thought otherwise, Slick."

"Right."

She grinned and then shrugged. "No idea. We'll get closer than here, however far it is."

"If we land in the smoke, we will not be able to keep our bearings. The smell and the silence of it will overwhelm our senses. It is what *bakemono* smoke does."

"Won't that be more fun than a barrel of piranhas?"

He unwrapped his witch chain and fastened himself to her, holding his sword in his right hand. "So we do not get separated."

"Let's go, then," she said, and walked back up the ridge a ways. She turned and wrapped her hand around his wrist. He did the same. "Just don't accidentally skewer me with that thing when we land. Ready? On the count of three. Run and jump. One, two, three!"

They lunged forward, running as fast as their Shadowblade magic allowed. Just before the wall of smoke, they leaped into the air. Alexander clamped his hand tight on Max's as he began to fall. She held him equally hard. They rose above the filmy white ocean, heading toward the light.

The milky smoke curled and twisted with phantom

shapes as they drifted above it, slowly sinking. They could not have been more than a hundred yards from the light when they dropped into the smoke.

"Close your eyes," Alexander told Max. "Keep them closed until we get to the farmhouse."

The white curled around them both. It felt like ghostly hands, as well it could have been. Although *bakemono* wraiths could touch, they were not physically dangerous until they took their human form, but they could lead people astray in the smoke and walk them off the edge of a cliff.

Alexander tried to keep himself facing the farmhouse. He jolted as he landed. A moment later, Max settled beside him with a gentle thud. He did not wait, but started off in the direction he remembered, slowly swinging his sword out in front of him to feel his way.

He had held his breath as he entered the smoke, and now he let it out, drawing another. It was cool against his skin, but it burned his nose and down into his lungs. His eyes itched, despite being closed, and his face felt tight, like all the moisture was wicking out of him. Not good. It would be easy to get disoriented and be turned into a dry husk within a few hours. The thought was frightening, given how long Max's family had been submerged in it.

He went as fast as he dared. Voices whispered, and there were growls and yips all around. He fought the urge to open his eyes. Although he had never encountered *bakemono* before, he had heard enough stories to know what not to do. Keeping his eyes shut was crucial to finding his way.

They were in the orchard. Low-hanging cherry limbs

batted him in the face. He kept one arm up to ward them away and swept the sword back and forth before him.

It was becoming harder to breathe. His lungs felt like they were filling with sand. He pulled his shirt up to cover his mouth and nose, but it did no good. The smoke went right through.

He counted his steps. They had been maybe a hundred yards from the light. He was going slowly, so he thought a hundred and fifty steps should put him in the right vicinity.

Something brushed his leg. He kicked out, hitting nothing. A hand pinched his ear. Another slid up his thigh to his stomach. He slapped them away, this time hitting flesh. There was a trill of laughter, sweet and silvery. *Obake* turned into beautiful humans to lure their prey. Another reason to keep his eyes shut.

He kept walking. He felt the tug of Max on the other end of the chain as she, too, knocked away attackers. Her breathing was labored like his own.

At last he thought he had gone far enough. He groped for Max. "I am going to look. You might not be able to trust me after that." He coughed, his tongue so parched he could not swallow. It felt like the sharp spines of a thistle were drilling into the back of his throat. It was nearly a minute before he got himself under control.

He opened his eyes. In front of him was a clear little hollow in the smoke. Inside it stood a trio of beautiful women. They were naked, their bodies curvacious and lush. Their faces were delicate, and their hair cascaded down their backs in riots of red-black curls. *Kitsune*. Fox *obake*. They had to be.

They saw him looking and smiled, sashaying toward him, licking their lips and sliding their hands over themselves erotically as they did. They could not disguise their eyes, though—they were hungry for blood. He smiled as if amazed and delighted and looked past them.

In the near distance, the smoke thinned. He could see the glow of the light. It shimmered and danced like a reflection on water. He was headed slightly in the wrong direction. He needed to shift left. He did, squaring his shoulders to his goal. All he needed to do now was walk straight for another twenty yards.

The three women had reached him now and were rubbing themselves on him like foxes scent-marking their territory. They licked his neck and stroked him through his jeans. They smelled of jasmine and honey.

"What's going on, Slick? Friends of yours?"

Alexander nearly jumped out of his skin as Max spoke. He jerked around, scowling. "You were not supposed to open your eyes. Now, come on. We have to be quick."

He shoved the *kitsune* away and strode on. They screeched and came at him. Their mouths were fanged now, and their fingernails were long and sharp. He knocked them aside as best he could, but did not stop. He did not dare get turned around in a fight. He kept his eyes locked on the light, not daring to look away for even a second. The smoke closed back around him. It was patchy in places, blindingly thick in others. Shapes danced in it, and lights flickered all around. He kept his gaze fixed on the one he had seen first.

The *kitsune* women continued to claw at him. One of them was ripped from his back, and he heard the crashing thud as she was thrown into the air, breaking branches before she landed. The second and third soon followed as Max came to his rescue. More howls and yips sounded, and there was a rustle and snapping twigs signaling dozens of scurrying bodies—maybe more.

"Come on. Hurry!" Three female *kitsune* could not offer much trouble to a Shadowblade, but if fifty or a hundred *obake* swarmed them, the two Blades would be overwhelmed by sheer numbers. It would not be long before they fell under the ravenous tide and were torn to bits.

He broke into a run, Max close on his heels. He stepped on something soft. It screeched, and Alexander fell to the side, losing sight of the light. He thrust to his feet as a flood of furry bodies squirmed and writhed around his legs. Dozens of mouths fastened onto his thighs, calves, and feet, pulling and yanking back and forth. Max was kicking and swearing. He bulled ahead, dragging her after him in the direction he thought he had been going. The smoke was thinner here. It had to be right. He prayed it was right.

The animals—badgers, raccoons, foxes, skunks, squirrels—chased after Max and Alexander. They clambered over one another in a frenzy, raking claws into their prey and snapping at the soft flesh. Something scrabbled up Alexander's back to his shoulder, and Max snatched it away as it fastened onto the flesh at the nape of his neck.

He chopped before him with the sword, shuffling more than running as he sought to keep his feet beneath him. The witch chain jerked and loosened as Max fought her way through. He heard the whine of her sword cutting through the air and the squalls of *obake* in pain.

They kept slogging through the shifting tide of bodies, panting as the smoke petrified their lungs. His head spun with lack of oxygen. How much farther? Alexander could not tell. Then suddenly they crossed a ward line. Fire swept over Alexander's skin and he sprawled into a ditch. The bottom was muddy. He leaped to his feet. Max stood in the mud, the witch chain pulled tight between them. Behind them, *obake* raged at the edge of an impenetrable magic circle.

The air was better here; the smoke wasn't as thick. Convinced the *obake* could not break the ward line, Alexander turned to see where they were.

Behind them was a sprawling white farmhouse surrounded by trees. Behind it were two long white barns. But they weren't what caught his attention. Twenty feet away was a bonfire. It was the light that had guided them. A single figure stood in silhouette before it. He came slowly forward. He was older, in his late sixties or early seventies. His hair was a bleached gray, and his face was angular and tanned, his eyes brown. Lines of exhaustion and worry dug furrows into his face. His gaze was fixed on Max.

"Anne?" he asked in disbelief. "Anne—is that you?"

Alexander frowned in confusion. Max looked stricken. Her clothes were torn from where the *obake* had clawed and chewed on her, and blood smeared the skin of her face and arms. She let the sword fall from her limp fingers.

"Hi, Dad. I'm back."

16

MAX FELT LIKE THE BOTTOM HAD JUST FALLEN out of the world. She'd known she would see her family, and yet nothing had prepared her for that moment when her father first looked at her and saw that she was alive. Thirty years after her supposed death, she was alive and still looked twenty-one years old.

She had seen her father, of course. From a distance, usually around Christmas and again at Tris's birthday in the summer. She had watched him and her mother and everyone else growing up and growing older. He stared at her now, shock making his mouth fall open.

"How? I don't understand," he said finally. "You look like you did—just like the pictures we have of you."

Then his face took on a look of dawning understanding and he said the last thing she ever thought she would hear from him. "You're a witch servant, aren't you? A Shadowblade, right? The ones who can only go out at night?"

It felt like he had punched her in the gut. The breath

went out of her and she couldn't speak. She gaped like an idiot.

"It makes sense. And of course, if you were a Sunspear, you couldn't be here now." He was talking more to himself than to her. He'd always done that. He liked to think out loud.

"How—" She swallowed the dryness in her throat that had more to do with facing him again than with the smoke. "How do you know about Shadowblades and Sunspears? How do you know about witches?"

"Why, I am one. Not all that strong, I admit, but I do all right. Now, Kyle, he's got some real juice."

Kyle. Her brother. The boy she'd never really known. He'd been born right after she left for college. He was thirty-three now, divorced and remarried, with a daughter from the first marriage and two stepsons from the second. And he was a witch. How had she never known that? But she'd watched from afar, never imagining that they were anything but ordinary.

"The witch blood had to come from somewhere," she muttered. Giselle had always told her that the spells that made Max a Shadowblade were made stronger by the few drops of witch blood running through her veins.

She jumped up out of the ditch, all too aware of the blood slicking her skin and her dirty, torn clothes. She fought the urge to smooth her hair and adjust her clothing. There wasn't much point, and a slow anger was starting to burn in her stomach. Why hadn't her father told her what he was? What she was?

"You must serve a witch. What are you doing here?"

"I came to get you, all of you. We heard the *obake* had

attacked here. It's about to get worse. You need to come with us back to Horngate."

"Is Horngate your covenstead?" he asked, scrutinizing her as if he was studying a rare bird.

He had not tried to hug her. That fact was not lost on her. He was treating her like an interesting scientific artifact, not his daughter. She looked around behind him.

"Where is everybody?" she asked, not bothering to answer his question.

"Inside. Everyone is going to be so surprised. That witch—Jim—he said someone was coming to help us. He never said it was you, Anne."

"My name is Max now," she corrected tersely. This was not going the way she'd expected. He was not angry, not resentful. Nor was he all that happy to see her. She remembered him from long ago—the way he would put his arm around her when they walked somewhere, the way he would rub her shoulders when she was studying intently for a test, the way he would always kiss her before she went to bed, even when she was twenty-one and thought herself too old for such sappy crap. But this man—he was more witch than father. And she was more Shadowblade than daughter. That hurt more than she ever thought it could.

She pushed the hurt down, into the cold abyss at her core where she put all things painful. She felt her mask fall into place, emotion smoothing away like sand washed flat and featureless by waves.

"Where is Jim?"

Her father frowned. "He's not doing so well. The smoke has affected him quite a bit, and he has bites that have become infected. Tris has been nursing him."

"Is there anybody else here?"

"Just your mother and me, Kyle and Tris and the kids, and your friend Jim. The hired hands tried to get out the first day. Oh, and, of course, the Leshii."

"Leshii?" Max repeated. Those were . . . she racked her brain, resisting the urge to scrape her hands through her hair. Leshii were forest dwellers from Russia. They were powerful in their own way, tricksters, with a love of trees. Like the *obake*, they could shape-shift, but took the forms of trees or grass. They didn't usually make friends with humans.

Her father nodded. "It's a family group. They've lived on this land for hundreds of years. When we bought it, we made friends with them. They helped our trees, and we did the things they needed. It's worked out quite well."

Max could only stare. Her father and brother were witches and friends with a family of Leshii. What did that make Tris? And her mother?

"We need to get moving," Alexander said, just as her father broke into a hacking cough.

It was a full minute or so before he gained control of himself, and when he did, he wiped off a spatter of blood on his pants leg.

"Smoke is getting to me," he said. "It's getting to everyone."

"It will kill you before long," Alexander said.

Her father narrowed his eyes at the other man. "Who are you?"

"Alexander."

"He's a friend," Max said. "Alexander, this is Peter." She couldn't bring herself now to call him Dad.

The two men exchanged wary nods of greeting, each eyeing the other suspiciously.

"Let's go into the house. Your mother will be over the moon to see you."

Right. Like he clearly was. Max followed him. Alexander fell in beside her.

"Are you all right?"

"Nothing wrong that a case of whiskey wouldn't cure." Not that she could get drunk. Her Shadowblade metabolism made it impossible.

He brushed his fingers over the back of her neck. She bit the inside of her cheek hard, her eyes burning with tears she refused to let go. Her chin lifted. She reached up and caught Alexander's hand, squeezing it once before letting go. His gentle touch threatened to shatter the armored walls protecting her emotions, walls she needed more than ever now.

The house was old, built at least a hundred years ago, if not more. It was three stories, with additions around the outside, dozens of gables, and a couple of turrets. A broad porch ran around three-quarters of it. Benches swung from the overhang, and a table and chairs were set up outside a pair of French doors. Inside the house and up close, she could smell the Divine magic in her father that the smoke and *obake* scents had obscured.

A long living room took up the front of the house. It was cozy, with hardwood floors, plush throw rugs, couches, and a flat-screen TV. The dining room was off to one side. A short hallway led to the kitchen, branching off to go upstairs and farther back into the house. Smoke hazed the rooms, despite the fact that the windows were closed tight. The air was stuffy.

Her father pushed open the swinging kitchen door. It was a modern room, with a large kitchen at one end and a family dining area at the other.

"Look who I found outside," her father announced dramatically, stepping to the side and making a flourishing motion at Max. "It's Anne."

"Max," she corrected automatically, stopping just inside the doorway. Alexander was just behind her, his chest warm against her back.

"Hello, everyone," she said, scanning the faces. She saw Kyle sitting at the table, his stepsons playing video games by the window. Beside him was Tris. Her mouth hung open in shock. Like Max, her hair was blond, though darker, more gold than Max's silver-white. It was graying now. She was slender and soft around the stomach. Her face was tanned and lined, and crow's-feet fanned out from her eyes. She stood, her wooden chair rumbling back across the tile floor.

"Anne? How can it be? You're dead. You died thirty years ago." Tears ran down her cheeks, and her chin crumpled.

Her husband, Paul, slid his arm around her, looking at Max with both curiosity and fear. Their youngest daughter, sixteen-year-old Sharon, stood behind him, staring at Max with wide eyes. She had Paul's black hair. The other one, Tory, was standing in the middle of the kitchen holding a cup of coffee. She was nineteen, with long blond hair. Beside her was Max's mother. She was tall, with broad shoulders and thick thighs. Her red hair had gone gray, and she wore it clipped short. She held a full coffeepot, several empty cups hooked on her fingers.

"Anne?" she said, the color bleaching from her face. She slowly went to the counter and set the coffee and mugs down with a sharp clatter. "Where . . . how?"

"Hey, Mom." Max's throat was knotted so tight she could hardly breathe. Her eyes burned hot with tears. She blinked them back.

"I don't understand," her mother whispered. "You're dead—murdered. The police found blood." She swallowed hard, one hand pressing against her throat. "So much of it. Like your body had been emptied. They said there was no chance you could have survived."

"She's a Shadowblade," her father declared confidently.

"A what?" Tris asked, her voice cracking. She'd stood up and was clinging white-fingered to her husband's arm.

"A witch turned her into a superwarrior of the night. She has superstrength and superhearing, but she can't go out in the day or she'll be burned alive."

Tris's eyes widened and her hand covered her mouth.

"Is that true?" Max's mother asked.

"It is," Max said, not missing the fact that her mother wasn't particularly startled by the notion of witches. Tris wasn't, either. Peter and Kyle were both witches. After forty years or so, there was a good chance they'd figure it out.

A tremor quaked through Max. Her father and her brother were witches. She was no less stunned by that fact than they must be to see her still alive. How had she not known? There was a ward shield around the house. She should have noticed that. But then, she had never come very close in case she was seen.

But Giselle had known.

The realization sent a jolt down to the bottoms of her feet, and anger whirled white-hot inside her. Everyone in the room blanched and stepped away as the power of her Prime filled the room with deadly rage. Kyle's boys hunched down, staring in fright.

She couldn't pull back her Prime or douse the storm that roared through her. She shifted, facing her father. He alone didn't look frightened. He looked more like a kid in a candy store. Max's lips curled as she bared her teeth. "You knew Giselle was a witch, didn't you?" she asked softly. "She was my roommate for more than two years. There's no way you didn't know."

He nodded. "Witches recognize each other."

"It didn't occur to you to warn me?" she asked, speaking each word slowly. She wanted to scream them.

"Warn you? What for? Oh!"

She watched as realization hit. There was a flicker of guilt in his dark eyes, so like her own.

"*She* turned you? But she was just a college girl."

Max ground her teeth together. "She was—is—a whole lot more than that."

"But she came to see us," her mother protested, stepping forward to stand beside her father. As if they were teaming up against her.

Hurt slashed through Max. She held herself still, though she felt like she was bleeding to death. "Giselle came to see you? When?"

"Many times. She was so sympathetic . . ." Her mother trailed away, pressing her fingers over her trembling lips.

"I swear, I will fucking kill her this time for sure," Max gritted. Instantly, her compulsion spells seized tight. She doubled over, feeling like her flesh was being peeled from her bones. She squeezed her eyes shut and bit back on her cries of agony. She didn't give in to the pain. She *would* kill Giselle, slowly, and enjoy every single second of it. Her body spasmed, and she sagged to her knees. She wrapped her arms around herself and tipped forward until her forehead rested against the oak floor. Her lungs felt full of ground glass; she could barely breathe.

"What's happening?" Tris demanded.

"Compulsion spells," Alexander said grimly. "It is what happens when a witch binds you and you break the rules."

His hands slid under Max's arms, and he picked her up gently, pulling her against his chest.

"You have to stop," he whispered, his hands rubbing her back. "You have every right to hate her, but this will not help you or your family. We have to get them out of here. That's why we came. Let it go. For now."

She convulsed as the spasms in her muscles increased.

"Max!" Alexander's voice was sharp and commanding. "Pull yourself together. You have work to do."

He was right. She knew it. She had to let it go. Giselle's further lies and betrayal didn't change anything about the danger of the *obake* or the spread of the wild magic from Shasta.

It took everything she had to push her hatred deep down inside where she didn't have to feel it. She began to relax as the hate was replaced by cool purpose. She pushed herself out of Alexander's arms.

"Thanks."

"If you want, I will cut her throat for you." His mouth was white-rimmed with fury and his eyes were icy.

"No need."

He nodded. "The offer stands."

"Thanks. But you're trying to get her to like you, remember?"

"I do not give a fuck."

She gave him a slow smile before turning back to her family. It was good to have someone in her corner.

"Are you . . . okay?" her mother asked, looking nervous, as if she didn't know whether she should offer to hug Max or run to the hills. "That looked—"

"I'll be fine," Max said shortly.

"I still don't understand," Tris said. "What about the blood the police found?" Her face was blotched red, and her jaw thrust out. She was pissed and afraid. Max could smell her fear. "It was yours. They tested it."

Max shrugged. "It was better for you if you thought I was dead."

"Better for us? Better for us?" Tris's voice was shrill. "How could it be better? God, I don't think I ever recovered from losing you. Do you know what it's like to think your sister was murdered? I loved you so much, and you were alive this whole time! Now you're standing there like the day you disappeared, acting like it didn't matter to you at all. Was it that great? Becoming this thing you've become? Why did you do it? To stay young? Is that it? You traded us for *that*?" she asked scathingly.

Her words hit like bullets. Max's fury reared up and words spilled from her in a torrent. "Did you see what just happened to me?" she spat. "Do you think that was fun? That I wanted that? If you do, then you are stupider than you look. I never wanted to be a Shadow-blade. But once I was turned, there was no going back. I stayed away because of you. All of you were better off if I was dead."

"Better off?" her mother asked. She had her arms wrapped around herself, and tears rolled down her cheeks. Max's father slipped his arm around her.

Max whirled on her. "Have you seen what's happening out there? The monsters in the smoke? The ones that want to eat you alive? They're maybe a three on the scale of scary shit I have to deal with every day. Did you want me bringing my new friends around at Christmas or Thanksgiving? Maybe for the Fourth of July we could put on a real show. Of course, if I'd had warning, I could have protected myself, but no one told me my best friend was a witch, did they? Or that witchcraft runs in the family."

She glared at her father, who, for the first time, looked a little shamefaced.

Max looked away and took a breath. She was wasting time. "Where's Jim?"

"In here," her mother said, and led Max through another door into a TV room. Jim lay on the couch inside a sleeping bag piled with blankets. He was shaking. His eyes were red-rimmed and his skin was sallow. He lifted a hand in greeting as Max came to crouch beside him.

"'Bout time you showed up. Thought you said you'd be here by dawn yesterday." He coughed, his throat sounding raw.

She waited until he was done.

"Are you going to be okay?"

He shrugged and snugged the sleeping bag tighter

around himself. His lips were blue, his chin speckled with blood from his coughing. "You know me. One foot in the grave most of my life. No point changing now."

She frowned. "How bad is it?"

He coughed again, and the sleeping bag and blankets pushed down. Bruises patterned the skin of his chest. She covered him again as his cough subsided. He drew a ragged breath, wiping his mouth and looking at the blood on his fingers.

"I got attacked coming in. Pretty sure I'm done for."

"The hell you are," Max said softly, brushing her fingers over his forehead. He was a seedy little man, with receding brown hair, a narrow chin boasting a scraggly beard, and a wicked sense of humor. "I'm going to get us out of here. Tonight. We'll find you someone to help."

"Gone too far, babe. I'm already gone, my body just hasn't agreed yet. Can't feel my legs. Cold. Coughing blood. I'm toast."

"Not if I can help it," she said, rising to her feet.

He smiled and took her hand in his weak grip. "Take care of yourself. Get your family out safe."

Her hand clamped around his. "You should have waited for me, dammit."

"The shield ward wouldn't have held long enough. Needed extra juice."

She nodded, a tear sliding down her cheek despite herself. She brushed it away. "Thanks. I owe you."

"Lucky you won't have to pay me back. Besides, I owed you big for what you did in Arizona. Consider us even." He began to cough again.

Alexander handed her a glass of water. She looked at him, startled. She nodded thanks.

"Here," she said to Jim, holding the cool liquid to his lips. He sipped and then pulled away, lying back on his pillows.

"I'll be fine. Go get to work."

She nodded. She felt she might snap apart at any moment. "I'll be back for you."

"See you when I see you," he said, and closed his eyes.

Max turned and brushed past Alexander, unable to take the pity in his eyes without completely losing it.

She stepped back into the kitchen and several hushed discussions fell silent.

"I don't know what Jim told you or what you've figured out, but here are the high points so I know we're all on the same page. Right now, we're surrounded by smoke, and it's full of shape-shifters that want us all dead."

Kyle and her father nodded.

"Jim told us they were shape-shifters," her father said.

"What do they want?" her brother asked. He was tall and angular, with the same pale hair as Max. He wore it in a short, military-style cut.

"Your land," Alexander said. He was leaning against the doorjamb, arms crossed, looking deceptively calm. He wasn't. "You might have been spared, but you practice the craft outside of a coven—right?"

Kyle and Max's father nodded, frowning at Alexander.

"That's right. We're solitary practitioners, for the most part," her father said.

"The Guardians don't know you exist. So your land and your lives are fair game. If they'd known about you, they probably would have tried to recruit you for their war," Alexander said.

"The Guardians?" Tory repeated.

She looked like Tris had at the same age, with long wheat-colored hair, a slender body with curves in all the right places, and a defiant curl to her lip, like she wasn't going to let anyone push her around. Exactly like Tris. She was looking at Alexander as if he was dessert. Max suppressed a sudden urge to warn the girl off.

"What war?"

"The Guardians oversee the magical world. They decided that humanity has done too much to harm magic. So they've ordered a war to cull most of humanity and bring magic back as a force in the world. Chances are they gave this land to the *obake* and the *bakemono* in exchange for helping them," Max explained. "This isn't the only place they're attacking. That's why I have to take you back to Horngate. You'll be safer there."

"That's your covenstead?" Kyle asked.

He looked eager, as did her father. The palm of Max's hand itched to slap them. This wasn't a game. People could die.

"It is. So I suggest you gather what you can't live without and only what you can carry, and get ready to go," she said curtly.

"How?" Kyle asked.

"That's what we need to figure out. You, me, Alexander, and . . . Peter," she said. Calling her father by his first name felt awkward and weird, but she couldn't call him Dad, either. He was a stranger now, just like the rest of them. They were afraid of her and of what she'd become. She couldn't blame them. But it hurt. More than she was willing to contemplate. She refused to let herself think about it.

Her father bustled everyone out of the kitchen. Her mother lingered, staring at Max.

"You look the same," she said finally.

"I'm not," Max said. It came out more harshly than she intended, but she was having a hard time managing her emotions.

"I see that." Her mother lifted her chin. "We missed you. Very much."

Max nodded. "I missed you, too." *So much*. But being here now, she realized she had missed something that never really existed. Her parents weren't who she thought they were.

"I want to hear about your life. If you will tell me. When we are safe."

Her voice was tentative, but she was reaching out. It wasn't the homecoming Max had dreamed of, but it was something. Not that Max could tell her much; there was too much her mother could never understand.

"Sure," she said. "When we're safe." But she hadn't been safe in thirty years.

Her mother left, and Max turned to her father, who was watching her and Alexander with sharp curiosity.

"What are you capable of?" Max asked abruptly, not bothering with manners. She was too pissed off. "Did you make the shield wards out there?"

Her father shook his head regretfully. "I'm a minor witch. Hedgewitch is what I'd be called in the old days. I can do small things, but I hired someone to make that ward line."

"And you?" she asked Kyle.

"I've got some power. Tell me what you need."

Max rubbed a hand over her mouth. The fastest way

to Horngate was to go back through Winters to get to the freeway. But the smoke would certainly kill Jim and probably everyone else. If the shape-shifters didn't get them first.

The only other way out was to take the road through the smoke, back to where she and Alexander had left their car. Hopefully they'd be able to outrun the *obake* and not get lost. It was shorter, but left them on the wrong side of Winters. They'd have to run for the coast and hope they got there before the crimson wind trapped them in the valley.

"Those are our two choices," she said, explaining her thinking. "Unless one of you has a better idea."

No one did.

"What about these Leshii friends of yours?" Max asked her father. "Will they help at all?"

He gave an embarrassed shrug. "They keep to themselves mostly. I tried to talk to them when the smoke descended, but they shape-shifted into grass and trees, and that was it."

"They are in as much danger as we are," Alexander said. "So long as the ward line holds, they will be safe enough, unless the smoke bothers them. But once it breaks, and undoubtedly it will, even if the Guardians have to send someone to smash it, then the *obake* will find the Leshii and kill them."

She stood up. "I'm going to talk to them. Can you show me where?"

"I will." Kyle stood.

She looked at Alexander. "Go see what we're working with for vehicles." She looked at her father. "And weapons. Anything you've got."

She headed for the front door. As she went through the living room, she noticed a picture of herself on the mantel. It had been taken on a trip to the ocean when she was nineteen. She was hugging Tris in the water. Both girls looked happy. She looked away. She wasn't that girl anymore, and neither was Tris. Nothing was the same.

She strode outside, letting herself flatten beneath the rising Shadowblade Prime. Human cares did not matter to the Blade, only war and killing.

"What the hell is that?" Kyle backed away from her.

"It's what I am. What I really am."

"But you're—"

She smiled, toothy and dangerous. "Fucking scary? I'm supposed to be. Show me the Leshii."

He led the way around the house and past the barns. He coughed frequently as the smoke chewed on his lungs. On the other side was a vegetable garden, the lush leaves wilted and curling black. At the far end was a compost heap, taller than Max was and grown over with wild garden plants. All around was thigh-high grass, and there was a single gnarled cherry tree.

"That's the father. Careful where you step. Somewhere around here in the grass are the mother and children and a couple of aunts or uncles." Kyle stayed at the foot of the garden while Max approached the Leshii tree. Her Shadowblade senses roamed over the grass, and she heard the muffled sounds of insects as they burrowed downward to escape the smoke.

She could feel the Leshii in the grass. In this form, she could pluck them and kill them as easily as stepping on a spider. She touched one, then another, then all five, brushing her fingers lightly over each stem. Then she stood before the tree.

"If I can find you all, the *obake* can, too. You aren't safe here. Sooner or later, the ward line will break. The Guardians won't let this place stand, not when they've decided to conquer it."

The tree shivered like it had been struck with an ax, then the lines of it blurred and pulled inward, shrinking into itself until the father Leshii stood before her. He was only three and a half feet tall, with an ancient face and green eyes the color of a summer pond. His skin was as pale as grass that's never seen the light of day, and the strands of his hair and beard fell about his head like willow twigs.

"Where is to go?" His voice was dry and earthy. "This is home for long time."

"Time to find a new one. I've got a place you can go, with trees and water and few humans. But we'll need your help to get out of the smoke."

"New home?" He considered, closing his eyes and tipping his head back.

Max waited. You didn't hurry fairies. One of the tall grasses lengthened and turned into a female Leshii. She looked like her husband, but without the beard. Her hair was fernlike.

She looked at Max, studying her. "We go," she said finally. "What must be done for you to help?"

"We need you to help us find our way through the smoke when we leave."

"No protection?"

Max looked at the two Leshii children and the two aunt Leshiis. The children had short, mosslike hair with tiny star-shaped flowers. The elders looked much like the mother.

"Keep your strength for yourselves. We'll help you all we can."

The father tipped his head, eyeing her. It was a measuring look, the same his wife had given her. "You ask for little."

"I'll ask for more if I need it."

"And we do not give?"

"Then we might not make it to safety. But it's your choice." She did not want to force them or make demands. She needed their help, and they needed hers.

"You promise much."

Clearly he was suspicious. She didn't ask for enough to warrant helping them get out of there and providing a new home. He didn't understand. There was a tit-for-tat notion of life in the Uncanny and Divine world. You didn't put yourself in the position of owing anybody anything. You paid as you went, or you were sorry for it later when the bill came and it was more than you expected or wanted to pay.

Max crouched down to eye level. "I've asked what's fair to ask," she said. "I promise you a place to live, but only if we all get out of here alive. So you have to give first. I'm asking you to make a leap of faith on the word of a stranger. That's a lot for you to give, as far as I'm concerned. I will ask for more if I need it. But right now, what I need most is eyes through the smoke. You protect your family. They are the whole reason you are trusting me, and if anything happens to them, then what's the point?"

The Leshii father put his hands on her face. They

were surprisingly soft and long, looking more like roots than fingers. He stared deep into her eyes. Finally, he nodded. "Agree."

Max rose to her feet. "We'll leave soon. Out the front gate. I'll meet you there."

She returned to Kyle and walked back to the house.

"They wouldn't hardly talk to us. Just to make the deal that we would let them be and they would help the orchard." He sounded slightly awestruck. "They wouldn't say anything when the smoke hit."

Max shrugged. "I had something to say they wanted to hear. And I'm scarier than you are."

"I'm a witch," he protested, sounding like a ten-year-old defending his honor.

Max smiled to herself. "You're a witch," she agreed. "But not a particularly frightening one. That's not a bad thing, if you ask me. But I was made to kill and I'm pretty good at it. That makes me a threat the Leshii can't ignore."

"Threats can't be all they respond to," he said dubiously, and once again broke into a cough. When he pulled his hand from his mouth, it was spattered with blood.

"I don't know about that. The world of the Uncanny and Divine is a world of danger, of give and take, kill or be killed. You don't make a lot of friends."

"Sounds lonely."

She shrugged, thinking of Niko and Tyler and Oz and the rest of her fellow Blades and Spears. And Alexander. For so long, it had been terribly lonely. And now—

She stopped dead. Family. They were her family more so even than her own parents and Tris and Kyle, who were strangers to Max.

"Is something wrong?"

She shook her head. "No. Nothing's wrong." She kept walking.

Tris was waiting on the porch. She paced, her arms crossed tightly over her chest. She turned as Kyle and Max approached through the acrid smoke.

"I want to talk to you," she told Max. Her voice was raspy from the smoke, and her breath rattled in her lungs.

"I'll go get ready," Kyle said, taking the hint that he wasn't welcome in this conversation.

Max stepped up onto the porch and leaned against the rail. "Whatever it is, keep it short. We don't have a lot of time." But it hurt, looking at Tris and seeing only anger.

"That was a great show in there, you know that? All the writhing about on the floor like you were in agony. Really convincing. But you lied. Dad said you have to want to become a Shadowblade; no one can make you do it."

"Technically, that's true," Max agreed. Her heart pounded against her ribs. This was so much harder than she'd thought it would be.

"So what the hell kind of a game are you playing? Why all the drama? Why not just admit you wanted to be—" Tris gestured stiffly with her hand, still clutching her elbows tight against herself. "Whatever you are."

Max bit her lips hard. "There's no game and I wasn't putting on a show. If I so much as think of trying to hurt Giselle, my compulsion spells punish me."

"Then why? If it's that bad, why did you do it? Just to be forever young? Were you that stupid?"

"Very stupid," Max conceded, her stomach churning. "But I didn't know what I was agreeing to. Not really."

Tris stopped and stared. "You're saying this was, what, an accident?"

Max ran her fingers through her hair. "I was drunk," she admitted. "She asked the questions then. Would I like to live forever? Would I like to never grow old? Would I like to be superhumanly strong? I thought she was joking, so I said sure. That was all it took. I woke up a month later, and I wasn't human anymore. I was this." She waved a hand at herself. "And so long as I promised to stay away from you, she promised she wouldn't have all of you killed."

That caught Tris up short. She covered her mouth with her hands. "Killed?" she whispered. "Giselle? But she couldn't mean it. She visited us. She wept for you."

"She meant every word."

"And there's no way out? No way to undo this? What if Dad and Kyle helped you?"

Max shook her head. "No. But, Tris, this is who I am, and I wouldn't go back now. Not even if I could. I'm—" She was going to say . . . *happy*. Holy mother of fuck— was it possible? In thirty years, she'd never been happy, never imagined it was even possible. But somehow it had sneaked up on her. Part of it was her ties to everyone at Horngate. So close she considered them family. Part of it was Alexander. Part of it was her strength and knowing that she could make a difference—protect the people she cared about.

"You like being a—" Tris motioned at Max's clothes.

Max looked down. Her clothes were shredded and she was covered in blood, hers and the *obake*'s. "If I wasn't a Shadowblade, then nobody would be here to help you now," she said, lifting her gaze to her sister.

"But still—"

"But nothing. I am what I am, and I like it. I might hate Giselle and the fact that she owns me, but the rest is good. " She was surprised at how much she meant it. "Now, c'mon, little sister. We've got to get out of here before the sun comes up and I fry."

"Would you really?"

Max snapped her fingers. "Poof. Me and Alexander both."

"Oh, my God. You can't go to the beach or watch the sunset?"

It was always the silly things people fixed on in a crisis. "No. But we can talk about it later. Go make sure your girls are ready."

Tris looked at her a long moment, as if she wanted to say something else, then went inside. Max sighed and rubbed her chest. The smoke was still eating at her lungs. They had to get out of here fast.

"How are you doing?"

Alexander stepped up onto the porch and leaned against the rail beside her. She'd been aware of him for a few minutes. She looked at him.

"I'll live. But I always do."

He brushed his knuckles down her cheek, and she leaned into his touch, her throat knotting with pain she didn't want to think about.

"It will get better."

"Maybe. But I'm not my parents' daughter anymore, and I don't know if any of them can get around that."

"You will have time to figure it out."

She shrugged. Maybe. She stood up straight. "We'd better go. What kinds of vehicles did you find?"

He stood and slid his hands delicately around her neck. She almost whimpered at the gentleness of his touch. It was so very opposite to the way she was feeling. He bent and brushed his lips against hers, and warming heat poured through her. He ran his hands down to her shoulders as he pulled away. She licked her lips, wanting more than a brief taste of him. He watched her, his eyes flaring. He stepped back, letting go.

"Just remember, I am not going anywhere," he said, still watching her lips. "And if you ever try to hide from me, I will not believe you are dead. I will find you. Count on it."

She stared at him. He meant it. And more than that. There was a promise under those words that made her stomach twist with both fear and longing. She licked her lips again, all too aware of the effect it was having on him and liking it a whole lot.

"You'd better," she said finally. "Don't let me down, Slick."

17

ALEXANDER HAD FOUND A PAIR OF PICKUP TRUCKS and a stock trailer. "There are a couple of little cars and an old Suburban. The gas tank is about empty on that one, and the *obake* would overrun the other two," he told Max.

She was wound so tight he was afraid she was near to snapping. She was holding herself under tight control, but he could feel her emotions churning. There was little he could do for her except watch her back.

She nodded. "We'll take just one truck and the trailer. Peter can drive and we'll put everyone else inside the trailer. The windows are small and the back is closed. That will keep the *obake* from being able to swarm them. They'll have to fight off the *bakemono*. Nothing will keep them out." The smoke creatures could slide inside a crack and shift into a flesh shape to attack.

"Are they up to it?"

"They'll have to be. Kyle can ride with them. I don't know if he knows how to use his magic to kill, but he'll have to learn fast. You'll ride on the running boards and try to keep Peter alive, and I'll protect the Leshii."

It was not a good plan, but he had nothing better to offer.

Max went back to the house to fetch her family, and he went back to the barn and found several lengths of chain. He had already filled the back of the truck with all the tools he could find that might serve as weapons. He returned to the trailer and hooked the chain up inside so that it could be locked from within.

A few minutes later, Max returned, leading her family. They were carrying an assortment of kitchen knives, rifles, and handguns. Max's face was flat and cold. It made his stomach drop.

Her mother had her arms wrapped around the two teenage boys, her face pinched. Tris was holding a butcher knife and an aluminum bat and looking terrified. Kyle and Peter were caught between excitement and fear, as if they were about to get on a roller coaster. Tris's two girls brought up the rear, carrying golf clubs and pulling small suitcases.

Alexander ignored them, going to Max, putting his hands on her arms, and holding her gently. He ignored the stares of her family.

"What happened?"

"Jim. He's dead. Coughed up a bunch of blood and then—"

She tried to pull away.

He tightened his grip. "I am sorry." He pulled her roughly against his chest, hugging her tightly. "He died well."

"He died because of me. He shouldn't have been here at all."

"He made his own choice. It is what friends do," he said against her hair.

For a moment, he felt her clutch him tight. Then she twisted away. "Let's get this over with."

She turned. "Everyone, remember what I told you. As soon as we cross the ward line, we'll be under attack. If I'm right and we're the only humans left alive in Winters, then there's likely to be quite a swarm of *obake* waiting. Be ready to kill them; they certainly won't hesitate to kill you."

She looked at her father. "Peter, you're driving. Alexander is going to guard you. He's going to kill everything that comes at you. The Leshii and I are going to lead the way. You won't be able to see much, maybe not even at all, which is going to make guiding you a bitch. But that's not the only problem. The smoke is going to try to trick you. It's going to give you illusions. You need to ignore them. Listen to Alexander and steer. If we get stuck in the smoke, we're dead. Are you going to be able to do that?"

Her father's childish excitement faded and he sobered. "I'll do it. How am I supposed to stay on the road if I can't see anything?"

"I'm still working the signals out," she said. "Get in."

He went to get into the front seat. Alexander motioned the others to get into the stock trailer. It was clean but for wisps of hay. The floor was wood and the sides were steel. Small sliding windows lined the upper half on both sides, with larger windows at the back. They were already closed and secured with twists of wire.

"Careful," he said before shutting the door. "The smoke will get thick in here. The *bakemono* can cast illusions. Make sure you know where everyone is before you attack. You are safe until they take human form. Then do not hesitate. You cannot have mercy, and you cannot hold back. They will kill you if you do not kill them first. Remember, they are no stronger than ordinary humans and will die easily enough."

They stared with eyes full of horrified denial. Four teenagers, a mother and grandmother, and a witch with untried power and skill. Alexander grimaced and hoped they would have the stomach to do what they had to do.

"Chain the door when I shut it. Good luck."

He swung the door closed and listened as the chain rattled and the lock snicked into place. He hoped they would do what was necessary to save themselves. Max and he could only do so much.

Alexander rattled the door to be sure it was secure, then returned to Max. The Leshii had appeared and now gathered around her. Max looked at the father. "I know you don't like metal, but I think your family is safer in the back of the truck."

He looked past her and then back and shook his head. "No harm to us from them."

He said "them" like he was talking about maggots. Alexander smiled and hoped the creature was not overconfident.

"Then that just leaves the problem of guiding the truck. The Leshii will have to guide Peter with their voices. Luckily, it is not far. Once we get to the main road, it is not even a mile to where we left the car," he said.

"A mile is a hell of a long way when everybody's out to kill you," she said.

"Should be exciting, then."

She grinned. "No doubt about it."

Max unwound the witch chain from her waist and laid her sword on the hood. She fastened the chain to the grille on the passenger side. Alexander did the same, threading his through two holes he punched in the driver door with his sword. Tethered to the truck, they could not get lost in the smoke.

"Ready?" Max asked.

Peter nodded. Sweat rolled down his forehead. His face was tense. Good. He was finally figuring out that this was no game. He turned his head to look at Alexander.

"I love my daughter. I never meant to hurt her. I never in a million years would have thought Giselle could do something like this. She was always such a sweet girl and I thought she was like me—a hedgewitch. Nothing more. I would have warned Anne—Max—if I had thought she was in danger." He faced the windshield again. "Tell her that for me, in case."

"I will," Alexander said. "We should go."

Max's father took a slow breath and nodded. "Right." He twisted the key and the truck rumbled to life.

"Nice and slow," Alexander reminded him, stepping up onto the running board.

The truck rolled forward, following Max and the Leshii. The two elder aunts held the hands of the children, and the parents walked just ahead. Pale green magic limned them all. Max walked to their right.

As if feeling Alexander's eyes on her, she turned. "Try not to get killed."

"Are you saying you would miss me?"

"Yeah, Slick. That's what I'm saying. You're like a boil on my ass that I've gotten used to."

"That is so sweet. Like a Hallmark card from hell."

She laughed. "I do like you, Slick."

"It is a start."

They had reached the entrance of the orchard, where the driveway cut through to the main road. The ward line glowed faintly against the wall of white smoke.

"Ready?" Alexander asked Peter.

The other man nodded jerkily, his jaw flexing and his hands knotting on the steering wheel as he stared ahead of him.

Alexander held his sword ready, counting again the number of grenades in his bandolier. There were four. And six flash bombs, all given to him by Maple when they'd left the dead covenstead. He doubted the latter would do much good against the *obake*, but he would not count them out yet.

Max looked over her shoulder and nodded at him. Just then, she stiffened, lifting her head as if smelling something. Alexander did the same. Diesel fumes and smoke overwhelmed his senses, but then he caught a whiff of something else. He put a hand on Peter's shoulder.

"Stop."

The truck jerked to a halt. "What's wrong?" Peter demanded hoarsely.

"Maybe something is right. Hold on."

Alexander unfastened his witch chain as Max did the same. He bounded over the hood to join her. She prowled back toward the house and he headed out to the left. He found the scent trail and followed it. Max veered to join him. They went around the side of the house on silent feet, approaching the intruders from behind.

"What in the hell are you doing here?" Max demanded.

Ivy, Oak, and Steel jumped guiltily and spun around. They were covered with blood, their clothes torn. The wounds they had suffered were healing, and they looked a lot better than they had.

"We thought you might need some help," Ivy said, flushing to the roots of her hair.

Max stared stony-eyed. "You're supposed to be on your way north."

Ivy lifted a shoulder in a defiant half-shrug, but did not answer.

"How did you even find us here?" Max demanded.

"Steel. He can find anything anywhere. It's one of his talents."

Alexander eyed the blond Blade appraisingly. He was one of the twins. He looked far less shy and diffident than before. Now he prowled about, sensing and searching.

"Where are the others?" Max asked.

"By your car. Waiting for us in the RV."

"Shit. Holy mother of fucking night." Max scraped her fingers through her hair. "What were you thinking? Have you seen what's coming down the valley? And you left your witches out there hanging?"

Again Ivy gave that shrug, but her expression was tenacious. "We owe you."

"Are you saying you don't need help?" Oak asked. His arms were crossed, and he stood hipshot, his brows raised, his chin outthrust.

"No, dumbshit. I'm saying you are too stupid for words," Max snapped. "All right. You're here. Let's get going."

"Can he find his way back to the cars on the road?" Alexander asked, still watching Steel.

Ivy nodded. "He's amazing. Plus Flint is back there. Because they are twins, they always know where the other one is. As good as GPS."

Alexander glanced at Max. "Put him in the truck with your father, and we do not have to have the Leshii."

Her lip curled in an animal snarl. "I'm not leaving them. I promised them a place to go."

"Of course not, but it means we can find our way without their help. We can go faster."

She gave a sharp nod and stalked away. Ivy hurried after, and Steel wound back and forth behind like a hunting dog. Oak fell in beside Alexander.

"How come you're both Blade Primes?" he asked suddenly. "I've been wondering since we found you."

"It is a long story."

"But you work together?"

"She is Prime. I am one of her Blades." Or he hoped to be. That was still to be determined.

You will be Prime.

Not a fucking chance.

"Never heard of a Prime serving under another Prime."

"And you have heard of everything, right?" Alexander's temper was rising.

Oak ducked his head and eased away, abashed. "No offense meant." Then, "Are you guys really going to let us stay at your coven?"

Is this all a trap? was the underlying question. That he had the balls to ask in the face of an angry Prime showed he was not a coward.

"Depends on you and your witches. Helping us will not hurt."

"That's what Maple said. That, and we all agreed we owe you. Bad karma to show up at the covenstead when we could've stayed and helped you."

"We are glad for the help."

Oak looked at Max and grimaced. "I could tell."

"She is letting you walk behind her. It means something."

The other man looked taken aback and then nodded slowly. "Our Prime was not given to thinking a lot about fighting. Patricia wasn't that kind of witch."

"I did not know there was any other kind."

"She liked to grow things. She was an artist, too. All the coven were. She didn't go looking for trouble. That's why it was a full coven even though she wasn't all that strong. She was good to us."

He face tightened with grief, surprising Alexander. He hadn't thought Oak was capable of anything besides anger.

Max reached the truck with Ivy and Steel.

"Get in the cab with Peter," she told the blond Blade, and turned to the Leshii. "We can go faster now without your help. You've got to ride. Can you do that?"

The father looked up at her. "We made bargain."

"We did, and I will stick to my end of it. But we have someone to guide us faster than you can, which means fewer chances for the rest of us to die. So you need to ride."

"In iron box." His voice was thick with distaste.

"I'm afraid so. It won't be long."

"Will hurt."

"I know." She waited.

Asking them to ride inside the trailer was a lot. Alexander knew she did not want them in the back of the truck. She would put Ivy and Oak there to keep any *obake* from breaking through the back window and attacking her father and Steel. That left no room for the Leshii.

The father looked at the truck and the trailer, then motioned for his family to follow. Max and Alexander followed to let the family inside. But the Leshii stopped at the front of the trailer. Then the mother climbed up the front of it. From her hands extended small tendrils that clung to the metal. She clambered up and reached down, and now her arms lengthened, turning into long, snakelike vines. She wrapped the two children and lifted them. Then the aunts and father followed her up. They sat on the top in a diamond shape, with the father and mother in front and back, the two aunts on the sides, and the children in the middle. After a moment, a green bubble of light rose around them.

Then, to Alexander's surprise, it pushed out, enveloping most of the trailer. The father looked down at Max. "Bargain?"

Never take a favor when you do not know the cost.

She nodded. "Yes."

As he expected, she appointed Ivy and Oak to the bed of the truck. Alexander took up his position again, fastening himself with the witch chain. Max took the passenger-side running board, punching holes in the door to anchor her chain.

"Still won't go fast," Steel mumbled.

Alexander was beginning to think he could not speak any louder.

"How fast?" Max asked through the window.

"Maybe thirty."

She looked across them to Alexander. "Do we need blindfolds?"

"The others came through without them. They might be too busy to worry about illusions."

"Then let's get on with it. Get us out of here safe, Steel." She squeezed his shoulder, and he nearly jumped out of his skin.

Alexander smiled to himself. Max had that effect. She was dangerous and scary. *Thank the spirits for that*. It kept her alive, and it was sexy as hell.

The truck rolled forward again. This time it did not stop at the ward line. Fire flickered through him as they crossed. Alexander hardly noticed. They were in the smoke now, and he could hear the coruscating howls of *obake* as they called one another to the hunt. His entire body tensed. There must have been hundreds. Thousands, even. They must have been gathering around the farmhouse, preparing to attack the wards. Lucky for them, their prey was coming out.

He firmed his hand on the sword and took a grenade from his bandolier, pulling the pin with his teeth and spitting it out. He heard the *ping* of pins hitting the bed of the truck as Oak and Ivy did the same.

The smoke swirled and moved, so thick it was like swimming in milk. Sounds seemed both close and far away. Steel murmured directions, talking nonstop to Peter, as if aware that the driver needed reassuring in the blinding smoke. "Straight ahead now, easy, steady, don't worry if you hit things, they need hitting, go a little left, not too much, that's good . . ." His voice was gentle, as if soothing a frightened animal.

Then Alexander ceased to listen.

Teeth and claws boiled up at him. They leaped up to his face and arms, ripping and tearing. He battered at them with the sword. The truck swerved and bumped as it ran over bodies. There were squeals and shrieks and whimpers. Oak swore and went silent as he fought the swarming *obake*. Alexander heard the whine of Max's sword and the wet smack as it hit flesh. A grenade exploded twenty feet away. Alexander tossed his. The explosions rocked the truck. Muffled screams erupted inside the trailer. But the grenades did little good. To be of real help, they needed to explode right beside the truck, which would blow them off the road.

Pain traveled up Alexander's legs. He had not expected so many *obake*. He kicked and slashed, drawing his knife and swinging with both arms. Still, the creatures climbed on him.

"Faster!" he called to Peter and Steel.

The truck lurched, and they bumped and heaved like they were on a deeply rutted road.

"Hold on!" yelled Steel, and then the truck turned sharply. Tires squealed as they caught the blacktop.

Obake fell away. Alexander clung to the frame of the truck to keep from falling off. He heard the patter of feet, and the ghostly hands of the *bakemono* caught at him without any effect. The truck swerved again, and Peter swore and coughed, as did Ivy and Oak. Steel continued his calm reassurances, his voice turning raw and raspy. Alexander's throat felt like he'd swallowed acid, and his lungs seemed to bubble without letting him draw a breath. The smoke was thickening, and his chest squeezed painfully.

Human hands grabbed at him. Men and women alike. Dozens of them. They clutched at him, dragging him down. He fell off the truck. Shrieks of triumph sounded from a chorus of *bakemono* throats. Fangs and claws gnawed and scraped at him. He was being dragged along the ground by the witch chain. *Obake* wrenched at the witch chain, then followed it down to his waist to untie it. He wrapped his wrist in the chain, gripping it tightly in case they succeeded, chopping at them with his sword as he did.

Screams filled the air and fists pounded him. They grabbed his hair and stabbed at his eyes. He bit down on the thumb that hooked into his mouth. His teeth cut through skin and Uncanny blood spilled across his tongue. He coughed and twisted away. Another thumb jabbed his left eye, driving in. His eye burst, and blood and fluid ran down his cheek.

He cried out in agony and kept fighting. It could not be much longer.

Bakemono straddled him. They had freed the witch chain from his waist and now clawed at his arm to make him let go. He used the sword like a club, battering at them. Every time one fell away, another solidified instantly in its place.

The truck veered. Alexander slid underneath, just in front of the rear tire. He pulled his feet up and bucked, knocking the two *bakemono* on top of him against the undercarriage. They fell away and screeched as the rear tire bounced over them.

Alexander panted. No more *bakemono* came to replace the others. He felt their ghostly caress over his body, but under the truck, he was safe. If he did not let go and if his skin did not completely shred away.

He held on with single-minded ferocity. His sword was gone. He reached up with his empty hand and gripped the chain. It was slick with blood and had cut to the bones of his wrist and hand. His body flamed with unending agony. Smoke condensed around him, and the *bakemono* pressed their wraith bodies against him. It was as if they'd poured lye over him. He moaned and clenched his teeth, clutching the chain with all the strength he had left.

How long that agonizing journey lasted, he had no idea. But suddenly the smoke vanished and the truck pulled to a stop. He gasped the clean air, too hurt to move. He felt like he was miles underwater. His head swam, and he could not let go of the chain.

Hands gripped him and pulled him out from under the truck.

"Holy fuck," said Ivy in a shocked voice.

"Can someone survive that?"

"Oh, good, Oak. Suppose he can hear you."

"Look at his eye." That was Steel.

"I didn't even know he went down." Oak again.

"Me either. Mother of night, it looks bad." Steel.

"Slick? Can you hear me?"

Max. She called him Slick. That meant he could not be so hurt that she had need to worry. Otherwise she would call him Alexander. He nodded and made a whimpering noise at the fire that spiraled around his body.

"Good. I have to get this chain off you."

He felt her yanking it loose from the truck. Then she unwound it from his hand, pulling it free from his flesh. Pain streaked through him, and he yanked away. She had an iron grip on him and didn't let go. A few more seconds and he was free. His arm throbbed. His body throbbed. Nothing did not hurt.

"Over here." He thought it was Maple. She sounded shaken.

"I'm picking you up, Slick. There's no way to do this that won't sting a little."

She pulled him up and slung him over her shoulder. His head dangled down her back. It was excruciating. He could not stop the sounds that slipped from his mouth. Mewling, whining noises, like baby kittens.

"This way."

A door opened and they went up steps inside somewhere. He was still whimpering. They turned into a space, and Max laid him down. It was soft, but he burned and burned.

"What kind of medical supplies do you have? We need warm water and towels. And sugar. He needs calories."

Max's voice was cool and deliberate. Alexander held on to that.

"If you like, I can tend him. I have some experience." It was the witch, Judith.

"Are you in any shape for it?"

"I am better than I was. I will do all that I can."

"Fine."

He felt her withdrawing. "Max," he croaked.

She leaned over him, her smell washing over him— sweat, blood, and pure Max. He breathed her in. "Slick,

I've got work to do. So shut up and let Judith clean you up. I'll be back."

There was nothing to say, even if he could. She had her family to see to. And he would heal. He had been hurt worse. He was sure of it. He just could not remember when.

18

MAX STEPPED DOWN OUT OF THE RV HER NEWLY adopted friends had arrived in, fighting the urge to puke. Alexander looked like hamburger. His crushed left eye was hanging out of its socket, his hand was half torn off, and what skin hadn't been grated away on the road was covered with bites and claw marks. The *obake* had pulled him down and no one had seen it; no one had helped him.

Guilt fought with fear. No. She would not be afraid that he would die. Judith was a triangle-level witch. She was in miserable shape, but she could help him. Max believed it. She refused not to.

She fought to push her fear down into the cold place where she kept all her pain, but it wouldn't go. It was too big. She couldn't get her mind around it. She was being ripped in half. She'd never felt anything like it before. Nothing had ever hurt this much.

Tears burned her eyes, but she didn't let them fall. She wasn't going to grieve; Alexander was going to live.

Gathering herself, she strode to where her family clustered in front of the truck. They stared at the white wall behind them and then at the Leshii, who had climbed down off the trailer. All but her father and Kyle, who were chattering in low voices, their excitement palpable.

Steel, Oak, and Ivy stood to the side in silence, looking at one another with vague smiles, their bodies stiff with pride. As well they should be. They'd fought a bloody battle and come out safe on the other side. Steel was wheezing, but was mostly unharmed. The other two looked like a stiff breeze would blow them over. Blood and wounds covered their arms and legs. They wore them like badges of honor.

Max checked the sky. From here, she couldn't see the coming wild magic. But dawn was arriving all too quickly. The RV was light- and dark-sealed, so she didn't have to worry about where to spend the day. One of Maple's three Spears could drive it. That left the truck, the car she and Alexander had been driving, and a little SUV that belonged to Maple's group.

She strode up to her waiting family. "Kyle and Peter, go into the RV. See if you can be any help." Her tone brooked no argument. They hurried to do as she said, no doubt driven more by curiosity than anything else. Max bit the inside of her lip to keep her temper. They were like children at an amusement park. Neither seemed to understand how deep the shit was they were standing in.

She surveyed the rest. Tris was hugging Sharon close, and her husband, Paul, held Tory. The younger girl was crying, and Tory was staring, her expression set as if she refused to let anyone see her fear. Max liked her. Max's mom held both of Kyle's stepsons. They looked terrified and lost.

They eyed her nervously. Max looked down at herself. Her clothes were ripped to shreds and she was covered in half-healed wounds. Her hands and arms were red with drying blood, and she could feel that her hair was plastered to her head with it. No doubt she looked like she'd bathed in the stuff. All in all, she looked like something straight out of a slasher movie.

Too bad. They were going to have to get over it. There was no time for squeamishness.

Still, she didn't speak to them immediately. She didn't have the energy for the drama.

She went to the Leshii instead. "You fulfilled your bargain. It is appreciated." She was careful not to say thank you. In the world of the Uncanny and the Divine, those words carried bindings that could be dangerous down the road. "You will want to ride on top of the RV." She pointed. "It will likely be most comfortable for you." That and fewer people might see them up there.

The father nodded and did as she suggested. Max turned to the three Blades. "You did good." She put a hand on Steel's shoulder and squeezed. He nearly jumped out of his skin, then flushed. "Without you, we never would have made it. Without all of you."

"Is Alexander going to be all right?" Ivy asked, looking at the RV. "I've never seen anyone—" Her throat convulsed, and she turned and puked violently.

"He's going to be fine," Max said, sounding more certain than she felt. Her stomach churned with worry, and she wanted to go back into the smoke and start slaughtering the little bastards who'd done this to him. "He's tough."

But was he tough enough? She'd survived worse on

Giselle's altar, but then, Giselle was a good healer and at full strength in those sessions. Alexander was as strong as she was, but Judith wasn't as powerful as Giselle, and she was severely depleted to boot. Max swallowed the bile that rose in her throat, forcing herself to focus on what needed to be done. "You three had better eat. You weren't in good shape coming into this, and I'll want you helping to drive until the sun comes up."

They nodded and climbed up into the RV.

"Where are you planning to take us?" Tris demanded from behind Max.

Max closed her eyes and took a deep breath before turning around. "Montana."

"And then what? What will we do there? We're not like you." It was an insult. Her gaze ran over Max and she didn't bother to hide her fearful repugnance.

Max glared at her sister, feeling the power of her Prime rolling off her as she rose back to the killing edge. Her fingers curled into claws. Tris fell back a step, her face turning white.

Max smiled. This was what she was. Dangerous. Terrifying. Strong.

"Is something wrong with me? I can't imagine what. Because of me and the rest of us who came to help you, you and your girls are still alive. We fought the battle. We sold our pain and our blood so you wouldn't have to. Maybe we even sold a life." Her fury was growing, fed by her fear for Alexander. "Maybe you wanted to stay in there and wait until the smoke suffocated you or the *obake* broke through the ward line and killed you all."

She felt her adopted Spears and Blades tumbling out

of the RV as if called. It was the power of her Prime. She ignored them.

"You're coming to Horngate because there is nowhere else you can be remotely as safe," Max said flatly. "I don't care if you want to or not. If I have to, I'll tie you up and haul your asses back in the trunk of a car. Your choice."

"You wouldn't."

"Actually, I would love to." Max grinned and it wasn't a nice expression.

"What about Kyle's daughter, Kristen?"

Max frowned. "Where is she?"

"She was with his ex-wife, Lynn, today. They were going to San Francisco. And Darla, his wife. She went to Placerville to visit her grandmother. We can't just leave them."

Max shook her head. "There's nothing we can do for them. Not now. They'll have to survive on their own."

Tris backed away. "The Anne I knew would never act this way."

"You're right. But I'm not her. *My* name is Max. Split yourselves up between the SUV and the Mustang. We're leaving the truck."

She walked away then, afraid she'd punch her sister.

"Flint and Steel, I want you at the wheels until sunrise. Then Eagle and Stone can take over. Understand this—I don't care what anybody says, they are coming with us to Horngate. Do whatever you have to to make sure of it. Got it?"

The Spears and Blades nodded. Black was starting to thread beneath the skin of the Spears—dark poisoning. She waved them inside before turning back to her sister and mother. Max didn't trust them not to try to escape, and tying them up would make things harder. Fine. There were ways around it.

She went to Tory and grabbed her arm. "You're riding inside."

"What?" The girl pulled against Max's hold, but she seemed more resentful than scared.

"You're riding in the RV. They won't go trying to run off if you're inside. They'll follow quietly or never see you again." Max looked at the two stunned women. "Right?"

She pushed Tory into the RV and stepped up inside without another word. Oak and Ivy followed.

The smell of blood filled the interior of the motor home. Max glanced at the narrow hallway. It was silent. Her chest tightened. She turned her attention to Tory, pointing her to a chair by the window. "Get buckled."

The girl stood a moment. "Is it really true you're my aunt?"

"Afraid so."

"And that guy who got hurt—is he my uncle?"

Max snorted. "Hardly."

"He's cute."

"Yeah." Max resisted the urge to tell the girl that Alexander would break her in half. "Buckle in."

Oak took the wheel and started the engine. Max looked out the window. Her mother, Tris, and Tris's younger girl had climbed into the SUV with Flint. Tris's husband got into the Mustang with Kyle's stepsons and Steel.

"Get going," she told Oak, then went to rifle the galley kitchen for food. She hurt, and her lungs felt like they wouldn't inflate. She wanted nothing more than to collapse in a heap, but she couldn't.

Forty-five minutes later, they were forced to change drivers. Max and the Blades retreated into the back of the RV, sealing the doors and locking the wards so they could not be opened from outside. She went down to the room holding Alexander, her father, Kyle, and Judith, sliding down the wall to sit outside.

Oak, Ivy, Steel, and Flint sat beside her. She frowned at them. "You should go get some sleep."

"We will," Ivy said, unmoving.

Max tipped her head back against the wall, closing her eyes. She could hear chanting—Judith. Alexander was silent. But as long as the witch was working her magic, there was hope.

Hours ticked past. The five of them kept their silent vigil. After a while, Steel tipped his head onto his brother's shoulder and fell asleep. Ivy rested her head on Oak's leg and followed suit. Not long later, Flint was snoring softly.

"Can't be comfortable," Max said, eyeing them with exasperation, though she was glad of their company.

Oak watched her. His eyes no longer had that feral ring they had had when they first met. Gone also was that psychopathic edge.

"One time, we found this cave up in the hills," he said, startling Max. "Patricia was excited. It went deep, one of those caves that's really a tunnel to someplace mystical. We couldn't get through unless we made it bigger. So some of the witches went in with a few of us Blades. Something happened and the roof caved in. We dug out, but Shana—one of the witches—was crushed. I didn't know how she could still be breathing. Didn't seem like a bone of her body wasn't broken. You could hear her lungs bubble, and her head was shaped kind of like a football." He shook his head at the memory.

"They sent for Judith. She saved Shana." He looked at Max. "Judith's triangle-strong, and she knows how to heal. She said Gregory should make it, too."

Max nodded. "Thanks. That helps."

The wait went on for two more hours. At last the door opened and Max sprang to her feet, the others with her. Her father came out first. He looked haggard, but his eyes sparkled. Kyle came behind. He looked less weary and more than a little satisfied. Judith swayed, exhaustion digging deep grooves into her face. She motioned for Max to come in.

Alexander lay on the bed. His chest was bare, and the rest of him was covered with a sheet. Much of the blood had been wiped away and his wounds were closed. His skin was pebbly and pink, but healing. His hands and feet twitched and jerked.

"He'll be okay," Judith said, her voice hoarse and cracking. "He's restless. You might see if you can reassure him. He needs sleep. Food, too, when he wakes up."

"Thank you," Max said as relief sluiced through her. Her legs shook. She bent over, catching herself on her knees. Her head spun, and her stomach lurched. She drew a long breath and let it out slowly, then straightened.

The witch patted her shoulder as she turned to leave. "No, m'dear. Thank you."

The door shut behind her. The room was tiny and smelled of sweat and blood. She reached down and ran her hand down the side of Alexander's face. He turned into her touch, his body going still. She made a face at the dried blood on her hands and washed them in the bucket of cool red water on the floor. She rubbed the rag over her face, washing away what she could, then slid into the little gap between him and the wall.

She pressed her face against his chest, sliding her arm over his stomach. Silent tears slid down her cheeks. For Jim, for the family who no longer loved her, and for nearly losing Alexander.

AT SUNDOWN, SHE WOKE. ALEXANDER HAD NOT MOVED, but his skin was smooth, and he slept easily. She frowned, smelling the brine of the ocean and the scents of sand and pine. She crawled out of the bed without waking him and went to the cab of the RV.

They were parked in a lot in front of a tall dune. Maple yawned as Max came out. Tory was sitting in her chair, and Kyle and her father had opened the door and were stepping out.

"Where are we?" Max asked.

"Oregon. Florence."

"You made good time."

Maple flushed at the praise. "There's a Fred Meyer here. I thought we should get some clothes for you and Alexander, pick up groceries and anything else we need. There's a shower in the RV, or we can go find a camp-ground and use theirs."

She was smart. Max dearly wanted to get cleaned up and put on fresh clothes. She grimaced. She still wasn't wearing underwear.

"Go get some sleep," she told Maple as Oak, Ivy, Flint, and Steel came out of the back, yawning. "I want three of you to go shopping," Max said. "Got a credit card? You'll be paid back."

They nodded. She made a list of clothing and sizes, guessing at Alexander's. Ivy, Steel, and Flint went, leaving Oak with her.

"Bring her," she told him, motioning at Tory.

She stepped outside. The wind was blowing and sand stung her skin. The ocean lay just beyond the big grocery outlet. They were parked off to the side. Her father and mother were talking heatedly in low voices. Tris was fuming beside her car, as Sharon walked up and down, stretching as she listened to music on her MP3 player. Paul was watching the two boys, who were climbing on the sand dune. Max grimaced. She wouldn't want to be around her sister right now, either.

Max nodded at Eagle and Stone, who were standing guard. "Go eat and get some sleep. And thanks."

They flashed smiles at her and climbed inside. Just like puppies.

She watched with disgust as Tris hugged Tory as if she was afraid the girl had been mauled.

"I'm *fine*, Mom. I just sat in a chair. I even wore a seat belt. Uncle Kyle and Grampa were there for most of it." Tory pushed out of her mother's arms and went to talk to her sister.

Tris marched over to where Max crouched in the shadows. She didn't want to be seen. Dressed as she was in bloody rags, someone would surely call the cops. She looked up at her sister, exhaustion weighing on her. She'd not slept well, waking every time Alexander so much as twitched or snored.

"If you're going to chew my ass, can you make it quick? I'm really not in the mood."

Her sister surprised her. "How is he? Your friend?

Steel told us how bad he was hurt. We didn't know."

"He's going to live, I think." Max looked down, drawing lines in the blown sand that powdered the parking lot.

"That's good." Tris didn't walk away. "Steel also told us what you did for them—for their coven." The last word fell stiffly from her lips, like she didn't like the taste. Probably she didn't.

"He told you a lot."

"He said if it wasn't for you, they'd have all died."

Max shrugged. "Maybe. Maybe not. They weren't going down easy."

Oak snorted. He was watching them from a few feet away. "Don't let her fool you. We were toast."

Max eyed him balefully. "If I want your opinion, I'll ask for it."

He tossed her a careless salute. "Yes, ma'am."

Holy mother of fuck. He was going to be as bad as Niko and Tyler. She could tell already.

"Anyway . . ." Tris said, trailing away.

"Yeah?"

She squatted down. "Is it as bad as you say?" she asked, her voice hushed. "All that end-of-the-world stuff?"

"Pretty much. Except the world isn't exactly ending. It just is going to be a whole lot different."

"We'll really be safe where you're taking us?"

"As safe as you can be, given what's happening. It isn't good to be an ordinary human right now. But then, you have some witch blood in you, too. Just like Kyle and me."

Tris was taken aback. But before she could answer,

the door of the RV swung open. Max stood as Alexander stepped out. He chest was bare, his hips wrapped in a towel. His gaze scoured the parking lot until he locked onto Max, taking in her matted hair and her bloody clothes. A shudder ran through him, and he strode to her. She didn't move. Everything about him smoldered like bottled lightning and her skin felt like she'd catch fire any moment.

He stopped in front of her. "You are all right?"

"Sure. Nice to see you upright, though."

More than nice. His skin was like satin over his shoulders and his stomach rippled with muscle. She wanted to trace the planes of his body with her tongue and fingers. She closed her eyes and shook herself. *Down, girl. Now is definitely not the time.* She didn't need to be the entertainment.

"What are you doing out here? You should be eating. You were pretty wrecked."

"I wanted to see you—to be sure you were all right."

"I'm fine. So go get some food."

"Have you eaten?"

She shrugged. "Soon enough. I sent Ivy, Steel, and Flint shopping. For clothes, too, since towels are out this season. But there's enough inside for you, and you need it. You took some massive healing." Her expression flattened at the memory.

"Do not do that," he said, gripping her arm. "Do not go away from me."

"I'm standing right here," she said. If he kept staring at her that way, she was going to rip away the towel and jump his bones in front of her family and anybody else who happened to walk by.

"You know what I mean. You withdraw inside and I cannot follow. I hate it."

"I'm not going anywhere, Slick." *Not yet.* But Scooter was waiting. She thrust the outlaw thought away, refusing to think of having to leave Alexander. Not so soon after nearly losing him.

She couldn't look away from his lips. He caught his breath.

"You are killing me," he muttered.

"Back at ya, Slick. Go eat. For my sake."

He hesitated, then bent and brushed his lips against hers and went back inside.

That slight touch was enough make her ache. She took a harsh breath and crouched back down to wait.

No one came near her again until Ivy, Steel, and Flint returned. They pushed and pulled six or seven overloaded carts. It was all stashed inside in less than fifteen minutes.

"There's a campground not far from here," Oak said, holding the directions that Maple had written on a pad of paper. "We can clean up and eat there."

"You've got the wheel," Max said, and climbed inside the RV. Alexander sat at the small table. He wore a pair of loose-fitting jeans and a red button-up shirt. He was eating from a container of ice cream. A dozen power bar wrappers littered the table around him.

When he saw Max, he shifted so that she had room to sit beside him. She did, grabbing another carton of ice cream from a sack and tearing it open. Before she could take a bite, he offered her a spoonful of his. Meeting the challenge of his look, she wrapped her fingers around his and slowly licked the chocolate-swirl ice cream from the spoon, then ran the tip of her tongue around her lips.

He made an animal sound deep in his chest and pulled away. "Maybe you should eat your own."

She smiled smugly. "I suppose you want me to sit on the other side of the table, too," she said, starting to stand up.

He clamped an arm around her, pulling her tight. "Stay put," he growled.

They arrived at the campground and Ivy handed Max a comb, towel, soap, shampoo, and clothes. Max glanced at Alexander with her brows raised. It wasn't—quite— an invitation to join her, but the idea of him naked and wet made her insides clench with want.

Abruptly she left, jogging to the bathroom.

She stayed there too long, delighting in the pounding heat of the spray. Ivy had also given her a washcloth, and Max scrubbed away the blood with hard strokes, then washed her hair three times. When she was done, she dressed in jeans and a soft long-sleeved green cotton shirt. She combed her hair and returned to the RV.

Inside, someone was cooking grilled cheese sandwiches, and Paul and Tris were barbecuing hamburgers on a grill outside. Alexander was sitting on the end of a picnic table. He saw Max and got to his feet, grabbing her hand and pulling her down to the beach. His hand laced with hers as he drew her along with urgent steps. They neared the water, and he turned and kissed her.

His arms wrapped around her and he lifted her against him. She locked her legs around his waist. His kiss was desperate and deep. His lips slanted over hers, his tongue delving inside her mouth as he tasted her.

After a few minutes, his touch gentled. He nibbled her lips and sucked lightly on her tongue as she moaned and slid her fingers over his scalp, dragging him closer.

His touch was scorching and turned Max's insides to liquid gold. She rubbed herself against him and jolts of pleasure flared through her body. He pulled away, nipping at her lips and kissing down the sensitive column of her neck. One hand slid up under her shirt to cup her breast. His thumb rubbed the nipple. She moaned as indescribable pleasure spiraled through her. He caught the sound in his mouth, kissing her again.

He set her down on her feet, pulling her shirt up. His lips fastened on her breast, where his thumb had caressed. He sucked and she felt the pull deep inside. Hot red embers swirled inside her and her legs trembled. She gripped his shoulders, then slid her hands down his back to knead his ass as he flicked her nipples with his tongue, first one, then the other. He groaned as she slid one hand around to cup his stiff length through his pants. It felt hard as iron. She squeezed and he thrust against her, then lifted his head and kissed her again, jerking her tight against his chest as his tongue twined wetly with hers.

She ran her hands up his back beneath his shirt, discovering the silky play of his muscles beneath his skin, grinding her hips against his as she did. He made a guttural sound in his throat. Her hands drifted lower beneath the waistband of his pants. She rubbed the firm, round contour of his ass beneath his loose-fitting jeans.

He leaned back and stripped away her shirt before she could protest. Not that she would have. Her head spun, and she wanted him so much she thought she might explode if he didn't get down to business soon. He grabbed her hands, held them behind her back, and went back to licking and sucking her breasts, kissing searing trails up her neck and back down. Her nipples were so hard they might have cut diamonds.

She twisted to get away, wanting to tear off his clothes. "You fucking tease," she groaned when he tightened his grip and laughed, then gently bit a nipple. She gasped and sagged against him as her body went up in flames.

He licked the edge of her ear. "I am not going to be a one-night stand you cannot remember the next day. You are never going to want to give me up," he murmured, then moved to her mouth again, kissing her with breathless hunger.

"Max!"

It was Ivy. Her urgent voice was a bucket of cold water. It barely cooled Max's heated flesh.

"Max! You've got to come on. There's a tsunami warning. We have to go."

"Of course there is," Max muttered. "Why wouldn't there be?" Then, "Coming!" Didn't she just wish.

Alexander had let go of her hands and settled his on her hips. He was panting, his chest rising and falling as if he'd been running a marathon. He slid his palms up her sides and rested them against the curves of her breasts.

"I think I might want to risk the tsunami," he said in a hoarse voice.

"Don't tempt me."

"But I want to tempt you. If we get back and you push

me away, I might jump off a cliff." There was no hint of humor in his voice.

"I won't push you away, Slick. I'm staking a claim."

She stood on tiptoe, leaning in and biting his neck until she tasted blood. He sucked in a breath, his hands returning to her hips and yanking her against him, rubbing his hard length into her crotch.

"You had better not change your mind," he said, and abruptly let her go, reaching down to pick up her shirt.

He shook off the sand and slid it over her head, kissing both breasts and thumbing her nipples once more before pulling it down.

She shuddered. "Not fair. You do not play fair."

"Who is playing?"

He grabbed her hand and kissed it, then started back toward the picnic area. Now Max noticed the wail of the tsunami sirens. The Guardians were really striking hard.

By the time they got back, everyone was already loaded. Oak was at the wheel of the RV.

Max climbed inside. Alexander had let go of her hand as they left the beach, and she missed his touch instantly. This was all the time they had. When they got back, she had a promise to keep to Scooter.

She sat and ate, her body still feverish from Alexander's touch. She didn't look at him, keeping her distance. She couldn't trust herself. By sunrise, they would near Horngate, and they were trapped in a vehicle with a half dozen other people, at least four of them with supersonic hearing. She wasn't going to have a screaming good time on a tiny cot while they listened in. She wasn't that much of an exhibitionist.

She ate randomly, stuffing herself with whatever came to hand. But eventually she was full. She looked at Alexander. She could no longer resist. He stood and held out his hand.

"Come on."

Her body still throbbed. She shook her head. "Not my style, Slick. I can't."

"I am not asking. Trust me."

She went because she couldn't say no. She didn't want to. For thirty years she'd done little but deny herself, and now that she was looking at an uncertain future with Scooter, she wanted to snatch a little happiness for herself.

He led them into the rear of the RV and resealed the wards, then led her back to his room. He shut the door and sat on the edge of the bed, still holding her hand.

"Sleep with me," he said. "Just that. Nothing more."

She wondered if he remembered exactly what she owed Scooter. That when they got to Horngate, everything was over. At least until Scooter was done with her, and she wasn't any too sure he ever would be. She didn't remind him. Their time was too precious to shatter with reality.

She lay down beside him. He turned on his side, pulling her against him. One hand came up to cover her breast. He kissed the back of her neck.

"If you start that, I won't be able to stop," she warned him.

She felt his lips curve. "Is that so bad?"

"I don't like an audience."

"Neither do I."

With that, he settled, his breath soft and warm on her shoulder as they drifted off to sleep.

19

MAX WAS WRONG ABOUT HOW LONG IT WOULD take to get to Horngate. So many people were fleeing from the tsunami and the eruption of Mount Shasta that the roads and the gas stations were choked. It was sunrise when they made it up the gorge to Kennewick and just an hour before dawn when they drove into Horngate.

The closer they got, the more uneasy and short-tempered Max became. She could hardly look at Alexander, and it was obvious it infuriated him. She was pushing him away, exactly as she had promised not to do. But she didn't know what else to do with herself. She felt a little like she was drowning. It wasn't fair to him. She knew it. But the thought of leaving him hurt worse than anything else she'd experienced in her life. She couldn't handle it. Not without pulling away inside herself. And every mile closer to Horngate made her ache more.

She sat in the passenger seat, her knees to her chest, her arms wrapping them tightly. Alexander sat on the couch, watching her from beneath heavy-lidded eyes, his Blade balancing on the killing edge. The magic of his

Prime filled the vehicle with an aura of choking power. Her own was wild and menacing. She felt trapped between her feelings for him and her promise to Scooter, and her Blade was raging against it.

They made everyone else twitchy. Oak drove with one eye on Max, his ears clearly straining for sounds of Alexander. His shoulders were stiff and he frequently veered over the rumble strip in his distraction. No one else wanted to be anywhere near them.

They reached Missoula all too soon, and Max realized that she was nearly out of time to say something to Alexander before they got to Horngate and Scooter claimed her. She fought for words, but her mind was frozen.

She had still not found any words when they wound up the road to Horngate and pulled to a stop in the parking area at the base of the mountain. Time was up. She stood and looked at him. He stared back, waiting. The message was clear. He'd made enough first moves. Now it was her turn. She couldn't. She went to the door and stepped out.

The first thing she noticed was the gray minivan. That meant the refugees from Weed had made it. That was good news.

"Max!" came Niko's sudden shout, and then he was beside her, grabbing her in a rib-cracking hug. "We thought something happened to you," he said, swinging her around before setting her on her feet.

"I'm not that easy to kill," she said. "You should know that by now."

He frowned at her. "What's wrong?"

"It's been a long trip. I'll tell you about it. But first, let's get unloaded."

He glanced up behind her. "Alexander. Good to see you back." He sounded like he meant it. That was good news, too. They were going to need each other soon. His gaze sharpened. "And these others?" Alexander had stepped down, and Oak filled the doorway. Niko tensed.

"He's okay," Max told him. "My family is with us, plus two witches—no, make that four," she said, her mouth twisting. She had not spoken with her father or Kyle since they'd helped to heal Alexander. She didn't know anymore what to say to them than she did to him. "There's also three Sunspears and four Shadowblades. A few others."

"Hitchhikers?" Tyler asked as he came up behind her. He eyed Oak warily.

"Something like that."

The cars opened and slowly emptied out. Her traveling companions gathered around Max, hemmed in by a wall of Horngate's Shadowblades and Spears. Oz came out of the main entrance with Giselle, Tutresiel and Xaphan flanking them. They started down the hill eagerly. Max waved.

There were gasps as the others caught sight of the angels. Max rubbed her arm where Scooter had marked her with his magic. How much time did she have left? She doubted he was going to wait very long.

"What's got you so uptight?" Niko asked. "Your Blades are raging. Both of you." He looked from Max to Alexander and back, frowning.

"It's been a tough week," Max said vaguely.

Alexander's unrelenting silence was getting to her. Damn, but she was a coward and an idiot. How could she have told him she wouldn't push him away and then done exactly that? How stupid was it to waste the few hours she had with him?

A flare of white heat along her arm warned Max. She reacted on instinct, spinning around. She caught Alexander's bitter gaze. "I'm sorry. I really did mean every word," she told him. "It hurt too much knowing what was coming." Weak excuse, she knew.

She didn't see his reaction. Magic flared in a brilliant borealis. Streamers of blue and white wound through the night. The air and ground shook as a hole in the world opened up and Scooter stepped right through. His smooth skin was coppery, his blue-black hair a shimmering curtain around his shoulders. Surprisingly, he wasn't entirely naked. His bottom half was clothed in red buckskin, and he wore a red vest. His black eyes spun with flecks of blue. Magic coiled around him in sensuous ribbons.

"It's time," he told Max. "I have waited. I will wait no more."

He held out his hand. Max looked at it. She could not refuse; he would not let her. Besides, a promise was a promise. She stepped forward, then hesitated, looking at Giselle. The witch stood frozen, her mouth drawn flat. She wasn't going to try to stop Scooter. Not that she could.

"Trust Alexander," Max said. "If I don't come back, make him your Prime."

Her glance flicked to Tutresiel. "Thanks for the gift. It came in handy. Maybe one day I'll pay you back."

He scowled, his silver wings lifting wide in what could have been anger.

She looked at Oz, then Niko and Tyler, and lastly Alexander. A knot filled her throat. For all of them, for finally figuring out what mattered and having to walk away from it. There ought to have been something profound to say, but she could only think of Jim's final words.

"See you when I see you."

She put her hand in Scooter's. Lightning ran up her arm and crackled through her body. The ribbons of his magic curled around her, binding her tight. Cold washed over her as the hole opened again. A black plain stretched before her, filled with crisscrossing strands of rainbow magic.

The last thing Max heard as she stepped into the web between worlds was Alexander shouting her name.

Desire is stronger after dark...
Bestselling Urban Fantasy from Pocket Books!

Bad to the Bone
JERI SMITH-READY
Rock 'n' Roll will never die. Just like vampires.

Master of None
SONYA BATEMAN
Nobody ever dreamed of a genie like this...

Spider's Bite
An Elemental Assassin Book
JENNIFER ESTEP.
Her love life is killer.

Necking
CHRIS SALVATORE
Dating a Vampire is going to be the death of her.